BAXTER HOUSE

GEORGE ENCIZO

This book is a work of fiction. Names, characters, places and incidents are the product of the author's imagination or are used fictitiously. Any resemblance to actual events, locales, or persons, living or dead is entirely coincidental.

ISBN-13: 9781523993819
ISBN-10: 1523993812

Library of Congress Control Number: 2016902617
CreateSpace Independent Publishing Platform
North Charleston, South Carolina

Printed in the United States of America

When care is pressing you down a bit, Rest! If you must—but never quit.

Author unknown

BAXTER HOUSE

CHAPTER 1

Afghanistan—2013

Although grateful for the downtime, the men of C Company 3rd Platoon at Camp Delaram were anxious for some action. Gunnery Sergeant Harding and Staff Sergeant Roger Pritcher—nicknamed Pritch—decided some healthy competition might be just what they needed to relieve their anxieties. The weather was mild so after lunch, the two sergeants tossed a coin and chose sides for a volleyball game. In the past, it helped distract from the boredom. After several hard fought games, their platoon leader, Second Lieutenant Jeffries, interrupted their fun.

"What's up, Sir? We got a mission?"

"We do, Gunny. We're to rescue a corporal who was captured after his supply truck was ambushed. Intelligence has all the info on his location."

"When do we go, Sir?"

"Tonight, Pritch. We roll at 2030 hours. Briefing's at 2000. Five Humvees and the entire platoon. Night vision goggles and make sure

Ramirez has plenty of rockets." He rubbed his arms. "I expect it will be cold tonight, be prepared."

"That's a lot of firepower, Sir."

"It is Gunny, but this guy's one of ours and HQ wants him back alive. There's not gonna be any prisoner swap."

"Don't worry, Lieutenant, we'll bring him back."

"I know you will, Gunny. That's why we were handpicked." The lieutenant grinned. "So, who won this time?"

"We did."

"That's because you cheated, Pritch."

The lieutenant shook his head. "It's a good thing you two are friends. Be ready to go at 2030."

They saluted and the lieutenant left.

"Another game, Brad, or do we let the men rest? I could use a shower"

"Me too. Let's let the men rest and clean up. How many missions does this make for us, Pritch?"

"Let me think. Hmm, this is our third tour together, so who knows? I've lost count anyway. Best we leave it that way. We don't want to jinx this one."

At 2130 hours, the convoy came to a halt three hundred meters from an encampment on the outskirts of Peshawar near the Pakistan border. As anticipated, the temperature was in the high thirties.

According to intelligence only a few Taliban were guarding the prisoner.

Lieutenant Jeffries ordered the drivers to stay with their vehicles and left four marines as backup for a quick retreat. The remaining thirty advanced cautiously wearing night vision goggles. They were assured by intelligence that the insurgents weren't expecting them.

When they were within fifty meters, several rounds hit the ground in front of them and kicked up sand. Another round hit Jeffries and he went down.

"Jeffries is down," Harding yelled into his mouthpiece.

"You're in command, Sergeant. You have your orders."

The sand made it difficult to see where the rounds were coming from. The marines immediately dispersed and sought cover wherever possible. When the dust settled, they cautiously approached further after getting the lieutenant safely out of harm's way. Several more rounds were fired by a large band of insurgents. The marines returned fire, and a fierce battle took place with bullets and dust flying everywhere. It sounded like fireworks on the Fourth of July.

"Shit!" shouted Harding. "I thought they told us we would surprise them. What kind of fucked up intelligence did we get?"

The voice in his headset said, "We can hear you, Sergeant."

"Yeah, well, can you see this? It's chaos here. We're under attack."

"Yes, we can; complete your mission, Sergeant."

"What the hell do you think I'm doing?" Then he muttered to himself, "Fucking asshole." He called out to one of his men. "Ramirez, can you hear me?"

"Yes, Gunny."

"Good. Fire a couple of grenades and make sure you do plenty of damage." Ramirez fired two grenades which were right on the mark. "Fire two more and save some for our escape," Ramirez fired two more grenades and took out several Taliban.

Ultimately, the marines prevailed and the insurgents took off running. Harding's platoon kept up a barrage of firepower. Eleven insurgents died but no marines. Two were injured including Lieutenant Jeffries.

Harding and Pritcher saw an insurgent running toward a small hut. They chased after him and aimed but both missed. They rushed into the hut and saw he was about to shoot the corporal. Pritcher took aim but the insurgent turned and fired at him. Harding shot the insurgent.

Pritcher took a bullet in his abdomen. He dropped his weapon, clutched his stomach and turned toward Brad. "Shit," he said and went down. Another marine entered.

"Ramirez, get the prisoner and I'll help Pritcher," Harding called out.

The voice in his headphone asked him, "Is the package secured, Sergeant?"

"Yes, it's taken care of."

"Don't delay, Sergeant, bring it home."

"We've got a situation here."

"Get your package home, Sergeant, that's an order."

Harding ripped off his headset and looked at the medic, "Fucking assholes, they don't give a shit about us. All they want to do is cover their asses. I'm surprised they didn't say stand down. Help me here, Jimmy."

They got Pritcher out of the hut and on the ground. Corporal Jimmy Mitchell tried desperately to stop the bleeding. Harding stood by as Mitchell worked feverishly to save his friend. Mitchell looked up and shook his head. Harding sat down next to Pritcher and held his head in his arms.

"Don't you die on me, Pritch, you hear me."

Sergeant Pritcher knew what he was about to say would be his dying words. "Sorry, Brad, there's nothing I can do about it. I need a big favor from you."

"Anything, Pritch, just ask."

"I want you to write a letter to my parents, and I want you to tell my mom I love her. Will you do it for me, Brad?"

"Don't worry, Pritch, I'll do as you ask." Harding's cheeks were wet with tears. He wondered why this had happened after all their time together. They had close calls before but never like this.

"Thanks Brad." Those were Sergeant Roger Pritcher's last words.

"Son of a bitch, why did it have to be you, Pritch?" He picked up Pritch's helmet and threw it. "Damn, those fucking intelligence guys!"

Harding and his men got the lieutenant safely into a Humvee and loaded Pritcher's body into another, and the kidnapped corporal in a third. Then they headed for base.

Suddenly from out of nowhere, a jeep with three insurgents appeared. They fired a rocket at the convoy and disappeared into the night. The rocket hit one of the Humvees causing it to overturn. The driver's arm was seriously injured, three other marines were also wounded and two died. Harding and his men were able to get the marines safely out of the Humvee before it burst into flames. They squeezed the driver, the wounded and the dead marines into the remaining Humvees and continued on toward base.

When the platoon returned to Camp Delaram, Harding honored his friend's request to write the letter. He sat at the make-shift desk and began. It was difficult but he managed to get a few words down—but with much heartache.

Damn, Pritch, if only I had gotten to the hut first. You might be writing this letter for me. Unlike you, I don't have a home to go to and my mother and sister would never know what happened—and my father and his father would probably say I told you so.

After a near fatal mission, the platoon members elected to write letters to their loved ones to be sent to them if they didn't return from the next mission. The letters were placed in a box and Pritcher was its keeper. Since Pritcher could no longer mail the letters, Harding took on the responsibility of mailing them—but decided to write a note to the family and loved ones of the other marines who were killed—and sent it along with their letters. A boy and a girl would grow up without their fathers and wedding plans would have to be cancelled.

Harding's letter was addressed to his maternal grandfather—the only person he felt would care about him.

He dropped his pen, rubbed his hands through his hair and rubbed the back of his hand across his eyes. After a moment he was able to put more words down. He folded the letter and sealed the envelope.

It was his worst day since joining the marines, and it would haunt him for the rest of his deployment. After seeing so much death and destruction, he questioned whether he still wanted to be a marine.

CHAPTER 2

Atlanta Airport—April 2015

Harding walked through the airport searching for a place to relax between flights and wandered into an airport lounge. He sat at a table, ordered a beer and pretzels and then watched the first round of the Master's tournament—content that danger wasn't lurking nearby. Two wannabe pro-golfers were wagering on the outcome of a forty foot putt by a real professional. The pro stood over the ball, stroked his putter and watched the ball rim the edge and drop in. As he raised his putter and pumped his fist, the two wannabees settled their bet.

The scene was a welcome relief from where he had been and where he was going. He had never played golf before but on rare occasions he enjoyed watching a match on television. He grabbed a handful of pretzels, took a swig of beer and contemplated what had brought him there.

After an emotional goodbye to his platoon and a brief period of R&R, Master Gunnery Sergeant Bradley Harding reached a decision about his career in the marines. First on his agenda, after submitting his itinerary, was a couple of stops in South Carolina and a thirty day leave before reporting to Parris Island—the final destination before his current enlistment ended. He planned to use the time to determine if there was someone and someplace where he could start a new life. It all depended on the outcome of a confrontation with a person from his past.

The sergeant was suddenly interrupted by the middle aged couple sitting at the next table.

"Excuse me, Sergeant, but are you deploying or returning home?" The man sitting at the table had short black hair, wore a tan shirt, jeans and brown sneakers. At his feet was their carry-on bag with the woman's light jacket draped over the handle.

Although he doesn't like these kinds of questions, there was something about this couple that made him want to be polite and respond. "I'm going home, sir." Not exactly the truth, but he wanted to say something.

"Forgive me for asking but were you ever in Afghanistan?" The woman had short blonde hair, wore glasses, a light blue long sleeve top, jeans and grey sneakers with a blue stripe. She wore little makeup and just a trace of lipstick.

Her question was one of the reasons he avoided discussions concerning his military exploits. It was always followed by were you in combat or did you see action.

"I don't mind you asking, ma'am. Yes, I was. Did you know someone who was there?"

The woman's eyes saddened. "Our son was there. We lost him two years ago. He died in his platoon leader's arms. We received a very nice letter from him. They were close friends."

"What was your son's name, ma'am?"

"Roger Pritcher." She could barely say his name. "You probably never met him, though."

His stomach tightened and his heartbeat quickened. He had met him but it was when he was last deployed. The memory of the events that took place the last time he was with him saddened Harding and he could barely respond.

As a mother of two, Mrs. Pritcher often had to use the remote and turn the television off to get their attention. Her son was the biggest offender as he walked around the house listening to music in his headphones. After a basketball game loss, he'd come home, get a Coke from the fridge, sit at the kitchen table and sulk. She'd walk in and could always tell that something was bothering him by the expression on his face. She saw that same look on Harding's face.

"Sergeant, are you all right?"

He wasn't but he didn't want to alarm her. "Yes, ma'am, I am. I actually did know your son. I was his platoon leader, and we were close friends. I'm the one who wrote the letter. Roger's last words to me were to tell you he loved you." He took a moment to swallow. "I'm sorry I didn't make it to his funeral. I would have liked to say it to you personally."

Mr. and Mrs. Pritcher stood up and walked toward him.

"It's okay, you had other matters to concern yourself with. Mr. Pritcher and I appreciate you taking the time to write the letter. May I hug you?

He felt guilty because the truth was that he met a woman in a bar, woke up the next morning in her bed and missed his flight. He spent the next two days and nights with her trying to forgive himself.

"Yes, ma'am."

He felt forgiveness in the arms of Mrs. Pritcher and the faint scent of her lilac perfume brought memories of his own mother.

She whispered, "Thank you so much, Sergeant. You don't know what this means to me and how happy I am. God bless you."

Mr. Pritcher reached out and took his hand. He was six feet two, built like a lumberjack, but Pritch had said that he was nothing but a giant teddy bear. His grip was strong and he had calluses on his hand—it felt like his grandfather's.

"Our daughter appreciates it too and thank you for your service."

"Thank you, sir, but it's your son who deserves the praise."

Unbeknownst to them, everyone in the lounge overheard their conversation and there were a few teary eyes.

Harding ordered another beer. Mr. Pritcher decided to have one with him and Mrs. Pritcher ordered another glass of iced tea. He said he would pick up the tab, but the waitress said there was no charge as all of their drinks were taken care of.

Without going into too much detail, he told them the purpose of the mission and what happened when they went into the hut. Then he amused them with tales about him and their son. Mrs. Pritcher wasn't the least bit surprised by her son's antics.

Mr. Pritcher checked his watch and stood up.

"Sergeant, we have to go it's nearly boarding time. We're glad we got to meet you. You be well, young man."

"You too, sir. Same to you Mrs. Pritcher."

"Stay safe, son."

Pritch's proud parents waved as they walked away.

Ten minutes later he got up to go to his gate. He waved goodbye to everyone as they all applauded him.

He boarded his flight to Charleston—the last leg of a long journey by airplane. If the flight went without a hitch, he would arrive at his destination in time for a late lunch. He took his seat, sat back, closed his eyes and tried not to think about what awaited him in South Carolina.

CHAPTER 3

At the Budget Car Rental station, Harding rented a small compact for a month with a drop off near Parrris Island. After paying, he asked the attendant where he could buy a South Carolina map.

"I have one here, Sergeant, but your car has GPS."

"Better give it to me anyway." She handed him the map. "Thanks, which way to my car?"

She gestured toward his right. "Follow the sign over there and when you get out of the terminal, there'll be a shuttle that will take you to the lot. Enjoy Charleston and South Carolina, Sergeant!"

"Thanks again."

She winked and gave him a two finger salute.

He took the shuttle to the lot where his rental waited. Before leaving, he turned on the GPS and put in Blocker's Bluff. He remembered it wasn't on any map many years ago when his grandfather had picked him up at the airport.

He followed the highway signs until he came to Highway 174 and headed south toward Beaufort. The last road he looked for was County Road 103 which would take him to Blocker's Bluff. He knew it was the right one because it was his birthdate.

When he saw the large green rectangular sign with white lettering on it for County Road 103 it was another surprise. The large wording announced, *Coastline Resort Community - Blocker's Bluff – Crofton – I95 - 2 miles.*

When he came to a stop sign, another sign directed him left to Blocker's Bluff and right to Crofton and I95. He wasn't sure he was in the right country since he didn't remember any of this. The highway was four lanes now but it was just an old paved road when he was last there.

He turned left onto 103, the only road that led into town. It was approximately thirteen miles to town and to the coast. Several miles later on his right he passed CR325 a road he knew went through the boondocks and to the next county. Further on, he noticed the well landscaped entryway for Coastline Resort Community. He drove on by and saw the golf course and some single family homes in the distance. He wasn't sure if he had made a wrong turn but suspected it was because he had been gone a long time.

In Blocker's Bluff at Willie's Diner, the only place in town to get something to eat, Chief of Police Molly Dickson and John Porter were enjoying lunch. Lying on the floor at Porter's feet was their dog, a four year old female golden lab. She was Porter's dog and Molly got to pick the gender when they got her. Molly and Porter had known each other since high school and were often together

Porter constantly asked her to marry him but she always refused. Not because of the bi-racial thing, but because he had anger issues when he returned from Vietnam. Several years ago she conceded defeat and agreed to marry him. In appreciation of her finally marrying him, he named his dog Miss Mollie—which she agreed to.

They were having a conversation about how peaceful things had become in Blocker's Bluff.

"It's nice that we haven't had any trouble like we did years ago with the former mayor."

"Yeah, let's hope it stays that way, Molly."

They were talking about the brutal homicides of Robert Parker, the former bank owner and mayor, and Linda Jacobs his bank manager. Both were involved in embezzling $150,000 from the bank to finance Parker's scheme to develop land he owned. Their bodies were found inside their homes. The investigation stretched all the way to Atlanta.

Parker had a partner in Atlanta. Her name was Melanie Tifton and she duped several investors out of $150,000 as part of their scheme. Melanie's body was found in the trunk of her car parked at a popular jogging trail. Her brother, Johnny, who was also involved, was found dead in a motel on a highway between Blocker's Bluff and Atlanta.

Melanie's assistant, Stephanie, described as a gorgeous blonde with a nice set and very shapely legs played a part in duping Tifton and Parker in their scheme. Stephanie's whereabouts and Parker's wife were still unknown as was the $300,000.

Parker's son and daughter inherited the land and sold it to Costal Resort. They used the money from the sale to reimburse the authorities for the stolen funds and sold the restaurant their father owned to a pair of long time employees who were now the proud owners.

It was those murders and Mollie's interview by a major cable news network that gained notoriety for the town.

Chef Willie, a tall black man, retired army chef and owner of the diner was also involved in the conversation. He inherited some land from a family member, sold it to Coastal Resort and used the money to purchase the restaurant and do some remodeling. He changed the name, added seating capacity, a larger freezer and increased the size of the general store. The outside of the restaurant didn't look anything like a diner. Chef Willie just didn't want folks to be reminded of Parker.

"Things sure have been good since then. For a retired school teacher, Wilma Patterson has been a good mayor. And I got to buy Parker's restaurant and it's all mine."

Miss Mavis, the chef's wife who was also retired military overheard his comment and shouted from the kitchen, "You mean it's all ours, Chef." Miss Mavis was in charge of the general store and the bakery.

"I hear you woman. Yes, it's all ours," he replied. Molly and Porter grinned.

"And give Porter's dog a treat," she yelled.

Miss Mollie sat with her paw raised.

Chef Willie grabbed a muffin and set it down by her. She gobbled it up in a New York minute.

Before long the road narrowed to two lanes. Longleaf pines and old oak trees covered with moss lined the highway and occasionally formed a canopy over it. Off in the distance beyond the trees were a number of farms and several small residential developments. They weren't there when he last visited. He came to a large sign that read—*Welcome to Historic Blocker's Bluff, est. 1867.*

The sign was new to him, but he remembered his grandfather once told him that the original town consisted of just a general store, a covered pavilion where farmers and fishermen sold or bartered their goods and a livery stable.

When he came to the site where the town cemetery was located, he turned in. The part-time caretaker sat on the bed of his truck under an old oak tree sipping from a bottle of water and taking a break from the afternoon sun. He stood when he saw Harding.

"Excuse me, sir, can you tell me where Travis Waverly's grave is?"

The caretaker looked him up and down. "I know where every grave is." He pointed to a small hill. "That's the Waverly family's plot over there next to the Baxter family's plot. Be careful where you walk, those are special folks."

Harding walked over to several graves and read the tombstones, especially of his maternal grandfather and grandmother. He read the inscription on the one for his grandfather.

TRAVIS WAVERLY
1933 – 2003
Loving Husband to Juliette
Father to Judy
Korean War Veteran and Loved by All

The date on the tombstone infuriated him. "Son of a bitch!" he mouthed. Then walked back to his car and waved to the caretaker. He slapped the steering wheel and shouted, "Damn, damn! Why couldn't father have told me about Grandpa's death?" He had to take a moment to steady his nerves. His anger and frustration were as bad as they were when his mother left and his father said there would be no more visits to Blocker's Bluff—not ever.

Eventually the road led into town and not much seemed familiar to him except the restaurant, and it wasn't called Parker's Restaurant like he remembered. The sign read, "Willie's Diner" and "General Store." Both sides of the street were lined with retail shops and a few offices.

He almost went through the stoplight in the center of town when it turned red and wondered what happened to the stop sign.

A car marked "Chief" was parked in front of the diner. He remembered the town's chief of police was named John Porter. However, his car wasn't as nice, and the sign on Porter's car looked like it may have been taped to the front door. He pulled into a parking space and sat in his car wondering what to do next.

The door to the diner opened and a black female with short grayish-black hair, sharply dressed in a police uniform, and a white male dressed in civilian clothes exited. Both were in their sixties. Although his hair was grayer and he now had a paunch, Harding recognized John Porter but didn't recognize the female and thought maybe she was his chauffeur.

The female went right to the driver's side while Porter opened the back door, and the dog jumped in. Then he entered on the passenger's side.

It seemed strange to him that the town had a real police car and if that was Chief Porter and his chauffeur, things really had changed. Last time he was here, they only had a one-man police force.

As the woman backed out of her parking space, she glanced at Harding and gestured a salute. He returned the salute but didn't know if she could see his uniform or was just being polite. He waited for them to leave before getting out of his car.

Chief Molly glanced at the rearview mirror and watched as Harding got out of his rental. She focused her attention on the road in front of her. "John, did you notice the rental car parked in front of the diner? The guy who got out of it was dressed in military garb." Porter was preoccupied with other thoughts and didn't hear her at first. She elbowed him on the arm. "John, did you hear what I said?"

He flinched and shouted, "Geez, Molly! Pay attention to your driving. Yes, I heard you. So the guy was in uniform, so what?"

She elbowed him again. "Damn, John, I was just making an observation. Don't get all pissy."

"Pissy? What the hell you talking about? I don't see what's so strange about someone in uniform. It's the way military personnel dress these days. Ain't you ever seen it before?"

Miss Mollie, their dog, covered her eyes.

As always, Molly ignored his attitude. "Not for a long time in Blocker's Bluff, and I noticed he was driving a rental. Okay, maybe I'm being paranoid, and he's just passing through. We can ask Chef Willie who he is next time we're there. That okay with you?"

Porter shook his head. "Sure, ain't no big deal but if it will satisfy your curiosity. When you get something stuck in your craw, you don't let go."

"Can't help it, that's the way I am."

"I know and maybe it's one of the reasons I love you."

"You think I'm a fool, but I know what's on your mind. You're just looking for sex."

He grinned. "You caught me."

CHAPTER 4

Harding removed his name tag from his shirt, put it on the seat, went into the diner and took a seat at the counter. A cute black waitress with a white apron tied around her waist walked over and gave him a menu.

"Here you go, sir, when you're ready to order call me." She winked at him.

Chef Willie stepped out of the kitchen. "Susie, I'll take care of him, you take care of the other customers."

She winked again and walked away.

"Just passing through, Sergeant, or staying a while?" asked Chef Willie.

He hesitated since he knew Chef Willie, but did he recognize him? "Don't know yet. Any place I can get a room for a day or two?"

"Miss Baxter rents rooms by the day. You passed her place coming into town. It's the gray house with the porch and rockers. You'll see the green sign at the end of the driveway. This time of year, I'm sure she has a room available. And they're reasonable too."

"Thanks, I'll go there after I leave here. This place is bigger than I remember and so is the town."

"You from here, Sergeant?"

"Fished off the coastline a number of times; ate here a few times too, but it was called Parker's Restaurant back then. Didn't a Parker own the bank?"

"Parker's long gone. I bought the place and added more seating. That development you passed on the way into town brought prosperity and a new mayor changed things." He beamed with pride. "And we're much larger in population then we were years ago."

"I wondered about that development when I drove by. It looks big and has a golf course. Is it just winter residents or are there year-rounds also?"

"Both. They keep me busy as do the townsfolk. The developers built a new access road to I-95, paved the road through town, and built us a new dock and a marina. Brings a lot more fishermen, also got a better filling station too."

Susie Watkins, the waitress, wiped the other end of the counter and pretended to arrange the napkin holders and salt and pepper shakers while watching Harding. He was aware of her interest, turned and smiled. She blushed.

"Town really has grown and prospered. So have you. I don't remember this place being as big as it is. I'll just have coffee and a muffin if it's okay with you."

"Sure, Susie, bring this young man a muffin, and I'll get his coffee." He poured a cup of coffee and Susie brought him a blueberry muffin. "That muffin is fresh made by Miss Mavis, my wife. You'll enjoy it."

"Thanks, it's awfully big, but it's how I like them."

Chef Willie decided he liked the marine and wouldn't charge him for the muffin. He noticed there was no nametag on his shirt.

"Damn that was good!" He finished the muffin, wiped his mouth and took a sip of coffee. "Guess I better take a ride over to Miss Baxter's place and get a room. What's the tab, sir?"

Chef Willie saluted him and grinned. "It's Chef Willie, and it's on the house, but next time you pay."

"I can't let you do that, sir. Please, let me pay."

"Nope, you take care and tell Miss Baxter I sent you."

"Thanks again. I'll probably see you for breakfast in the morning. You still serve a big breakfast?"

"Absolutely, you come by around eight thirty, that way you'll miss the crowd."

Before leaving, he turned to Chef Willie and asked, "Say, I noticed the police car that left earlier. Was that Chief Porter with a chauffeur?"

"Nope, Porter hasn't been the chief for some time. That was Chief Molly Dickson. She's Porter's wife. Told you things have changed."

He wondered what other changes were in store for him.

CHAPTER 5

Harding almost missed the hidden driveway but when he saw the sign that read—*Baxter House-circa 1891-Crofton Historical Society,* he turned right and saw the two-story house with weathered siding, a front porch, and windows facing the front yard. It was a welcome sight to him. The house was built by Miss Baxter's great-grandfather and had been remodeled several times by Harding's grandfather, Travis Waverly. It still retained its historical significance.

The long dirt driveway led to a garage out back. The door was up just like it had always been when he was a boy. The green Crown Victoria that his grandfather had purchased for Miss Baxter was parked inside. He pictured his grandfather in the garage tinkering with the car and sometimes a lawnmower.

He parked next to a compact car, got out of his rental, and was immediately struck by the sweet smell of jasmine. The hot afternoon temperature brought back memories of the long hot summers visiting with his grandfather as a young boy. He remembered how he used to pick wild violets, bring them to Miss Baxter and trade them for a piece of rhubarb pie with ice cream on it, and the times he mowed the yard for a whole pie.

Occasionally he'd see a black girl, two years younger than him, visit Miss Baxter. She always wore jeans and her hair was always in braids. He thought she looked like a tomboy. Miss Baxter referred to the girl as her granddaughter. He couldn't remember her name, but he remembered her. Sometimes they would play together while Miss Baxter cleaned his grandfather's house. They'd sit on the porch and she would serve them pie and ice cream. He enjoyed the girl's company and took a liking to her.

He had been just months away from his thirteenth birthday when his parents divorced. His father got custody of him and his sister, and he was no longer allowed to visit Blocker's Bluff. His mother returned there after the divorce and dropped her married name. When Travis Waverly died, he didn't go the funeral as he wasn't told of his death.

He knew his grandfather often visited with Miss Baxter by himself and occasionally spent an evening or two with her. His two fondest memories of Blocker's Bluff were sitting on her porch and going fishing with his grandfather.

He walked up to the front door and rang the bell.

An elderly gray-haired black woman answered the door. "Can I help you, young man?"

Miss Baxter was thinner than the last time he saw her, and her facial features showed her age. Twenty years had a way of changing the body and its appearance, but he recognized her just the same. She still wore white sneakers and a dress that fell well below her knees. A white apron was tied around her waist. Her hands were thinner and showed signs of arthritis. Also her hair was much grayer, but she had that same welcoming smile.

"Yes ma'am, my name's Roger Pritcher, and I'm in need of a room for a couple of nights."

The woman stepped outside, lowered her reading glasses to her nose, looked him up and down taking notice of his uniform. "I've got a room if you're interested. It's on the second floor and faces east so you'll be able to see the sunrise. The bathroom is down the hall. You share that with other guests. There's only one boarder right now so you won't have much of a wait. It's thirty-five dollars a night."

"I'll take it, ma'am, and Chef Willie told me to say hello."

"If Chef Willie sent you, then it's only twenty-five dollars. I suppose you've already had lunch so no need me fixin you something. Come on in. You got any bags, young man?"

"Yes, ma'am, I do. I appreciate the discount, but I can pay regular price."

"Nonsense. It's twenty-five dollars take it or leave it. You get one meal, breakfast or supper. Breakfast is at seven thirty and supper's at six o'clock. The other guest will join you."

For twenty-five dollars, he felt he was getting quite a bargain. Maybe he might come back after he took care of the matter in Beaufort. And he would have to get used to folks around here still calling dinner supper except on Sundays and certain holidays.

"Okay, ma'am, I'm having breakfast at the diner in the morning, so I'll have supper this evening. My bag is in the car, I'll go get it, ma'am."

"And stop calling me ma'am. I ain't that old. Call me Miss Baxter or Miss Lottie."

"Okay, Miss Baxter. I'll be right back. You don't have Internet access by any chance, do you?"

"Of course I do. I may be old, but I'm no dinosaur. My guests appreciate it, and my granddaughter uses it when she visits."

"Thanks. I may need to use it."

"You go right ahead."

He trotted off to his car, retrieved his bag, and followed her. His room had a queen-sized bed and a sitting area with a small desk for writing. He plugged in his iPad then searched the name Judy Harding on Google.

There were no links, so he decided to try her maiden name. He found several links for Judy Waverly. One showed her as an independent real estate agent and another showed her as a member of the sales force at Coastline Resort. He clicked the one for Coastline Resort. Not much background information was available, just her bio for the Resort. Then he tried the site that had showed her as an independent realtor.

It gave the name of her agency, how long she was in business, sales experience, and contact information. She was also listed as a member of the town council. The contact information was similar to the Coastline site.

He copied the information and logged off the Internet. What he was going to do with it he hadn't decided. He had another priority to take care of before doing anything about his mother.

He joined Miss Baxter and her other guest for supper in the kitchen promptly at 6:00. The kitchen seemed larger then he remembered and there was ample room for the table with seating for eight. Where there used to be an entrance to the dining room, now there was a closed door with a small sign on it that said "private." He took his place at the table and reached across it to shake hands with the other guest.

"Evening, my name's Br-r… Roger Pritcher. What's yours?"

The middle-aged black gentleman sitting across from him shook his hand. "Name's Marvin Johnson. I'm leaving in the morning for Charleston, how about you?"

"I'm staying a few days then I have business in Beaufort."

Miss Baxter brought the food to the table and joined her guests. She served them each a full plate and filled her own. The three of them enjoyed the meal of southern fried chicken, mashed potatoes, and collard greens followed by a slice of apple pie with vanilla ice cream. After supper, he and Mr. Johnson went outside and sat on the porch. When Harding passed by the large living room, it reminded him of the Sunday mornings after church when his grandfather brought him there for brunch with Miss Baxter, her daughter, and granddaughter. The little girl was all dressed up on those occasions, looking pretty in her yellow dress, and didn't look anything like the tomboy he had played with.

The two men sat on rockers looking off in the distance. There were still remnants of a sunset on the horizon as it shined through the tops of the longleaf pines and live oak trees in the near distance.

"It's beautiful, isn't it, young man?"

"Yes, sir, it certainly is. I could sit here all night and watch that sunset."

They sat back in their rockers and enjoyed the sight in front of them.

"Have you stayed here before?"

He had never spent a night but did spend plenty of evenings chasing lightning bugs.

"It's my first time. How about you?"

"First time this year, but I stay here three times a year. I'm the regional vice president for East Coast National Bank. Blocker's Bluff's branch is in my territory so whenever I'm passing through I stay here. Next stop Charleston then home to Charlotte. Where are you going from here?"

"After my leave is up, I'll be going to Parris Island, sir. I'm in the marines, and that's my final base."

"How long have you served?"

Too long, he thought. "Almost twelve years, sir."

"Are you going to stay until retirement?"

After another tour in Afghanistan, Harding decided to leave the marines when his enlistment ended. He requested Parris Island be his next base of operations. Because of his combat experience, his request was accepted. He would transition out at one of the field training battalions where he would train recruits and receive transition classes to assist him toward civilian life.

"No, sir, I'm getting out in six months. Seen too much war, and I need to get on with a new life."

"When I came home from Vietnam, I felt the same. You know what you're going to do after you get out?"

He hadn't given much thought to what he would do. He had a college degree and maybe it would help him find something.

"Not really, sir."

Mr. Johnson reached into his pocket, took out a business card and handed it to him. "You call me and maybe I can help you. It will be one veteran helping another one. I was lucky to retire after twenty-one years in the army, and I understand your frustration."

"Thank you, sir, I just might do that."

Mr. Johnson stood up. "Roger, since it's nine o'clock, and I'm leaving in the morning for Charleston, I'm going to turn in. Goodnight, young man."

"Goodnight to you, sir. I'm gonna sit a while." He gazed at the sky, and soaked in the night air as he wondered if coming here was the right thing.

CHAPTER 6

Harding woke from a deep sleep feeling refreshed and invigorated. During the night he opened the window to let fresh air in and now the curtains were blowing in the cool breeze. He hadn't had a good night's sleep in a very long time nor had he slept in a comfortable bed. He turned on his side and peeked at the clock on the nightstand. It read 8:00. He rolled over onto his back, looked up at the ceiling, and glanced around the room. Twenty-five dollars a night with one meal didn't seem like a fair exchange for the owner. But he was happy to have a room all to himself

The sounds of the birds chirping their morning song comforted him. Waking up in war zones was nowhere as peaceful as it was here. He sat up, reached for the robe hanging on the back of the door and put it on. The old wood floor felt much better than the sand floor in his tent in Afghanistan. He grabbed the towel and a bar of soap from the small table in the corner. He opened the bedroom door, checked the hallway, and proceeded to walk down the hall to the bathroom. Before opening the door, he knocked gently to make sure no one was inside, and then opened the door and entered.

The bathroom was tiny but at least looked nothing like the latrines he was used to. A small sink, toilet, and a bathtub were pretty much all it offered. He removed the robe, stepped into the tub, closed the curtain, turned on the shower and let the water fall over every part of his battle-worn body. He had forgotten how good it felt to take a shower in private in a safe environment. When he finished showering he dried off, slipped on the robe, opened the door, peeked down the hallway and went back to his room. He reached into his suitcase, took out a pair of shorts, a military T-shirt and the only pair of sneakers he owned, and dressed. Hopefully, he would still be able to make breakfast at Willie's Diner.

It was now eight-fifty and way past the time he wanted to go to the diner, and he was hungry. He walked down the stairs, something else he hadn't done in a long while. When he reached the bottom, Miss Baxter was standing there.

"Good morning, young man. Looks like you overslept."

The sound of her voice made him feel melancholy since he hadn't been greeted in the morning like that in a very long time.

"I guess I did. I haven't slept in a bed like that or in a room of my own in almost a decade, except in a hotel. It felt like I was almost at home."

"Well, I'm glad you were comfortable. You going to the diner or would you like me to fix you something?"

Longing to tell her who he was and have breakfast with her like in the past, he decided to simply accept her offer. "I thought breakfast was earlier and I missed it."

"It was, but I don't mind fixin' something for you. Anything special you care for?"

Her question triggered fond memories. "Eggs and bacon would be nice but whatever you have will do. I don't want to take advantage of your generosity, ma'am."

"Young man, you're not takin' advantage of anything. I just want you to be comfortable like you're in your own home. Come,

I'll fix you a breakfast that will last you the whole day, and tonight you'll have supper here. No arguments!"

He wished it were possible to be in his own home, but this was the next best thing. Now he knew why his grandfather had spent so much time here.

"Thanks, ma'am. Those are words of comfort to me."

She laughed and led him to the kitchen.

"There's fresh coffee on the stove. Pour yourself a cup and have a seat."

The smell of the fresh coffee was intoxicating. He poured himself a cup and sat at the table. He noticed the sturdy wooden chairs were the same ones he sat on decades ago. He chose the one that had "BH" carved in the seat.

"Ma'am, these chairs look kind of old. Have you had them long?"

Busy fixing scrambled eggs and bacon, she responded over her shoulder. "Goin' on thirty or forty years now. They were made special for me by a man handy with his hands."

His grandfather was a carpenter among the many talents he had, so he guessed he had made them.

Miss Lottie brought him a plate of eggs and bacon with two links of sausage, toast and homemade peach jam. When he saw the plate, he felt like getting up and hugging her. She used to fix him a plate like that when his grandfather brought him here early in the morning.

"Eat up son, and if you want seconds, I can make more."

"Thanks, ma'am. Everything looks really good."

"Tastes good, too, and stop callin' me ma'am. I said for you to call me Miss Baxter or Miss Lottie didn't I?"

He remembered the girl's name was Lottie, just like her grandmother's. "Do you mind if I call you Miss Lottie?"

She looked at him suspiciously. "I prefer you did. You know when you say that, it has a familiar ring. Must be my imagination, else I'm getting old." Both smiled.

He hoped she still didn't recognize him and continued to eat his breakfast. She began cleaning up the previous tenant's breakfast dishes.

"Thank you for the breakfast, ma'am. I haven't eaten like that in a long while."

Her eyes twinkled. "So, what have you decided to do the rest of the day?"

He hadn't thought much about it; maybe he'd wander into town or relax on the porch like old times. "I haven't decided yet, ma'am."

"Didn't we agree you'd call me Miss Lottie. No more ma'am."

If his memory was correct, that was what she told him to do that last summer. "Sorry, just can't shake being polite. I think I'm going to sit out on the porch. Doesn't seem like it's too hot yet, so if it's okay with you, I'll have another cup of coffee and go sit out there. Can I help you clean up before I go?"

"No, you go on out and relax. You seem like you could use some relaxation. You're probably a bit war weary."

Yes, he was war weary, he thought. He filled his cup, excused himself, and went out to the porch. He looked up at the ceiling and chuckled when he saw that she still hung bags of water to shoo away the flies. She always told him and her granddaughter not to stick pins in them to splash each other, but they did it anyway.

He leaned forward in the rocker with an elbow on a knee and held the coffee in one hand. He surveyed the yard and noticed the grass was getting tall and in need of mowing. He wondered who mowed it and pictured himself doing the chore.

Miss Lottie opened the front door and carefully stepped onto the porch with a pitcher of lemonade, two glasses and a small basket of muffins.

"Here, let me help you."

She handed him the tray. "Thank you. Set it on the table. I thought I'd join you but not with coffee. It won't be long before it warms up and lemonade goes better with the muffins." She poured two glasses, handed him one, and sat down next to him. "Peaceful out here ain't it."

"Yes, ma'am, I mean, Miss Lottie, it sure is. It almost feels like home."

"You've been away a long time, haven't you?"

"Yes, a very long time, too long in fact. I've forgotten what it's like to just sit and relax with no worries."

"Well, you got no worries here so just relax. I'll keep you company. It's nice to sit with someone out here."

He turned his head away from her as a tear slipped from one eye. He wiped it with the back of his hand. "I see your lawn is getting up high. Who mows it?"

"My granddaughter mows around the house and garden and a neighbor does the rest once a month with a ride-on mower. Lottie comes on weekends with her son, Thomas. She's a schoolteacher in Crofton. She ain't got a husband 'cause he was killed in Iraq. He was in the army. She manages well for a single mom. Poor girl, first her father up and leaves her, then her mother caught the cancer and she died. It's tragic."

Now he knew what happened to the girl, but he felt sad that she had lost her husband and mother. He always called her Brat and she referred to him as Bratly. Maybe he would get to meet her but not this weekend because he had to go to Beaufort for a reunion with one of his injured comrades.

"Since I don't have anything to do the rest of the day, do you mind if I mow it? It's been a while since I mowed a lawn and the exercise will do me good." Not only would it be good exercise, he thought, but it would be another fond memory for him.

"You don't have to, but if it would make you feel better, the mower's in the garage. Be careful because it's a really old garage and could use some work."

"I'll be careful and thanks for letting me do it."

They stayed on the porch until it was near lunchtime. Miss Lottie got up, placed the glasses and his cup on the tray along with the empty basket of muffins and went into the house to start preparing lunch.

"You join me in the kitchen for lunch. I'll call you when it's ready. The lawn can wait until afterwards."

"First I'm gonna check the mower and see if it runs."

CHAPTER 7

As Molly drove through town, Porter looked out the window admiring the cozy little town that he grew up in. The rows of vacant stores were now a haven of specialty shops. Numerous artists and writers had been attracted to the small town charm. Poets had also found inspiration while observing the morning sunrises. A number of fancy vehicles were parked angling toward the storefronts. Business had been good for the shopkeepers.

Passing the police station, he fondly recalled spending nights sleeping on the small cot in the back room. Now there's a separate room with a comfortable bed and a decent bathroom with privacy.

"Molly, I was just thinking about how things used to be here. Lot of progress since the murders, and you got a comfortable bed for tomorrow night."

She glanced around the center of town admiring all the changes including the stop light. She also remembered nights spent in that awful cot and the tiny room.

"Yeah, I remember what it was like. Funny how those murders years ago changed things."

"This town has come a long way since its beginning. It was built by farmers and fishermen like our grandfathers. They worked from dawn to dusk to eke out a living. Folks back then were good hard working people who looked out for each other."

"They still do. That's what makes this town a great place to live."

Porter watched as two tourists came out of a gift shop and walked to their car.

In the rear seat, Miss Mollie rolled over on her back and covered her eyes as if saying, these old farts are getting maudlin now.

"All this talk is makin me hungry, Molly. Let's go eat."

She pulled up and parked at the diner. Porter opened the back-door. Miss Mollie leaped out and ran to the entrance and sat, waiting impatiently.

Molly laughed. "Looks like she's hungry too."

"She's always hungry when we come here. You buyin' or am I?"

"I'm on duty so you have to buy or I can let the town pay."

He put his arm around her, pulled her close and said, "Then I'm buyin', 'cause I love you."

She removed his arm and stepped away. "Stop, I'm on duty, no fooling around"

"I know, but we will tonight because I'll be back on the island tomorrow night with Miss Mollie."

"What are you gonna do there"

"Maybe do a little fixin' up and then maybe a little fishin' for Sunday night supper." Miss Mollie barked several times. "Okay, we're coming!" Porter shouted.

The only patrons in the diner were an elderly gentleman and his wife. Both lived at Coastline Community and they must have come to town to shop. Porter and Molly waved to them. Susie had just finished waiting on them and was now behind the counter.

"Afternoon, Chief, you too, Mr. Porter, are you folks having anything to eat or just coffee?"

"Afternoon, Susie, we're having a late lunch," Molly replied. "What's available?"

Susie handed them a menu. "We've still got some items left that are on the menu, or would you care for something else? Take a look while I get a couple a glasses of water and some utensils."

Porter and Molly glanced at the menu but nothing interested them except the burgers and fries. Susie came back with napkins, utensils, and two glasses of water and set them down then took her pad and pencil from her apron pocket.

"What did you folks decide?"

"We're just gonna have burgers and fries and a patty for Miss Molly," replied Porter.

Susie looked down at Miss Mollie, wrote the order and put it in the window for Chef Willie. He grabbed the order and noticed Porter and Molly.

"Chief Molly and Porter, what you doin here so late?"

"We was making rounds and got hungry, so we came here. Can you make those burgers quick?"

"Sure can, Chief."

Seven minutes later, Chef Willie delivered their order personally and they were really big, especially the amount of fries.

"Damn, Chef, that's one hell of an order."

"You both can handle it. I made a special for patty Miss Mollie. Can I give it to her?"

"Go ahead 'cause she looks like she's gonna jump at it."

He set the saucer on the floor, Miss Mollie went after the patty and it was gone in a New York minute. Chef Willie went back to the kitchen to prep for supper. Porter and Molly ate their burgers, he paid the bill, tipped Susie, and then they said goodbye. They were almost out the door when Molly stopped, turned, and walked over to Susie.

When Susie saw the expression on Molly's face, she became concerned—like when the principal caught her smoking in the girl's bathroom and worried she was going to be expelled from high school. "What's the matter, Chief? Did I make a mistake on the bill?"

"No, Susie, you didn't. I have a question for you. Yesterday after we left, I noticed a soldier in uniform come in here. Do you know who he was?"

Susie scratched her head with the pencil, took a moment to think and then remembered Harding. "I saw him; he was kinda cute, but I didn't wait on him, Chef Willie did. He's staying at Baxter House. Chef Willie sent him there. Is there a problem?"

"No problem, just curious. You take care now."

"You too, Chief."

Porter gave her a curious look. "What was that all about?"

"Just curious about that soldier yesterday, that's all."

He shook his head. "You just can't let some things be, can you?"

"No, I can't."

On the way to their house, she drove past Baxter House, slowed down as she passed it, and made a mental note of the car parked in the driveway.

Porter turned and glanced out the window. "Why are we slowing here?"

"That soldier's staying there. Chef Willie sent him there. I just wanted to check if he was."

Porter put his right hand on his knee and looked at her. "So he's staying there. Ain't no harm in it and if Chef Willie sent him, then it's okay."

She ignored him and drove on by.

CHAPTER 8

As he walked toward the garage, he noticed the remnants of a garden behind the house that was in need of raking and tilling. Weeds had taken over and it appeared to have been ignored for quite some time. Miss Lottie always took good care of it before, but she was no longer able to keep up with the necessary care. He walked through a few rows, kicked the soil, bent over, pulled several weeds, tossed them away and then wiped his hand on his shorts.

She watched from the window, and wondered why he'd taken an interest in the garden. Then she remembered there was a young boy who helped her in the garden and they picked the rhubarb to make pies for him and his grandfather—for after they mowed the yard. He turned and walked toward the garage. Miss Lottie went to her bedroom and looked out the window.

He could smell remnants of gasoline and old sawdust when he first entered the garage. His grandfather's workbenches that he used when making furniture were still there. Old doors and windows were stacked up in the rear and there were handsaws hanging on the walls. The lawnmower was parked against the wall. He pushed it out of the garage and checked to see if it needed gas. Under the workbench was a gas can; he picked it up and filled the mower's tank. Then he tugged on the starter cord and the mower came to life.

She watched him start the mower and wondered if he was that young boy. She walked into the pantry, stuck her head out the door and called out to him. "Young man, lunch is ready."

He walked inside, went to the sink, washed his hands, and sat down at the table.

"Miss Lottie, I thought you told me I only get one meal a day. This makes two so far."

She wiped her hands on her apron. "That's right, but lunch is because you're gonna be mowing the lawn. You need some energy 'cause that's a big job and too much for one person."

After lunch, he thanked her and went back to the garage. He found a clean rag on the workbench and put it in his back pocket. Then he pushed the mower out of the garage, down the driveway, and started it. He worked south to north across the yard, reversed, and came back repeating it over and over.

Thirty minutes later his forehead was drenched in sweat, so he paused to wipe it with the rag. Miss Lottie sat on the porch, watched and remembered that his grandfather used to do the same thing when he was mowing.

He took a set of ear phones from his pocket, put them on and continued mowing. He had country music on his playlist and Alan Jackson was singing—"Where Were You When the World Stopped Turning?" He stopped mowing and wiped his brow.

On that infamous day, he was in his apartment getting ready for his first law class at the University of Virginia when the first tower was struck. He watched the events unfold and never made it to any of his classes that day. He felt compelled to do something for his country, but his father and his paternal grandfather convinced him to complete law school. Two years later at the start of his third year, he still felt compelled to serve his country. A few of his classmates had joined the military as JAG officers, but he wanted to see combat like his paternal great-grandfathers and maternal grandfather had.

He informed his father that he was enlisting in the marines. Both his father and his grandfather vehemently objected as they opposed the war and disliked both the president and the military. Neither of them had ever served. It was his grandfather's words that really stunned him, and his father echoed them.

They said serving in the military was for someone else's son to do. He had an obligation to his family and to their law firm. His father shouted at him that if he enlisted, he would no longer be welcome in his house.

He shouted back that it was his decision and if they couldn't find it in their hearts to respect it, then that was their problem. He told them to tell his sister, EmilyKate, that he loved her and would miss her.

Before leaving, he overheard his grandparents speak of his mother and her father, Travis, in a not so flattering way. He left the house that day and never looked back.

He was sent to Parris Island for training and deployed to Iraq. Six months into his deployment, he killed his first insurgent. It took him several days to come to grips with killing another human being. But shortly thereafter on another mission, he killed several more during a firefight in which he saved some of his fellow marines. He eventually wrote a letter to his sister hoping she received it; unfortunately he never got a reply.

Miss Lottie wondered why he stopped mowing. When he resumed again, she became concerned that something was bothering him. She got up and went inside to make some sweet tea, left it in the refrigerator and went back to watching him. Halfway through the yard, he decided to let the remainder wait until the morning. As he pushed the mower toward the garage, he waved to her. She brought the sweet tea from the kitchen on a tray and a towel for him to use. He left the mower in the garage and joined her on the porch.

"It's too hot to do any more, it's more than I can handle. I'll finish in the morning." He wiped his forehead and arms with the rag.

"I brought this towel for you to wipe off with." She handed him the towel. He sat down and took a glass of sweet tea.

"Thank you, this hits the spot."

She sipped her tea. "You can let the rest go. My neighbor will finish it and my granddaughter, Lottie, will appreciate what you did. You've done enough already and should relax." She studied his facial features and recognized them at last. They resembled those of Travis Waverly.

"That was relaxing for me. I haven't done it in a very long time." He leaned back in the chair, took a sip of tea, and admired his work.

"Where is your home, young man?"

He wasn't sure where his home was or eventually would be since he hadn't thought much about it since leaving Afghanistan. But felt she didn't need to know that. "I'm originally from Virginia, but my home has been with the marines the past decade or so."

"Are your parents still in Virginia?"

He had to be careful not to give himself away. "My father is but not my mother. My parents were divorced when I was much younger."

"That's sad. Have you written to them?"

"No, I haven't. When I joined the marines, my family objected and there were harsh words. The marines have been my family ever since." *And that was okay with me.*

"Well you should at least try to contact your mother. Every mother worries about her children, especially in times of war. You think about it."

He turned his head away and wiped his eyes with the towel. "I will, Miss Lottie, soon. Thanks for the advice."

She noticed him wipe his eyes. He wasn't fooling her; she knew he was Travis' grandson Bradley Harding and not Roger Pritcher and must have a reason for keeping it a secret. "You've done enough for today. You're supposed to be relaxing not working."

"I actually enjoyed the work, but you're right I've done enough for today. It's nice to have someone like you to talk with, especially not about war."

"I'm happy to keep you company. After supper if you'd like, we can sit out here and chat or you can watch the television. You could go into town and walk around or go to Crofton. They have a movie theatre there and you can catch a movie or just walk around. You should probably do that, it would be better for you."

He scratched his neck. The last movie he watched was under a tent in Afghanistan and it wasn't very enjoyable. "I might just go into Crofton. It's straight out 103 if I remember the exit when I came here."

"Yes, it is. I'll fix a light supper so you can get there in time for the show. After the movie stop in the ice cream parlor and get yourself something. They only sell homemade ice cream, and it's really good. My Lottie takes me there when we shop in town."

He grinned. *Grandpa made homemade ice cream, too, and man was it good.* "Thanks, that sounds like a nice idea, I'll do that. If I get back early enough, I'm going to sit here and enjoy the moonlit sky. What are you going to do?"

"I'm going to talk with my Lottie and great-grandson on Skype. She set it up for me and we have fun with it, especially Thomas and me." She touched his arm. "If I'm up, I'll join you. Go shower now, you'll feel better."

He went to his room, showered and dressed. Then he opened his laptop and did some more research on Judy Waverly.

Later after supper, he left for Crofton. As he drove off, he noticed a car turn into a familiar driveway and stop. He slowed and watched as the driver got out and walked to the mailbox to retrieve her mail. He drove on by and she waved to him, he waved back. She was his mother, Judy Waverly, and the house belonged to his grandfather.

In Crofton, he found the theatre, parked, walked to the ticket booth and purchased a ticket, a small bag of popcorn and a small Coke, found a seat and watched the movie. After the movie, he went to Bonnie's Ice Cream Parlor room and ordered a banana split with all the trimmings. Since it was nine-thirty, he decided to go back to Baxter House. He slowed when he passed his mother's house.

Miss Lottie sat on the porch with several candles burning. "You're home early, young man."

"Yes, I decided the night was too pretty not to enjoy. May I join you?"

"Come take a seat. I'll get you some tea. Be right back."

He took a seat in the rocker next to hers. She brought him a glass of tea and some homemade cookies and handed them to him.

"Beautiful evening, isn't it, young man?"

The light from the citronella candles sparkled off her face. It felt as though he was sitting with the maternal grandmother he never met. His paternal grandparents were very distant and the only family time he and his sister had with them was briefly on Thanksgiving and Christmas. But those holidays were cold and uneventful, especially after his parent's divorce.

The moon was above the tree line and lit the entire yard. A few lightning bugs glowed and an owl screeched in a nearby tree. He was intoxicated by the beauty of the scene.

"It certainly is."

"After lunch tomorrow would you drive me into town? I want to stop at the farmer's market and get some fresh fruit and vegetables. If they have any rhubarb, I'll buy some and make a pie. You ever tasted rhubarb pie, young man?"

"I can't say I have, but I'll try anything once." *Oh, man I can't wait.* He had a slight grin on his face. "I'd be happy to take you into town. If I had a boat and a fishing pole, I'd go out in the morning and catch some fish for supper tomorrow."

That grin when she mentioned the rhubarb pie confirmed that he was Travis' grandson. "Well, I bet you'd catch a plenty."

Those three little words were the ones she used when he and his grandfather returned from a morning of fishing. "You boys catch a plenty?" she would ask. He watched more lightning bugs.

"When will you be leaving, young man?"

"Probably Sunday afternoon. I'll rent a motel room in Beaufort and do my business some time Monday morning." He would have liked to say never, but he had to go to Beaufort and then Parris Island when his leave was over.

"No need for you to rent a motel room. You could stay here Sunday night and drive in the morning. It's only about an hour or so drive. I'd welcome your company a little longer."

He leaned back on the rocker. "I'm going to take you up on your offer and stay the extra night." Another night just might prepare him for what awaits in Beaufort.

CHAPTER 9

At nine-thirty, Molly and Porter went to their bedroom. Molly went into the bathroom to change clothes. She selected the nightie that she wore on the night of their wedding. Molly wanted to impress Porter and give him something to take back to his island tomorrow.

Their master bedroom wasn't that large. It accommodated the queen-sized bed they slept in, two nightstands and a chair. She didn't change the bed for a larger one after Porter started living with her. She also kept the pretty floral bedspread and curtains from when she was single.

"You look nice in that nightie. Guess that means we're having sex."

"You're a crazy son of a bitch, Porter."

"Yep, and I'm crazy in love with you. Now turn them damn lights out."

In the morning, Molly woke before Porter, let Miss Mollie out, and then made a fresh pot of coffee. She showered, selected a fresh uniform, dressed, and put on her holster. Since they were going to the diner for breakfast, she decided to wake Porter up. Afterward she'd take him to his boat. Porter was snoring like a fog horn.

"Porter, wake up you damn fool, you sound like a ship's fog horn and you're making the walls shake," she shouted.

He sat up immediately as though hit by a bolt of lightning. "What the hell! Dammit! You scared the hell out of me. What's the matter with you woman?"

She laughed. "The neighbors are complaining about the noise. Get up and shower; it's time to go to breakfast."

"You could have just tapped me on the shoulder."

"Yeah, but that wouldn't have been any fun. You should have seen your face. Look at Miss Mollie, she enjoyed it too."

Miss Mollie was rolling on the floor.

"I'll get even with you two one day, just wait."

"Yeah, yeah, come on, get up."

He showered and dressed. Miss Mollie waited impatiently for him to get ready.

"Okay already, I'm ready. Let's go 'cause now I'm hungry."

"John, you got everything you need?"

"Yep." He grabbed his bag, slung it over his shoulder, and followed Molly and Miss Mollie out the door.

The morning air was still a little crisp, but the sun was starting to warm the day. The sky revealed the aftermath of a gorgeous sunrise. Miss Mollie hopped into the backseat and Molly drove to the diner.

"Looks like you're going to have a nice morning for your boat ride to the island."

He glanced up at the sky. "Yep, and maybe calm seas, too."

Molly parked, and he opened the rear door for Miss Mollie. She leaped out and ran to the diner and waited for them.

"Looks like she's hungry too, John."

Molly and Porter found seats at the counter. Miss Mollie sat by Porter's feet. Susie walked over to greet them, but Chef Willie stepped out of the kitchen and waved her off.

"Morning you two, guess you want your usual breakfast?"

"Morning, Chef Willie. Yes, we do, and Miss Mollie will have her usual too," replied Porter.

"Chef Willie, has that soldier been in lately, the one that's staying at Miss Baxter's?" She wondered if he knew anything more about him.

"Why you so interested in him, Molly? He ain't done anything wrong, and, no, he hasn't. He's a marine and must be eating meals at Baxter House."

Porter also wondered why she was so interested in the marine. "Yeah, Molly, what's with all the questions about him? He's probably back from Afghanistan. Give him a break."

She elbowed him in the arm. When her eyebrows pulled downward and her mouth pursed, he knew that meant she was annoyed.

"I'm just curious that's all. You know how I am."

Porter rubbed his arm. "Are you gonna hit me every time I question you? Give the man a break. He may be on leave from the war. Let it rest."

"Porter's right, Molly, he probably is on leave and just passing through. And he don't need any trouble from you."

She decided to drop the subject for now. "Okay, I know when I'm outnumbered. You gonna fix our breakfast or keep nagging me, Chef Willie?"

Chef Willie laughed and winked at Porter. "Sure, won't take but a few minutes."

Miss Mollie covered her eyes with her paws and whimpered as if saying, give me a break, will ya.

Meanwhile at Baxter House, Harding had just finished breakfast and was clearing the table while Miss Lottie washed the dishes and pans from the morning's meal. The door to the back porch was open letting in the fresh air. He was restless to get started mowing the rest of the front yard before it warmed up and the heat made it difficult.

"I'm going to start on the yard before it warms up."

She turned from the sink, dried her hands on her apron, and asked, "Don't you want another cup of coffee first?"

"No, thank you, I think I've had enough. I best get started."

"Take this small towel with you. When you're done, I'll have some sweet tea for you and I'll join you on the front porch. Don't overdo it, young man."

"Thanks, I won't."

He went out the backdoor, walked to the garage and pushed the mower to the front yard. Then he paused before starting it, took a breath of fresh air and remembered helping his grandfather mow. His grandfather always bet him that whoever finished last had to give his extra piece of Miss Lottie's rhubarb pie to the winner. He always won because he had the smallest amount of yard to mow, and he knew she would have an extra piece saved for his grandfather.

He removed his shirt, set it on the porch, and put his earphones on. Then he pulled the starter cord and began mowing. The smell of fresh mowed grass was like therapy for him, and the country music in his ears completely relieved his mind of any thoughts about the war. Half-way through his chore, perspiration rolled down his face. He stopped periodically to wipe his forehead and face with the small towel he kept in his back pocket.

Miss Lottie sat on the porch and watched him. She remembered the times when she watched Travis Waverly and his grandson mow the lawn. The young boy would stop and wipe the perspiration just like he was doing. It was then that she knew for certain he wasn't Roger Pritcher, but Travis Waverly's grandson and for some reason he didn't want her to know. She wasn't going to take issue with him over his secret as she felt he must have a reason for it.

When he finished mowing, she handed him a fresh towel to wipe the perspiration. He was six foot two and all muscle just like his grandfather was at his age. On his right shoulder was a tattoo of the Marine Corps insignia. It reminded her of the 82nd Airborne Paratrooper tattoo that Travis Waverly had on his right shoulder. He wiped himself dry, put on his shirt, and sat down on the porch. Miss Lottie handed him a glass of sweet tea.

Back at Willie's Diner, Molly and Porter were just finishing breakfast and about to leave.

"I'll see you later, Chef Willie, I'm pulling an all-nighter so it will be just me for supper and breakfast in the morning."

"What about you, Porter, what will you be doing?"

"I'll be spending the day and tonight on Porter's Island, so I won't see you until sometime Sunday. Thanks for breakfast."

Chef Willie handed some bacon to Miss Mollie. "You folks have a good day."

Miss Mollie leaped onto the rear seat.

"Let's go, Molly."

She drove to the dock and parked. He opened the door for Miss Mollie and grabbed his bag. Molly walked them both down to his boat.

"I'm gonna miss you, John."

"I'll miss you too."

He took her in his arms and gave her a long kiss and then he and Miss Mollie boarded his boat. Molly waved as they pulled away. She wiped a tear from her eye and then went back to her vehicle and drove to the police station to check in with her assistant.

Since she had some time on her hands Molly decided to visit Miss Baxter.

"Adrian, I'm going to take a drive over to Baxter House. I'll stop back before lunch."

"Okay, Chief, I'll be here."

When she turned into Miss Baxter's driveway, she and Harding were on the porch. Molly waived and walked over to them.

"Morning, Miss Baxter."

Miss Lottie stood up. "Morning, Molly. What brings you out here?"

Molly turned and looked over at Harding. "Just passing by. Is that your new guest?"

"You're not checking up on me, are you, girl?"

"No, I was just curious."

Miss Lottie put a hand on Molly's shoulder. "You always were a curious child. No need checking on me. He's a very nice young man and his name's Roger Pritcher. Don't you be bothering him now, you hear me?"

Molly registered the name in her mind for later use. "Why would I bother him, Miss Baxter?"

"Because you're too curious for your own good, that's why. I made some sweet tea, would you like a glass?"

"Don't mind if I do."

He got up and gave her his seat. "Morning, Chief. Miss Baxter, I sure could use another glass of sweet tea."

"Be right back." She went into the house and came back with a pitcher and a glass for Molly. She filled both their glasses.

"Thank you."

"Yes, thanks, Miss Baxter. How did you know I was the chief, young man, aside from the uniform and my car?"

"Chef Willie told me when I had lunch at his restaurant the other day."

Miss Lottie gave her a look that told her to stop and so she did. "Well, I got rounds to make, so I best get going. Thanks for the sweet tea, Miss Baxter. See you around, young man."

"Probably so, Chief."

"Remember what I said, Molly."

"Don't worry about me, Miss Baxter."

She stepped down off the porch, went to her vehicle, turned, and waved goodbye.

He got up and sat in the rocker next to Miss Lottie.

"Nice girl, but she's too curious for her own good. After you clean up we can go to Crofton and shop if you still want to, young man."

"I still do, but I'd like to sit here a bit longer with you."

Molly felt like a scolded child after leaving Baxter House, but her nagging suspicious nature wouldn't let her dismiss the concern she had about Harding. She decided that when she had time at the police station, she would look up Roger Pritcher on the Internet. She also wanted to see if she could get information from his rental's license plate.

He went into the house, showered, dressed, and then went to the kitchen to get Miss Lottie. She was putting dishes and glasses in the cabinets. He watched and was reminded of when his mother used to do the same thing after meals.

She sensed his presence and turned around. "You ready, young man?"

"I'm all set if you are."

"Let me get this apron off and get my purse, then we can go."

They went out the front door and to his car. He opened the door for her and waited until she was seated with her seatbelt fastened. He closed the door, got in and then drove to Crofton. As they approached Judy Waverly's house, Miss Lottie glanced out the window.

"Nice young lady lives there and I knew her father. Poor girl, no mother should have to go through what she did."

He had always thought the divorce was an amicable one even though there was the possibility of infidelity.

"What happened to her?"

"I'm not certain, but her father said there was a divorce and she had to give up custody of her children. It broke her father's heart because he never got to see his grandson after the divorce. Broke her heart too."

He wanted to ask her more of what she knew about Judy Waverly but didn't want to seem too curious. It might reveal his real identity.

"That's really a shame."

Miss Lottie turned and faced him. "Yes, it is."

They drove to the Crofton farmer's market. There were close to twenty vendors selling their products including several produce stands, bakery goods, ice cream and a few craft tents.

"Miss Lottie, do you mind if I get me a sticky bun? I haven't had one in a long time."

"You go right ahead. I'm going to look at the fruit and vegetable stands."

After he got his sticky bun, he joined her as she selected fresh vegetables, some fresh rhubarb, and strawberries. Those were the main ingredients for her strawberry-rhubarb pie. The remaining ingredients she already had at home. When she finished shopping, she handed the bags to him.

"Did you enjoy your sticky bun?"

"Yes, I did, but I can't wait to have a piece of rhubarb pie."

She placed a hand on his arm. "You won't have to wait long. I'll bake one this afternoon and you can have a slice this evening."

Later in the day, Molly relaxed in the police department reading one of her favorite fiction novels. When she came to a chapter where the lead character searched the Internet for information on a subject, she decided to do the same on Roger Pritcher. She Googled his name and got several results. The one that interested her the most was the one about a marine's obituary.

Staff Sergeant Roger Pritcher, loving son of Robert and Georgia Pritcher, died serving his country in Afghanistan on June 15, 2013. Sergeant Pritcher had served two tours and was part of a rescue mission that saved the life of another marine who was captured by the Taliban. For his dedicated service, he was awarded a medal for bravery and the Purple Heart posthumously. Family and friends celebrated his life with a memorial service at the Norcroft Lutheran Church. Sergeant Pritcher had an older sister and a niece and nephew.

Molly had read enough and was confused by what she learned. She decided to call the rental agency to see if she could learn whose name was on the rental agreement. Unfortunately, Budget Car Rental told her that information was confidential. She surmised that it most likely wasn't Roger Pritcher.

So who really was the marine staying at Baxter House? She wondered.

CHAPTER 10

As he approached Porter's Island, Porter noticed a strange boat docked near one of the houses belonging to the Coastal Resort Community. He usually knew when someone was in residence and the boat didn't seem like any he had ever seen before. Also, the folks there usually gave him a heads up when someone would be in residence.

"Wonder who's staying at that house, Miss Mollie?"

Miss Mollie's ears went up. She was probably thinking to herself, h*ow* the hell would I know? I'm just a dog.

"Later on we'll go over there and introduce ourselves. Maybe find out how long they're staying."

He slowly pulled up to his dock and was about to secure his boat when he noticed two men walking toward the resort dock. He couldn't make out who they were because of the distance.

Porter motored over to the other dock to see who they were. When the two men saw him approaching, they quickly tossed two bags into their boat. He cautiously pulled up to the dock, and he and Miss Mollie got off. One of the men was in his mid-forties and weighed roughly two hundred pounds. The other man seemed younger and much lighter with an unshaven face. Porter made a mental note of the name on the boat's stern, *Greybeard*.

"You fellas staying in that house over there?" he called out.

The heavier man motioned for the other one to get on their boat.

Porter walked closer and asked again. "I asked if you were staying at that house. Any reason you're not answering?"

Porter thought the big guy was reaching for a gun, so he charged him like he was an opposing quarterback back when he played linebacker in high school. He hit the guy in the stomach with his shoulder, and he fell backwards. Porter landed on top of him. Miss Mollie charged the one on the boat, but he fired his gun at her and she went down yelping. Porter heard the shot and her yelp. He immediately got up to go to her aid. As he turned toward Miss Mollie, he was hit on the head. A burst of pain erupted in his head. He stumbled forward, saw the planks of wood from the dock and landed on them just before everything went dark.

"Why the hell did you shoot the damn dog, Lloyd?"

"Because it was coming at me, that's why, Wilbur."

"Get rid of that damn gun, now."

"But it's—"

"Now, damn it, Lloyd!"

Lloyd tossed it overboard; they finished loading the boat, and they headed north away from Porter's Island.

When Porter came to, he was surprised to find himself lying on the dock face down. A bolt of pain caused him to touch the back of his head. His hand came away with a trace of blood. He raised himself up carefully, almost went back down but managed to right himself. His memory was foggy but he suddenly remembered Miss Mollie's yelp and looked around for her. She was lying on the dock and there was blood on her left shoulder. He walked toward her on wobbly legs. When he reached her, he knelt down beside her and checked to see if she was alive. Fortunately, he was able to feel a pulse, but the blood concerned him. He checked her wound and it seemed as though the bullet had just grazed her shoulder, but it had done enough damage that she would need medical attention, and she was probably experiencing shock.

He rubbed her gently to let her know he was there. He had to get her back to Blocker's Bluff and hopefully Dr. Meyers would be available to treat her. He carefully gathered her in his arms and struggled to get her onto the boat. When both were safely on the boat, he laid her on the floor and then covered her with his shirt. Next, he reached for his cell phone to call Molly.

Molly was an avid reader of Robert Parker books. She was sitting at her desk reading the latest Jesse Stone novel when her phone rang.

"John, what's up? You miss me already?"

"Molly, Miss Mollie and I were attacked and she was shot. It's not that serious, but she's in shock and needs Doc Meyers' help. Can you get hold of her? I'm on my way back to Blocker's Bluff."

Molly did her best not to panic, but she was really worried. "John, are you all right?"

"I was knocked unconscious, but I'm more concerned with Miss Mollie."

"Okay, I'll get hold of Doc Meyers, and we'll meet you at the dock. Make sure you use your running lights."

"Don't fret, they're already on."

He pulled away from the dock and headed toward Blocker's Bluff. Fortunately the sea was calm as he navigated his way, but his vision was somewhat impaired. His head ached from the blow, and he was struggling to stay conscious but he knew he had to for Miss Mollie's sake.

Molly called Dr. Myers and was fortunate to get hold of her at her home because it was Saturday and she had the weekend off. She was the town's part-time physician and Vet. But she was actually a well-respected pediatrician with privileges at several hospitals including Crofton Regional Hospital.

"Chief Dickson, how can I help you?"

"Doc, I have a situation and need your help. John Porter and Miss Mollie were attacked on Porter's Island. He was knocked unconscious and Miss Mollie was shot. Don't know how bad it is, although John says it's not that serious. Hell, nothing is serious with him. Can you meet us at the dock? He is on his way there now."

"I'll get my medical bag and meet you there. Should I call an ambulance?"

"I don't know, but whatever you think is best. Porter won't like it, but the hell with him."

Dr. Myers laughed as she knew how Porter would react to seeing an ambulance there for him, but she was worried about Miss Mollie.

"I'll call for an ambulance."

"Thanks, Doc. I'm on my way now."

Dr. Edna Myers, the daughter of the mayor, was forty-two years old and had known Molly and Porter since she was a child. She knew about Porter's anger issues but respected him for all he did for the town, especially during the hurricanes. Dr. Myers was the one who had to put Old George, Porter's last dog, to sleep, and he had a hard time dealing with it.

"Robert, there's a problem down at the dock. Porter and Miss Mollie need my help. Depending on how serious the situation is, I may not be back tonight. If not, you have a good golf match tomorrow."

Robert Myers, her husband, was the overall project manager at the Coastal Resort Community. He got up from watching television, walked over and hugged her.

"You go do what you have to, honey. I'll be okay. Take care of Miss Mollie and Porter too."

Molly turned her flashers on and sped to the dock. She searched the horizon for Porter's boat. Dr. Myers arrived shortly after she did. An hour later, they saw the silhouette of his boat on the horizon.

Two hundred yards from the dock, Porter's boat slowed but kept approaching. On board, Porter could barely see the dock as his vision was still impaired, but he used the lights from the dock to guide him there. When he was close enough, he throttled down, shut the engine off, and let the boat glide to the dock. Molly, Dr. Myers, and two EMTs watched as the boat drifted to a stop ten feet away.

"John, can you get closer?" shouted Molly.

"I can't see too well. You're gonna have to pull me in."

"Okay, hang on a sec. Woody, get that landing loop over there."

Woody Stevens, one of the two EMTs, had known both Molly and Porter since he was a teenager. He grabbed the landing loop and extended it as far as it would go. Then he hooked the railing of Porter's boat and pulled it up against the dock. Molly secured the boat and Dr. Myers and Woody climbed onboard.

Dr. Myers checked on Miss Mollie's wound. "Woody, get her on the dock so I can check on Porter then I'll take care of her."

He picked up Miss Mollie and handed her to Andy Johnson, the other EMT. Andy placed Miss Mollie on the dock near Molly. Dr. Myers took a pencil flashlight out of her bag and stepped in front of Porter. She shined the light in his eyes and told him to follow the light as she moved it from right to left.

"You're pretty, you know that, Doc?"

She laughed. "Are you making a pass at me, Porter?"

Molly called out. "He probably is, but that means he's okay. Get him on the dock and come look after Miss Mollie, Doc."

Porter winked at the doctor and attempted to stand. "Damn, guess my legs are a little weak and my head aches." He put his hand on the back of his head.

"You may have suffered a concussion, Porter, and you're going to have a bump back there. Woody, help him off the boat."

"Let me help you, Chief." He took one of Porter's arms and placed it over his shoulder.

"I ain't the chief, Woody. Molly is and don't forget it."

Woody grinned. "Anything you say, now let's get you off this boat."

Porter put his foot on the step-up. Woody put his hands on Porter's butt and gave him a shove. Molly and Andy pulled him onto the dock. She ordered him to get on the gurney.

"I'm okay damn it. It's Miss Mollie I'm worried about."

"I am too, but you do as I say, and don't give me any lip."

Porter got on the gurney. Andy turned his head and smiled. Dr. Myers and Woody did the same.

"Take my bag, Woody, so I can get off the boat."

"You need any help, Doc?"

"Please, but keep your hands off my ass." She put her foot on the step, Woody put his hands on her hips and Molly and Andy reached out to grab her, but she hesitated. "Oh, go ahead, Woody."

Molly and Andy pulled on her arms as Woody placed his hands over her soft cheeks and gave her a gentle shove up and onto the dock. She turned and winked at Woody as he handed her the medical bag. His face and ears turned pink so he turned away. Andy looked away and laughed.

"Porter, you okay?"

"Yeah, Doc, I'm okay. See to Miss Mollie."

Dr. Myers checked first to determine Miss Mollie's heartbeat and inspected the wound. "Her heart's beating a little rapid, and she may be in shock. I'm going to give her something to calm her. Then I'll dress the wound. It doesn't look that bad, but it's the trauma that I'm worried about." She cleansed the wound area, shaved the hair, applied an antiseptic, applied a few stitches, and then bandaged the wound. Miss Mollie remained calm as the doctor treated her and after a while the sedative slowed her heartbeat. "She's much calmer now. I think she'll be okay, but she needs to rest. I think she should spend the night at my office, Molly. I'll stay with her, and we should get Porter to the hospital."

"I ain't going to no hospital. I'm okay. I'll stay with Miss Mollie. You can look after us both. Molly has to take care of her police duties."

"Damn thickheaded old fool. What do you think, Doc?"

The two EMTs looked away, put their hands to their mouths and stifled laughs.

Dr. Myers held back a laugh. "It's okay with me as long as he doesn't make another pass at me."

"If he does, you let me know, and he'll need more than a night in a hospital." The EMTs couldn't resist laughing and so did Dr. Myers.

"Okay then, you two wheel him up to the ambulance and take him to my office."

Porter took one look at the gurney and decided he wasn't going to let them haul him up the steps in it.

"You ain't hauling me up in that thing, Woody. I can walk up those stairs."

Woody looked at Molly and Dr. Myers for an answer.

"Wheel him to the stairs and help him up the steps. Is that okay, Doc?" asked Molly.

Dr. Myers was still concerned that he might not be able to make it up. She looked up at the steps to the bluff and then at Porter.

"Woody, can you get him up those steps by yourself?"

Woody looked at Porter and the steps. "I'm pretty certain I can."

"You okay with that, Porter?"

Porter looked up at the steps and scratched his head. "Yeah, I'm okay with that. He looks strong enough to help me. Right, Woody?"

"Sure, Chief, no problem."

Porter slapped him on the back of his head, "I ain't the chief. Molly is. Stop calling me that, dammit!"

Woody rubbed his head. "Ouch. Okay, Mr. Porter, whatever you say."

"And I ain't Mr. Porter either. He was my father. Call me John or Porter, understand?"

Woody looked to Molly. She mouthed Porter, and he understood. "Okay, Porter, you ready?"

"What about the dog, Doc?" asked Andy.

"She goes with me," shouted Porter.

Woody picked up Miss Mollie and gave her to Porter. He wrapped his arms around her and they wheeled the gurney to the steps. Andy took Miss Mollie and carried her up the steps and to the ambulance. He poured some water in his hand and let Miss Mollie sip it.

"Don't worry, girl. You're gonna be okay. Doc's gonna look after you."

Miss Mollie thumped her tail and whimpered.

"Okay, Woody, let's go." Woody put his arm around Porter, and they started up the stairs.

Molly turned to Dr. Myers and whispered, "Stubborn old fool."

"I heard that, Molly," shouted Porter.

"You two always talk like that, Molly? Don't you two ever talk nice and romantic like?"

"That's how we talk nice to each other. You don't want us to talk like we do in bed do you?"

Dr. Myers laughed, and she and Molly followed Porter and Woody up the stairs. Woody had Porter sitting in the ambulance. Miss Mollie was inside it resting.

"How much do I owe you, Doc?" asked Porter.

"You can buy me breakfast at Willie's Diner in the morning if you and Miss Mollie are okay."

"I'd hug you if I was standing, Doc."

"Wow, Porter, what would Molly and my husband say if I let you?"

Molly grinned. "You could tell him his wife said it was okay this time."

They all laughed. Dr. Myers left and followed the ambulance to her office. Molly followed after them.

At the doctor's office, the EMTs wheeled Porter and Miss Mollie in and then left. Porter set Miss Mollie down on a comfortable blanket. Then he lay down on the small bed in the examining room.

"Say goodnight to him, Molly, and go do what you do as the chief of police."

"Thanks, Doc. John, can you tell me more about what happened so I can take a statement?" He told as much as he could remember. "That's good for now. Tomorrow you can tell me more. I'll see you in the morning. I love you, you old bastard." She gave him a kiss. "You scared the hell out of me."

"I love you too. See you in the morning. Me and the Doc are gonna have a party here." He put his head down on the pillow and drifted off to sleep. Dr. Myers grinned.

"Old fool. Have a good night, Doc. He's all yours."

"Thanks. Now I have to call my husband and tell him that I'm spending the night with another man. See you in the morning, Molly. They'll both be okay."

They looked over at Porter. He was sound asleep and snoring. Miss Mollie stirred and thumped her tail.

"Don't think you have anything to worry about with him. You know you're pretty special for doing this."

"No problem. I like you guys, and I love Miss Mollie."

Molly drove to the police station to continue her all-nighter.

Earlier, Miss Lottie and Harding were busy in the kitchen making rhubarb pies. She had all the ingredients on the table and was making the dough. He watched as she mixed the ingredients and rolled the dough out with an old wooden rolling pin. She was reminded of the times when her granddaughter, Lottie, and young Bradley would sit in her kitchen with their chairs reversed, their legs straddling them and their heads perched on the back of the chairs. Their eyes bulged as they watched her assemble the pies and then put them in the oven. She would stick her finger in the flour and dab a spot on each of their noses making them giggle.

While the pies cooled, he and Miss Lottie ate supper. When they finished, she sliced them each a piece. Then they sat on the porch with pie and a glass of sweet tea.

"Nice night to sit out here, young man."

He ate a bite of pie and took a sip of his sweet tea. "Yes, it is and even nicer with you sitting here with me."

Her cheeks turned suddenly warm and a wee bit red as she wiped her eye with the back of her hand. Travis Waverly used to say something similar to her decades ago.

"That's the sweetest thing anyone has said to me in a very long time."

He reached out and touched her hand. "I mean it, Miss Lottie; you deserve to hear it often."

Later they said goodnight and he went to his room. Miss Lottie washed the dishes and put them away. Then she went to her bedroom and retrieved three aged light sepia-colored photographs. She sat on the bed, touched the photos gently with her fingers and wiped her tears with the back of her hand.

CHAPTER 11

Porter slept peacefully during the night and periodically Dr. Myers checked on him and Miss Mollie. Both seemed to be doing just fine and in between, she managed to get some sleep herself. Molly spent most of the night at the police station and occasionally made a quick drive around town and over to the Coastal Resort Community. Everything was peaceful, and she made her last trip just before sun-up and then drove to Dr. Myers' office to check on Porter and Miss Mollie.

Dr. Myers checked Miss Mollie's bandage, rubbed her head, and asked, "Good morning, would you like to go out?" Miss Mollie gave her an uninterested look. "How about some water?" She raised her head. "Okay, I'll get you some and then you just rest." She got Miss Mollie some water. "Here you go, girl. Now I'll make a pot of coffee then check on Porter."

Porter opened his eyes and saw a pretty face staring down at him. At first he thought he was in heaven or he was in another woman's bedroom and worried what Molly would think.

"Morning, how do you feel?" asked the woman.

Then he realized he was in Dr. Myer's office. "Fine, I guess." He smelled fresh brewed coffee.

"Can you sit up?"

He rubbed his head. "I think so."

"Hold my arm and try."

"Thanks Doc." He grabbed her arm and pulled himself up. "Damn, that coffee sure smells good."

"I'll get you a cup. Be right back." She grinned. "Don't go away."

"Where am I going to go, and how's Miss Mollie?"

"She's fine and resting on her blanket." He looked over at Miss Mollie. She had her head resting on her paws, and her eyes looking up at him. "I cleaned her wound and changed her bandage, but she wasn't interested in going out. I think she should rest here a few days." She brought him a cup of coffee.

"Thanks, Doc." He looked down at his feet and was glad his shoes were still on. Molly had told the doctor not to remove them if she valued her life.

"How's your head feel?"

He rubbed his head. "A little sore, but thank goodness I had a good night's sleep. Help me off this bed so I can check Miss Mollie." She held his arm as he got off the bed and kneeled down in front of Miss Mollie. "How are you feeling, girl?" She licked his face. "You know I would always have your back."

Molly arrived at the doctor's office, stepped out of her car and glanced up at the sunrise.

"The beginning of a new day, let's hope it's better than the end of the last one."

She went inside and was pleased to see Porter and Miss Mollie awake.

"Morning, looks like you two are okay." She walked over and gave Porter a kiss and then kneeled down and petted Miss Mollie.

"It's good to see you, Molly. Doc Myers took good care of us."

"Morning, Molly, guess you can tell that my two patients are okay. Would you like a cup of coffee? I can pour you one."

"That's okay Doc. You've done enough for us already. I'll get my own."

Dr. Myers walked over, gave Miss Mollie a treat, and kissed her on her head. Miss Mollie raised her eyes up at her as if saying, thanks Doc for taking care of me.

"Say Doc, you up for that breakfast at the diner?"

"Let me do a quick check on you first, Porter." She checked his bruise, shined a light in his eyes, and pinched him on the cheek.

"Hey, why'd you do that?"

She winked. "Would you rather I kissed you?"

Porter laughed. "If you did, Molly might have shot you."

"No, I wouldn't have. Not after what she did last night. What say we go to breakfast?" Molly paused. "Say, Doc, why don't you call your husband and have him join us?"

"I would, Molly, but he's playing golf with a men's group at the country club. He joins them once a month as a public relations thing. They have a late breakfast after golf at the club. On second thought, maybe I should stay here with Miss Mollie. You two go ahead without me."

Harding was up and already shaved and dressed when he went downstairs to have breakfast. He smelled fresh coffee and something sweet as he entered the kitchen. She was wearing her apron and setting a place for him.

"Good morning, what's that sweet smell?"

She turned. "Good morning, young man. I made some sweet rolls for us, and I've got waffle batter ready for breakfast. Pour yourself a cup of coffee and have a seat."

"Mm, mm, sweet rolls and waffles. I haven't had them in a long time." He walked over to the coffee pot and poured himself a cup. Then he stood in front of the backdoor and looked out. "Looks like it's a pretty morning."

She poured some batter into the waffle iron and closed the lid. "It certainly does. What are your plans for today?"

He looked out at the weed infested garden and wondered if at some point he should clean it up some.

"I think I might go into town and walk around. Maybe stop at Willie's Diner for lunch. Chef Willie seems like a nice person to talk with."

She lifted the lid on the waffle iron, took the cooked waffle out with a fork and placed it on a dish. "I got a waffle ready for you. Come sit down and get it while it's hot. There's butter and syrup on the table. Fix your waffle the way you like it, and I'll make you another one." She set the plate on the table, went back to the stove and poured more batter onto the waffle iron.

He turned, walked to the table, and sat down. Then he poured a heap of syrup over the waffle but skipped the butter and took a bite. She watched as he did and remembered that when he was a child, he didn't like butter on his waffles and neither did his grandfather.

"Oh, this is good. I like my waffles with lots of syrup on them."

She took the other waffle out of the waffle iron. "Give me your plate and you can have another one and then I'm going to make me one." He handed her his plate and she put the waffle on it. "After that one, you have yourself a sweet roll."

He took the dish and smothered the waffle with syrup. "You're spoiling me, Miss Lottie."

"You deserve it." When her waffle was ready, she put it on her plate and joined him at the table. She spread some butter over the waffle and poured some syrup on it. "Don't forget to have a sweet roll."

He grinned, ate the last few bites of his waffle, and reached for a sweet roll. He wiped it in the syrup just like his grandfather used to do. Her cheekbones raised. She ate her waffle and then had a sweet roll.

"What are you going to do today, Miss Lottie?"

"My granddaughter and her son are taking me to church. You're welcome to join us."

He hadn't been in a church for well over a decade. He had gone to services several times with his platoon, but it was in a tent and the chaplain was sometimes of a different faith depending on when they could get to service in the combat zone.

"It's been a long time since I was in a church. I don't think I'm ready for that. Thank you for asking anyway."

She remembered that Travis Waverly wasn't much of a churchgoer either, and she had to take him and Lottie to church with her when he visited his grandfather.

"You're welcome. Maybe one day you will be. You might even get to meet Lottie and Thomas. You'll like that boy, and I bet he would like you too."

He was hoping that he would but was also concerned that she might recognize him after all these years. However, he would like to meet her son and maybe toss a ball with him. If Thomas' father was alive, that's probably what they would do, just like Harding's maternal grandfather did with him.

"I'd like to meet him, no boy should be without a father. I bet he was a good man, Thomas' father."

She reached across the table and put her hand over his. "He was, and he was good for Lottie, especially after her mother passed away. You would have liked him." She wiped her eye with her napkin. "Enough already, it's making me sad, and I don't want to feel that way. You go sit on the porch and I'll bring you the rest of the sweet rolls for your coffee." She got up and started clearing the table.

"Let me help you." He grabbed his plate and utensils and put them in the sink and then topped off his cup and went out onto the porch.

A short time later, she came out with the sweet rolls and a cup of coffee for herself. She sat down next to him and handed him the plate.

"You know Miss Lottie; you make me feel like I'm almost home. I'm going to miss you when I leave in the morning."

They turned and faced each other. "I'm going to miss you too."

He wanted to stand up and hug her but felt it would be inappropriate so he refrained and sipped his coffee and took a bite of the sweet roll.

Molly and Porter walked into the diner and took seats at a booth. Chef Willie was surprised to see they were alone.

"Good morning, where's Miss Mollie?" he asked.

Molly told him what happened the night before and that Miss Mollie was okay, but she was staying at the clinic with Dr. Myers.

"How about you, John Porter, are you okay too?"

Porter rubbed the back of his head, closed his eyes, and grimaced.

"You okay, John?" asked Molly. "You're not feeling woozy are you?"

He leaned his head back and took a deep breath, "No, but my head still hurts a little."

"Are you sure?"

"Yes, let's order breakfast."

Molly rubbed his back. "If you're really not up to this, we can go home."

"I'm okay, Molly. Chef Willie, give me eggs, bacon, and home fries and a cup of coffee too."

Chef Willie looked from Porter to Molly. "Is he really okay, Molly?"

"Damn fool wouldn't say if he wasn't. Give him what he wants. I'll have the same."

Chef Willie grinned, turned, and went back into the kitchen to prepare their breakfasts. Miss Mavis stepped out from the kitchen to see what the commotion was.

"What's all the fuss about? Is there something I should know?"

Porter repeated his story to her including that Miss Mollie had to stay at Doc Myers' clinic a few days.

"Who would do such a thing like that?" she asked.

"I think they were a couple of burglars." Porter turned to Molly. "Gonna have to tell Mr. Myers 'cause they was into one of his houses."

"Is that what happened? Did you see who they were, John?"

"Yeah, but with all that happened last night, I forgot to tell you. I got a good look at them, and I saw the name on their boat too."

"Well, what was it?"

"I believe it was *Greybeard*."

Molly took out her notebook and wrote it down. "Since the island isn't in the county, we'll have to call the Coast Guard. Looks like Commander Edison is going to be doing some fishing pretty quick. We can call him after breakfast."

"Sounds like a good idea but wait until later because after breakfast I'm gonna take a nap. You check on Miss Mollie."

Chef Willie brought them their breakfasts and a special treat for Molly to take to Miss Mollie.

"What about me, Chef Willie? Didn't I save Miss Mollie?"

Molly kissed him on the cheek. "You sure did, and I'll make it up to you later."

CHAPTER 12

Miss Lottie's granddaughter, Lottie, turned into the driveway and approached the house as Harding was leaving for town. He waved to her and she waved back.

"That must be Grandma's guest, Thomas. Maybe he's going to church by himself. We'll ask Grandma."

"Is he the marine, Mom?"

She touched his leg. "Yes, he is." She drove up to the house and parked. Miss Lottie waited on the porch for them. Thomas ran up to greet her.

"Good morning, Gramma." He hugged her. "We passed the marine on our way in. Is he going to church too?"

She squeezed him close to her. "No, Thomas, he isn't. He's going to town to walk around and have lunch. You want a sweet roll before we leave?" She looked at his mother, who smiled and nodded that it was okay.

"Oh boy! Are they in the kitchen? I'll get one myself. You want one, Mom?"

"No, son, you go ahead, but hurry because we have to leave." Lottie walked over and hugged her grandmother. "How are you, Grandma? How is it with that marine as a guest?"

"I'm fine, child, and he has been a big help. He mowed the yard and did a little weeding. We went shopping yesterday and made rhubarb pie when we returned. You and Thomas can have some when we get back from church."

Lottie's eyebrows lifted. "Thomas will like that and so will I. You ready to go?"

"Yes, but we had better call Thomas. He's probably eaten more than one sweet roll by now."

Both laughed and Lottie called out, "Thomas, come on we have to leave and no more sweet rolls, young man."

Thomas put his third sweet roll back on the plate and frowned. "Aw shucks. I'm coming, Mom." He left the kitchen and went out onto the porch.

"Thomas, help your grandmother."

She shooed him away with her hand. "I can take care of myself, Thomas, but you can go open the door for your mother and me."

He jumped off the porch, scampered to the car and opened the doors for the ladies. Lottie drove them to church.

Harding parked at the diner and started walking through town. He was still amazed at the stoplight which was more for pedestrian use than for the intersection. It was a way that folks could get across the street from the diner to window shop at the specialty stores. The storefronts were all remodeled and they resembled a street scene from *It's a Wonderful Life*. He walked past the police station and stopped when he came to a realtor's office. The sign read, "Waverly Realty—Call for an Appointment." *This must be Mom's office.* Displayed in the window were several of his grandfather's pictures of the town in the 1920s. He continued walking, looking in every store window and then proceeded down toward the bluff and the dock.

"The way it looks now would make a pretty postcard," he said as he walked down the street and past the gas station, which looked like it was from the 40's.

When he reached the bluff, he was amazed to see that the parking area was now paved over with concrete and there was a three foot seawall. The boat ramp was gone and there was a marina so boat owners could lower their boats into the water. He took it all in then paused to look out to sea.

"It's just as pretty as it was back when Grandpa brought me here. The new dock is something else, though, and so is that marina."

He walked down the steps to the dock and looked at each boat. One of the boats named *Miss Mollie* didn't seem secure so he unfastened the lines and used the landing loop to put it properly in its space and secured the boat.

Molly stood with her hands on her hips and watched from the bluff as he secured the boat. Initially she was going to call to him as he started to unfasten the ties, but decided to wait and watch him. She checked her watch and saw that it was almost lunchtime.

Maybe he isn't a bad person, but I still would like to know who he is. She turned and drove home to check on Porter.

Harding looked out to sea remembering when he and his grandfather used to leave the dock early in the morning to fish. He reminisced for a while, checked his watch, and saw that it was close enough to lunchtime so he walked back up to the bluff. He watched Molly's car as she drove through town.

"Wonder if that was the chief. I could swear someone was watching me while I was tying up Porter's boat."

He walked back toward the diner. When he passed the novelty shop, he looked in the window and saw the postcards. Miss Mavis had them made specially with *Greetings from Blocker's Bluff* printed on them.

As soon as he entered the diner, Chef Willie immediately greeted him.

"Morning, Sergeant, haven't seen you since Thursday. Where you been keeping yourself?" Chef Willie wiped his hands on the towel on his shoulder and gestured for him to take a seat.

"I've been staying at Baxter House and eating my meals there. I also did some chores for her. I'll be leaving tomorrow. Thought I'd come in and walk around town and have lunch here. You got anything special?"

Chef Willie handed him a menu. "I can make you whatever you want since I just got some new provisions in. What'd you feel like?"

He sat up straight and scratched his head. "Can you fix me some fried chicken and potatoes?"

The chef grinned. "That's one of my specialties. You got it, fried chicken and taters coming up. I got some cheese grits from this morning so I'll put them on your plate too."

While he waited for his lunch, Susie came over and poured a glass of water for him. She gave him utensils, a napkin, and a wink.

"Thanks, Susie, I appreciate that."

Susie flirtatiously smiled. "You remembered my name. That's so sweet."

He winked back. "How could anyone forget someone as pretty as you?"

She blushed and walked off to serve the other customers sitting in the booths.

Chef Willie brought him his lunch and set it down in front of him. "Wow, that's a lot of chicken, Chef Willie."

He wiped his hands with the towel and grinned. "You're a big boy and look like you could use a big meal. Enjoy yourself."

Harding picked up a piece of chicken, bit into it. "Man this is good." Then he continued to eat his lunch and Chef Willie went back into the kitchen.

Susie came over and asked if he needed anything else. She gave him a coy look as she asked.

"Not right now, Susie, but thanks."

"Anytime, you just call me." She wrote her name and number on a napkin, handed it to him and walked off.

After he finished his lunch, he paid the check and started to leave.

"Don't forget to call me," Susie said and winked. He winked back.

He drove back to Baxter House, parked, and walked toward the garage. He stopped, turned, and walked over to the garden out back of the house. He looked at all the weeds and then went into the garage and found a pitchfork, a rake, and a hoe, went back to the garden, and started weeding.

After church and a stop at the Food Mart, Miss Lottie, Lottie, and Thomas went home to her house. She had purchased some much needed groceries for her kitchen. When they pulled into the driveway, they noticed his car parked close up to the house.

"Looks like your marine's back from town, Grandma."

"Yes, and I wonder where he is."

They got out of the car and each of them carried a bag of groceries into the house and set them on the kitchen table. Thomas walked over to the backdoor and looked out.

"Gramma, the marine's tending to your old garden. Can I go out and watch him?"

"Go ahead, but don't disturb him. He likes to fool around in that garden. Why, I don't know."

Thomas opened the door, stepped outside, and walked over to him. He turned when he noticed Thomas and waved. Thomas waved back. "Why you doing that?" he asked.

Harding stopped, pushed the pitchfork in the ground, put a foot on it and replied, "Why am I working this garden? Is that what you're asking?"

Thomas rubbed his head. "That's what I asked. Ain't nothing ever gonna grow there. You're wasting your time."

"You think so, huh?"

"Yeah, I know so. Ain't nothin growing there since my Dad used to care for it."

Harding looked carefully at the boy and wondered if his weeding was bringing back sad memories.

"Well, your dad must have been some gardener. And something is growing. See here."

He motioned for Thomas to come over and look. Thomas walked over and looked down where he pointed.

"You mean those rotten old tomatoes? What good are they?"

He put his hand on the boy's shoulder and laughed. "Those aren't tomatoes. Those are rhubarb. You ever had rhubarb pie?"

Thomas' eyes lit up and his head snapped back. "No shit, really. Oops, sorry that slipped out. I didn't mean to say that, especially on Sunday."

Harding just grinned. He had slip ups like that when he was Thomas' age. "I didn't hear anything, but have you ever had rhubarb pie?"

Thomas laughed. "Yeah, I love it. My gramma makes the best. We're having some now, you want to join us?"

"I know she does. I had some last night, and it was downright good. Maybe I should let you all be since your family."

"My gramma and my mom won't mind. I'll go ask. You wait here, I'll be right back."

Harding shook his head and laughed. "I ain't going anywhere." He continued with the pitchfork, using the hoe to pull some of the weeds and then raked them into a pile.

While Harding and Thomas where talking, Lottie watched from the backdoor window. When Thomas came charging toward the door, she stepped away.

"Here comes Thomas, Grandma, and he looks excited."

Thomas leaped the steps and bounded into the house. "Momma, Gramma, can the marine have pie with us? Please say yes."

Miss Lottie nodded yes. "Okay, Thomas but only if he wants to. You go ask him and be polite."

He jumped up and down. "Yippee. Thanks, Mom. Don't worry he'll say yes. He already tasted Gramma's pie and he liked it too." He turned and went out the back door.

Miss Lottie smiled and so did Lottie. "What do you think, Grandma? Will it be okay? He is so excited."

"It'll be fine. The marine's a very nice young man and been too long fighting wars and needs some peace. Thomas will be good for him, and don't you fret none." She felt that the marine would be good for Lottie as well—but wouldn't say who he was.

"I guess you're right but watching him out there, he reminds me of someone. Can't say who, but watching him working that garden seems familiar."

"Maybe you're thinking of your husband."

Lottie glanced out the window and eyed the marine. "No, Grandma, it's someone from the past, I think. Let's set the table because here they come."

Miss Lottie watched her closely as she started to set the table and wondered if Lottie saw signs of Travis in the young man.

Thomas ran up to Harding and shouted, "They said yes. Will you join us? Say yes, please."

"Calm down, Thomas. That's your name right?"

Thomas looked at him curiously. "Yes, how did you know?"

"Your grandma told me. If I say yes, will you settle down?"

Thomas put his hands on his hips and gave Harding a stern look. "Hey, I'm a kid. I'm supposed to get excited."

Harding laughed. "Okay, you win. I'll have pie with you."

Thomas jumped up and down, almost fell and shouted, "Yippee. Say what's your name, you know mine or do I just call you Marine?"

He almost said Brad but caught himself. He didn't want to lie to the boy but had to. "Call me Marine. I like hearing you say it, okay?"

"Okay, Marine, let's go have some pie."

Harding stuck the pitchfork in the ground, and laid the hoe and the rake on the ground face down. He put his hand on Thomas' shoulder and they walked toward the house.

"Mom, this is my new friend, the marine. He likes it when I call him that. Marine, this is my mom and you already know my grandma."

He took a deep breath when the boy introduced him to Lottie. She didn't look anything like the skinny tomboy he once knew. Her braids were long gone, and her dark hair was now shoulder length. She still looked pretty as ever in a dress and was captivating. He stepped forward and extended his hand.

"Nice to meet you and you can call me Marine too, Lottie."

She looked into his eyes and realized who they belonged to. That kid she used to play with, the one she gave her first kiss to and also had a crush on. She stepped forward and took his hand and held it gently.

"It's nice to meet you, Marine. Grandma speaks highly of you. Thank you for helping her and for mowing the yard. I appreciate that you did, and I'm sure Thomas does too. Right, Thomas?"

"You mowed my gramma's yard? Really? Thanks, Marine."

Harding and Lottie's eyes were focused on each other, and he laughed. "You're welcome, Thomas. Are we going to have pie now?" He wanted to deflect the topic away from him because he could tell that Lottie was studying him.

Miss Lottie watched and knew she had to get Lottie to stop focusing on him. "Yes, you all sit down and I'll cut the pie. Thomas, you want a big slice?"

He was the first one to sit and handed her his plate. "Yes, Gramma, and give my friend the marine a big slice too."

Miss Lottie decided to cut everyone a big slice, pour four glasses of sun tea and join them in a pie feast. They all sat and ate their pie, but all the while, Lottie kept looking at him. He knew that she was watching, and tried to avoid eye contact.

"Good pie right, Marine?"

"Sure is, Thomas."

Lottie looked at him then at her grandmother. She knew that he was Brad.

Miss Lottie understood and frowned at her.

After he finished his pie, Harding got up to go back out in the yard and finish the garden.

"Well, I've eaten enough pie for now. I have to go finish weeding. Miss Lottie, you have a few rhubarb plants coming up. I weeded around them. Maybe you'll be able to pick them when they're ready and make pies with them."

She hadn't known about the rhubarb because she hadn't been in the garden in several years and was pleased that she still had some.

"That's wonderful, now I'll have to look after them."

"I'll do it for you, Gramma, whenever Mom and me come over. Can I, Mom?"

Lottie looked at Harding and then at her grandmother. "Okay. We'll let it be your chore. What do you think, Grandma?"

The three turned toward Miss Lottie who was smiling. "I'd like that, Thomas. Your daddy used to take care of that garden for me. Yep, it's your chore now."

Thomas got up, walked over and hugged his mother and then hugged his grandmother. Harding said goodbye and went out back to continue weeding. Thomas followed behind him.

"Can I help you, Marine?"

He put his hand on Thomas' shoulder. "I'd let you, but you're wearing church clothes, and your mother wouldn't like you getting them dirty. Why don't you just watch?"

Thomas frowned. "Aw shucks, okay, Marine."

Miss Lottie and Lottie cleared the table and washed the dishes while Thomas watched Harding. Lottie looked out the window and at Harding.

"Grandma, I know who he reminds me of."

Miss Lottie was suddenly concerned that if she did, she might reveal his secret. "You probably just think he reminds you of someone, Lottie."

Lottie placed her hand on her grandmother's. "He reminds me of Mr. Travis' grandson. I think his name was Brad. We used to play together when Mr. Travis visited you." She searched her grandmother's eyes for confirmation, but Miss Lottie turned away. "You know, don't you?"

She put her hand on Lottie. "Yes, you're right, that's who he is. For some reason he's using another name. I don't think he wants anyone to know his real name. Let's keep his secret. Okay, Lottie?"

Lottie kissed her on the cheek. "Okay, Grandma."

"Thank you, Lottie." She pulled Lottie close and kissed her on the cheek.

"I better go get Thomas now. He has some homework to do. We'll come again next Sunday and maybe Saturday. I love you, Grandma."

"I love you, too. Go get Thomas and say goodbye to the marine." They winked at each other and then Lottie opened the backdoor to call Thomas.

"Time to go, Thomas. Say goodbye to your marine friend."

"Okay, Mom. I gotta go now, Marine. Will I ever see you again?"

"I'll be back here in a few days maybe we'll see each other. You better go now."

Thomas stepped close and put his arms around Harding. He was startled by the boy's actions and looked up at Lottie. Her eyes lit up.

"Bye, Marine."

"Bye, Thomas."

Thomas turned and ran to his mother. She waved to Harding and he waved back. Lottie waited a moment and watched as he jabbed the pitchfork into the ground and rocked it back and forth before lifting the weeds out of the ground. When he started whistling as he worked, she shook her head and grinned. Mr. Travis and his grandson used to do the same thing. Then she went into the kitchen.

He had over half the garden cleared of weeds and a pile of them that he had accumulated. He added more weeds to his pile.

Lottie and Thomas left by the front door. He ran and opened the car door for his mother.

"He's becoming a fine young gentleman, Lottie."

"Yes, he is. We'll see you next Sunday. We'll try and get here Saturday too." She kissed her grandmother and walked to the car.

Miss Lottie watched as they drove off and worried if Lottie would keep their secret.

CHAPTER 13

Molly's house was built decades ago and constructed using cinder block with a stucco façade. Porter and Eddie McClellan had enclosed two sides of the carport with cinder block and put up shelving. One wall had a window to allow light in. The roof was three years old having been replaced from funds Molly received when she sold acreage she owned to Coastal Resort Community. Parked inside was her red pickup truck.

She parked in the driveway and went into the house. "John Porter, you awake? She shouted.

Porter jolted upright and screamed, "What the hell? Dammit, Molly, you scared the hell out of me."

"Get up you old fool. It's lunch time."

"I gotta take a shower first."

Molly grinned. "I do too. Want to take one together?"

Porter got off the bed, walked over, and hugged her. "You bet. Come on."

They stripped, entered the bathroom, and showered together.

"How's your head feel?"

"It feels much better and so does something else."

She grinned. "Later we can make up for last night if you're up to it."

"You bet your sweet ass I am." He wrapped his arms around her and lifted her off the floor. After showering, they dressed. Molly made them sandwiches and they sat at the kitchen table and enjoyed lunch.

"So, how was your all-nighter?"

"Except for that thing with you, it was quiet, thank goodness. You want to talk about what happened?"

He took several bites from his sandwich and drank some iced tea. "Not much more to say than what I did last night. Think we can check on that boat or do you want to call Edison?"

She rubbed her hand over her chin. "I can Google the name, but maybe we should call Edison. You still got his home phone number?"

Porter went into the bedroom, grabbed his wallet, came back, and sat down. He looked through his wallet and found Edison's business card. Edison's home phone number was written on the back.

"Got it right here." He handed the card to Molly.

"You want me to call him?"

"Why not? It's official business, isn't it?"

She raised her eye brows. "I'll call him after we finish eating."

"Good idea, Molly."

She broke a piece of bread off of her sandwich and threw it at him. "Smart ass!"

After lunch, Molly dialed Edison's number. She got his voice mail, so she left a message telling him to call and it wasn't an emergency.

"He probably went to church with the family then lunch. It's what he generally does on Sunday's when he isn't on duty." Porter walked into the living room, sat down on the couch and turned the television on. "You want to watch television with me?" She joined him on the couch. "Come here and snuggle with me." He wrapped his arm around her and pulled her close. She rested her head on his shoulder. "I love you, Molly."

"I love you to, John." The doorbell rang. "Wonder who that is?"

"Don't know. Want me to get it or do you want to?"

"I'll get it." She peeked out the window to see who it was before opening the door. "Afternoon, Mayor. What brings you here?"

Mayor Wilma Patterson was still dressed in her church clothes and wearing her large brimmed Sunday hat. "Don't call me Mayor, Molly. I'm not here on business and we've known each other since we was kids, so call me Wilma. I heard Miss Mollie was shot and Porter was injured. I came to see how he is. You gonna let me in or just stand there?"

Molly stepped back. "Can't help it 'cause you're my boss."

Mayor Patterson shushed her away. "Oh, cut the crap, Molly. Where's Porter?"

Porter shouted from the living room, "I'm in here, Wilma. Come on in."

She walked into the living room. "How're you doing, Porter? My daughter told me what happened."

He scratched the back of his neck. "I'm much better. Thank goodness for your daughter. She took good care of me and Miss Mollie. You tell her that I said she's one hell of a doctor."

"Thanks, Porter. I'll let her know you said that. I have to go now, I just wanted to stop by and see how you were doing. Molly, can you see me out?"

Molly glanced at Porter and walked the mayor to the front door. "What's up, Wilma?"

"Any idea what happened?"

"According to John, two guys were robbing one of the CRC houses and when he confronted them, there was a fight. One of them shot Miss Mollie and the other knocked John unconscious. He managed to get the name of their boat. I have a call to the Coast

Guard to see if they can track down the owner. I'm waiting for a call back from Commander Edison."

"Sounds like you have it under control. Good. I'll see you at the next council meeting. Take care, Molly."

"Thanks, Wilma, and thanks for stopping by."

"My pleasure."

Molly went back to the living room, sat on the couch and snuggled up against Porter.

"That was nice of her to stop by."

"It was. She's a nice lady, John. So is her daughter."

"Yes, they are. I'm glad we know them." He pulled her head against his shoulder and leaned his against hers. An hour later the telephone rang and Molly answered.

"Molly, it's Edison. What can I do for you?"

"Good afternoon, Commander. We need your help."

"Must be important official business since you called me commander. How can I help you, Chief?"

Porter and the commander were fishing buddies, and Molly first met him five years ago when they worked a drug smuggling case off the coast of Porter's Island. His full name was Morris Edison but Porter always called him Mo.

Porter asked her to let him have the phone.

"Hold on, Commander, Porter wants to talk to you." She handed him the phone and stepped aside.

"Hey, Mo, how are you?"

"I'm fine, Porter, but what seems to be the problem?"

Molly circled her hand telling him to speed it up. He waved her off.

"Miss Mollie and me had an altercation with a couple house robbers on the island."

"Geez, Porter. Are you two okay?"

Molly again signaled for him to get on with his story. "Yeah, but we need your help tracking them down. I got the name of their boat. Maybe you could check it out."

"Sure, what's the name?"

"It's *Greybeard*, and I got a good look at both of them, enough that I could identify them if they're ever caught."

"Okay, Porter, I'll get on it, but it will have to wait until tomorrow when I'm in the office. That okay with the chief?"

He looked at Molly. "Is tomorrow okay with you?" She shook her head. "She says tomorrow is fine. Thanks, Mo."

"No problem, Porter. You guys take care."

"Yeah, you too, Mo." Porter and Molly went back to the living room and snuggled on the couch.

"You know, John, we're getting too old for this."

"Too old for cuddling? Hell no we're not!"

She slapped him on his knee. "No, you damn fool. I mean police work."

"You'll be retiring soon enough, Molly."

"I know, but I'm not sure I'm going to wait that long. This thing with you has got me thinking. Maybe it's time to let Eddie takeover."

"Why don't you let Eddie handle the case with the commander?"

"That's not a bad idea. You can introduce them and we can play a supportive role."

"When Mo calls tomorrow, we'll run it by him. Now let's get back to snuggling."

She gave him a coy look. "We could go to bed and do more than cuddle."

He jumped up and pranced toward the bedroom. "Hot damn, woman, come on." Molly danced after him.

Miss Lottie made baked chicken, green beans, mashed potatoes, and biscuits for their evening meal. She had the table all ready and went to call Harding.

"Dinner is ready, young man." Since he didn't respond, she repeated her call. "Dinner is ready, young man."

He was deep in thought about his trip to Beaufort. "Sorry, I was thinking about my trip tomorrow and didn't hear you."

"That's okay, but you should stop thinking about it for now and come eat your dinner. Tomorrow's another day."

He stood up and took a drink of sweet tea. "You're right, tomorrow is another day." He followed her into the kitchen. She fixed his plate and handed it to him. "Oh boy, that's a lot of chicken."

She waved a hand at him. "Nonsense, you need the nourishment after all you've done for me. Working in that garden is hard work. Eat up—there's more when you want it." She fixed her plate and sat down.

He reached over and grabbed a biscuit. "Oh boy, these look good. I really miss homemade biscuits." He took a big bite and recalled how she used to bake them for him and his grandfather, also for him and Lottie when they were kids.

"I'm glad you like them. When you come back, I'll make them for you. I can make some for your breakfast if you'd like?"

"You do realize that I haven't eaten this much food in a very long time. You're fattening me up, Miss Lottie." He took another bite of the biscuit, ate some chicken, green beans, and mashed potatoes, and then wiped his mouth with his napkin.

"I'll take that as a compliment. After dinner we can sit on the porch with some sweet tea if you'd like too."

"I'd like that."

They finished their meal and Miss Lottie cleared the table and he went out onto the porch. When she finished putting the dishes in the dishwasher, she poured two glasses of sweet tea placed them on a tray with the rest of the biscuits and joined him.

"Young man, would you get the door for me?"

He opened the door and took the tray from her. She handed him his glass of sweet tea and the dish of biscuits.

"You might as well finish these or they'll go to waste."

He grabbed two biscuits, took several bites and a sip of sweet tea. "You're spoiling me, Miss Lottie."

She sipped her sweet tea. "I'm glad I am because you deserve it."

He ate all the biscuits and they enjoyed the last of a sunset as it silhouetted the tops of the trees against hues of an orange, red, and yellow sky. Loggerhead Shrikes sang their nightly tune to them.

"I'm going to miss sitting here with you."

She adjusted the shawl over her shoulders. "I'm going to miss it too, but you'll be back and we can do it again." She looked away and brushed a tear from her eye. He did the same. Two hours later they got up and went inside.

"Good night, Miss Lottie."

"Good night, young man." She went to her room, sat on the bed, and shed tears.

CHAPTER 14

Monday morning, he packed for his trip to Beaufort and really didn't want to go, especially after meeting Lottie and Thomas. He wanted to get to know them both more. Maybe when he came back he'd get the opportunity. But for now he had other matters to attend to. Beaufort wasn't going to be a pleasant trip, but he had promised Corporal Towning's friend that he would stop and visit. He grabbed his bags and went downstairs for breakfast.

He set his bags down by the front entrance and walked into the kitchen. "Good morning, Miss Lottie. Whatever you're making sure smells good."

She lowered the flame on the stove, turned to greet him, and smiled. "Good morning. I'm making you scrambled eggs, bacon, and hash browns. There's fresh coffee and some biscuits on the table. Help yourself. I take it you're all packed to leave. I'm gonna miss you."

He walked over, poured a cup of coffee, sat at the table, and grabbed a biscuit. "I'm all packed and my bags are by the front door. I'm gonna miss you too, but I'll be back shortly."

She used the spatula to put his eggs on a plate and did the same with the hash browns. She grabbed a small towel, tossed it over her shoulder, wiped her hands on her apron, turned, and set the plate in front of him. She was about to kiss him on the top of his head like she did when he was a child, but refrained just in time.

"You be sure and call me in case I get guests to fill up the rooms. I'll save one just for you. Any idea yet when you will be back?"

He picked up a strip of bacon, ate it, and put some eggs on his fork. "Either Wednesday afternoon or Thursday morning," he replied. "Depends on how things go in Beaufort. Is that okay with you?"

She had hoped it would be sooner. "Thursday is fine. I'll keep the day open for you. Whatever you have to do there must really be important for you."

He ate a strip of bacon and a forkful of eggs. "I made a promise to someone and I aim to keep it. It's something from my time in Afghanistan." He wanted to tell her more but decided not to. But he knew it would have made him more at ease if he had someone to talk to about the situation.

She fixed herself a plate and joined him at the table. "Whatever it is, I'm sure you're doing a good thing. How was your breakfast?"

He cleaned his plate and finished his coffee. "It was great. Excuse me while I get another cup of coffee." He filled his cup, sat back down, and picked up a biscuit. "These things are great, too." He took a bite and a sip of coffee. "I'm not sure I'm prepared for what I'm going to do, but it's something I have to do. Maybe when I get back I'll tell you about it."

"Only if you want to." She finished her breakfast and put their plates in the sink. Then she sat down with him and picked up a biscuit. "When you get back, I'll make more of these for you."

He picked up another biscuit, and took a bite. "I'm looking forward to it."

They sat in silence with their coffee and biscuits. Both of them felt sad because of his leaving. After a while, he stood up and put his cup in the sink.

"I guess it's time for me to leave. Will you walk me to the porch?"

"Certainly, you didn't think I wouldn't, did you?"

"No, I just wanted to be sure you did." He left the kitchen, picked up his bags, opened the front door, and stepped out onto the porch. She followed behind him. "Let me put these bags in the car and I'll come back and say goodbye." He put the bags in the car and returned to the porch. "Guess this is goodbye for now." He was about to hug her, but she stiffened. "Sorry, Miss Lottie, that was inappropriate of me." He extended his hand. She took it in both her hands and gently rubbed her fingers over his hand.

"No need to apologize. You drive safely and come back safe and sound."

He stepped off the porch, got into his car, backed up and turned it around. But before he left, he rolled the window down and waved to her.

When he reached the end of the driveway, Miss Lottie sat down in a rocker and looked up toward the heavens. "Lord, Travis, what am I supposed to do?" She covered her face with her hands and wept.

As he drove toward Highway 174, he slowed down when he reached Judy Waverly's house. He wanted to take one more look at the house where he'd spent summers with his grandfather.

Judy was just coming out of the house when she noticed his vehicle slow down. "I could swear I've seen that car go by several times and slow down. Wonder who that is? Oh well, I've got an appointment to get to." She got in her car, backed out of the driveway and drove off in the same direction that he went.

When he passed the Coastal Resort Community, he read the sign that said, *You're Leaving Blocker's Bluff Come Back.*

"Damn right, I'll be back." He looked in the rearview mirror and rubbed tears from his eyes with the back of his hand. "Damn,

I wish I could stay in Blocker's Bluff forever." He turned left onto Highway 174 and headed toward Highway 17 and Beaufort.

Molly and Porter decided to sleep in Monday morning and not go to Willie's Diner for breakfast. Instead they chose to eat at home. Porter was having a bowl of miniature shredded wheat and raisin bran cereals without milk and a strawberry Pop Tart. Molly was having a bowl of Raisin Bran cereal with milk and an apple Pop Tart.

Porter ate the last remnants of his cereal and took a bite of his Pop Tart. "What should we do today?"

She finished her cereal, lifted the bowl, and drank the remaining milk. "We have to talk to Eddie about your case and we still have to wait on Edison. Maybe we should call Doc Myers to see if we can get Miss Mollie."

"That's a good idea, and I think we need to go talk with Bob Myers at Coastal Resort, because those two guys were coming out of one of their houses. They need to check on the house."

"I forgot about that. Why don't we go there after breakfast?"

"Sure, and I do have to go back to the island because I need to check on the cabin. I think Edison might want to go out to the crime scene, so it can wait. What do you think?"

She got up, grabbed their dishes and put them in the dishwasher. "Let me call Doc Myers, and I'd rather we wait because you're not going there alone. Soon as you're ready we can go over to Coastal." She called Dr. Myers and she said Miss Mollie was feeling good and they could come get her. "Let's go get Miss Mollie."

"I'm ready if you are."

They left the house and got into Molly's chief's car. She backed out onto the street and headed for the road into town. Molly's neighborhood had five other houses almost all similar in size to hers. Three of them were occupied by folks who worked in Crofton, one worked at the marina, and the other was retired. He was in his driveway pulling on the cord to start his mower. He suddenly threw his hat down on the ground, kicked the mower, and started cursing.

Molly and Porter laughed as they had seen him do it on numerous occasions.

"Why doesn't the damn fool just buy a new mower?"

The neighbor saw them go by, waved, and went back to pulling the cord. He finally got the mower started.

"Because he's a stubborn old fool just like you."

"I may be stubborn, but I would have bought a new mower by now."

"Okay, I'll give you that one."

She turned right at the end of the street and started toward town. As she pulled onto the roadway, she noticed Harding go by on his way to Beaufort. She didn't say anything just kept on going, but when she reached Miss Baxter's driveway, she turned in.

"Why are you turning in here I thought we were going to get Miss Mollie and then to the station?"

"I have to make a quick stop here."

"This isn't about that marine, is it?"

She ignored him and drove up to the house. Miss Baxter was still sitting on the porch when they arrived and waved to them. They walked up to the porch. Porter walked behind Molly.

Miss Lottie got up from the rocker and stepped forward to greet them. "Good morning, Molly, what brings you here? Morning, John Porter."

"Good Morning, Miss Baxter. Molly wanted to stop by."

She glanced at Molly, and her expression wasn't a pleasant one. She suspected Molly was there about the marine and curtly asked, "Well, Molly, what can I do for you?"

Molly paused considering her words carefully. "I want to talk to you about that marine, Miss Baxter. I don't believe who he is because I did some research on him."

She shook her finger at Molly and scolded her. "You look here, Molly Dickson. I told you to mind your own business, didn't I?"

Molly's eyes almost fell back into their sockets and her hands went to her hips. "I'm just looking out for you."

She shook her finger vehemently and shouted, "I don't need no looking out for, and I don't want you poking into that young man's business. It's none of your's. You never could mind your own business and was always nosy, even as a child. You go on now and don't you be bothering me or that young man. You hear me?" Molly opened her mouth to say something, but Miss Baxter stopped her. "You go on, get off my property and don't come back until you learn to mind your own business. John Porter, you best teach your wife some manners, you hear me?"

Porter grabbed Molly by the arm and tugged at her. "Yes, Miss Baxter, we hear you. Come on Molly, there's no need for you to continue this." He suspected that she had good reason to protect Harding and figured it had something to do with her, Judy and Travis Waverly. "Molly, listen to me you may be doing more harm than good, trust me."

She pulled her arm from him, turned, and pouted off to the car. Miss Baxter went inside the house.

"Why did you do that, John?"

He didn't want to reveal his suspicion because he knew she would only keep digging if he did. "Just listen to me. If you persist with this marine thing, you're going to wind up hurting some people and you don't want to do that."

She slammed her hands on the steering wheel and yelled, "What are you talking about, Porter?" When she called him Porter it was usually because she was angry.

"Listen to me, I'm not certain, but I think I understand why Miss Baxter is protective of that marine. It's just a hunch, but I'm asking you to drop it just like she wants you to. Please, Molly, do it for me."

She turned to face him. "You're serious, aren't you?"

"Yes, please, Molly. I remember what it was like when I came home from Vietnam and had to put up with those damn protestors. Give the man some space, please."

When Porter said please twice in a row, she knew he was real serious. "Okay, I'll do it, but I ain't gonna like it."

"Thanks, besides don't you have enough to be concerned with?"

He was right. Porter and Miss Mollie's attack needed to be dealt with. "Okay, you win."

"It's not about winning, it's about what's right." He stroked her hand.

Molly conceded defeat and drove to the clinic where they picked up Miss Mollie. She was so excited to see them and leaped onto the back seat. Three nights away from them was wonderful, but she was ready to go home.

"It's good to see you, Miss Mollie, but you could have at least said hello," said Porter.

"Yeah," said Molly.

Miss Mollie barked.

As they pulled up to the police station, Molly's phone rang. She looked at the caller's name and showed it to Porter before answering.

"Good morning, Commander, do you have some information for us? Porter's here with me, and I've got you on speakerphone." Porter gave her a grin and a thumbs-up hoping to change her mood. "So do you have something for us?"

"I've got a name for the owner of that boat, but I'm not sure it's any good. I've also got a picture of the owner. I'll send it to you, and Porter can see if he's one of the guys who attacked him and Miss Mollie. I'm sending it to your phone now."

Molly and Porter waited for the photo. "Mo, it's Porter, you want to go out to the island and look around? We're gonna go talk to the manager at Coastal Community and see if he wants to go too."

"Sounds like a good idea. When do you want to do it?"

"Hold on, we'll call you back after I look at that picture."

"Okay, I'll be waiting."

Molly opened the text and showed it to Porter. "Is he one of the guys, John?"

He carefully looked at the picture. "No, he's much older than the two who attacked us. Let's call Mo and tell him. Then we can go see Myers and arrange a trip to the island with the both of them."

Molly closed her phone but saved the text just in case they might need it later, and then called Commander Edison.

"So, Chief, any help? Was he one of the guys?"

"John says, no, he's not. We're going to go talk to the manager at Coastal and then we'll call you when we can all meet on the island. You okay with that?"

"Call me when you know. Porter, you and Miss Mollie okay?" Miss Mollie stood up and barked real loud. "Guess that means she's okay, how about you, Porter?"

"I'm fine too. We'll call you. Take care."

"You too."

Molly hung up and was about to get out of the car but hesitated. She put her hand on Porter's arm and asked, "John, am I really nosy?"

He put his hand over hers and considered his answer carefully. He knew for certain that whatever he said was going to get him in trouble so he decided to just be honest.

"Yes, you are. But that's not such a bad thing because it makes you a good chief of police. However, you don't know when to back off and sometimes it makes you frustrating to be around. Take, for instance, this thing with Miss Baxter and that marine. It's obviously personal to her and that's why she reacted the way she did. You need to learn to understand when something's not in your best interest to continue with and learn to back off."

It was at that moment that Porter realized why Miss Baxter was so protective of the marine. He remembered that Judy Waverly had a son that visited her father during summers and he and his grandfather were often at Baxter House. Now he knew who the marine was and for some strange reason the two didn't want Judy or anyone else to know who he was. "Molly, trust me here because I really think it's important that you do. You need to let it be. Can you please do that?"

She looked him square in the eyes and could tell he was serious and for the first time in her life she was about to let her curiosity be set aside—although it would nag at her insides for having done so.

"I get your message, but I don't like having to do it. I'll drop the matter as you ask. Let's go talk to Eddie."

Porter grasped her hand and squeezed it. "I know it's difficult for you, but you're doing the right thing." He leaned over and kissed her. Porter opened the door to let Miss Mollie out.

She leaped out of the car. If she could speak, she'd say, he's so right this time, and I can't believe she gave in. Hell must be freezing over.

The inside of the police station was much different than it was when Porter was chief and when Molly first took over. During the past five years, significant remodeling was done. Molly had her own desk area as did Eddie and Adrian. There were now two bathrooms, one for the staff and another for those who were spending a night or so in jail. An additional jail cell was added in the event there were prisoners of a different gender. The room that the bed was in for all-nighters was much nicer than sleeping in the cell as Porter and Molly had to. All of it was accomplished by knocking down a wall between the jail and the store next door with funds provided by Coastal Resort Community.

Eddie was just hanging up the telephone when Molly, Porter, and Miss Mollie entered. "Hey Chief, what's up, are you checking up on us?"

Miss Mollie walked over to Adrian, sat down, and gave her a paw. She reached into her desk drawer, took out a snack, gave to Miss Mollie and shook her paw. "There you go, girl. It's good to see you up and around." She looked at Miss Mollie's bandage and then rubbed her belly. Miss Mollie reclined next to her and hoped for another treat.

"Eddie, this thing with John and Miss Mollie, I want you to take the lead. I'll back you up. You okay with that?"

He looked over at Miss Mollie and then at Porter. "Sure, Chief, just tell me what to do."

Porter sat down in the empty chair in front of Eddie's desk. Molly pulled the one from in front of hers and sat down. "We've already been in touch with Commander Edison of the Coast Guard because Porter's Island isn't in our jurisdiction or the county's. I'm going to call Bob Myers at Coastal and arrange a visit to the island with him and the commander. I want you to be there with us. He'll most likely take it from there, but you'll be our coordinator with them."

Eddie rubbed the back of his neck, raised his eyebrows, and grinned. "I can handle that. Any ID yet?"

"The commander sent us a picture of the owner of the boat, but he's not the guy who attacked us. He's much older than both of them," replied Porter.

Eddie rubbed his chin with his hand. "Could he have lent the boat to someone or could they be employees of his, Porter?"

Porter and Molly exchanged glances. "We hadn't thought of that, which is why I want you as our coordinator," replied Molly. "I'll call Myers now and see what he says." She dialed Bob Myers and he answered right away.

"Chief Dickson, to what do I owe a call from you? Anything to do with my wife and what happened Saturday night?"

She looked at Porter and Eddie. Porter mouthed for her to put it on speakerphone.

"Nothing to do with your wife, but it's about what happened on Porter's Island. We'd like to arrange a meeting there with you and Commander Edison of the Coast Guard. The island isn't in our jurisdiction so the Coast Guard will have to be involved. Since the incident involves one of your homes there, we need you to be there. Got any problem with that, Bob?"

Bob Myers was considering her request, the possibility that the home may have been ransacked, and the possibility that there was damage to the interior.

"No problem here. When do you want to do it? I can do it this afternoon or tomorrow."

"Let me call the commander first and I'll call you back. Eddie McClellan will be coordinating it for the police department. You're familiar with him already."

"No problem, Chief. Eddie's a good police officer and knows his stuff. I await your call. Say hello to Miss Mollie for me."

They hung up and Porter looked at Molly. "Doesn't anybody care about me?"

Eddie turned his head to stifle a laugh as did Adrian. Molly giggled.

"Yes, but they're more concerned about Miss Mollie." He shook his head and raised his hands in surrender.

Molly called Commander Edison and arranged for a meeting on Porter's Island after lunch. She called Bob Myer's back and set it up with him. He invited them to have lunch with him at the resort.

"Okay, now that that's all taken care of, we'll all go to the resort for lunch together and then we can take Porter's boat to the island."

CHAPTER 15

Beaufort—Monday

As he approached the city limits, he reached into his pocket and took out the directions that Corporal Towning's partner, Laurie Robinson, had sent him. He put her address into the GPS system and let it guide him.

A while later, the GPS said to turn left onto Clear Oak Street. The neighborhood had a number of moss-draped live oaks and Sabal Palms. He pulled into the driveway and the GPS navigator said—*you've arrived at your destination.* It was a white one-story sixteen hundred square foot bungalow with a garage. He walked up to the door and rang the bell.

When the door opened, he was stunned to see the most amazing looking woman that he had ever seen. She was thirty years old, five foot eight, with brown eyes, short brunette hair and attractive looking. She'd known Corporal Towning prior to Towning's enlistment. They kept in close contact by mail until Towning was injured.

"Good morning, you must be Sergeant Harding, I'm Laurie Robinson. Please come in."

She extended her hand. It felt soft against his calloused hand. Her eyes lit up when she smiled. He asked himself, *is this what a goddess looks like or is she an angel sent from heaven?*

"Are you going to give me back my hand, Sergeant?"

He let go of her hand and his complexion suddenly changed to a pinkish color. "Sorry, it's just that I didn't expect someone as good looking as you, Miss Robinson."

She grinned. "Are you always so forward with women the first time you meet them? And please call me Laurie."

"I'll call you Laurie, if you'll call me Brad.

They both laughed. "Okay, Brad, you win. Come on in. Jessica's in the den."

He looked around the house. "Nice digs, Laurie. You own or rent it?"

She beamed with pride. "I own it. My parents sold it to me when they retired and moved to Florida. They hold the mortgage which makes it easier to afford. I grew up in this house."

"Good for you, you must be proud of your parents. I wasn't so lucky with mine."

His remark struck her as odd. "We all have our crosses to bear, Brad. Let's go see Jessica."

Corporal Towning sat in a recliner watching television. She had on sweat pants, socks, and a shirt that had one sleeve cut off at the elbow. The shirt was wrinkled and looked like it had been slept in for several days, and it was obvious she wasn't wearing a bra. Her hair was long and unkempt as opposed to Laurie's.

Laurie put a hand on his arm, stopped him, glanced quickly at Towning and whispered, "It's all she does, every day. I just wish I could get her to go outside, but she refuses. She doesn't even put on shoes or brush her hair. I hope you can be of some help. Anything would be better than this."

He gave her hand a light squeeze. "I don't know what help I can be, but I'll try."

She tightened the grip on his hand, and he could see the pleading in her eyes. "Thanks, I'll take anything."

He approached Towning and stood beside her. "Good morning, Corporal Towning."

She kept her eyes focused on the television set and barely acknowledged his presence.

"I'm not a corporal anymore," she replied. "I'm a civilian. Remember they sent me home, gave me a medical discharge and a small pension. You can call me Jessica." She scrunched up in the chair, remained focused on the television and surfed the channels.

"Okay, Jessica, but you have to call me Brad." He moved a chair close and sat down. "Can you at least look at me, Jessica? We did serve together."

Several days after Harding's platoon returned from the rescue mission, he made a special visit to Kandahar Combat Hospital to visit his lieutenant and the other injured from his platoon. He made a special visit to Lance Corporal Jessica Towning who was the driver of the Humvee that was hit by the rocket resulting in severe damage to her left arm and shoulder—which resulted in her losing the arm. On the table next to her bed were a number of unanswered letters. They were from the same person who had previously sent letters to her.

The corporal opened her eyes and looked up at him. "Hey, Gunny thanks for stopping by."

"How are you doing, Corporal?"

She glanced at her left shoulder. "How do you think I'm doing? They're sending me home with a purple heart and no arm." She looked at her left arm. "It's bullshit."

He dismissed her comment as the beginning stages of PTSD and there was nothing he could do except offer encouragement. "Yeah, maybe it is, but you deserve the medal, and home will be good for you."

"That's more bullshit, Gunny?"

"Call me Brad, Jessica, since you're practically a civilian. You got some letters to open, need any help?"

She glanced at the letters and turned her head. "No thanks, but you could do me a favor and throw them away for me. I'm not in the mood to read them. Would you do that for me please?"

"Sure. I'll let you rest. If I can get back to see you, I will."

He picked up the letters, but he didn't throw them away. He felt that someone was waiting for an answer so instead when he got back to his tent, he wrote a letter about her injury, put it in a package with the letters and mailed it to the addressee.

Towning turned and faced him but kept her hand on the television remote and gave him a blank stare. "Okay Brad, I'll acknowledge that but what are you doing here?"

He had mixed emotions about being there. If he had only protested more when she was assigned to his platoon or passed her off to another one, or assigned a different driver for the mission, maybe he wouldn't have to be here. But then he might be visiting another marine. He had no training for this, and the tension was building up inside him. Maybe he shouldn't have come, but he had made a promise to Laurie.

"I'm here because as far as I'm concerned you're still a member of my platoon and always will be. That means I owe it to you to be concerned about what you're dealing with. Believe me, I have my own demons to deal with." He had never mentioned to anyone that he was dealing with the hell of war and all those tragic losses were weighing heavily on his mind.

She put the remote down, looked him in the eyes and realized that what he said was something she had never thought about. He was suffering as much as, if not more, than she was.

"I'm sorry, Brad, I forgot about what also happened that day, but you still have both your arms." She gave him another icy stare. "Look at me, what good am I to anyone? They wouldn't even let me stay in the marines."

Laurie winced at the sound of her words. She had seen a lot of wounded military personnel and even some deaths as a nurse at the Naval Hospital, but the effects of Towning's PTSD hurt her deeply. She wiped her tears and tried her best to control her emotions.

He reached out to put his hand on Jessica's, but she pulled it away. "Believe me being a marine isn't everything. There's more in life." His words were out of his mouth before he realized that what he said may have been the wrong thing.

She turned her head to avoid eye contact with him. "That's easy for you to say. You have both your arms."

He had no answer for her. "I'm getting out in less than six months. I've seen and had enough. It's time I did something else." He bit his bottom lip. "When my leave is up, I report to Parris Island until I'm discharged. After that I don't know what I'm going to do or where I'm going."

She swiveled in her seat, put one leg under the other, and said, "But I thought you were going all the way. What about what's happening now in Iraq?"

He took a chance, extended his arm again and put his hand over hers. This time she didn't pull away. Laurie clasped her hands to her chest and took a deep breath.

"I don't have it in me anymore, and I just can't stomach the way things are being conducted in Washington. I'm no good as a leader if my heart's not in the fight. And I'm starting to resent the command structure, especially since that phony prisoner swap."

"It pissed me off too. That last mission we were on was worth doing and if I could, I'd do it over again but not for a stinking deserter."

"Look, Jessica, I made this trip just to visit with you. I'd like to spend the day with you, even tomorrow if you'll let me. We can have pizza for supper. How does that sound?"

"What do you think, Laurie?"

"I think that's a good idea, Jess. I took the next couple of days off in case you wanted to spend more time with the sergeant."

"Hey, I thought we were on a first name basis?"

"Sorry. I forgot. So Jess, are we having pizza?"

"What the hell, why not?"

"Great, but first I have to go get a hotel room for tonight," he said. "Then I'll come back and we can order that pizza."

"You're not leaving so soon are you, Brad? You just got here."

"I guess I can stay a while longer, but do we have to watch television?"

She turned the television set off. "No, we don't have to. We can talk about what you've been doing since you got back to the states. It feels strange calling you just Brad."

He squeezed her hand. "Not as strange as calling you Jess, Corporal Towning."

They both started laughing. Laurie turned and left the room in tears, but they were happy ones.

He told Jessica about his visit to Blocker's Bluff and why he was going back there. She listened and suddenly realized how fortunate she was to have someone to come home to, unlike him.

"I hope you and your mother reconnect. Family's important." Laurie shivered at her comment. "Don't waste too much time because you never know what could happen." She realized that she was dispensing advice and that she wasn't one to give it because she had been ignoring both her mother and the one person who had been there for her.

"I don't plan to. I'm just working up the courage. Maybe after I leave here, I'll do it and stop back and let you know."

They continued conversing while Laurie went to her room, showered, and dressed in comfortable clothes.

He checked his watch and saw it was 4:00. "I'd better leave now and get a hotel room."

"Why don't I go with you? That way I can show you how to get to the nearest hotel. We can get that pizza and bring it home. There's a great place that I know of."

"If you don't mind, Laurie, I'd appreciate your company. You won't miss me while I'm gone will you, Jess?"

She slapped him on the arm and laughed. "Go on get the hell out of here."

Before he started the car, Laurie put a hand on his leg. "Thanks Brad, that's the first time she's laughed since she's been here. She never even smiled much less carried on a conversation with me."

He put his hand over hers. "Has she gone to PT, counseling or anything?"

"No, she refuses to, and I don't know what to do. If I could at least get her to counseling, I know it would help."

"Does she have any family?"

"Her mother lives in Charleston. Jessica went there as soon as she came home, but her mother freaked when she saw Jessica's arm was missing. Jessica couldn't deal with it. She showed up at my doorstep and asked if she could stay with me." Laurie looked away for a moment. "I didn't want her to end up homeless so I let her move in with me. She's been here ever since and calls her mother once or twice a month. Her mother does most of the talking. My parents came to visit for Christmas, but Jessica stayed in her room the whole time they were here. I guess I'm her family now."

"Wow! That's got to be really hard on you. Let's see what a few days with me visiting does. Now where are we going?"

She removed her hand, turned away, and wiped her eye. He backed out of the driveway.

"There's a Comfort Suites not far from here. Take a right onto 128. It's near the intersection of 128 and 21."

He followed her directions, drove to the hotel, parked, and went in to register. Then he drove around to where his room was located and parked. He left his overnight bag in the room and returned to the car.

"Okay, Laurie I'm all set, where to now?"

She gave him directions to Bardo's Pizzeria and Restaurant a mile and a half from her house. It was located within a small cluster of retail shops that included an East Coast National branch. He wondered if it was in Marvin Johnson's territory.

"Man, this place smells great," he commented. The smell of garlic and marinara sauce greeted them.

"I love the smell and they make the best pizza in Beaufort County."

A hostess greeted them. They said they were ordering takeout, so she directed them to the takeout counter. Laurie ordered a large pizza with several toppings and a side order of breadsticks and meatballs. Since it would be twenty minutes until their order was ready, they ordered a couple of beers and found seating.

"You don't look like the type who drinks beer, Laurie."

"I wasn't always, but being a nurse can sometimes change a person." She tapped his bottle. "What made you join the marines?"

He took a sip of his beer. "Well, 9/11 happened, and I felt the need to do something for my country. I was in law school when I enlisted. What made you become a nurse?"

"My parents wanted a boy they could mold into a sailor like them, but they got me instead. After high school, I decided on my own to become a nurse. It's been a rewarding career so far."

He wondered if he should use the remaining time he had in the marines to plan his life after the military. "How did you and Jessica meet?"

"We met at the university library. We were both studying and started talking and soon became really good friends." She started peeling the label off her beer. "Now I'm like her caregiver, and it hurts to see her like she is. Today was a relief for me because you made her laugh."

"I'm glad you asked me to come. While I'm here, you can lean on me if you'd like." He hoped she would because he was finding himself becoming attracted to her. "I'm happy you're there for her." He tipped his beer to hers.

He couldn't help looking at her and wondered what it would be like to hold her in his arms, kiss those lips and feel the warmth of her body next to him. He reached across the table and placed his hand on hers. "Too bad I'm not a civilian yet, I could be more helpful."

"Thanks Brad, you're doing enough for now." She removed her hand. "It looks like our pizza is ready."

He paid the bill and drove to her house. Towning was watching television but when she smelled the pizza she turned it off.

"Hey, that pizza smells good. Did you get it at Bardo's?"

Laurie grinned. "We sure did. Are you going to sit with us at the table or are you going to eat it there by the television, Jess?"

She got up out of her chair. "I'll have mine over here with you guys."

Laurie and him pressed their lips tight. They were glad that Towning finally got out from in front of the television.

He set the pizza on the table and Laurie got plates and forks.

"Anyone want a beer?" Laurie called out.

"Come on, Jess, have a beer with us. One beer won't hurt."

"Okay, but just one."

Laurie went to get them each a beer. As she walked away, she pumped her fist in front of her so Towning couldn't see it and whispered, "Yes!"

They ate their pizza, had another beer, and made dumbass jokes about nothing in particular.

"Jess, it's ten o'clock. Time I went to the hotel."

"Will you be back tomorrow?"

"Yes, but it will be after lunch. I have something I have to do first."

Laurie walked him to the door. "Thanks, Brad, for everything."

"You're welcome and maybe tomorrow things will be even better. Goodnight, Laurie."

She reached out and put a hand on his face. "Goodnight, Brad." The soft touch of her hand felt soothing.

After he left, Laurie cleared the table, put the dishes and forks in the dishwasher and took the empty piazza box to the garbage. When she came back, Towning was watching television.

"Goodnight, Jess. I'm going to turn in; it was a long day for me. I'll see you in the morning. I liked Brad, he's a nice guy."

Jessica changed channels, gave her a wave with the back of her hand and said, "Yeah, he is. Goodnight."

Laurie went to her room, got into bed, and wept. Later that night, Towning went to her room and climbed into bed.

By the time Harding arrived at his hotel room, he had decided that there must be more he could do for Jessica. Before going to bed, he watched a little television and became interested in a commercial about the Wounded Warrior Project and another about dogs for veterans. He opened his laptop and searched the Internet for the dog site "CARV—Companion Animal Rescue for Veterans." When he found the site, he viewed some of the dog pictures and stopped when he came to the one named Sarge. The dog intrigued him so much that he decided in the morning he would visit the place and check out Sarge.

At two-thirty in the morning, he woke drenched in sweat. He had a nightmare about that day in Afghanistan when Towning's Humvee was struck by a rocket. He hadn't had any nightmares since he left Kuwait, and it was the same one that Towning experienced almost every night.

CHAPTER 16

Porter's Island

Porter eased his boat up to the CRC dock. Molly and Eddie leaned over the side and secured it as he shut the engine off. Eddie got on the dock, checked the moorings, and then helped Molly.

"Can I help you, Mr. Myers?"

"No thanks, Eddie. You may want to help Porter and Miss Mollie though." He got off the boat and stepped onto the dock. Miss Mollie leaped off the boat and landed on the dock beside him. "Damn, she's good."

Porter started to get off the boat and Eddie offered him a hand. "If you want to keep that hand, Eddie, you best get it away from me. I ain't crippled." He stepped onto the dock, and they all watched as Commander Edison pulled up behind them.

"See you all got here before me. Someone tie me up." He tossed a line to Eddie. He grabbed it and secured the commander's boat. "Good catch. You must be Eddie. I'm coming on shore." He climbed onto the dock. "I'm Commander Edison." He extended his hand to Eddie and Bob Myers.

"I'm Bob Myers and you can call me Bob. Coastal Resort Community owns this dock and the three houses."

"Nice to meet you too, Bob. Porter, is this where it all happened?" He looked around the dock and up at the houses.

Porter showed him where it had happened and explained it in as much detail as he could. He pointed to the spot where Miss Mollie was shot and rubbed the back of his head.

"I noticed the name on their boat when we pulled up."

"You and Miss Mollie were pretty lucky, Porter. It could have been worse." The commander looked for a shell casing and a slug but there weren't any. He looked toward the homes. "Was anything taken from the houses?"

"We haven't checked yet, but Mr. Myers can let us in," replied Molly. "Eddie's going to be the lead on the case."

Another Coast Guard boat pulled up to the dock. Everyone watched as two people stepped off the boat. "Those are my forensic investigators," Edison said. "Let's let them check the houses. Mr. Myers, could you let them in, please?"

Myers led the investigators toward the house that Porter said he saw the perpetrators coming from. The door was jimmied open so he let the investigators go in first. They had him check the house for anything missing while they checked all the rooms. Then they went to the other houses. Since there was no sign of forced entry, Myers opened the door and they checked both of them for evidence.

The investigators and Myers reported back to Edison. "They took the laptop we provided for guests and a small television from the master bedroom. Nothing was taken from the other houses," said Myers.

"Not a very lucrative haul," remarked Eddie. "They're probably amateurs or were more interested in using the house for a place to stay."

"Commander, we dusted for prints and checked the beds for DNA. Apparently someone slept in them. It looked like they tried to make them look like nobody did," said the female investigator. "Anything else you want us to do?"

"No, but get back to me as soon as you have some results. You can take off now. Thanks for your help." He held his hand up and said, "Wait one." They stopped. "Porter can you give them some kind of description of those two guys?"

He gave as much of a description as he could. The investigators wrote it down and then left.

"Maybe they were just using the house to party in," said Eddie.

"Possibly, Eddie, but why here? They might have been hiding out for some reason or used the place for a meet," remarked the commander.

"A meeting for what?" asked Porter. "You're not thinking drugs again are you, Mo?"

"Could be, Porter, otherwise why attack you?"

"You think it was revenge from what happened years ago. Is that it, Commander?" Molly asked. "If it was, then why didn't they do more harm to him than just knock him out and leave?"

The commander rubbed his jaw. "Good question, Chief. What do you think, Porter?"

Porter puckered his mouth. "I don't buy the revenge angle. What do you think, Eddie?"

Eddie tilted his head and put two fingers to his forehead. "The more I think about it, the more I agree with Porter, sorry, Commander."

"Maybe you're both right and maybe we'll get lucky when we get the evidence results."

"Let's hope so," said Molly.

"Guess we're all done here. When are we going fishing, Porter?"

"When Molly can take a weekend off."

"Chief, I can take your next few Saturdays for you if you want to go fishing with them." Eddie said.

"That's awfully nice of you, Eddie, but your wife's pregnant and you should be home with her."

That's when Eddie surprised them. "I've been meaning to tell you, Chief. She had the baby Sunday night." His grin spread from ear to ear. "I'm the father of a beautiful little girl named Rose. My mom and dad came to help until Rosemary can go back to work and until Rose can go to daycare."

Molly put her arm around him and kissed him on the forehead. "Congratulations, Eddie. Why didn't you say something sooner? I wouldn't have put this case on you."

"Chief, if I'm going to take over when you retire, I need to handle situations like this, even if it interferes with my personal life. I signed up for this job, and I intend to do my best just as I did in the army."

The commander extended his hand. "Let me shake your hand, Eddie, and congratulate you. I'm proud that you'll be coordinating this case with me."

Porter slapped him on the back. "Well I'll be damned, Eddie, congratulations, you son of a gun."

"Thanks, Porter, I appreciate it and thank all of you."

"Okay, now that the celebrating is over, we best get back to work," interjected Molly. "Commander, when you have something for us, you know where to call Eddie."

"Will do, Chief," he answered and then boarded his boat.

"Let's get Bob back to his office," Porter said.

They boarded Porter's boat. He pulled away from the dock and headed for Blocker's Bluff. He pulled up to the dock and Eddie secured the boat.

"Eddie, I'll take Bob back to Coastal Resort, and you can finish your shift. Tell Rosemary congratulations from me."

"Thanks, Chief, I will. See you, Mr. Myers, you too Porter and Miss Mollie."

"Take care, Eddie, and give my congratulations to Rosemary," Myers replied.

Molly dropped Myers off at Coastal Resort and drove to the diner for an early supper. They told Chef Willie about their trip to Porter's Island, their meeting with Edison, and the investigation. Then she told him about Eddie and Rosemary.

"Eddie is now officially a daddy. Rosemary had a little girl Sunday night and they named her Rose. Ain't that something?"

He slapped his towel against his hand. "That sure is. Miss Mavis, come out here we got something to tell you."

Miss Mavis wiped her hands on her towel and tossed it over her shoulder. "What you got to tell me? Is Molly with child?"

Molly almost fell off her seat, and Porter laughed. "Miss Mavis, you know better than that."

"If you two would have tied the knot a long time ago, you might have been. Now what do you want to tell me, Chef?"

He held her head in his hands and kissed her on the lips. "Rosemary had her baby. They named her Rose. Ain't that something?"

Miss Mavis actually blushed—something she rarely did. "It sure is, and you're an old fool kissing me like that in front of these children."

He put his arm around her and pulled her close. "They ain't children, and we're too old to worry about foolishness, Mavis Caldridge."

Molly and Porter raised their eyes. It was the first time they had ever heard Miss Mavis' last name.

Miss Mavis hit him with her towel, turned, and went back into the kitchen. Chef Willie handed Porter and Molly menus. They both ordered the special, and Chef Willie gave Miss Mollie a cookie.

She gobbled down the cookie and barked.

Chef Willie brought their meals from the kitchen and a special treat for Miss Mollie. He set their plates in front of them, reached down and gave her a small plate with baked chicken, gravy, and a biscuit freshly baked by Miss Mavis.

She chomped on it and licked her plate clean.

Molly and Porter finished their meal and left.

"What's the plan for tonight, Molly?"

She gave him a sheepish grin. "What do you think it is, lover boy?"

He braced himself against the dashboard and shouted, "Lover boy? Where did that come from? I hope that means what I think it does."

She put a hand on his thigh, rubbed it, and grinned. "You know it does."

He wondered why she was suddenly so affectionate. It had started right after Saturday night.

CHAPTER 17

Beaufort—Tuesday Morning

He researched the CARV website again. It gave him an idea for something that might help Towning. He wrote the address on a piece of paper and called Laurie.

"Laurie Robinson, how can I help you?" Since she hadn't recognized his number, she answered formally.

"Laurie, it's me, Brad. Don't let Jessica know I'm calling. I need you to do me a favor."

She walked into the living room. "Good morning, sir, what can I do for you?"

"Are you where you can talk?"

She whispered, "Yes, she can't hear me, but I'll act as though you're my superior. What's this favor you want?"

"I need you to meet me at the address I texted you. I'll explain when you get there. Trust me, it's for Jessica."

She wasn't sure what he wanted but decided to go along with him. She spoke loud enough so Jessica could hear her. "Yes, sir, I can be there in twenty minutes. Thank you for calling." Then she whispered, "It may take me longer, since I have to change clothes. I hope you know what you're doing."

"I hope so too. See you in twenty or thirty."

She called out to Jessica, "Jess, I have to go to the hospital for a little while. Will you be okay?"

Laurie closed her eyes and almost cried. After finishing dressing, she again called out to Jessica. "I'm leaving, Jess." As usual, there was no response.

She wasn't familiar with the address he texted her so she put it in her GPS and followed the directions to a small business district. She parked in front of the building with the sign on it that read CARV—Companion Animal Rescue for Veterans. She wondered what he was up to and hoped he knew what he was doing. He was talking with a slender woman dressed in a white lab coat when she entered.

"Laurie, I'd like you to meet Doctor Jennings. Doctor, this is Laurie Robinson."

Doctor Jennings was fifty years old with short black hair, black glasses, a hint of makeup and lipstick. "Laurie, I'm pleased to meet you."

"Pleased to meet you, Doctor."

"Please call me Ann. Since you're a nurse, my guess is that you're not the veteran the sergeant has been telling me about. And with that knockout smile of yours, you're certainly not suffering from PTSD. But your eyes suggest that you're feeling the stress from dealing with someone who is." Laurie's eyebrows went up. "Why don't we go into my office and you can tell me about your veteran."

"Sure, but I'm curious how did you come up with all that so quickly?"

"Twenty years as a navy nurse and twelve years as a veterinarian working with veterans. I've seen it all, and I'm sure as a nurse you've seen a lot too."

"I have, but I'm sure not as much as you have."

The doctor sat behind her desk. "Okay Laurie, tell me all about this veteran and we'll see if I can help."

Laurie told the doctor what it had been like the past year with Jessica. "She gets up in the morning, dresses, has breakfast and then sits in front of the television all day and night. When I'm on duty, I don't know if she eats anything. I'm pretty sure she doesn't because there are never dirty dishes in the sink or the dishwasher." Laurie put her hand over her heart.

"You okay, Laurie?" asked Brad.

"Yes." She looked down. *Not really, but they don't need to know how I truly feel.*

Dr. Jennings listened, all the while observing Laurie's body language, tone of voice, and the expression on her face.

"Okay, I can see this is having an impact on you too. I'm guessing you and Jessica were close at one time, am I right?"

Laurie looked at Brad. "Yes, we were and it hurts me to see her like this." A tear rolled down her cheek.

The doctor handed her a box of tissues. "I'm sure it does. All right, you've convinced me that we may be able to help. Let me tell you what we do here. We match veterans with PTSD or those who are living alone, hence the name companion, primarily with dogs we feel would be a good fit. Normally the veteran comes to our shelter and we try to match them with a perfect fit."

"Doctor, Jessica won't come here," commented Laurie.

"Okay, that's going to be difficult in her circumstance. Let me ask you this. Are you willing to adopt a dog and try to get Jessica to become comfortable with it?"

Brad put a hand on Laurie's. "Dr. Jennings, we would like to try it for a week and see how it goes."

"That's really not how this works, Sergeant. It's not a maybe or maybe not; it has to be a commitment."

"I'm on leave for three more weeks, after that I can check up on them weekly. My enlistment is up in six months and I have more leave time coming. If it doesn't work out, I'll take the dog."

"Are you suffering from PTSD?"

He closed his eyes. "It's possible because I've been having some nightmares lately."

"How can I be sure you'll take the dog? And where it will it stay while you're away, Sergeant?"

He thought of Thomas. "In Blocker's Bluff, there's a ten-year-old who will take care of the dog for me." He considered Baxter House or his mother's house but first he had to reconcile with her. "The dog can stay at his grandmother's house. I'll stipulate it in the documents if it's the right dog."

"Are you sure, Brad?"

"Yes, I have to do this for Jessica's sake."

"You two would make a nice couple," said the doctor. Laurie winced. "Okay, I'm going to give you guys a chance, and I'm placing my faith in you, Sergeant."

"You have my word, Doctor, and I won't disappoint you."

"What about you, Laurie, are you willing to make the commitment?"

"Yes, if it's the right dog."

Dr. Jennings crossed her arms and studied them both. "I know how Laurie met Jessica but how did you meet her?"

His heart started to palpitate because he hated reliving what happened again. He wiped his brow, looked down and then at the doctor. "I was her platoon leader, and she was on a rescue mission when her Humvee was hit. In a way, I feel responsible for her just like I did for all my men and woman."

"That's an awful lot of responsibility to take on."

Laurie put her hand on his. She had wondered why he was so concerned about Jessica. This was the first she'd learned that she was injured during a mission led by him. "She's right, Brad. That is a lot to take on."

"It's not an easy task that you're doing." He squeezed her hand.

"Okay, you two have convinced me to give it a try, but it will be with a very special dog. You may change your minds after you see her. Her name's Sarge. She was given the name by her previous owner, who was also a veteran. He took her when she was a puppy and had her for three years until he passed away. She needs someone who will love her because she'll love whoever gets her."

"I actually saw her picture on your website last night. It's why I came here, but I didn't read up on her."

"Hmm, if you had you might not have come. Are you ready to meet Sarge?"

"Yes, you ready, Laurie?"

"You've made me nervous now, Doctor. I'm wondering what I'm getting myself into."

The doctor got up from her desk. "Wait here, I'll be right back." She went to the kennel and returned with a dog on a leash. The dog stood next to the doctor's right leg.

"Laurie, Sergeant, meet Sarge."

She was a mixed breed, white with brown spots and captivating eyes that were masked in brown. Sarge's tail wagged back and forth and her legs shivered as though she was excited to see them.

They both covered their mouths and gasped. "She only has three legs, Doctor."

"I told you she was special, Laurie. Want to change your minds? You can, but tell me now because I don't want to waste Sarge's time."

He put his arm around Laurie. "We're not sure how Jessica will react to her. She doesn't have a left arm, and it could be traumatic for her."

"Maybe," the doctor replied. "But the reason Sarge is special isn't just because she only has three legs, it's because her previous owner only had one. Even though they only had three years together, Sarge made them special for him. I think she can do it for Jessica, but it's up to you two."

"How do you know the years with her owner were special?"

She crossed her hands over her heart. "Because he was my husband, Laurie."

Laurie and Brad froze for a moment.

"I'm sorry, forgive me for asking."

The doctor raised a palm up. "That's okay, Laurie, but it's time Sarge introduced herself to you two. Sarge, go introduce yourself to them."

Sarge walked over to Laurie first. Laurie was nervous at first but knelt down in front of Sarge and introduced herself.

"Hello, Sarge, my name is Laurie. I'm thinking about taking you home to meet someone special, but I don't know if I should. Can you help me out here?"

Sarge sat down and extended her right paw. Laurie took it and let Sarge lick her face.

She looked into Laurie's eyes, and could see the pain. Laurie couldn't help staring into Sarge's eyes. Sarge licked Laurie's face again. Tears rolled down her face and Sarge licked at them.

"We'll take her, Doctor."

"Are you sure?"

"Yes, Brad, who could resist her? Why don't you introduce yourself to Sarge?"

He knelt down in front of Sarge. She extended her right paw to him. He took it, and then rubbed the top of her head and let her lick his face.

"I'm glad to meet you, Sarge. It looks like you're going to have a new home." He stood up. "We'll take her, Doctor."

Laurie hugged him and stepped back. "Sorry, that was inappropriate of me."

He laughed it off. "Don't apologize. I was going to hug you."

"Since that's settled, let's get the paperwork completed and you can take your dog home. Guess you'll be leaving us, Sarge." Sarge barked. "Sergeant, why don't you and Sarge go for a walk while Laurie and I start the paperwork?" She handed him the leash and he and Sarge went outside.

Laurie gave the doctor Jessica's personal information and her home address. Then the doctor and Laurie shook hands. Harding and Sarge came back from their walk.

"Good luck and you call me if there are any problems, Laurie."

"Thanks, Doctor, I will."

The doctor gave him a pat on the arm. "You did good, Sergeant, now come sign the papers."

"Thanks, so did you, Doc."

He signed the papers with the stipulation that he would take Sarge if it didn't work with Towning.

The doctor walked over to Sarge, bent down and kissed her on the top of her head. "So long girl. You take care of these two." She patted Sarge's head. "I'm gonna miss you." She watched as they left.

Sarge jumped into the backseat and Laurie drove home. He followed behind in his car. At the house, Sarge carefully jumped out of the car.

"What do we do now, Brad?"

He scratched the back of his head. "I'm not sure but let me take Sarge inside. I have an idea. Go along with me."

"I hope this works. I really appreciate what you're doing for Jess."

"I'm doing it for you too."

She turned her head, opened the front door, and let him and Sarge enter.

"Hey, Jess, guess who's back?" he yelled, but Towning ignored him. He leaned down and whispered into Sarge's ear, "Okay Sarge, let's see what you can do. She needs your help." Sarge walked over to Towning, sat down by her, and put her chin on Towning's thigh.

"What the hell! Where did you come from?" she exclaimed.

"She's mine, Jess. Her name's Sarge. I thought maybe you and Laurie could keep her for me until I get out. I can visit her every week to see how she's doing. What do you think? Laurie already said yes."

Sarge put her right paw on Jessica leg and stared into her eyes. She turned to ignore Sarge. While he and Laurie waited for her response, she shocked them by putting her hand on the back of Sarge's head and petting her, but curtly replied, "Whatever."

"Does that mean you're okay with it?"

"If you want to, Laurie." Sarge jumped onto her lap and started licking her face. "Hey, take it easy there." Jessica put her right arm around Sarge and that was when she saw Sarge had no left front leg. "Is this some kind of sick joke, you two?"

"No Jess, Sarge is a special dog."

"What's so special about her? She only has three legs."

"That's what makes her special," answered Laurie. "Her previous owner only had one. He raised her from a pup."

Jessica gave Laurie an icy stare. "What happened to him? Did he give up on her?"

"No Jess, he passed away not too long ago. She's a rescue dog," answered Harding.

"And what, you're gonna recue her or do you expect me to?"

"Dammit, Jess," shouted Laurie. "No, she's going to rescue you. She's my dog, not Brad's. Give her a chance, please." Laurie waited for an answer hoping it would be the one she wanted.

"If you want to keep her, fine, but you have to take care of her and walk her."

"She doesn't need to be walked just let out to do her business. The yard is fenced in so that won't be a problem. Does that mean you're okay with her staying?"

Laurie looked to him. He mouthed, "Wait."

"I guess so." Sarge rolled over on her back, rubbed up against Jessica and licked her face. "Damn dog sure is affectionate." She rubbed Sarge's belly and kissed her.

He signaled for Laurie to step back. "I have another idea. Why don't we leave them alone for the afternoon? You and I can do some sightseeing. I've haven't had a chance to tour the city, and you could be my tour guide. What do you say?"

"Do you think it would be okay?"

"I can hear you two. Go ahead, me and Sarge will be fine."

They were excited that Jessica was okay with them leaving her alone with Sarge.

Laurie went to her room and changed into jeans and a t-shirt. When he saw her, he raised his eye brows, and shook his hand indicating, "Wow."

"Jess, we'll be back before dinnertime. Anything special you want for dinner?"

"Pizza's fine."

He and Laurie left and she got behind the wheel of his car. "Where to first, Brad?"

"You're the tour guide so wherever you want to take me is okay." He reached into the glove compartment, took out his camera and fastened it to his belt. "If we're going sightseeing, I might as well take some pictures."

"How about we start with the Historic District?"

"Sounds good to me."

CHAPTER 18

Laurie and Harding began their walking tour starting with the Historic District. He reached down and took her hand. Her first thought was to pull it away, but it felt good having someone hold her hand. She locked her fingers with his and turned his way. Her eyes twinkled.

She led him all around the district, touring the antebellum homes and mansions. Next, they went to the Marine Corps Air Station and toured the museum. He took lots of pictures. Then they walked along the water watching the boats. When they came to a wooden bench facing the water, they sat down to rest.

He leaned back against the bench. "You know so much about Beaufort, did you grow up here?"

She leaned back with him. "I actually did. My parents and I used to walk around the city on weekends and have lunch in the District. Those were good times. What about you, where is your home?"

"I'm originally from Virginia, but I haven't been back there since I joined the marines." He hesitated before continuing. "My parents divorced a long time ago. My mother lives in Blocker's Bluff up the coast, and I'm planning on reuniting with her."

"What does that mean?"

He watched a sailboat go by before answering. "After my parents divorced, I never saw her again. I don't know what happened and she never tried to see me after it was final. Her father lived in Blocker's Bluff, and I used to visit him in the summers. But after the divorce, I never got to see him again. He died years later."

She put her hand on his thigh. "I'm sorry and I hope you get to reconnect with your mother."

He stood up and handed her his camera. "Enough reminiscing. Take my picture, Laurie." He stood on the bench, put one foot on the back and posed as though he was Atlas. "How's this?" She laughed and snapped the picture. He stood with both feet on the bench and strummed an air guitar. "Take another one."

"You're crazy."

"Okay, now it's your turn." He took the camera and motioned for her to get on the bench.

"No way, I'm not going to do what you did."

"Oh come on. Have some fun. Get up on the bench."

He held her hand and helped her up onto the bench. She made like she was Hulk Hogan. He snapped two pictures.

"Okay, that's it."

He took her hand and helped her down. They gazed into each other's eyes. He felt like kissing her, but she looked away.

"Brad, we've got company."

An elderly couple watched and applauded them.

"Would you take a picture of us, sir?" Harding handed him the camera.

"Sure, but then you have to take a picture of us."

"You got it, sir. Come on, Laurie, he's going to take a picture of us together."

"I'm not sure we should do this."

"It's just one picture. Come on don't be a spoil sport."

"Okay, but you're like a kid, you know that?" He stood next to her.

Before the gentleman took their picture his wife whispered something in his ear. "You're right, Agnes. Put your arms around each other like you like each other."

Laurie was reluctant. "One picture, Laurie, I promise." They put their arms around each other.

"There you go now." He took their picture. "Now turn and face each other. Come on don't be bashful."

"Brad, please, no."

"Sir, we'd rather not."

"Oh, come on, just one picture. You're not afraid of each other, are you?"

He turned and put his palms up. "I don't think he's going to let up until we let him, Laurie."

"But this is the last one. I mean it!"

They faced each other. The woman walked over, put a hand on their backs, and pushed them closer. "That's much better now. Okay, Arthur, take their picture and this is definitely the last one. We don't want to annoy this nice couple."

Laurie winced when she called them a couple. He gazed into her eyes and could tell there was loneliness in them, but there was also hope and a promise of a better life.

She gazed into his deep blue eyes and saw the heartache in them but sensed compassion and strength of character. *If only this wasn't contrary to regulations,* she said to herself.

The gentleman took two pictures. He showed his wife the pictures. She put two fingers to her mouth and smiled.

"Okay, young man, now you take one of us."

They exchanged cameras. The couple embraced, leaned their heads forward, and touched their foreheads together. Harding took two pictures and handed the gentleman his camera.

"Thank you. I hope you two have a nice day."

"Pardon me, sir, but how long have you two been married?"

The corners of his mouth went up. "Forty-six years. She was my nurse in Vietnam. She's been nursing me ever since. Can you believe she resigned her commission to be with me?" He took his wife's hand and they walked off.

Laurie turned her head away. "You're not mad at me are you, Laurie?"

She watched the elderly couple as they walked off. "No, I'm not. How about we get a glass of wine and a snack? We can go to Blackstone's Café."

"Sure. Are you okay, Laurie?"

"Yes, it's just that they reminded me of my parents."

He held her hand as they walked to the Café, found a seat near a window, and placed their order with the waitress.

"You're a good tour guide, Laurie. I don't think I would have seen as much if I was by myself. Thanks." He put his hand on the table.

She put her hand on his. "You're a good tourist, Brad."

They gazed into each other's eyes and then she removed her hand. When they finished their wine and cheese and crackers, they walked back to the car. Laurie started to get in the car as he held the door for her but suddenly stopped, put her arms around him, kissed him, and pulled back.

"Sorry, that was inappropriate of me."

"No need to apologize." He walked around to the other side smiling and got in next to her. "Where to now?"

She leaned over and kissed him again. "Can we go to your hotel room?"

"Are you sure?"

She kissed him again. "Yes."

She drove to the Comfort Suites and they went to his room. Both needed the comfort of one another. As soon as they were in the room, they undressed and were quickly on the bed kissing each other. He reached down, cupped a breast and put the nipple in his mouth. She put a hand on his head. Then he began kissing her until she arched her back and raised her hips.

"Oh, yes!"

They changed positions as she raised her knees so he could cover her body with his and she welcomed him to her. Her body quivered when she felt him inside her. She wanted all of him, wanted him to erase the past year of living with Jessica and the loneliness. She pulled him to her taking more of him.

He plunged into her, taking what she offered. He needed this, needed her, and needed the sex. It had been a long time since he bedded a woman and she was going to be all his. He didn't care; he just wanted, needed and demanded all of her.

He was taking her: taking all of her and showed no sympathy. But she didn't want sympathy she wanted to be loved and didn't care about the consequences. Suddenly she was leaving her body, floating somewhere in time and space. She knew not where but it was wonderful. People were holding hands, smiling at each other, hugging and kissing.

She wrapped her legs around him and dug her fingers into his back. He went deeper and his heart started pounding

"More please!"

She floated back into her body and let out a soft scream. Her body shivered then calmed as the warmth of his offering lovingly flowed into her.

For her it was a release of the frustration from caring for an ungrateful Jessica, and the feeling that it was a mistake to have given her a place to live. For him it was a release of the heartache from the death of Roger Pritcher and the injury to Corporal Towning.

Suddenly it was over and she opened her eyes—he was gone. Then she felt her hand in his and his body lying next to her.

"I'm sorry I didn't mean to be so eager." She breathed deeply. "It's been so long since anyone held or kissed me. Can we just hold each other for a while?"

"Sure." He cradled her in his arms.

She rolled over, put her head against his chest, a hand on it and straddled him with her leg. He felt the wetness from her tears on his chest, put an arm around her and gently stroked her back. She felt the beating of his heart and his heavy breathing, looked up at him and gazed into his eyes.

She saw sadness in them; he saw loneliness in hers. But he saw something else. He saw the woman that he knew he loved.

"Thanks, Brad."

He leaned his head down and kissed her on the mouth. She put her head back against his chest. He pulled her closer and breathed in the scent of her hair. It had the aroma of lavender and violets, and was intoxicating. Suddenly they were making love again.

They both lay side by side and gazed up at the ceiling. She wondered if she had made a mistake coming to his room and if she crossed a fine line. She got out of bed; showered, wrapped a towel around her and went back to the bedroom to dress.

He sat on the bed, listened to the shower running. When she came out of the bathroom, he went in and took a shower. He wrapped a towel around him and walked back to the bedroom. He watched as she started dressing and couldn't help but notice she had a gorgeous body.

"I don't mean to be inappropriate, Laurie, but you're smoking hot."

She swiveled into her jeans, fastened her bra, and glanced at him.

"Thanks, it may be inappropriate, but I appreciate the comment. No one has ever complimented me like that." She looked at him, and grinned. "You're not so bad yourself."

His color turned a shade of pink when he realized the towel was on the floor. He scooped it up and covered himself.

"Thanks, I liked holding you, and I would have been content to hold you forever."

She looked away. "I wish you could, but you can't. We both know we've already crossed the line."

"That's one line I'd gladly cross any day."

Her shoulders stiffened as she gripped the buttons on her blouse. "But I can't, I've too much to lose, and I'm not going to throw it all away because of a lapse in judgment and an afternoon's indiscretion."

"What are you talking about?" He was totally confused.

The silence in the room was deafening. She finished buttoning her top.

"We should go get that pizza now."

He dressed, they left the room and drove to the pizzeria in silence. She focused on her driving, and he stared out the window. Neither wanted to bring up the subject of what had happened in his hotel room. The only distraction was the smell of the pizza.

She pulled into her driveway and they walked into the house practically ignoring each other. Jessica and Sarge were playing on the floor. As soon as she saw them, she got back in her chair and turned on the television. Brad and Laurie managed to grin.

Laurie set the pizza and breadsticks on the dining room table, got plates, forks, and napkins and put them on the table. "Anyone for a beer?" she called out. "We still have a few left. Last call."

He raised his hand and yelled, "I'll take one. What about you, Jess? Are you and Sarge joining us?"

Sarge barked at Jessica, put her head on her thigh and stared into her eyes. "Sure, why not. She won't leave me alone if I don't."

Laurie felt like dancing. She was ecstatic that Jessica was going to join them again. It was a new twist in their relationship. Meals were always her serving Jessica in front of the television and conversation was nothing but how was your day and her replying—how the hell do you think it was. She hoped this was going to be the start of something new. Laurie got three beers and joined them.

He felt a sense of accomplishment. When he first arrived there, he didn't think he could help Jessica. Maybe her getting up from in front of the television was a first step in a journey of a thousand miles to overcome her situation. If she could do it, maybe he could take a first step in his journey toward dealing with the situation with his mother in Blocker's Bluff. At least, he hoped so.

"How was your tour, Brad?"

Laurie turned away. Jessica looked at her and then at him.

"It was real nice. Laurie was an excellent tour guide."

Jessica took a slice of pizza and bit into it. "Good. You two make a lovely couple."

"Jess, we just walked around, that's all."

"I know, what did you think I meant?"

"Nothing," Laurie curtly replied. "Forget I said anything."

He sensed the tension between them. "Jess, how did it go with you and Sarge while we were out?"

She peeled off some pizza crust and gave it to Sarge. "We managed okay. She's a fun dog, but we'll see."

They ate their pizza and took turns giving Sarge some crust. At 7:00, Brad said he was tired and was going to his hotel room. Laurie walked him to the door.

"Goodnight, Sergeant. Thanks for everything."

He put his hand on her arm. "I had a good time, Laurie, and I hope things work out with Sarge tonight. I'll see you in the morning." He shouted, "Goodnight, Jess."

"Good night, Brad. Thanks."

He and Laurie pumped fists and he left. She went back to the dining room, cleared the table, and put the dishes and forks in the dishwasher. Jessica and Sarge went back to the television. Laurie opened her laptop and did some research before retiring for the night. At ten o'clock, she closed her laptop and got up to go to bed.

"Goodnight, Jess. I'm turning in."

"Goodnight, Laurie. Sarge and I are going to turn in too."

She shed a tear since it was the first time Jessica said goodnight to her and didn't stay up watching television.

"Maybe you should let Sarge out before you turn in."

"Come on girl, time to go out."

When Sarge came back in, she noticed that Jessica and Laurie went to separate bedrooms. She left Jessica's and went to Laurie's.

"What are you doing here, Sarge? Aren't you sleeping in Jess's room?"

Sarge walked over to her bed, sat down and barked and then repeated it several times.

"What's the matter, girl? Do you want me to follow you? Is something wrong with Jess?"

Sarge barked again, turned, and started toward the door. Laurie got out of bed and followed her. Jessica was on the bed in her pajama bottoms struggling to get a clean super-large t-shirt on. Her breasts and the stub were clearly visible. Jessica looked up and saw Laurie standing there.

Laurie looked down. "I'm sorry, Jess. Sarge acted like something was wrong. I'll go back to my room and leave you alone."

"Wait. Don't go."

"Are you sure?"

"Yes. Please sit next to me, and could you help me with this damn shirt?"

Laurie sat down next to her, crumpled the shirt and Jessica slipped her right arm into the sleeve. They stood up, Laurie pulled it over Jessica's head, over her shoulders and down over her hips.

"There you go. I'll let you get some sleep now."

Jessica put her hand on Laurie's arm. "No, don't go. I'm sorry, Laurie."

"For what? You haven't done anything wrong."

"Yes, I have." She wrapped her arm around Laurie and put her head on her shoulder. "I'm sorry for ignoring you and treating you like you don't exist." Sarge got up and lay down in front of them. "I'll do whatever you want. I'll go to physical therapy, counseling, whatever. Just don't give up on me." She had tears in her eyes.

Laurie put her hand on Jessica's cheek. "Jess, I'd never give up on you. I'll always be here for you." She took a chance and put her arms on Jessica's shoulders. "I love you, Jess." She pulled Jessica against her.

"I love you too, Laurie. Will you stay with me tonight?"

"If you're sure you want me to."

"Yes, I do."

"I'll be right back." She went to her room and turned the light out. Sarge followed her. Jessica turned the bedroom light out and they got into bed.

Sarge leaped onto the bed and got between them. "Guess we're having company."

They both put an arm around Sarge. "Looks like it. Goodnight, Jess. I guess we're keeping Sarge.

"You're damn right we are. Goodnight, Laurie. Goodnight, Sarge." Sarge snuggled her head under Jessica's arm. "You know, Laurie, Brad really likes you."

"Jess, please don't do this. Not tonight."

"I just want you to be happy."

Sarge rolled over and put her nose against Laurie's shoulder.

"I am happy. Let's not go through this again, please."

Sarge rolled back over toward Jessica. It was as though she was watching a tennis match.

"Okay, I'm sorry, goodnight."

Laurie rolled over on her other side and shed tears on the pillow. She liked him too, but nothing could become of her feelings toward him.

That night with Laurie and Sarge in bed with her, retired Marine Lance Corporal Jessica Towning slept the night away without a nightmare.

Unfortunately, Harding wasn't as lucky. At two-thirty in the morning he woke drenched in sweat. This time his nightmare was about Corporal Roger Pritcher dying in his arms. He sat on the edge of the bed with his head in his hands and cried. Twenty minutes later he got up, showered, and paced the room before getting back in bed. He grabbed his camera and started thumbing through the pictures from their day in Beaufort. When he came to the close up of the two of them, it caused the stress of his nightmare to ease. He stayed focused on the picture and then thumbed back to the full shot and kept alternating between the pictures of her. He laughed when he came to the one of her flexing like Hulk Hogan.

"I love you, Laurie Robinson, and you're going to be mine one day."

He turned the camera off, rolled over on his side and caught a whiff of the woman who he had spent the afternoon in bed with and who he loved. He closed his eyes and drifted off to sleep—contented that he'd found the woman of his dreams.

In the morning, he showered and dressed, went down to the restaurant and had a late breakfast. He then packed his bags, paid his bill, and drove to Laurie's house.

She opened the door and was radiating a huge smile. "Good morning, Sergeant. We have good news for you."

Her smile warmed him as did her eyes. And her lips, the ones he kissed yesterday, made him want to take her in his arms and never let her go. What news could she have? It would be really good news if she said she loved him.

"Come in, Jess has something to tell you."

When he walked past her, he smelled that same scent that she left on his bed and enabled him to sleep and dream of her last night.

He looked around for Corporal Towning but she wasn't there. Standing in front of him was a gorgeous brunette, her hair nicely combed, her lips a light shade of pink, a sparkle in her eyes and glamorous legs. Sarge sat at her feet.

The woman shouted, "We're keeping her, Brad."

"Does that mean for good or until I come back?"

Laurie put an arm on his shoulder. "For good, Sergeant."

"For good, Gunny," echoed Jessica. Then Sarge barked.

"Sounds like it's unanimous. I'm happy for you, Jess."

"Thanks Brad. Be happy for Laurie too."

Laurie and he exchanged glances. "I'm happy for Laurie, too. Damn Corporal, you're gorgeous."

Her cheeks turned pink. "You think so?"

"Yes, I do, especially your hairdo. And those shorts reveal your dynamite legs." She crossed her legs. "And you're smoking hot."

"Stop, you're embarrassing me. Laurie helped me this morning. She said she would help me every day."

He looked at Laurie and she winked.

"Corporal since I came all the way here for you, can I at least get a hug?"

She looked at Laurie then back at him. "Okay, but please don't hurt me."

"I'd never hurt you." He stepped closer and gently wrapped his arms around her. When he put his hands on her back, she stiffened. He stepped back.

"You should give Laurie a hug."

Laurie shook her head. "No."

"Jess… that might not be appropriate."

She mouthed, "Thank you." He mouthed, "You're welcome." Sarge brushed up against his leg.

"Since you're obviously in good hands here, I should probably be on my way. I'll be back next Wednesday just for the day to see how it's going. And Laurie, you should call Dr. Jennings and let her know about Sarge."

"She will, Brad. I have to let Sarge out. Laurie can say goodbye to you. Thanks again for having my back." She saluted him and then she and Sarge left him there with Laurie.

"Come on, Sergeant, I'll walk you to your car."

As he was about to get in his car, she extended her hand. He wanted to kiss the back of it and pull her into his arms—but just held onto her hand.

"You're one hell of a guy, Sergeant. If things were different, I'd fall head over heels for you."

"Oh, well then, I guess you should know that I'm already head over heels for you, Laurie. But I promise to respect you until I'm a civilian." He winked at her. "Be happy, Laurie. I'll see you next week."

She put a hand over her mouth and blushed. Then turned and walked toward the house, stopped, and turned around.

"Sergeant, one more thing, we're going to visit her mom this weekend. You're next."

He raised his hands. "Why do I have to meet her mom?"

"Not hers, yours."

"I'm working on it."

"Stop working on it and do it. That's an order."

He snapped to attention and saluted.

"Yes, ma'am."

CHAPTER 19

Blocker's Bluff—Wednesday Afternoon

Judy Waverly had just wrapped up her meeting with two prospective home buyers at Coastal Resort Community and a sale looked promising. The couple that she met with was in their early sixties, and the man was considering retirement from a major accounting firm in Ohio. She had already taken them for lunch and a tour of the town. They were impressed with its cozy small town charm.

She saved the best for last and took them to Willie's Diner for lunch. They not only enjoyed their meal, but were impressed by Chef Willie's personal greeting and attentiveness. It reminded them of where their roots were as they both came from small rural Midwestern towns where folks went out of their way to be friendly.

"Miss Waverly, we're really impressed by Coastal Resort and Blocker's Bluff. I think Mrs. Anderson and I will be buying a home here. If you don't mind waiting a few weeks, we'll be back to select one." Judy smiled. "Thank you for making time for us. You're very professional and if you and Chef Willie are what folks are like around here, then we've found the right place to retire."

He extended a hand to Judy and they shook. His wife did the same.

"Thank you, Mr. and Mrs. Anderson. I can assure you the folks who live in Coastal Resort are friendly as are those who live in Blocker's Bluff. I was born and raised there, so I can vouch for it. My family has been here since the 1800's. Most folks here are descended from tenant farmers or sharecroppers. The chief of police is descended from the town's first mayor." Judy beamed with pride. "And there's no shortage of veteran here."

"That's nice to know. Wasn't there an incident there some time back?"

Judy had hoped the incident she was asking about had been forgotten, but it was part of what put Blocker's Bluff on the map, and she had privileged knowledge of the events that took place.

"Yes, there was, Mrs. Anderson, but at the time Blocker's Bluff was just a tiny town and not even on any map. Since then, Coastal Resort Community has played an important part in reviving the town as well as the county. The population of Blocker's Bluff was less than one thousand and now it's almost five thousand. There wasn't even a stop light in town." Judy smiled when she mentioned the stop light.

"Well, that was in the past and like Mr. Anderson said, we're impressed with Coastal and Blocker's Bluff. It's also nice to know that you're a native of Blocker's Bluff. You make an excellent ambassador, Ms. Waverly."

"Thank you, Mrs. Anderson. I look forward to seeing you again. Let me walk you out."

Mr. Anderson waved her off. "That's okay. We've already taken enough of your time. We can see ourselves out. Come on, love, let's let this nice lady get back to work."

"Isn't he sweet? After all these years he still calls me love."

After they left, Judy sat down, turned sideways at her desk, stretched her legs out, and smiled feeling satisfied. At fifty seven, with short brown hair, wearing a knee length black skirt, white blouse and a slender figure she still looked classy as ever. She checked her appointment book and saw that she had the rest of the afternoon free, so she decided to go home early and do some housework. She grabbed her briefcase, left her office and told the administrative assistant that she was leaving for the day.

Harding turned onto 103 and headed toward Blocker's Bluff. As he drove past the Coastal Resort Community, he considered turning into the entrance and visiting the sales office to see if his mother was there, but decided he wasn't ready just yet to meet her so he continued on. As he drove by, Judy Waverly was just coming out of the entrance and turning onto 103. When he approached her driveway, he slowed down and glanced toward her house. The garage door was down and he wondered if his grandfather's ride-on mower was inside. Judy's yard was well manicured. Someone either mowed it for her or she used the ride-on and did it herself. He checked his rearview mirror and saw a car approaching behind him so he continued on his way.

Judy noticed the driver slowed down near her driveway. She recognized the car as the one she'd seen several days before and was curious as to why it did.

"I wonder why that same car slowed down by my driveway again. Could be someone who's interested in buying my house? If it is, they're out of luck because I have no plans on selling." Judy's curiosity got the best of her and she decided to follow the car.

Her car was behind him at a safe distance. He could see that the driver was a female but couldn't make out who she was. When he reached Miss Lottie's driveway, he signaled left, slowed down, turned, and drove up to the house.

When Judy saw him turn into Miss Lottie's driveway, she felt relieved that the driver was probably looking for Baxter House and had possibly mistaken her address for it.

It's nice to see that Miss Lottie has guests. Dad would be pleased to see that she's doing okay, especially after losing her daughter, Clarice.

Clarice Baxter was like her baby sister and they played together at Baxter House after school until Judy started high school. Then they only saw each other on weekends because Judy made friends at school—but they were still close—and Clarice kept her secret when she found Linda Jacobs and her together that one time.

Judy was deep in thought and hadn't realized that she was in town and came to a stop when the light turned red. She decided since she was in town to stop at the general store and get some dessert for tonight—and maybe one of Miss Mavis' pies.

When the light turned green, she turned right and parked in front of the general store. Molly, Porter, and Miss Mollie were walking across the street toward the police station. They saw her; she waved and went into the store.

The inside of the general store had rows of shelves stocked with jams, relishes, canned goods, chips and such. There was also a supply of candy for the children. Over the counter medicines were also sold. A pert-time pharmacist came in twice a week to service customers. The back wall consisted of bakery goods such as bread, pies, cookies and more.

Miss Mavis was behind the bakery counter putting fresh baked goods on the shelves.

"Well I'll be, Miss Judy, how are you child?" Miss Mavis had always addressed her as Miss Judy or child—and with a warm smile.

"I'm fine, Miss Mavis, how are you?"

Miss Mavis came around from behind the counter. "I'm just fine. You come here and give me a hug. I ain't seen you in a while." She wrapped her arms around Judy and squeezed her tight.

Miss Mavis' hug always made her feel warm and comfortable. "Don't squeeze the daylights out of me, Miss Mavis."

Miss Mavis put a hand on Judy's cheek. "Any news about your children?"

Judy's joy turned to heartache as she thought about her children and having not seen nor heard from either of them in over twenty years. She just wanted to be like other mothers enjoying their children as they grew up. "No, Miss Mavis. I've written my ex a number of times, but he doesn't answer my letters. A friend told me that my daughter lives in California and Bradley is in the military. I'm at my wits end and considering giving up trying to get him to tell me."

Miss Mavis rubbed Judy's arms. "Don't you give up, child. Something good is sure to happen. Trust this old woman. I've got just the thing to make you smile. Come, I just baked some oatmeal cookies, your favorite, and I've got fresh baked apple pie. You always liked my apple pie."

"Thanks, Miss Mavis. It's why I stopped in. I need some dessert for tonight and apple pie is just the thing. I'll have one of those oatmeal cookies too."

"Levina, get Miss Judy an oatmeal cookie and wrap one of those apple pies for her."

Levina Horton had been with Miss Mavis since 2010 and was hired when the general store was remodeled. She was a single mom who after high school didn't have the grades to get into college. Miss Mavis hired her for the store, but she also waitressed at the diner. Levina handed Judy the cookie and then took an apple pie from the shelf, wrapped it, and gave it to her.

"Thank you, Levina. How's your daughter doing in school?"

"She's doing great, Miss Judy. Thanks for asking."

"Miss Mavis, I heard something about an incident on Porter's Island last Saturday. Was it about Porter?" asked Judy.

"Yes, it was; he and Miss Mollie were attacked, but they're okay. Oh, and Sunday, Rosemary and Eddie had a little girl they named Rose."

Judy's eyes sparkled. "Wow, that's fantastic. Is she going to stay home or will she let Wilma and Levina's mother care for her?"

"Don't know. I only just found out about it from Molly. How come you're getting home so early?"

"I had a good sales appointment today and decided to take the rest of the day off. The people were impressed with Chef Willie, and they may just buy a house because of him. I noticed Miss Lottie has a guest for tonight. I'm glad she's keeping busy."

"She is. Last week she had a young marine staying with her. Chef Willie sent him there. Seems he has been in town before. Chef Willie said the young man told him that he used to fish off the coast and came to the diner for lunch when it was Parker's. He also knew that John Porter was once the chief of police."

Judy suddenly remembered the car that kept slowing when it passed her house and recently turned into Miss Lottie's driveway. Could it be, she wondered?

Miss Mavis noticed Judy's complexion suddenly changed and she was clutching at the pie and her cookie.

"Miss Judy, are you okay? You look like you just saw a ghost."

Judy felt dizzy and a weakness in her knees. She dropped the pie and the cookie. Miss Mavis immediately put her arms around Judy to steady her.

"Levina, get me some water. Hurry, girl." She guided Judy to one of the two chairs that were for customers when they waited to be served.

Levina grabbed a bottle of water, came from around the counter, and handed it to Miss Mavis.

"Here you go. Sit down now and drink some water."

Judy took the cap off the bottle of water and drank some. "Thank you, I feel better now." She handed Levina the bottle of water.

"What came over you? Are you sure you're okay?"

"Yes, Miss Mavis, maybe my sugar was low and it made me lightheaded. I'm sorry about the pie and the cookie. Could I have another? It might be good for my sugar level."

Miss Mavis put the back of her hand against Judy's forehead. It felt clammy. "Levina, bring me a towel." She put a hand on Judy's shoulder. "Don't you fret about the pie. We'll get you another one and a cookie too. Levina, get Miss Judy another cookie and wrap another pie for her."

Levina got a towel and another oatmeal cookie and handed Miss Mavis the towel and Judy the cookie.

"Thank you, Levina. I'll pay for both pies, Miss Mavis."

Miss Mavis wiped Judy's forehead, turned, and shook her head at Levina. "Nonsense, both are on me. And don't you make an issue of it."

Judy took several bites of the cookie and placed a hand on Miss Mavis' hand. "Thank you, Miss Mavis."

"Can you stand up now? If not, you sit a while."

"I feel much better, and I can stand." Miss Mavis held her arm as Judy slowly got to her feet and finished the cookie. "This cookie was really good. Can I have a dozen to take home with me?" Then she smiled. "I'll take them to the office with me tomorrow, and you must let me pay for them."

"You certainly may. Levina, put a dozen of those oatmeal cookies in a bag for her. My goodness, it looks like I'll have to bake some more."

Judy walked over to the bakery counter. Levina handed her the pie and bag of cookies. Judy winked at her. "Thanks Levina, you take care now."

Levina winked back. "You take care too, Miss Judy."

"Thank you, Miss Mavis. I'll have a piece of apple pie as soon as I get home. I'm all right. Thank you for looking out for me."

Miss Mavis ran her hand down the back of Judy's head. "We have to look after each other. It's what we do in Blocker's Bluff, and it's what makes this town special. You drive carefully now, and don't you give up on locating your children."

Judy felt more in control and considered using Miss Mavis' comment about the town being special in her next sales pitch. "Blocker's Bluff is special, and I'm not going to give up on locating my children, Miss Mavis."

"Good for you, now go on home and relax."

Judy set the pie and cookies on the passenger seat. Before starting the car, she thought about the marine who Miss Mavis said had stayed with Miss Lottie and realized why she almost collapsed in the store. Could it be possible that the marine was Bradley, and he had come in search of her?

She put a hand to her cheek and said out loud, "What if it was him? How could I find out and how would I approach him or he approach me?" She rubbed her hand over her mouth and down to her chest. "I could ask Miss Lottie, but what if I'm wrong? It could be embarrassing or only make it more difficult for me." She slammed her fists on the steering wheel and yelled, "Why does he have to be such a son of a bitch after all these years?" She sat back in her seat, rocked her head back and forth and started crying.

An elderly couple who had been in town shopping pulled up in front of the diner and noticed Judy in her car.

"I wonder what that's all about, Frances?" the man asked.

"She's probably upset, Warren."

"What makes you say that?"

She shook her head. "Warren, a woman can always tell when another woman is upset. Let's leave her be and go have dinner."

"If you say so, Frances. Anyway, I heard this place has great food and a personable chef." He took her hand and led her to the entrance.

Judy grabbed a tissue from the package of Kleenex on her console and wiped her tears. She reached for the car keys, and almost started the ignition, but stopped. "Then again, would Bradley forgive me if he knew the truth about me? Maybe I'll wait and talk to John Porter. He might know who the marine is. I'd ask Molly but she's too nosy." She slammed her fists against the steering wheel again. "Dammit, dammit, dammit!" she shouted.

CHAPTER 20

Miss Lottie was rolling pie dough for a rhubarb pie for tonight's guest when she heard the sound of a car pulling into the driveway. She wiped her hands on her towel, covered the pie dough with a towel, and walked out onto the porch to greet her guest. Seeing that it was Harding caused her to break into a big smile. She almost leaped off the porch to run and greet him like she did when his grandfather came to visit decades ago.

He got out of his car, grabbed his bag from the backseat, and waved to her. "Good afternoon, Miss Lottie. It's good to be back." It really was good to be back with the woman he once thought of as his grandmother. For now there were two women in his life that he adored, Miss Lottie and Laurie Robinson. Maybe before he saw Laurie again there would be another—his mother.

"Good afternoon, young man. Welcome back. I saved your room for you."

He set his bag down on the porch, felt like hugging her but thought better. "Thank you. Do you happen to have any sweet tea?" Her smile warmed his heart.

"I certainly do. Take your bag upstairs and then come into the kitchen and I'll pour you a glass. You can watch me make a rhubarb pie for tonight's dessert."

Now he really felt like taking her in his arms and kissing her. He put a hand over his heart and exclaimed, 'You certainly know the way to a man's heart, Miss Lottie."

She clasped her hands and remembered that Travis used to say the same thing to her, and she always replied, *there are many ways to a man's heart, sir.* Then Travis would take her in his arms.

"I hope things went well for you in Beaufort."

He wanted to shout out to her about meeting Laurie Robinson and how wonderful his afternoon with her was. But he wasn't ready to reveal his feelings to anyone about how he felt about Laurie. He also didn't want to talk about Corporal Towning yet because he wanted to savor the welcome back from Miss Lottie.

"Things went well. Maybe this evening I'll tell you about it."

She could tell from his false smile that there was something he didn't want to share with her yet. Travis Waverly did the same thing when he told her about Harding's mother's divorce and the cause. She gave him an understanding nod and opened the door for him.

"It may have to wait until tomorrow because we have another guest tonight. Mr. Johnson will be here before suppertime."

He remembered the conversation with Mr. Johnson when he was last there. Maybe he'd ask him about his dilemma with Laurie.

"Okay, I'll be right down." He grabbed his bag, entered the house, climbed the stairs and went to his room.

She went back to the kitchen and removed the towel from her pie dough. She finished rolling it, carefully placed the bottom crust into a pie dish and put the rhubarb and strawberries that she had previously cut up into the dish. When he joined her, she was just rolling out the rest of the dough for the top crust.

"Here I am, Miss Lottie. Is there anything I can do?"

She set the rolling pin aside. "Would you like to cover the pie?"

He wrinkled his forehead and rubbed his jaw. "I don't know. I've never done it before. Are you sure I won't ruin it?"

She wiped the rolling pin with the towel and tossed the towel over her shoulder. "You won't ruin the pie. Come here and I'll show you what to do."

He walked to the table and stood in front of the pie. "Okay, what do I do?"

"You cover the pie with the top crust. Here I'll show." She got behind him. "Now carefully pick up the dough and set it on top."

He did as instructed, carefully covering the pie. "That was easy, now what?"

She moved the pie from in front of him. "I like to crimp the edges with my thumb like this." She made several thumbprints. "Now you do it."

He used his thumb and crimped the edges. "What's next?"

"We take this knife and cut little x's in the top to let the steam escape." She made the cuts. "You take that brush and dip it in that wash and then brush the top. When you're done, you can put the pie in the oven. I already set it at the proper temperature. I'll open the door for you. After it's done I'll sprinkle some cinnamon over it just for you." His eyes lit up. She walked over, opened the oven door, he put the pie in and shut the door.

"Easy as pie, Miss Lottie, high five." He raised his hand, but she looked at him as though he was crazy.

"What does that mean, young man?"

His eyes lit up. "You slap my hand. Come on now, you can do it."

She shook her head and slapped his hand. "You're a damn fool."

He thought back to the time when she said something similar to his grandfather after seeing him tickling her. They didn't know that he was watching from the back door. He covered his mouth with his hand so they wouldn't hear him giggle, closed the door, went out back and told Lottie what happened. They promised each other it would be their secret.

"Sit down now, and I'll pour us a glass of sweet tea."

He sat at the table. She poured two glasses of sweet tea and joined him.

"Miss Lottie, there's something I must tell you."

She put a hand up before he could say anything else. "I think I heard a car pull up. It must be Mr. Johnson. I best go greet him. Whatever you want to say, young man, will have to wait until later or in the morning. Will that be all right with you?"

His lips pressed tight. "It can wait. I'll join you on the porch." He felt disappointed because he had decided to tell her the truth about who he really was. But it could wait until the morning after Mr. Johnson left. He set his glass down, got up, and followed her to the porch.

As Marvin Johnson got out of his car, he waved to Miss Lottie and Harding. "Good afternoon, Miss Lottie. Good afternoon, Sergeant. I see you're back."

"Mr. Johnson, I have sweet tea all made. Would you like a glass out here or would you like to sit in the kitchen? We made a rhubarb pie for tonight's supper."

His eyes were suddenly wide and glowing. "You sure know how to please a man, Miss Lottie. I'd prefer to sit out here, if you don't mind?"

She grinned. "You and the young man sit, and I'll bring your glasses out. I'll join you for a spell, but then I have to take care of that pie and start supper."

Harding and Mr. Johnson sat, and she went back into the house and returned with three glasses of sweet tea on a tray. Mr. Johnson stood up and took the tray from her.

"You take my seat, Miss Lottie, and I'll sit next to this young man."

She sat and took a glass. Harding took a glass too. Mr. Johnson set the tray on the little table, took a glass, and sat down.

"Sure is nice and peaceful here. I love coming back here. After supper, I'm going to sit out here. Maybe you two will join me?"

Miss Lottie sipped at her tea. "We can have our dessert here if you two would like."

Harding rocked back against his chair, took a sip of his sweet tea and turned in the direction of Mr. Johnson. "I'd like that. What about you, Mr. Johnson?" He would rather have some alone time with Miss Lottie to tell her who he was, but he knew it wasn't going to be possible.

"I'd like that too."

She leaned back on her rocker. "Now that that's settled, let's enjoy the rest of the afternoon." An hour later, she stood up and so did the two men out of respect for her. "Gentlemen, please stay and relax. I have to fix supper now. I'm making chicken fried steak and gravy. Instead of mashed potatoes I'm making cheese grits to go with green beans. Does that sound good?"

They bumped fists and said in unison, "Oh boy does it, Miss Lottie!"

She shook her head and grinned, amused by their boyish antics. "I guess that means you like what I'm cooking." Then she went into the house. When supper was ready, she called the men in and they sat together at the table and had supper. After they ate, the two men went out onto the porch.

"So, Sergeant, how was your visit to Beaufort?"

He turned and his eyelids raised. "I met someone, Mr. Johnson, and I think I'm in love."

Mr. Johnson grinned. "You just met her and you think you're in love already?"

"Yes, sir, I think I am."

"What about her, does she feel the same way?"

He didn't know, but that wasn't going to stop him from feeling the way he did for her. "Not sure. But I think, no, I'm sure that I love her."

Mr. Johnson remembered the day he was sure that he first fell in love with his wife. He had only known her for a day, but he knew she was the one and it would take time for her to realize he was the one for her.

"Sometimes the heart acts in mysterious ways but if I were you, I wouldn't push her. You should go slow and give her time."

He pondered Mr. Johnson's words. "That sounds like good advice since you would know better than me. Anyway, it will be a week before I see her again. Maybe she'll miss me like I'm already missing her." He decided to change the subject. "Mr. Johnson, how come you're back in Blocker's Bluff so soon?"

"The branch manager here gave birth Sunday night, and I came here to determine if we need to bring in someone to take her place until she returns. Fortunately, today she told me that she will be back part-time in three weeks. The senior teller seems quite capable of managing things and besides the manager will be readily available. Everything worked out fine, and I get to see my bride tomorrow."

"I'm glad it all worked out for you."

Mr. Johnson got up from his rocker. "Sergeant, I'm going to turn in, so I'll say goodnight. Will I see you for breakfast? I have to leave by nine o'clock."

"I should be up by then. Goodnight, Mr. Johnson."

"Goodnight, Sergeant."

Harding sat for another hour and then went into the house to say goodnight to Miss Lottie and turn in. She was still in the kitchen putting dishes away and getting things prepared for the morning's breakfast.

"Goodnight, Miss Lottie."

She turned and faced him. "Goodnight, young man. Sleep well. Will you be down for breakfast in the morning?"

"Yes."

He went to his room, got into bed, reached for his camera and thumbed through the pictures of Laurie. "I love you, Laurie Robinson, and I am going to wait however long it takes. Even if it's until I'm no longer a marine. Then you will be mine. I promise you."

CHAPTER 21

After breakfast, Marvin Johnson got up from the kitchen table to say his goodbye to Miss Lottie before leaving for Charlotte.

"Miss Lottie, I'm going to take my leave now. I have a bit of a drive ahead of me. As usual, my stay was pleasant. You're a wonderful hostess."

She turned from putting dishes in the dishwasher and grinned. "Thank you, Mr. Johnson. Will you be back soon?"

"I may be back next week since I have to check to make sure everything at the bank is going well, plus I need to go to Beaufort to check on things there. I'll call to let you know when I'm coming. Tell that young marine goodbye for me. I can tell he has some issues to deal with, and I hope he can manage to deal with them."

She nodded agreement. "He does and hopefully he can. You're very observant."

His head tilted to one side. "I've seen it in his eyes. It's the same thing I've seen in many a young soldier returning from combat. It's called post-traumatic stress disorder. Hopefully he gets the help he needs, but I think being here helps him some. You have a calming effect on people."

"So do you, Mr. Johnson. I've seen how comfortable he is talking with you."

"Guess it comes with being a parent. So long, Miss Lottie."

"So long, Mr. Johnson, you drive carefully."

Harding had overslept because during the night he woke from a dream about telling Miss Lottie the truth and coming face-to-face with his mother. Both frightened him. He entered the kitchen as Mr. Johnson was pulling out of the driveway.

"Good morning. Guess I missed Mr. Johnson. Sorry to be late for breakfast." He walked over to the coffee pot and poured himself a cup.

"That's okay, young man. Mr. Johnson said to tell you goodbye. He may be back next week." She watched him take a seat at the table and then looked into his eyes to see what it was that made Mr. Johnson comment about his stress disorder. She didn't know exactly what he had seen, but she definitely could see sorrow in his eyes. Whatever he wanted to tell her yesterday could wait until he was ready to. "Would you like eggs or waffles this morning?"

He was trying to decide if now was the right time to tell her his real name, but he was finding it extremely difficult. The last time he was this nervous was just before his first combat mission. But that had deadly consequences, and this wasn't as serious because there was no chance of physical harm

"Waffles would be fine." He decided to wait until after breakfast to tell her.

"Good, you sit and relax while I fix your breakfast." She sensed his apprehension and chose to avoid asking him what he wanted to tell her.

He took a sip of coffee and tried to relax, but his nervousness was more obvious as he repeatedly closed his eyes and kept rubbing the back of his neck. She ignored his behavior but wondered if it was one of the signs that Mr. Johnson had noticed.

She made him two waffles and fixed him a small dish of grits that were left over from Mr. Johnson's breakfast. Set his plate in front of him and put syrup on the table. He poured an enormous amount of syrup over the waffles, cut a large piece from one, tilted his head back, opened his mouth wide, and put it in his mouth just like his grandfather.

With a mouth full, he mumbled, "I love your waffles, Miss Lottie." He also wanted to say that he loved her too, but the words wouldn't come out, not yet anyway.

She smiled and nodded her head. "I'm glad you like them. Would you like me to join you?"

"Please do."

She poured a cup of coffee, sat down across from him, watched him finish his waffles and then start on the grits the same way Travis Waverly did.

When he finished his grits, he got up and brought his dish and silverware to the sink. He poured a fresh cup of coffee and sat across from her. As he sipped his coffee, he kept scratching his chest with his fingers. He was obviously nervous and she noticed.

He finally decided that now was the right time for him to tell her who he really was. He set his cup down, put his hands on the table, and leaned forward. "Miss Lottie, I have a confession to make." She set her cup down and sat upright in her chair. "My name isn't Roger Pritcher. My real name is…"

She reached over, put a hand on his and said, "I know who you are, young man."

When she squeezed his hand, he felt the tenderness from it, and could see in her eyes and hear in her soft voice that she was speaking from the heart.

"You do?" He was caught off guard. "How?"

She set her cup down and placed her other hand over his. "I've known for a while now. You've got a lot of your granddaddy in you. Your name is Bradley, and your mother's name is Judy."

His jaw dropped and he leaned forward to apologize. "Yes, it is. I'm sorry I lied to you."

She patted his hands. "You didn't lie, son, you just didn't want me to know for some reason, and I suspect it has to do with your mother and what happened a long time ago."

He lowered his head to his chest then looked up. "It does, and I want to talk to her, especially to ask why she didn't write me and tell me that my grandfather had passed away. She knew how much I loved him."

She wanted to tell him the story behind his mother and father's divorce, but she felt it wasn't her place to do so. If Judy wanted to tell him, it was up to her. However, she would make sure he knew that his mother never stopped thinking about him and so did his grandfather. She removed her hands from his, folded her arms, and looked directly at him with scolding eyes.

"Whatever happened between your parents is for your mother to tell you, but she did write your father and asked him to tell you. She even asked if she could send you a picture of you and your granddaddy." Her revelation surprised him. "I was with her when she did it and suggested the picture. I don't know what happened, but she never got an answer and thought you were angry with her."

He hadn't known about the letter and the only reason he knew about his grandfather's death was because he visited the gravesite. His face turned red and his nostrils flared.

"I was never told about the letter." He didn't understand why his father didn't tell him or why his grandparents also didn't.

Miss Lottie's nose wrinkled and her lips curled in obvious disgust. Travis was right about his father and his family when he told her about how they treated Judy during the divorce.

"You need to talk to your mother and ask her what happened. She never stopped loving you and the two of you need to reconcile."

He swallowed hard and his hands began to tremble. This was all new to him and a lot to deal with. He wasn't ready to meet his mother yet. "I will, but I need a little more time. It's just that I never knew this." His anger was now directed toward his father and his grandparents, and he knew he would never forgive them.

She recognized that same angry expression that Travis had when he got angry, especially when he told her that he would never see young Bradley again because of the divorce. She was able to calm Travis by telling him to be patient and think things through. There may be more to the situation, and he needed to get all the information before flying off the handle. If he was like his grandfather, she had to be the same way with him.

"You're angry right now," she said softly. "And it's best you wait until you're ready to talk with your mother. Maybe a day or two and then you can talk to her." She put her hands on his to calm him.

His features softened, but his voice reflected the emotions that he felt. "You're right, Miss Lottie, it's best I did. You were always like a grandmother to me, and I cherish the days I spent with you, Lottie, and my grandfather." Then he asked, "Would you be offended if I asked for a hug?"

Her eyes sparkled. "I'd be honored to hug you. Come give me one like you used to."

He walked over, wrapped his arms around her and squeezed her tight. Just the way his grandfather did. He had practically squeezed the breath out of her like Bradley was doing.

As he held her tight, he caught a hint of baby powder and couldn't resist saying what was in his heart. "I love you, Grandma."

She breathed deeply. "I love you too but only call me grandma when it's just the two of us."

He squeezed her tighter, stepped back, and kissed her on the cheek. "God, how I miss hearing that. Okay, only when we're alone."

Her cheekbones went up. She put a hand on his cheek, kissed him on the forehead, and stepped back. "I best get to cleaning the kitchen and the dishes. You get another cup of coffee and when I'm done, I'll join you. Go on now."

He laughed remembering the last time she told him—go on now. It was his last summer in Blocker's Bluff and neither of them knew if they would ever see each other again.

CHAPTER 22

Molly was getting dressed for their breakfast at the diner. Porter was still asleep, and Miss Mollie was waiting to be let out. She leaned over and tapped Porter on the shoulder. "John, are you going to breakfast with me or are you sleeping in?"

He opened his eyes and smiled at her. "You go ahead. I'm sleeping in. I've got some things to do in the garage. Maybe I'll have lunch with you."

She eyed him apprehensively and was dumbfounded that he wasn't going to have breakfast with her. Since she was running late, she had to hurry and let Miss Mollie out and then be on her way.

"Are you okay, John?"

He rolled over on his side. "I'm fine, Molly, you go ahead."

"Okay, I'll call you about lunch." She was still concerned but leaned down and kissed his cheek. "Come on, Miss Mollie, I'll let you out." When Miss Mollie came back in, Molly left.

When Porter was certain she was gone, he got out of bed, went into the bathroom, showered, and then dressed.

"Okay, Miss Mollie. You ready to do this?"

Miss Mollie looked up at him, tilted her head, lay down and covered her eyes. She knew trouble was coming..

He opened one of the kitchen cabinet doors and retrieved the spare set of keys hanging on a hook. "Let's roll, Miss Mollie. Time we became independent." Miss Mollie followed him out the door to the carport. He opened the door to Molly's pickup truck, she jumped in and he got behind the steering wheel. "Let's see now, if I remember right, R is for reverse and D is for drive."

Miss Mollie put a paw over her eyes.

He shifted into reverse and carefully backed out of the carport and down the driveway. When he reached the end, he checked left and right before backing into the street. He shifted into drive and carefully turned to his left making sure to avoid the neighbor's garbage cans. A neighbor across the street waved to him. He waved back and drove down the street.

Molly parked in front of the diner, went inside and took a seat at the counter.

"Good morning, Chief. Is Porter joining you?" asked Susie.

Molly reached for a menu. "Not this morning, Susie, maybe for lunch. He has some things he wants to do at home."

Susie brought a glass of water and utensils and set them in front of her. "Well, you tell him we missed him. Are you having your usual this morning?"

"Yes, and I'll tell Porter you missed him." She gave her a wink.

Susie wrote down her order, went to the kitchen window and put the slip on the hook for Chef Willie. When he looked at the order and saw that it was only for Molly, he came out of the kitchen.

"Morning, Molly, where's Porter?"

Her shoulders slumped. "Geez, I come to breakfast by myself and everyone wants to know where Porter is. Can't I have breakfast by myself?"

Chef Willie's eyebrows lifted, wondering why she was being so defensive. "I'm just asking, that's all. I'll start your breakfast."

"Sorry, I didn't mean to snap. I'm just feeling on edge lately since that incident with him and Miss Mollie."

Chef Willie looked out the window at the parking lot and said, "Well, it looks like you're going to have company after all, Molly. Here come Porter and Miss Mollie. They just drove up in your truck."

"What the hell you talking about? Porter doesn't drive. I don't even think he has a license anymore."

"Maybe so, but take a look because here they come now."

She turned in her seat, glanced out the window, saw her pickup parked outside and Porter and Miss Mollie walking toward the entrance.

When Porter and Miss Mollie entered, Susie greeted them. "Porter, I thought you weren't coming in for breakfast? Good morning, it's good to see you."

He winked at Susie. "Good to see you too, Susie. Changed my mind and decided to have breakfast with the chief." He started toward Molly, but she got up and walked toward him. His smile resembled a clown's face, but the expression on Molly's face changed it to a frown. "Morning, Molly."

Miss Mollie saw her expression and knew enough to get out of harm's way, so she wandered off by Susie.

"Don't you be morning me, you damn fool. What the hell's the matter with you?" Porter turned and retreated for the exit. "Don't you turn your back on me, John Porter!"

He turned around held his hands up surrendering. "What did I do now, Molly?"

Miss Mavis heard the commotion and came out of the kitchen. Chef Willie put his finger to his mouth and whispered, "Let them be."

"You trying to kill yourself? What were you thinking driving my truck? You don't even have a driver's license and you could have killed Miss Mollie too." She walked over and pounded her fists against his chest. "Ain't it bad enough I almost lost the two of you on that damn island of yours?" She shoved him with her hands. "Now you go and do this. Don't you give a damn about me?"

Porter realized it wasn't about him driving the truck. It was about the incident on the island. He had wondered why she was so caring toward him ever since it happened and now he understood. Molly was experiencing PTSD and his driving the truck was the catalyst that brought it to the surface.

There were seven customers in the diner. Two fishermen that had come in for breakfast were sitting at the counter. They got up and started to leave, but Chef Willie motioned for them to stay. The other five were sitting in booths. They all stopped what they were doing and watched the scene as it unfolded. All of them knew Molly and Porter, but none had ever seen her so hysterical.

Porter grabbed her by the wrists and pulled her close to him. "Molly, stop worrying. Miss Mollie and me are okay." She placed her head on his shoulder and started to cry. He rubbed her back. "If I'd a known you'd get this upset, I wouldn't have driven here. But, Molly, I ain't going nowhere, and please don't fret about me."

She wiped her tears with her hand, stared directly into his eyes, and replied, "John, I can't do this anymore."

His eyebrows drew together and he was off guard. "What does that mean?"

She looked around the diner and everyone lowered their heads. "I can't be the chief anymore, and I need a long vacation away from all this."

He leaned in and kissed her softly on the cheek. "We'll take a vacation just as soon as the commander tells us he caught those two. I promise you." He held her face in his hands and rubbed her cheeks. "I love you, and whatever you want to do is okay with me."

Her features softened and she kissed him. "I love you too." Then she smacked him on the arm. "But that don't solve the problem of you driving without a license."

He reached into his back pocket, pulled out his wallet, took out his driver's license and handed it to her. "Yes, I do. I renewed it a while ago and I've been practicing driving in our neighborhood." Everyone in the diner was smiling. "Are we okay now? Everyone's watching."

She laughed. "Yes, you damn fool." Then she turned and faced the customers. "There, are you all happy now?" Everyone gave her a thumbs-up as they knew what she had just experienced. The fishermen were a retired policeman and a retired fireman. Two of the other customers were a retired military man and a retired nurse. Miss Mavis went back into the kitchen. Chef Willie stood in the doorway and grinned. "Come on let's go have breakfast. Miss Mollie, you can join us even though you're his partner in crime."

Miss Mollie lowered her head and looked up at her with eyes that pleaded innocence because she was a dog.

Molly shook her head. "Pathetic."

They ordered breakfast and something for Miss Mollie. After breakfast, Molly followed Porter home. He parked the truck in the garage, joined her and Miss Mollie in the car and they were off to the police station.

"You know, Molly, now that I can drive you don't have to chauffer me everywhere."

She looked at him and stopped the car. "You don't like spending the day with me?"

"I do, but I need to do some things on my own now and then."

She scratched the back of her head. "What would you do? You can walk into town. We've done it lots of times, besides you and Miss Mollie could use the exercise."

"Hell, Molly, you could make a shopping list, and I could go to the E-Z Market and get our groceries and some beer for me. It would save us the trip and we'd have more time to ourselves."

"You old fool, you're crazy. Okay, I'll make a damn list."

"At a girl, Molly. Look, aren't you glad I didn't walk to town? It's starting to rain."

CHAPTER 23

Coast Guard Headquarters—Thursday Afternoon

Commander Edison sat at his desk in the Coast Guard station reviewing the report sent to him via email. He wasn't satisfied with the way Porter's case was going and the results so far. He wanted an answer as to who the two men were who attacked Porter. The commander was a stickler for detail and he just didn't feel the explanation from the old man about his boat was complete. It lacked some important elements. Why didn't the old man know where his boat was and how could it have been taken from the marina so easily? Something was missing, and it didn't sit well with him. He contacted the investigative team and had them go back and talk to the man.

After a lengthy discussion with the old guy, he finally relented and told them that he lent the boat to his two nephews. They were supposed to be using it to start a fishing business. He hadn't heard from them in over a week and believed they may be off the coast of North Carolina—somewhere near Cape Hatteras. Their names were

Lloyd and Wilbur Burldy. He also owned a gun, but he kept it on the boat as a precaution.

The commander instructed the investigative team to search every marina and port from Charleston to Cape Hatteras. They put out an APB and a search was started using Coast Guard cutters, response boats, and utility boats. The commander had a lot of pull and when he wanted something done, it got done.

At a small marina on the coast near Morehead City, a coast guard utility boat spotted the *Greybeard* moored. The police were asked to investigate and were sent the description of the men that Porter provided. At the Fishtail Bar, the officers approached the bartender asked if he'd seen anyone who matched the description they had. The bartender nodded toward two men and two females. The approached the two and the two women who were lavishing themselves with drinks. The officers asked the men if they if they were the owners of a boat named *Greybeard.*

They said no and the officers replied, "In that case, I guess you won't mind if the Coast Guard impounds the *Greybeard* docked outside."

"Hold on a second. You don't have to do that," said Lloyd.

"Yeah, we ain't done nothing," added Wilbur.

"Not according to the information we got about an incident in South Carolina."

"We didn't mean no harm. We was just partying." Wilbur looked at the two women. They got up, turned and went to the ladies room.

"We're sorry, can we just forget this?" asked Lloyd.

"That's not going to happen. Since the boat's not yours, we're taking it."

Lloyd and Wilbur relented and said it was their boat and it belonged to their uncle. They were taken into custody, turned over to the Coast Guard, and the boat was impounded.

Commander Edison phoned Eddie McClellan and told him the good news. Eddie called Molly to relay the commander's information.

"Chief, I have good news. Those two guys who attacked Porter and Miss Mollie were arrested in North Carolina."

"Hold on, let me put you on the speaker so Porter can listen. Go ahead, Eddie."

"The two are brothers, and they were using the house to party with two women. Porter when you confronted them, they panicked. The two women were in the house tiding up and when they heard the shot, they came running out. They finished loading their boat and headed north."

"Eddie did the guy who hit me have a gun?"

"No, he hit you with the laptop they stole from the house."

"Dumb son of bitch. I hope he broke the damn thing." Porter rubbed the back of his head.

"They're both in jail as we speak charged with breaking and entering, theft, and endangering a life."

"Thanks, Eddie, appreciate the heads up," said Molly.

"You're welcome, Chief."

"At least the case is over and you can relax." He winked at her. "See, me driving myself to breakfast was a good omen."

She put both hands on her head exhausted. "You really are a crazy son of a bitch."

"Now you can retire."

"We'll talk later."

"Why aren't you excited?"

She bit her lower lip. "There's still that other matter."

"What other matter?" Molly looked at Adrian. "You mean that marine?"

She placed her hands on her hips. "Yes."

"Dammit, Molly, I thought you agreed to drop the thing about the marine." She crossed her arms and stood defiant. Adrian got up and went outside. "Molly, I love you, but if you persist with your obsession with that marine, you're gonna upset some people in this town."

She was stunned. "What are you talking about?"

"You heard me, and I'm one of them. You just had to go and upset Miss Baxter. Isn't that enough to make you stop?"

"I can't help myself. It's who I am."

He decided to tell her who the marine was but not all the specifics. "Molly, he's Judy's son."

"What? But I—"

"She was married and then divorced. It was like twenty years ago. A lot of people in this town are grateful for Travis Waverly's carpentry skills, including your parents. Some of your furniture was built by him—he helped my dad and me move the cabin on the island after that last hurricane." Molly's eyelids shot up. "Travis was a good friend of mine—he wouldn't like you dredging up old secrets."

"What do you mean old secrets?"

"That's all I'm saying." He took a defiant stance. "If you don't drop it right now, I'm taking Miss Mollie, and we're gonna stay on the island till you come to your senses. I mean it, Molly because you're going to piss off a lot of people, including me."

Her lips trembled, and she grabbed the desk to steady herself. She nervously considered his demand. Porter had never threatened to leave her before.

"Make up your mind, Molly." The look in his eyes was menacing.

Miss Mollie crawled under a desk. She knew this was real serious and didn't want to get caught in the middle of their argument.

Molly shook uncontrollably. Porter had struck a nerve and she had to do something she had done only once before. It was when she decided to follow her parent's advice and reject his marriage proposal because they didn't want them to be the first bi-racial couple in South Carolina. He was so angry he didn't speak to her for almost a year and nearly reenlisted in the army. She came close to losing him and Miss

Mollie last Saturday and now he was threatening to leave her. She couldn't let that happen.

She sniffled. "Please, John, don't do that. I promise I won't say anything more. I mean it, give me another chance."

He took her in his arms. "Okay, but only because I love you."

She sniffled again. "I love you too. You really wouldn't have left me, would you?"

The look in his eyes told her he meant what he said. He kissed her on the mouth. "Yes, I would have. It would have killed me, but it's that important, Molly."

CHAPTER 24

Harding was satisfied with just relaxing on the porch with her and was in no hurry to go putter around in the garage. He leaned back on the rocker contented and drank some coffee. Suddenly the sky turned overcast and they could feel a slight drop in temperature. Miss Lottie went inside and got a shawl to drape over her shoulders. He didn't mind the change in weather as he had been through worse in Iraq and Afghanistan. When he was a boy, he enjoyed sitting on the porch watching the summer rain, especially with Lottie.

Miss Lottie snuggled in her shawl. "It looks like we're going to get some rain. Are you warm enough?"

"Yes, I like when it's like this. Lottie and I used to enjoy sitting here and watching the rain."

The sound of thunder boomed in the distant sky, and it started to rain. They moved their rockers back against the house. Rain spilled out from the downspout and into the garden. A hummingbird came to the feeder hanging from the downspout.

"Lottie and Thomas sometimes sit here when it's raining." The rain started coming down in buckets and clattered on the old tin roof. "You got any plans for today?"

He thought about the Crown Victoria in the garage. "Do you still drive that car parked in the garage?"

"Sometimes, but I haven't in a while. Lottie does most of my shopping for me. Occasionally I've driven into town to visit Miss Mavis and get some cookies." She sipped her coffee. "Why? You want to drive it? I'm not sure it'll even start."

"I was just wondering. You mind if I take a look at it?"

"Your granddaddy used to tinker with that old thing. You remember when he bought it for me?"

"I sure do. If memory serves me right, it was raining that day too."

"Yes, it was. I was really surprised when you two showed up with that car."

"You sure were. He joked that you were his queen and he bought you a crown."

She laughed. "You remember that?"

"Yep. Grandpa was a good man, wasn't he?"

"Yes he was, and I'm sure he would be proud of you." She reached over and put a hand on his arm.

"Thank you, but I wish I had more time with him. I should have been here for his funeral."

She gently rubbed his arm. "That's in the past now. Let bygones be bygones. You're here now and your mother needs to see you."

He covered her hand with his and gave her a doleful look. "I'm still not ready yet."

"Take your time but don't wait too long. You never can tell what will happen."

The meaning of her words bothered him because time had taken a number of people from him and always unexpectedly—like Roger Pritcher.

"I'm going inside and start fixin lunch." She stood. "I'll call you when it's ready."

"While you're fixing lunch, I'm gonna look at the car. Maybe it will start."

"Don't you fret if it won't. It's not like I'm going to drive it anytime soon. You'll find the keys hanging in the garage. Do you want an umbrella?"

He almost laughed when she said the keys were hanging in the garage. It was something that hadn't changed about her and Blocker's Bluff. She trusted most people and didn't worry about someone stealing the car. Residents also trusted each other and felt safe in their homes, and it's what made Blocker's Bluff a great place to live.

"I don't mind the rain, but I'll wait until it lets up a little."

Miss Lottie went inside. When the rain let up, he went around to the garage. The keys were hanging inside the doorway on an old rusty nail. He tried the ignition, but all he got was the familiar clicking sound of a dead battery. He popped the hood and took a look at the engine. It could use a cleaning, but that wasn't something he could do, so he checked the sparkplugs. They needed cleaning too—but better yet new ones. Since he still had time before lunch, he cleaned the sparkplugs, checked the oil, all the fluids, and the tires.

Miss Lottie called out to him. "Lunch is ready, Bradley." He put the hood down, found a clean rag, wiped his hands and entered through the pantry.

"I couldn't get the car to start. It needs a new battery. I'll go to the garage in town and buy one after lunch."

"You wash at the sink and then sit down and have lunch. I made you a big sandwich with chips on the side." She set his plate on the table. "You don't have to go to all that trouble. The car can wait."

He washed his hands and sat down. "I know, but I want to. Maybe we can drive into town tomorrow in the car." He picked up his sandwich, took a huge bite and ate some chips.

She sat down across from him. "I could use a few things from the general store and it would be nice to say hello to Miss Mavis. Don't eat so fast you'll choke on your food."

He grinned, took another huge bite and swallowed. "After lunch I'll go into town. It looks like the rain is over." He finished his lunch, went into the garage, took the battery from the car, put it in his and drove into town.

Molly, Porter, and Miss Mollie finished their lunch and said goodbye to Chef Willie. As they crossed the street to the police station, Harding drove by. Molly watched as he passed.

"I saw him go by, Molly. Don't say anything. Remember your promise."

"I wasn't going to say anything, just observing that's all."

"You don't just observe, you always comment."

"I'm keeping my promise. I mean it. Let's take a ride through Coastal Resort and see if anything is happening. Most likely nothing is though."

Harding pulled up to Ollie's Garage, parked, and carried the old battery in with him. Ollie Jackson, the proprietor, had been a mechanic in the air force during the Vietnam War. He slid out from under the truck he was working on.

"Whatcha got there?"

"It's from Miss Baxter's car. I'd like to buy a new one."

"Miss Baxter's, huh? Ain't seen her driving that old Crown Vic in a long time. As old as it is, you'd think there'd be more miles on it." He looked Harding up and down. "You a guest of hers?"

"Yes, sir, I am."

"You that marine?"

"I am. Does the whole town know about me?"

Ollie wiped his hands on a rag. "Most folks know who stays at Baxter House. You look familiar. Are you from around here?"

"I used to visit a long time ago. Do you know Travis Waverly by any chance?"

Ollie's eyes lit up. "Hell yeah! Travis was a friend of mine. Helped me out quite a few times. Shame what happened to his daughter and his grandson."

Harding set the battery down on the ground. "What happened, if you don't mind my asking?"

Ollie sat on an old crate. "Have a seat and I'll give you the short version." Harding grabbed a crate and sat down. "Something happened with her marriage, and Travis never saw his grandson after that. It broke his heart and broke his daughter's too. She still lives in town. Real nice lady, that Miss Judy. She brings her car and her daddy's truck in when there's something she can't fix on them. And she works on the old ride-on mower that she uses to mow her yard." He smiled. "Hell of a woman, that Miss Judy."

He never would have imagined his mother doing mechanical things. In Virginia, his father would have admonished her for even dirtying her hands in the garden.

"Do you know her?"

"No, sir, I don't. I heard some good things about Mr. Waverly, which is why I asked about him."

"Lots of people say good things about him. Now let's see to getting you a battery for Miss Baxter. Now that's one nice lady. You know she prefers I call her Miss Lottie."

"Me too, and she certainly is a nice lady. I'm glad Chef Willie referred me to her. I love her cooking, especially her rhubarb pie."

"Oh man, now that's good eatin!"

Ollie grabbed the old battery and put it in a bin with other old batteries, used parts, and tires. "Company comes by every so often and empties the bin for recycling at their cost" Then he searched for a replacement. "Here we go. It's gonna cost forty-eight dollars and eighty-nine cents. Do I charge it to Miss Lottie or you paying?"

"I'm paying. Do you take credit cards or just cash? I could use a set of spark plugs too."

"Prefer cash if you have it, and it'll be fifteen dollars for the sparkplugs.

He opened his wallet, took three twenties and a five and gave them to Ollie. "Here you are, sir. Don't worry about the change." He put the battery in the trunk of his car and left.

Ollie watched him drive off. "That boy sure looks a bit like Travis. I wonder if he's Travis' grandson."

He pulled into Miss Lottie's driveway, got the battery and sparkplugs from the trunk, and carried them into the garage. He set the battery in place, attached the cables, changed the sparkplugs, and then got behind the steering wheel. He crossed his fingers, turned the ignition, and beamed when the car started.

"You the man, Brad." He gave two thumbs up, let the engine idle for a while, shut it off and went to tell Miss Lottie the good news.

She had just finished cleaning the kitchen and poured herself a cup of coffee when he came in through the pantry.

"Got it started, told you I would. Now we can take that ride into town tomorrow."

"Good for you. You're just like your granddaddy. He always got excited working on that car. I'm having a cup of coffee and going to sit on the porch. Would you care to join me?"

"I sure would, let me get a cup."

Later that afternoon, Lottie and Thomas came to visit. Miss Lottie and Bradley were sitting on the porch sipping sweet tea when they saw her car pull into the driveway.

"Isn't that Lottie's car?"

Miss Lottie stood up and waved. "Yes, it is, and please don't call me grandma now. I don't want to answer questions from Lottie and Thomas."

"Okay, but she has to know sooner or later."

"Patience, Bradley, everything in due time."

Lottie parked behind his car. Thomas got out of the car and ran to the porch with his baseball glove in hand.

"Hey, Marine, you want to have a catch?"

"Thomas, where are your manners? Say hello to Grandma first. Maybe the marine wants to sit."

Thomas made like he was throwing the glove on the ground. "Good afternoon, Gramma. You gonna sit there or play catch with me, Marine?"

"Thomas, what did I tell you?"

"It's okay, Lottie, I'll play catch with him." He got up and stepped off the porch.

"Good afternoon, Thomas," said Miss Lottie. "You go easy with the marine. Don't throw that ball too hard." Harding laughed.

Lottie joined her grandmother on the porch. "Afternoon, Grandma. That boy is becoming attached to the marine."

"I hope he doesn't get too attached because he only has a few more weeks left here. You want some sweet tea?"

"No thank you. Has he told you who he is yet?" Lottie sat down next her.

She covered Lottie's hand. "Yes, he admitted to being Bradley Harding and Miss Judy's son."

She put her hand over her grandmother's. "Does he know about Grandpa Travis?"

Miss Lottie pulled her hand away. "What are you talking about, child?"

Lottie grabbed her arm. "Grandma, I know that he was my momma's daddy."

"Why are you saying that?" She was worried that her secret was out.

Miss Lottie's mother, Clarice Baxter, was a single mother. Her husband, Cyrus, was a member of an obscure Negro parachute infantry unit that volunteered to jump behind enemy lines as part of the

D-Day invasion. To this day the unit was still a well-kept secret in military records. Most of its members never saw action the day of the mission because they were gunned down in the air by an enemy machine gun nest. Cyrus was one of the unfortunate who was killed. His remains rest in a field somewhere in France.

To make ends meet, Clarice cleaned houses for the white folk in Blocker's Bluff and a few in Crofton. She was also a mid-wife and had birthed many of Blocker's Bluff's children, both white and black. When her daughter was old enough, she helped her mother. One day, Clarice was approached by a young father whose wife had taken ill and needed someone to help care for her and his daughter.

She was unable to help him but said her daughter would be able to, provided he picked her up at her house and brought her back in the evening. Travis Waverly was a Korean War veteran and a carpenter who built several houses in Crofton and did some remodeling in Crofton and Blocker's Bluff. His business kept him busy and he often worked past suppertime.

Lottie Baxter became a godsend for him. She looked after his sickly wife, made sure his daughter Judy was cared for, and kept house for him. After Travis' wife passed away, she spent more time looking after the house and Judy. She became like a mother to her. Lottie was twenty- four when Travis Waverly's wife died, and he was thirty. Occasionally when he had to work late, Lottie would spend the night at the Waverly house.

A year later after working well into the evening, Travis came home late one night. Lottie had supper prepared for him, and Judy was already tucked in bed. After supper, Travis and Lottie sat on the porch.

"Lottie, have I told you how grateful I am for all you've done for me?"

"Every day, Mr. Travis, and I'm happy to do it. Miss Judy is a pleasure to look after."

"What about me, Lottie?"

She smiled. "You're a distraction, Mr. Travis."

He stood up. "Lottie, stand up I want to give you a hug in appreciation?"

"Mr. Travis that would be inappropriate."

"Lottie Baxter, the hell with appropriateness. Stand up." He grabbed her hands and pulled her into his arms. Then he kissed her—a long lingering kiss.

Nine months later, Clarice Baxter was the mid-wife for the birth of her daughter's baby girl at Baxter House.

Travis made a promise to Mrs. Baxter that he would take care of Lottie and be a father to their daughter Clarice, named after Lottie's mother, and they would never want for anything. A promise he repeated to her on her dying bed years later.

"Grandma, don't be mad at me, but after momma died, I saw you in your bedroom crying. You were holding a picture. When you went to fix supper, I found the picture and looked at it. It was of Great Grandma, you, Mister Travis, and a young girl. I'm sure that was momma." She rubbed her grandmother's arm, smiled, and continued, "It's, okay, Grandma, he treated me kindly, and I always thought of him as my grandfather. You're not angry, are you?"

She rubbed Lottie's hand. "No child, certainly not, yes, he was your granddaddy and Bradley's too."

"That means Brad and I are cousins and so is Thomas."

"Yes, child, you are." She wiped a tear. "You're not angry with me for keeping it a secret, are you?"

She rubbed her grandmother's arm again. "Absolutely not, I'm happy. Did you love him?"

Miss Lottie leaned back in her chair, looked up at the sky and smiled. "Oh, so much. He made my heart flutter."

Lottie gently slapped her arm. "Grandma, really!"

"I sure do miss him. He was… how do you say it?" Her eyes lit up. "He was my rock." Then she whispered, "We can't tell Bradley though."

"What about Miss Judy, does she know?"

"No, and we can't tell her. It might break her heart."

Thomas threw the ball to Bradley and he threw it back. Miss Lottie and Lottie watched as they played catch.

"Hey, Marine, want to come to my ball game tomorrow? You can bring my gramma."

He turned toward the porch and raised his palms up at Miss Lottie. He thought back to high school, when no one ever came to watch his lacrosse game—which was why he considered going to Thomas' ballgame.

"What do you say, Miss Lottie?" He nearly called her grandma. "Can we go to Thomas' game tomorrow?"

Lottie looked at her grandmother. "Say yes, Grandma, and then I won't have to come by and get you."

Thomas yelled, "Please, say yes, Gramma."

"Okay, but you have to hit a home run for me."

"Woohoo, Marine, you'll get to see me hit a home run for my gramma." Then he stuck his fist out. Bradley raised his hand to high five him. "What's that? Don't you know anything? You're supposed to bump fists with me."

"Thomas, mind your manners."

"It's okay, Lottie." He bumped fists with Thomas.

Thomas bumped fist and then opened his hand and said, "Boom!"

"What was that?"

"I exploded your fist, that's what."

Bradley laughed, wrapped his arms around Thomas and hugged him.

"Hey, you're gonna squeeze the life out of me, Marine."

They laughed as did Miss Lottie and Lottie.

"You gonna stay for supper, Lottie? It would be nice having us all together."

She was enjoying watching him and Thomas playing catch. "Sure, it will be like family night."

"Yes, it will. Is tripe soup okay?"

Lottie gagged. "Yuck, no way, Grandma. I'll just go to KFC."

Miss Lottie laughed. "You always fell for that. I've got some meat in the refrigerator for burgers, and I'll make fries. Thomas loves my burgers and fries."

"Now you're talking. I love them too."

Miss Lottie called out to the boys, "You two keep playing. Lottie and me are going to make supper."

"Are we having burgers and fries, Gramma?"

"Yes, Thomas, and watermelon too."

"Woohoo, Marine, you'll love my gramma's burgers and fries and we're having watermelon too!"

The two women went inside and prepared supper. When it was ready Lottie called Bradley and Thomas in. They washed their hands and all four sat down like a family and had supper together.

When they finished, Miss Lottie gave Thomas watermelon and then they all had ice cream. The adults sat and had coffee.

"Gramma, can I watch your television? *Wheel of Fortune* is on."

"Go ahead."

"Thanks, Gramma."

"Thomas, after *Wheel* we have to go home. It's a school night."

"Okay, Mom."

While Thomas watched television, the adults talked. Lottie couldn't resist telling him she knew who he was.

"Brad, how long are you going to keep your secret?"

He almost choked on his coffee but spit it into his cup.

"Lottie, what's the matter with you?"

"It's okay, Miss Lottie. Actually I'm glad she knows. Did you tell her?"

"No, Brad, she didn't. I could tell when you were gardening out back. You haven't changed the way you use a shovel. Have you talked to your mother yet?"

"I'm working up the courage to. Damn, Lottie, it's good to be honest with you. I could never keep a secret from you."

"That's because you were easy pickings."

They all laughed. He got up and walked around to Lottie. "Give me a hug, Brat."

She stood up. "Sure, Bratly."

"Stop that you two. You're acting like kids."

"Yes, Grandma," they both said. Miss Lottie laughed as did Bradley and Lottie.

He wrapped his arms around Lottie and hugged her tight just as he did that last summer before his father came and took him back to Virginia. She ran off crying and screamed, "I hate you Bratly!"

Neither woman commented about him calling Miss Lottie, grandma.

"It's been a long time, Bratly. I'm glad you're here."

"Me too, Brat." She looked at her watch. "It's almost eight, I better get Thomas home."

"It sounds like he's watching Jeopardy."

"He never watches Jeopardy, Grandma. He hates that show."

They went to see what Thomas was doing and found him sleeping on the couch with Jeopardy on the television.

"I'm going to have to wake him."

"No, don't, Lottie, I can carry him."

"You sure, Bratly?"

"Yes." He picked Thomas up and carried him out to her car. Lottie said goodbye to her grandmother and went to open the door for him. He put Thomas in the car and closed the door. Lottie walked up to him, hugged him, and kissed him on the lips.

"Thanks, Bratly."

"You're welcome, Brat. I'll see you tomorrow." He walked back to the house with a spring in his step and went into the kitchen.

"Feel better now?"

"Yes, I'm gonna sit on the porch."

CHAPTER 25

Friday morning after breakfast, Miss Lottie sat next to Bradley as he drove the Crown Victoria into town and to the general store. She imagined herself sitting next to Travis Waverly when he drove her into town. Travis would cover her hand with his and they would talk about their daughters.

"Your granddaddy used to take me into town in this old car."

"The only time he drove me in this car was when we first brought it to you." He reached across and patted her hand. She placed her hand on his.

"He used to do the same thing with his hand." She smiled at him and he returned her smile.

When they pulled up to the general store, Molly and Porter were crossing the street on their way to the police station.

Porter waved. "Well, I'll be damned."

Molly kept walking. "Who was that?"

"That was Miss Baxter and her boarder. Haven't seen that old Crown Victoria in a long time."

"I saw them too, but I'm keeping my promise."

"Molly, it's okay to wave hello."

"Well, it's too late now. What are we going to do this weekend since I'm off as of this afternoon?"

He reached down and grabbed her hand. "How about we spend the weekend on the island? I need to go there anyway."

"Sounds good to me. We can leave as soon as I'm off."

"I have a feeling I'm gonna get lucky this weekend."

She elbowed him, and they walked hand-in-hand to the police station.

"It's nice to see those two acting like young lovers" Miss Lottie said.

He thought about Laurie and wished they were them. "Yes, it is, Grandma."

"Remember now, call me Miss Baxter while we're here."

He grinned. "Can I hold your hand?"

"You're just like your granddaddy. No, you can't."

He reached down anyway, touched her fingers, and they walked to the general store. He opened the door for her and followed her inside.

"Miss Baxter, do you mind if I go around to the diner and say hello to Chef Willie while you shop?"

"Go right ahead. I'll have Miss Mavis call you when I'm ready."

When he entered the diner, Susie greeted him with a great big smile. He took a seat at the counter and ordered a slice of apple pie.

When Miss Mavis saw her enter the general store she was surprised.

"Well, I'll be damned if it isn't Miss Lottie Baxter. Good morning, what brings you here today?"

"Morning to you too, Miss Mavis. I need some cookies for my grandson's game tonight. I forgot to bake some and his team likes to have cookies after the game."

Miss Mavis came from around the counter, walked over to Miss Lottie, and hugged her.

"You're gonna squeeze the daylights out of me girl. What's new in town?"

"Oh my, a lot has happened," replied Miss Mavis. "Was that the marine who's staying with you?"

"Yes, how did you know?"

"Just about everyone who matters knows. You know something, Miss Lottie? Miss Judy was in the other day and I was telling her about him. Strangest thing, all of a sudden she turned white and almost fainted. I swear it was as if she'd seen a ghost."

Miss Lottie and Miss Mavis had known each other a very long time. Miss Mavis knew about her and Travis Waverly.

"Can you keep a secret?"

Miss Mavis scrunched her eyes. "Girl, you know I can. Does it have to do with that marine and Miss Judy?"

She whispered so Levina couldn't hear her. "He's her son."

"Oh my lord, does she know?"

"No, he hasn't spoken to her yet."

"Well after what happened the other day, he best get to it. There's something else I have to tell you. It's about Molly and John Porter."

Miss Lottie's forehead furrowed. "What happened?"

"John Porter and his dog were attacked on Porter's Island. The dog was shot and Porter suffered a concussion."

"Are they all right?"

"Yes, but yesterday he drove Molly's car here with the dog. She got really upset and started hitting him on the chest. He had to calm her. Seems she was overreacting to what happened. Never saw her act like that."

"The attack and him driving must have caused her to breakdown."

"She broke down all right, in front of everyone in the diner. They made up but it was something." She reached for Miss Lottie's arm. "Enough gossip, come I'll get you those cookies. Anything else you need?"

"You have any sticky buns? He likes them too."

"I sure do. Does he know about his granddaddy and Lottie?"

"No, and I'm not going to tell him"

Miss Mavis put two dozen assorted cookies in a box and four sticky buns in another box and handed them to Miss Lottie. She paid and asked Miss Mavis to poke her head in the diner and tell the marine she was ready.

Miss Mavis stuck her head in the kitchen and told Chef Willie to tell the marine that Miss Baxter was ready to leave.

"Sergeant, Miss Baxter is ready to leave."

"Thanks, Chef Willie, and thanks for the pie."

"You're welcome and come back and see me soon. Say wait." He saluted Harding. "Thanks for your service, Sergeant."

He returned the salute. "I will, Chef Willie." He got up, winked at Susie, and walked around to the general store. Miss Lottie handed him the two boxes and they left the store.

"What's in the boxes?"

"Cookies for Thomas' game tonight, and I got some sticky buns for you."

"Wahoo! Thanks, Grandma."

He opened the door for her and then got in the car and drove home. The smell of the cookies and the sticky buns made him want to open a box and have one. Instead, he reached over and patted her hand.

"I love you, Grandma."

"I love you too."

After an early supper, he and Miss Lottie drove to Crofton for Thomas' ballgame. When they passed by Judy's driveway, she was getting the mail. Miss Lottie waved as they went by. Judy waved back and watched them drive on. When they arrived at the ball park, they found Lottie and sat next to her.

Miss Lottie sat behind home plate so she could pay attention to the umpire's calls. When Thomas came to bat, she yelled, "Knock it out of the park, Thomas!"

The first pitch was called a strike. Miss Lottie stood up and yelled, "That weren't no strike. You wearing your glasses, Devon?"

The umpire called time, stepped back, took his face mask off and turned to see who was yelling at him. He knew it was Miss Lottie because she did it at every one of her grandson's games. Thomas stepped from the batter's box embarrassed and lowered his head.

Lottie shook her head. "She does it all the time. Grandma, stop, you're embarrassing him."

Miss Lottie sat down. "Ain't nothin ever embarrassed that boy, 'cept the time he showed up for your prom in that old run down truck of his. No granddaughter of mine was getting in that thing all dressed up and looking pretty."

The umpire yelled, "Play ball!" Thomas stepped into the batter's box and waited for the next pitch.

Lottie leaned over and whispered in his ear, "That poor boy was so embarrassed. Grandma wouldn't let him take me to the prom in his truck. She made us take her car, and I had to drive. There I was all dressed up and driving my date to the prom."

Miss Lottie shook her finger. "Don't think I didn't notice that as soon as you were out of the driveway you switched with him." She furrowed her brow and continued, "Good thing nothing happened or both of you would have felt my wrath."

He wrapped his arm around Lottie, leaned in, and whispered, "I love being here with you two."

She glanced into his eyes and for a brief moment said to herself—*I wish we weren't cousins.*

Miss Lottie watched nervously and then interrupted them. "You two gonna just talk or watch the game?"

The tone of her voice clearly gave them her message, so he removed his arm.

Thomas steadied himself for the next pitch. The pitcher released the ball, and Thomas knocked it over the left field fence.

Miss Lottie, Lottie, and Bradley stood and clapped.

"Way to go, Thomas!" shouted Miss Lottie.

Thomas got two more hits, caught two fly balls, and his team won the game.

Miss Lottie grabbed the box of cookies and turned to Lottie. "Take these cookies to Thomas' coach, Lottie." She normally did it herself, but she didn't want to leave Lottie and him alone.

Lottie took the cookies, lowered her head, and said, "Okay, Grandma."

She knew the frown on her grandmother's face meant that she was in trouble. When she was a youngster and got that look, she always lowered her head to avoid eye contact. She walked over to Thomas' team's dugout, handed the cookies to his coach, and waved to Thomas. He grabbed two cookies from the coach, said he wanted to join his family, and asked for permission to be excused. His coach told him to go ahead.

"You did real good tonight, Thomas."

"Thanks, Coach." He put the cookies in his back pocket, jumped the fence, and caught up with Lottie. "Coach said I did real good, Mom."

She wrapped her arm around him and rubbed her hand over his head. "You sure did. Your dad would be proud of you."

"Think he was watching?"

"I'm sure he was." She looked up and smiled.

"I got two cookies, one for me and one for the marine." They walked over to where Miss Lottie and Bradley were waiting. "Gramma, I got a home run for you."

She wrapped her arms around him. "You sure did, I'm so proud of you."

"Hey Marine, I did good tonight."

"You sure did." He stuck his fist out; they bumped fists and exploded them.

"I saved you a cookie." He reached into his back pocket for the cookies, but got mostly broken pieces. "Oh well, at least I meant to."

"It's okay, I'll take whatever you have."

They munched on the broken pieces and then they walked to their cars.

"See you tomorrow, Marine."

"You too, Thomas. Ask your mom to bring you by early and we can do some gardening."

Lottie's eyebrows hiked up as she smiled. "We'll come by after lunch and then Grandma and I can go shopping. That okay with you, Grandma?"

"That's a good idea." She grinned, and Lottie knew she was forgiven.

When he passed Judy's driveway, he slowed, looked left and said, "I'm going to talk to my mother on Sunday."

She touched his arm. "That's good, I'm proud of you."

He pulled into her driveway, got out of the car, and opened the door for her. He reached down and took her hand and they walked up onto the porch.

"I'm going to sit a spell."

"I'll pour us a glass of tea and join you." She went inside and returned with two glasses a sticky bun and some cookies. "I saved these for us."

She sat down, gave him his glass, the sticky bun and a cookie. They relaxed on the porch and enjoyed watching the lightning bugs and the sounds of cicadas. Later, they both turned in.

He slept peacefully that night with dreams about Lottie and playing catch with Thomas.

CHAPTER 26

Beaufort

Laurie took Jessica and Sarge to their first physical therapy session and Jessica to her second session with a counselor Friday morning at the Beaufort Naval Hospital. Jessica's first counseling session was for evaluation purposes. Her second would be more in-depth in a group of people. The first physical therapy session was meant to acclimate Towning to her situation and expose her to other amputees. Its intent was to let her see that her situation wasn't unique and that there were scores of things that she could accomplish having only one arm. Special attention would be paid to teaching her the kind of clothes that she should buy and how they would make it easier for her to dress herself.

Laurie had arranged the counseling sessions for Jessica and was permitted to attend the first session but no more. She was also allowed to attend the physical therapy session as was Sarge, who was to become an important part of both Towning's physical therapy and counseling sessions.

During her second counseling session, Jessica mentioned that on Saturday she was going to Charleston to visit her mother who she hadn't seen in over a year. She also told the group why it had been so long since she last saw her mother.

"Jessica, are you sure you want to take Sarge with you?" asked Doctor Davidson, the psychologist and counselor. "It might not be a good idea since you said your mother freaked out when she saw your arm missing. It may be too much for her to absorb, especially since Sarge has only three legs. Maybe you should consider leaving Sarge behind."

She hadn't thought about how her mother would react to Sarge. "It's possible she may not be comfortable seeing the two us, but I would feel more comfortable having Sarge with me." Sarge got up off the floor and sat beside her. Jessica reached down and rubbed her back. "She's the reason I'm here, sir."

"No, Jessica, the reason you're here is because you need help. Sarge is your companion not your keeper," replied Doctor Davidson.

Sarge stood up and walked in front of Jessica. When she bent down to rub Sarge's head, Sarge licked her face.

"I think Sarge is telling you that it's okay to go without her."

Sarge licked her face again. She ruffled Sarge's ears. "Are you sure you don't mind, girl?" Sarge barked, sat down, and looked up at her. "Okay, I guess that means yes."

"Okay, then that's settled. Jessica you happy with the program we've laid out for you?"

"Yes sir. I feel more confident now and I've only been in the program two days. I know it's going to be difficult adjusting to doing things on my own, but I'm going to do my best to succeed."

"Good and everyone in the group is here to support you. If no one has anything else to discuss, that's it for today. I'll see you all on Monday. Have a nice weekend."

The members of the group stood and started to leave. On her way out, Jessica was approached by one of the members.

"Jessica, my name's Robbie Waters." He was twenty-six and was injured in Iraq before the troop withdrawal and had been attending counseling sessions the past two years. "I wanted to introduce myself and wish you luck. It's good you're attending the sessions and getting physical therapy. I wish I had started counseling sooner, but I'm glad I did and it's been good for me." He reached out and offered his hand.

She smiled and took his hand. "Thanks, Robbie; it's nice to meet you. I'll see you Monday."

"Say, maybe one day we can have coffee after a session?"

Her eyes sparkled. Robbie's offer, although just to have coffee, was the first time a guy had asked her for a date in a very long time.

"Sure, Robbie, maybe we can. But not until after I've had more sessions and as long as Doctor Davidson says it's okay.

Doctor Davidson was locking the door to the room and overheard them. "It's okay as long as you keep it to a coffee date."

"Guess it's okay, Jessica." He winked at her. "See you Monday."

Her eyes lit up. "See ya, Robbie. I've got to go, my ride's here."

Earlier that morning after dropping Jessica and Sarge at the Naval Hospital, Laurie had spent time at home on her laptop researching PTSD. She had sensed that Harding was exhibiting some of the signs that Doctor Davidson had mentioned during Jessica's first session. She recognized how tired he seemed, possibly from nightmares, and when he talked about Jessica's accident it was as though he was experiencing flashback. The positive thing she noticed was that he had no problem with feelings toward others, especially toward her. However, that could be due to PTSD. She also wondered if what happened between them was just raw emotion, brought on by the stress of caring for Jessica. Somehow, though, she felt that some of it was because she had feelings for him but knew that nothing could come of them due to her situation.

Her cell phone rang. It was Jessica calling, and it was time to go to the hospital and get her and Sarge. "Hi, Jess, how did your session go?"

"It was great." Laurie sensed that Jessica was excited and something good must have occurred. "I'll tell you when you get here. See you in a bit."

"I'm om my way, Jess."

She grabbed her keys, locked the front door, and left. Jessica and Sarge were waiting at the patient pick-up space when she arrived. She and Sarge were like a couple of kids skipping as they approached the car. Sarge leaped into the back seat and Jessica got in on the passenger's side sporting a huge grin.

"Look at you two, you both seem happy. What happened in session, Jess?"

She buckled her seat belt and turned. "One of the guys in my group asked me to have coffee with him one day. The counselor said it was okay as long as we keep it to just coffee for now." She patted her thighs and grinned.

Laurie put a hand on Jessica's thigh and winked at her. "That's great, Jess. Are you going to have coffee with him?"

"Yes, as soon as he asks me. His name's Robbie Waters and he seems like a nice guy, but I just met him so we'll see. Sarge liked him too."

Laurie pulled away from the curb and drove out of the parking area and onto the street. "Good, next up is our trip to Charleston tomorrow to visit your mother."

Jessica's excitement change to foreboding. "About that, Laurie, the counselor doesn't think I should bring Sarge. My mother may not be able to handle two amputees."

Laurie braked as a pickup truck cut in front of her and signaled for a right turn. After the truck made its turn, she continued on until she came to a red light.

"How do you feel about not taking Sarge?"

The light turned green and Laurie slowly proceeded across the intersection.

"I'm okay with it, and Sarge is too. It's probably the wise thing to do."

Laurie also felt it was a good idea not to bring Sarge and continued driving home.

Before getting out of the car, Jessica asked, "Want to take Sarge for a short walk with me?"

"Sure, I'd love to."

Jessica held the leash as they walked down the street. After four blocks, Sarge acted as though she'd had enough walking so they turned and walked back home.

Jessica grinned and asked, "How about I make us lunch? It's about time I earned my keep."

Laurie's mouth opened wide. "Wow, that would be wonderful and you're not earning your keep, this is your home too."

"I know, but I can't stay here forever. Someday I'll have to be on my own. Maybe even move to Charleston if my mom would take me back."

"One step at a time, Jess, let's see how tomorrow goes first." Laurie knew that one day Jessica would leave and she would be alone again but wanted it to wait until Jessica was ready or her mother accepted her as she was.

"You're right, one step at a time. That's what my counselor said too. I'll go make us lunch. Peanut butter and jelly sandwiches okay?" She laughed. "Just kidding."

Laurie also laughed. "You're getting a sense of humor, Jess. That's good. After lunch, I have to start getting ready for my four o'clock shift."

Jessica went to the kitchen, opened the refrigerator and checked its contents. "There's some tuna fish left over from yesterday and a few slices of tomato. Is a tuna sandwich okay with you?"

Laurie was on her laptop Googling directions to Towning's mother's house. "That's fine with me and a bottle of water also. There should be some in the fridge."

She printed the directions to Jessica's mother's house, set them on the dining room table, and then they sat and had lunch. After lunch, Laurie went to her bedroom, showered, dressed in her nurse's uniform, went to the kitchen and grabbed her keys.

"I'm off, Jess. Don't wait up for me. I'll see you in the morning."

CHAPTER 27

Blocker's Bluff—Saturday Morning

Judy stood in her living room glancing at the picture of her and her father taken two years after the divorce. Next to it was another picture taken decades ago of her father and her son Bradley, the summer before the divorce. There was an aching in her chest when she picked it up and held it in her hand. She placed her hand over her heart, closed her eyes, and recalled how sad it was to watch her father when he last held the picture in his hand and touched the image of Bradley.

Her father was heartbroken that he would never see his grandson again, and he was bitterly angry, not at her—but at her husband for the conditions of the divorce. She had told him everything about it, and he was sympathetic toward her.

He knew about her sexual preferences since she was in high school but when she married, he thought that they had changed—but he loved her anyway.

Her world slowed down as the memories of her father and son brought tears to her eyes. She took a series of deep breaths, wished for another place in time, tightened her fists, and decided she was going to go to Baxter House to find out if Miss Lottie's guest was Bradley.

If he was, she'd tell him the whole truth about the divorce. Whatever happened, she'd accept the result—and if he doesn't forgive her for the past—she'd just have to accept his decision.

She wiped a tear. If he could get beyond what happened, she'd be elated. She clasped her hands together and straightened her back. She was now resigned to the fact that just getting to see him and knowing that he was okay—would be enough for her.

She grabbed her keys and purse and walked out of the house and to her car. She was determined and planned to just walk up onto Miss Lottie's porch, ring the doorbell, and ask her if she could talk to her guest.

After breakfast, Miss Lottie put the dishes in the dishwasher and set it on normal wash. He poured himself another cup of coffee and was going to sit on the porch.

"I'll bring the rest of the sticky buns out and join you."

"Could you make another pot of coffee to go with the buns?"

She smiled. "You're just like your granddaddy. I will, you go sit."

He stepped out of the house, took a seat in the rocker, rocked back, sipped his coffee, and breathed in the fresh morning air—content with his surroundings. Miss Lottie came out shortly thereafter with a tray that held a pitcher of coffee, a cup, and the sticky buns. She set the tray on the table, filled his cup, poured one for her and sat down.

He gave her a grin, drank some coffee and put his cup on the tray. "Sure smells good out here."

She was about to reply but noticed a car turn into her driveway and head toward the house. "Looks like we have company. I wasn't expecting anyone and Mr. Johnson isn't due back until Wednesday. And please call me Miss Baxter."

The Toyota Camry approached, and he could see that the driver was a woman. "Maybe it's one of your lady friends."

They both stood and watched in earnest as Judy pulled up behind his car and hesitated before getting out. She took a deep breath, exhaled, and realized that if she was going to do this, it had to be in front of the marine. She opened the door, stepped out of the car, brushed her fingers through her hair and steadied herself.

Come on Judy you can do this. It just seems like a mile, but it's only twenty-five feet and the figures waiting on the porch aren't wolves waiting to attack. One is Miss Lottie, the woman who raised you. He, on the other hand, could be Bradley.

She continued her journey toward the porch. His hard expression reminded her of his father on the day he told her that she could never have contact with her children. She worried that after all these years, he may tell her to go to hell and walk away. If he did, she felt she deserved it.

She started up the steps. *It's not Mt. Everest, Judy, it's only three steps. You've done it a hundred times before.*

He realized who she was and watched as she walked up to the porch. It felt like that dream he used to have of an evil stepmother leaving me in the forest in the dark of night. He'd see the red tail lights from her car get smaller and then disappear from sight.

He rubbed his arm. *Wait, maybe the woman approaching is the fairy godmother coming to rescue me and take me home. Or she could be my mother, but will she leave me again like she did before?*

"Good morning, Miss Lottie, may I join you?"

"Yes, Miss Judy, you certainly may. You know you're always welcome here."

Judy rubbed her arms and looked around. She had to keep going, one step at a time because no one was going to help her.

His arms were straight by his side, his fingers curled and his back arched—just like a wooden soldier.

She extended her hand to him. "Good morning, young man. My name is Judy Waverly." She studied his features, especially his eyes. She wanted to see if they were the color of her father's—and they were.

He crossed his arms and gave her a cordial nod. "Hello, Mother." That was it, just hello, Mother. After all these years, it was the best he could come up with.

He thought maybe she might turn and walk away. It might have been a waste of his time coming here if that was the best he had. If she rejected him, he deserved it.

Judy suddenly felt nauseous. It really was her son, and after all these years, he didn't send her away. Her face turned white and her knees felt weak.

"Miss Judy, I think you best sit down. Help me, Bradley." Miss Lottie took one arm and he took the other. Together they guided Judy to a rocker and had her sit down.

She looked up at him, crossed her hands over her chest, and gasped. "Bradley, oh my God, is it really you?"

He sat down, rested his elbows on the arms of the rocker and crossed his hands over his stomach. "Yes, Mother, it is."

Miss Lottie put a hand on Judy's shoulder. Judy put her hand over it. "You and Bradley talk while I go get you a cup and we can all have some coffee."

Judy removed her hand from Miss Lottie's. She avoided eye contact with him. He sat down, crossed his arms, and sat back in the rocker. When Miss Lottie came back with Judy's cup, she stood in the doorway to watch as he and his mother ignored each other.

Judy wondered what she should say to him. Their silence was deafening. She rubbed her arm with her hand, turned her head toward him, and asked, "How long have you been in Blocker's Bluff, Bradley?" There was more she wanted to say to him—but didn't know how he'd react. At least she said something—now what would he say?

He had a lot of unanswered questions, but worried if this was the right time to ask. He kept his head straight forward, avoided her eyes.

"Since Wednesday last week, except for a visit to Beaufort." And he couldn't even take the time to visit his own mother. He turned, looked beyond her and said. "How have you been, Mother?" He realized that was a dumb question—and he couldn't even look at her—no wonder she left him.

"I've been fine. How is EmilyKate?" she answered. She was concerned if she could maintain her composure—and wanted to tell him how she really felt after not seeing him for over two decades—but his indifference was starting to irritate her.

Now he had a dilemma, because he hadn't seen or talked to his sister in twelve years—but she hadn't seen her much longer than he had. He sat up straight in the rocker and bit his lip.

"I haven't spoken with EmilyKate since 2003 when I enlisted in the marines. She and Father said they wanted nothing to do with me because I enlisted. Father and grandfather said I wasn't welcome in their homes anymore."

She wasn't surprised, because it was the same thing they said to her. "Oh dear, I'm so sorry. It's all my fault." She clenched her fists and said to herself, *that son of a bitch!*

He didn't know that if he reached out and took her hand, if she would rebuke him? He sat firm in his chair and exclaimed, "No, Mother, it's not. They didn't like that I was enlisting in the military. It had nothing to do with you." He was at least being honest—but he could have taken the chance and held her hand.

She put a hand over her heart, and rocked her head back. Those self-righteous bastards! She thought.

Miss Lottie watched and didn't like the way things were going between mother and son. This wasn't how she wanted their first meeting to go—and realized she had to do something. Travis would want her to. She opened the door and stepped out onto the porch and handed Judy a cup.

"Why don't you pour us some coffee?" She sat down, and watched as Judy filled their cups. She glanced over at him. "Bradley, hand your mother a sticky bun. Go on now, do as I say." She knew he was anxious for answers, but this wasn't the time to bring up past wounds. He'd have to wait until another time—now it was time for them to get comfortable with each other.

He looked down, picked up a napkin and a sticky bun and handed it to his mother. *Can't she see I have other questions?* He asked himself.

"Thank you, Bradley."

"You're welcome, Mother." He grabbed a sticky bun, leaned back in the rocker and took a bite.

"Bradley, aren't you going to offer one to Miss Lottie?"

He reached for a napkin and a sticky bun.

Miss Lottie held a hand up. "No, thank you, I'm fine with my coffee." She rocked back on her rocker, took a sip of coffee, and gazed across the yard. At a nearby feeder, two robins hovered over the feeder and then flew off. Mornings were when she and Travis enjoyed sitting as the sun rose above the rooftop and cast its shadow over the garden, creating a glisten on the bushes. "It's so peaceful out here. Mr. Travis used to enjoy sitting with his feet up on his handmade stepstool and drinking coffee or sweet tea, especially after breakfast."

Judy remembered when she and her father would sit together on mornings like this—and he had a stepstool at home just like the one he used here.

"He had me open that window and put the radio in it so he could listen to music. Then he'd stretch out and hum a song or two," Miss Lottie said. "He never sang because he had a terrible singing voice." She laughed. "Lord, when he did sing, the birds all took off." She rocked back and forth and watched as Judy's mouth formed a big smile.

"I remember him doing that too after breakfast or after we mowed the yard, Miss Lottie," said Bradley.

"That's right and he would watch you and Lottie play in the yard just like your momma did with my Clarice when they was children. Your momma was a tomboy back then."

"No, I wasn't, Miss Lottie. Clarice was the tomboy."

"You were both tomboys." The mood on the porch had changed to one of fond remembrances—which made it much better now that they were at least talking. "Your daddy always whistled when he was working in the garage. Do you remember what it was that he whistled?"

They pursed their lips and spontaneously started whistling together. "Whistle while you work, whew who, whew who, who, who. Whistle while you work, whew who, whew who, who, who."

Miss Lottie's eyes brightened and her mouth broadened as she listened to mother and son whistling together as a duo. "You two sound just like Mr. Travis. If he were here, he would whistle with you. If memory serves me right there was a time or two when he did whistle with you when you was children."

They stopped whistling, turned to face each other and grinned. Judy raised her hand to high five him, but he extended a fist bump.

She misunderstood his gesture, so she lowered her hand and looked straight ahead. She thought he was going to punch her—and became concerned that he might be angry with her. He did the same. However, the failed gesture of camaraderie didn't change the mood as both were still grinning.

Judy drank some coffee. "Those were wonderful times, Miss Lottie. Whatever happened to that stool?"

"It's in the living room. I use it when I read and watch television."

"I wish Dad was here now."

Bradley looked up and grinned. "I do too, Mother."

She rubbed her eyes with her fingers and he handed her a napkin. "Thank you, Bradley."

Miss Lottie rocked back and forth. "Sadly he isn't, but you two are and it's time you made new memories. Miss Judy, can you stay for lunch?"

She looked at her watch. "I wish I could, but I have an appointment that I have to keep. It will take most of the afternoon."

He shook his head and frowned. He had hoped to spend more time with her—but felt she was abandoning him again.

Miss Lottie noticed his disappointment. "You're welcome to come for supper tonight. Lottie and Thomas will be joining us."

Judy looked over at him. He looked so somber and she considered that maybe he wanted her to. "If it's all right with Bradley, and I won't be intruding, I'd love to come for supper."

His frown changed to a slight grin. "It would be nice if you could join us, Mother."

She pressed her fingers to her lips, made soft eye contact with him, and asked, "What time should I come by?"

Miss Lottie set her cup down and clasped a hand to her chest. "Is five thirty okay? That way all you children can talk and Bradley and Thomas can toss a ball."

He was certain that Thomas would want to play catch.

"I can be here by then. I don't really want to leave, but I do have to go. I'll see you this evening, Bradley." She got up as did he.

She offered him her hand and he held it loosely. "Goodbye, Mother. I'm glad we had this time together."

He realized his mistake and that he was as bad as his father.

She had hoped he would have hugged her—but all she received was a handshake. She turned and stepped off the porch and started toward her car.

Miss Lottie shook her head at him. He hunched his shoulders, turned his palms up, and said, "What did I do, Miss Lottie?"

"Young man, you go walk your momma to her car and say a proper goodbye. And make sure you open the door for her." She shook her hand at him and tilted her head in Judy's direction. "Go on now!"

"Okay, geez." Just like when he was a kid and she scolded him. He stepped off the porch and caught up with his mother. "Mother, wait! I'll walk with you."

She turned around. "You don't have to."

"I want to." They walked together toward her car. Miss Lottie sat on the porch and swiped her cheek.

He held the car door open for her. "Thank you, Bradley. I can't wait to see you again." She started to get in the car, put her hand on his arm, gave it an affectionate squeeze and made eye contact with him.

He didn't want her to leave. "I'm so sorry I never wrote you, Mother. Are you sure you have to go?"

She put her hand on his cheek and rubbed it gently. "Yes, I do, but I'll see you later and it's okay that you didn't write. You had other things to worry about. Everything is going to be okay now."

But he really had no plausible excuse. He wiped his tears. "May I hug you?"

She cupped her mouth to hide her joy. He put his arms around her and squeezed her tight. His embrace felt like the one her father gave her as he met her at the airport when she arrived home from Virginia shortly after the divorce.

Her arms were outstretched—and she wasn't sure what to do—so she went with her instincts and wrapped her arms around him.

Just like with Mrs. Pritcher, he felt comfortable in her arms and he she had that same scent of lilac perfume.

Miss Lottie rocked back and forth, formed a steeple with her fingers, gently clapped her hands, and looked up. "Travis, everything's going to be okay. Just like I always told you, patience is all it takes."

Judy patted his back and said softly, "Bradley, I have to go now."

He didn't want to let her go. "I'm sorry, Mother. I just don't want you to leave." Sadly he released her from his grip.

"It's okay, I don't want to go either, but I have to." She rubbed her hand over his cheek again and then got in the car.

He watched as she backed up, turned, and drove off. Then he walked back to the porch with moisture on his cheeks.

Miss Lottie stood up when he stepped onto the porch. "You okay, Bradley?"

"Yes, I am now, but can I have a hug?"

She hugged him tightly. "Feel better now?"

"Yes, thank you."

"Good. Now, since your mother's coming for supper, we need to go shopping and get some fixings to make a rhubarb pie. She loves it just like you and your granddaddy." He laughed. "We can go after lunch. I'll make us sandwiches."

His face lit up. "Sounds good to me."

CHAPTER 28

Laurie and Jessica left Beaufort Saturday morning for their trip to Charleston and the visit with Jessica's mother. They left Sarge at home like the therapist suggested. Jessica sat in silence the whole trip looking out the window. Laurie wondered if she was worried about the visit.

"Jess, what did your mother say when you called her?" Jessica just kept looking out the window. "Jess, did you hear me? What did your mother say? Oh, Jess, you didn't call her, why not?"

"Because I didn't want her to say not to come."

Laurie reached over and put her hand on Jessica's leg. "She may not have."

Jessica looked down at Laurie's hand. Laurie pulled it away. "You don't know that, Laurie. Besides what difference does it make?"

"I don't know. Guess we'll find out when we get there."

For the rest of the trip both said nothing.

When Laurie pulled up to Jessica's mother's house, there was no car in the driveway and the curtains on all the windows were closed. She parked on the street and they sat in silence.

"Jess, are we going to ring the bell or would you rather leave?"

"Give me a minute."

A minute turned into ten. Someone pulled a curtain aside and peered out of the window. Laurie noticed.

"Jess, someone's home, I just saw them look out the window. Come on let's go ring the bell." Jessica sat still. Laurie unfastened her seat belt and opened her door. "I'm going. Are you coming with me?" She got out of the car and started toward the house. Jessica followed her.

Laurie rang the bell. She rang it again and finally the door slowly opened. Mrs. Towning stood in the doorway.

"Hello, Mom."

"Jessica? Oh dear, it's been so long. Give me a hug."

Jessica hesitated and then stepped into her mother's arms. When Mrs. Towning realized that Jessica's left arm was missing, she stepped back and covered her face with her hands. She waved her hands and said, "No! No! I can't do this—I'm sorry, Jessica."

Jessica stepped back. "It's okay, Mom."

"No it's not. I'm really sorry, Jessica."

Jessica turned and walked off. "Forget it, Laurie. This was a bad idea. Let's go back to Beaufort."

Laurie looked at Mrs. Towning and then at Jessica. "No, dammit! We're not leaving, Jess." She barged into the house. "Mrs. Towning, you can't just let her leave. She's your daughter and she's going through a rough time."

"I'm sorry, but I can't help her."

"Yes you can!" Laurie shouted. "She lost an arm, but it could have been worse. She's hurting and I've watched her drown in her sorrow long enough." Laurie put her hands on her hips. "She started therapy and counseling to deal with her situation, Mrs. Towning. She's making the most of it."

Mrs. Towning crossed her hands over her heart. "I don't know how to help her, and believe me, I feel sorry for her."

"Don't feel sorry for her. She doesn't need your pity. She needs her mother and your love for God's sake."

Mrs. Towning's head snapped back. "You don't mince words do you, young lady?"

"Not when it comes to Jessica. Do you want her to leave? You may never see her again."

"Okay."

"Okay, what, Mrs. Towning?"

"I'll talk to her, but what do I say?"

"For starters you can invite her into your home and ask her how she's doing. Then you can work your way to telling her you love her. In time I hope you'll learn to accept her disability and hug her. She needs you."

Mrs. Towning stepped out of the house and shouted, "Jessica, wait!" Jessica stopped and turned around. "Don't leave. Come inside, so we can talk, please."

"Are you sure, Mom?"

"Yes, honey, I am."

Jessica slowly walked up to her mother. "You don't have to hug me, Mom. I understand."

"Give me some time, honey."

"Take all the time you need, Mom. I can wait."

"It doesn't mean I don't love you because I do."

They both started to cry, walked into the house, and sat in the living room.

"Would you young ladies like some iced tea or a soft drink? That's all I have."

"Mom, we'll both have iced tea."

Mrs. Towning went to the kitchen and poured three glasses of iced tea. Jessica followed her.

"Mom, let me carry mine. You bring Laurie's."

She put a hand on Jessica's. "Honey, I really do love you."

"I know, Mom."

Mrs. Towning suddenly did the unexpected and wrapped her arms around her daughter. "Oh, honey, it's been so long. I'm so sorry that I let you leave. I should have been more of a mother for you." She no longer cared about Jessica's missing arm. "I'm just happy we have a chance to start over. Maybe one day you'll consider moving back here."

Jessica was surprised. "Maybe" She'd have to think hard about it. "We both had a hard time dealing with this. I'm just learning to deal with it myself. I got a dog, Mom, and she's helping me."

Mrs. Towning put her hand on Jessica's cheek. "You have a dog, really?"

"Well, technically she's my former platoon leader's dog and Laurie's, but they got her for me. Maybe one day you can meet her."

"Maybe. Let's go join your friend. Laurie's her name, right?"

"Yes, Mom, she's been there for me since I left home and I love her." Mrs. Towning looked confused. "Not that way, Mom. Like a sister."

"I don't care what way. I'm just grateful she was there for you when I wasn't. Let's go." They walked back to the living room and Mrs. Towning gave Laurie her iced tea. "Laurie, thank you for what you've done for Jessica, and I'm sorry for not acting like a mother before."

"It's okay, Mrs. Towning, I understand." She smiled at Jessica. "I'm happy to have been there for her."

"Jess, honey, tell me about your therapy and your dog."

"Her name's Sarge, Mom. And she's special. She worked with another veteran before me. I just started therapy and counseling this week, but I'm making strides even though I have a long road ahead of me."

"You'll do fine, honey. You always were a fighter. I have faith in you. You're not going to do this by yourself. I want you to visit me whenever you want, and I might come visit you if it's okay with you, Laurie."

"We'd love that, Mrs. Towning. You can come whenever you'd like. I'll sleep on the sofa and you can have my room."

"Nonsense, I can't let you do that. I'll get a hotel room."

Jessica couldn't believe what she was hearing. In less than an hour, her mother was offering to come visit her.

"Mom, if you can manage to come during the week, you can take me to my sessions. I go on Monday, Wednesday, and Friday. Maybe you could come Thursday night and go with me Friday and stay the weekend."

"I can do that, honey. I have quite a few vacation days saved up and it's a good excuse to take some."

"Great, Mom. Laurie, isn't that great?"

"Yes, Jess, that's great. We can give your mother a tour of Beaufort."

They talked for another hour and then Mrs. Towning made them a late lunch. After lunch, Laurie and Jessica got up to leave.

"Mrs. Towning, do you have a computer?"

"I have a laptop, why?"

"I'm going to give you my email address, so you can email Jess. If you let me see your laptop, I'll load Skype on it, and you and Jess can have video conversations."

"I'd love that. Let me get my laptop." She went to her office and brought the laptop to Laurie. She loaded Skype on it and her email address.

"All you have to do is click on Skype and then Jessica. Select video call and wait until she answers. Pick a good time to call, and I'll make sure she's available. Maybe we can get Jessica her own laptop and email account." She looked at Jessica. "What do you think, Jess?"

"I've got the money for it."

Laurie gave Mrs. Towning her laptop and they said goodbye. Mrs. Towning hugged and kissed her daughter and then hugged Laurie. They waved goodbye as they got in the car.

"Thanks, I'm really grateful for what you did."

"You don't have to thank me, Jess. I'm glad I was there for you."

"I love you, Laurie."

"I love you too but don't even think about kissing me."

CHAPTER 29

That same Saturday morning on Porter's Island, the sun shining through the windows woke Molly. She checked the time on the clock and realized they should have set the alarm last night. But they were too busy with other things to think about the alarm.

She shook Porter's shoulder. "John, wake up it's time to get up if we're going fishing."

He rolled over and put his arm around her. "Damn, Molly, when you said I'd get lucky last night, you really meant it. That wasn't just lucky, that was awesome."

"It was, but we have to get up now."

He kissed her on the mouth. "Want to do it again?"

Friday afternoon after Molly finished her workday they drove home, packed a bag, and went to the general store for provisions. Chef Willie made them two big take-out meals and then they made their way to Porter's Island. They shared one of the meals, gave Miss Mollie a treat, sat on the porch, and watched the sunset. Later they spent a romantic night in bed.

"Not now. Wait until tonight and we'll both get lucky again. We have to get up, shower, and eat breakfast if you want to go fishing. And Miss Mollie needs to go out."

"Promise I'll get lucky tonight?"

"Yes, now get up."

He grinned from ear to ear. "What do you say we take a shower together and save on water?" He winked at her."

"Okay, but no fooling around."

They showered together and reluctantly he didn't fool around. After the shower he took Miss Mollie for a walk and after breakfast they went fishing.

Bradley and Miss Lottie left Blocker's Bluff to shop in Crofton so she could purchase fixings for a rhubarb pie and other things for tonight's supper. After she did her shopping, he wanted a sticky bun so they stopped at the vendor selling bakery goods. He bought the biggest bun the woman had. She put the bun on a sheet of bakery paper and gave it to him along with two napkins. He thanked her and then he and Miss Lottie walked to his car.

"That's a big bun you got. You're not going to spoil your appetite for pie tonight, are you?"

He wiped his mouth and mumbled, "Absolutely not. I'm going to enjoy a big slice of rhubarb pie after supper."

"You're just like your granddaddy." He laughed and they went home.

She spent the day preparing rhubarb pies for desert and fixing supper. He tinkered with the Crown Victoria.

Lottie and Thomas arrived early and Bradley and Thomas worked in the garden. Lottie watched as the two shoveled, pulled weeds, and threw dirt at each other. She recalled how she did the same with him when they were youngsters—afterward Miss Lottie would give them cookies and lemonade.

"Grandma, do you have any cookies and some lemonade?"

"There's a few left and lemonade in the refrigerator, why?"

"Those boys are filthy, and I want them to take a break. I'll bring them cookies and lemonade." Miss Lottie gave her what cookies she had left. Lottie poured two glasses of lemonade and went out the pantry door. "Hey you guys, take a break. I brought you cookies and lemonade."

They stopped working and wiped their dirty hands on their pants.

"Thanks, Lottie, we can use the break. Thomas is a workaholic."

"What's a workaholic, Marine?" He took a glass of lemonade, shoved the whole cookie in his mouth and munched on it.

"Thomas, you're going to choke on that cookie."

He mumbled, "No I won't," in words barely audible.

Bradley took a bite of his cookie. "A workaholic, Thomas, is someone who doesn't want to stop working like you."

"Oh, Marine." mumbled Thomas.

"Thomas, he has a real name. You don't have to call him marine."

"What's your real name, Marine?"

"It's Bradley, Thomas, but you can call me Brad."

"Okay, Brad, but I'm gonna call you Marine."

He rubbed his hand over Thomas' head and laughed. Lottie laughed too and went back into the house.

"The boys are enjoying themselves. Brad is like a kid with Thomas."

Miss Lottie checked the roast in the oven. "I'm glad they are, but they have to start cleaning up because Miss Judy will be coming soon."

"I'll go tell them. Do you need my help?"

"Yes, the potatoes have to be mashed and the salad has to be prepared. The pies are cooling so they're all taken care of. Go tell those boys to start cleaning up."

Lottie called the boys. They were splashing each other with the last of their lemonade and kicking dirt at each other. She should have yelled at them but instead she couldn't resist laughing.

"Hey you two children, stop that. It's time to clean up for supper. You both need to take a shower."

"Aw, Mom, do I have to?"

"Yes, Thomas you do. There are clean clothes in the bag in the living room. You go first and then Brad you next."

"Aw, Mom, do I have to?"

"If you want rhubarb pie, you have to." She shook her head. They started to walk into the pantry, but Lottie stopped them. "Take your shoes off first. Grandma won't like you tramping dirt into the house. Go on now both of you."

Thomas went upstairs to take a shower while Bradley sniffed at the pies.

"Don't even think about it, Bratly. You're a big baby you know that?"

"Aw, Mom." She smacked him on the arm. "Ow! That hurt, Brat."

"Good, you deserved it. Now go on upstairs and get ready to shower. Go on, get." She shooed him away with her hands.

"Aw, Mom, do I have to?"

She grabbed a towel and twisted it. He quickly left and went upstairs.

"He's like a big baby."

She handed the salad bowl to Lottie. "He always was around you."

Lottie reflected back to when they were young. She had that secret crush on him and could twist him around her little finger.

Thomas put his dirty clothes in the living room and went into the kitchen. "Here I am all clean. Is it suppertime yet?"

"My goodness, Thomas, you look handsome," said Miss Lottie. She wiped her hands on her towel, walked over, and gave him a hug and kiss. "Not yet, Thomas, we're waiting for Miss Judy, Bradley's mother. You go watch the television."

He went into the living room and turned the television on. Bradley came down a bit later and walked into the kitchen.

"What did you do with your dirty clothes, Bratly ?"

"They're in my laundry bag upstairs. Why, Brat?"

"Go get them and I'll wash them with Thomas's dirty clothes."

"You don't have to. I can do them tomorrow."

"Do as I say and go get them."

"Aw..." He stopped when he saw the twisted towel in her hand. "Be right back."

"You're mean to that boy. Just like when you were kids."

"He likes it, Grandma." They both giggled.

He grabbed Thomas' dirty clothes; put his and Thomas' in the washing machine and set the wash cycle. He joined Thomas watching television. He didn't want to be around Lottie and get scolded again.

At 5:20, Judy arrived and rang the bell. Bradley got up to let her in.

"Evening, Bradley." She was dressed in slacks and a light blue blouse—the clothing she wore to work—holding a box of sticky buns. "I brought these for you. Miss Mavis said you'd enjoy them."

"Thank you, Mother. You look nice. The ladies are in the kitchen. Thomas and I are watching television."

She was disappointed that he didn't at least offer her a hug or a kiss on her cheek. "I'll bring these back. You go back to watching television."

He realized he hadn't properly greeted her, especially since she was his mother. Maybe it was because of how he was raised in Virginia—proper with no outward emotional displays of affection. Unfortunately, his timing was off—she had already gone into the kitchen.

"Evening, Miss Judy, you look real pretty."

"Thank you, Lottie. I brought these sticky buns for Bradley." Lottie set them on the counter.

Miss Lottie wiped her hands on her dish towel. "Evening, Miss Judy, we're glad you're here." She reached out and took Judy's hand.

"Is there something I can do to help?"

"No, you're a guest tonight, and guests don't have to help."

She placed her hand on Miss Lottie's. "But I feel like family and family is expected to help."

"You can make the salad, Miss Judy," said Lottie.

"I can do that, I was always assigned to make the salad when I was a youngster."

They set the kitchen table so they could eat like a family.

"The table looks nice," said Miss Lottie. "We'll eat here since we're practically all family." Lottie winked at her.

They put the meal on the table and called the boys in. Thomas sat next to Bradley and Lottie sat across from him next to Judy. Miss Lottie sat at the head of the table and then they passed the bowls around.

"Hey, Marine… I mean, Brad. You want to play catch after we eat?"

He rubbed Thomas' head. "It's okay, Thomas, you can call me marine."

Lottie winked at him. Miss Lottie and Judy smiled at each other.

"Miss Judy, are you really the marine's mother?"

"Yes, Thomas, I am. You know, when I was your age, I used to eat meals at this table with your grandmother and your mother's mom."

"Really?"

"Yes, I really did. Miss Lottie was like a mother to me after my own mother passed away."

"And Bradley and I ate meals here when we were your age, Thomas. Grandma raised me after my mother passed away," added Lottie.

"Wow! That makes us all like family then."

"Yes, Thomas, we are," Miss Lottie said and in more ways than one—she thought as did Lottie.

After everyone finished eating, the boys went out front to play catch. The ladies started clearing the table.

"Lottie, why don't you go watch the boys. Your grandmother and I can cleanup."

"Are you sure, Miss Judy?"

"Yes, go on now."

"Okay, besides those boys need watching anyway."

Miss Lottie and Judy cleared the table; put the dishes in the dishwasher and the leftover food in the refrigerator. Judy reached for Miss Lottie's hand.

"What is it, child?"

She brushed away a tear. "Thank you for giving me a chance with my son."

"Well you two still have a ways to go yet."

"I know we do. Miss Lottie after mom died, you practically raised me. I believe you knew what I was like in high school, but you never judged me."

"Wasn't my place to judge."

"You were like a mother to me, and I've always loved you. I think you loved me, too, just like you loved Clarice, my sister." Miss Lottie covered her mouth with her hands. "I always suspected it, and Dad confirmed it. He told me about the life insurance policy and the annuity he purchased for you. And he showed me the marriage certificate." Miss Lottie crossed her hands over her heart.

"John Porter's father married you, and Chef Willie and Miss Mavis were witnesses. I'm betting John Porter also knows your secret." She rubbed her eye. "In essence you're my stepmother, but I consider you my mother." Both shed tears. "Dad also said he told you the real reason for my divorce and why I couldn't see my children ever again. Also how you eased his anger toward my ex." She touched Miss Lottie's arm. "I'm so happy, and I love you."

Miss Lottie gathered Judy into her arms. "I love you too, and I've loved you like a daughter." Judy buried her head against Miss Lottie's shoulder. "It's okay, child, everything will be all right. But we mustn't tell the children. They might not understand."

"I think they would but if that's what you prefer, we'll keep it a secret."

"Now that Bradley is here everything will be all right."

"But what do I tell him?"

"Just tell him you made a mistake and spare him the details. When the time is right, you tell him the truth. Trust me, your daddy would want you to do it this way."

Thomas had come into the house to use the upstairs bathroom. When he came down, he thought he heard someone crying in the kitchen. He barely heard what they were saying, but he saw his grandmother consoling Judy. He went back outside.

"Momma, I think Miss Judy was crying and Gramma was comforting her."

Lottie wondered if it might have been about Miss Lottie and her grandfather. "Thomas, I'm sure Miss Judy was just happy that she got to join us tonight. She hasn't seen her son in a long time because he was in the military."

"Like when dad came home and comforted you?"

"Yes, Thomas, I'm sure that's what it was."

He jumped off the porch and yelled, "Hey, Marine, your momma's happy that you're back from the military."

Lottie shook her head. Bradley looked at her. She grinned.

"I'm happy too, Thomas."

"Okay, boys, it's desert time," Judy called as she and Miss Lottie brought a platter of pie slices on paper plates, a pitcher of sweet tea, and glasses onto the porch. Lottie got up and helped them.

The boys leaped onto the porch, grabbed a plate of pie, a glass of tea, and sat on the steps. The ladies sat in the rockers. After he finished his pie and tea, Thomas got up and went inside to watch television. Bradley followed him.

"They're like two kids, Lottie."

"Yes, Miss Judy, they are." Lottie checked her watch. "I didn't realize it was so late. I have to get Thomas home."

"Why don't you stay the night, Lottie? I don't like you driving in the dark."

"Grandma, I'm a big girl now."

"Yes, but I'm concerned for Thomas."

"Okay, if you really want me to."

The ladies sat and enjoyed the evening making small talk about when they were youngsters. Lottie enjoyed listening to Judy talk about spending nights at Baxter House and stories about her mother. Miss Lottie enjoyed listening too.

Lottie checked her watch again. "I think it's time Thomas went to bed. I'll be right back." She went into the house. Bradley and Thomas were both asleep on the couch. She was about to wake Thomas, but Bradley stopped her.

"Don't wake him, Lottie. I'll carry him to your car."

"We're staying here tonight. Can you carry him upstairs for me?"

"Of course."

He picked Thomas up and carried him upstairs to one of the bedrooms. Lottie started to undress him, but he woke up, undressed himself, and then lay down on the bed. Lottie covered him.

"Goodnight, Marine, goodnight, Mom," he murmured.

"Goodnight, Thomas."

Lottie closed the door behind them.

"You did a good job with him, Brat."

"Thanks, Bratly. His daddy would be proud of him."

"He'd be proud of you, too." He wrapped her in his arms and held her tightly. She cradled her head against his shoulder. "If only things were different, Lottie."

"Yes, if only." She was thinking about their family situation. He looked into her eyes and couldn't resist kissing her. "We'd better go back downstairs before they wonder what's taking us so long." They started down the hallway.

Miss Lottie and Judy were still on the porch. "If things were different, Miss Lottie, those two would make a nice couple." She placed her hand on Miss Lottie's.

"Yes, if only they were."

"It would be nice if I could call you Momma, Miss Lottie sounds so formal."

She rubbed Judy's hand. "Momma is okay when no one is around, but Miss Lottie is better."

Bradley and Lottie joined them on the porch.

Judy looked at her watch. "It's late and I have to work tomorrow, so I'm going to go home now. Bradley, would you walk me to my car?"

"Yes, Mother." Judy said goodnight to Miss Lottie and Lottie and stepped off the porch.

When they reached her car, she put her hand on his arm. "Can you come by tomorrow, so we can talk? I have to go to work after lunch, but the morning is fine."

"I can come by after breakfast. Miss Lottie and Lottie will be going to church. Say ten o'clock?"

"Good. I'm happy we got to spend some time together, Bradley."

"I am too, Mother."

"I love you, Bradley."

He bundled her in his arms. "I love you too, Mother."

She kissed him on the cheek, got in her car and drove off. As he watched, he rubbed his eyes.

CHAPTER 30

After Miss Lottie, Lottie, and Thomas left for church Sunday morning, he left the house. When he stepped off the porch, there wasn't a cloud in the sky and the fresh air lifted his spirits—the start of a new day and possibly the beginning of a new life. Birds were chirping and there was dew on the grass. He could use some exercise, so he decided to walk, and take the time to contemplate what awaited him.

The azalea bushes in front of her house were still in bloom. A willow oak shaded the house. Judy was dressed in shorts, wearing a wide brimmed hat, gloves, and was tending to her garden. She had dirty knees and a smudge of dirt on her face. Earlier, she had mowed the yard with her father's ride-on mower. The garage door was up and he could see the mower and his grandfather's truck. He pictured her in jeans, dirty hands, and a grease smudge on her face as she tinkered with the mower and the truck. When he was a youngster in Virginia, there were gardeners who took care of the landscape.

"Good morning, Mother."

"Bradley, you startled me, and you're early. I'm glad you're here." She reached out to embrace him, but he hesitated, so she dropped her arms. "I must look a mess."

"You look fine Mother. Can we go inside and talk?"

"Sure." She was tired of his formality. Why couldn't he just call her Mom?

She still had the furniture that his grandfather made. Some of it had been recovered, but he knew his grandfather's work. The faux blinds on the large picture window let in the natural light.

"Your grandfather replaced all the windows and put picture windows in here, the kitchen, and the den." The pie crust table that his grandfather made was placed by the front window with a doily and a small bouquet of red roses arranged on it. Facing the fireplace was the frayed sofa where Judy and her father sat in front of a fire with their feet propped up on the coffee table, a bowl of popcorn between them, a beer in one hand and their favorite book in the other.

"We spent many a cold night on that old sofa." He glanced toward the fireplace at the pictures of her parents and her children on the mantle. "Come, I'll give you a quick tour." She led him to each room and stopped when she came to a bedroom. "Recognize this room, Bradley? It's the one you slept in when you visited your grandfather." His gazed shifted to one of the walls. "That fishing rod was yours. Your grandfather put it there to remind him of you." He focused on the fishing rod. "You remember when you and he would go fishing in the early morning?"

August—1994

At almost every hour, Bradley glanced at the clock to see if it was time to get out of bed. He eventually drifted into a sound sleep—but was awakened by a gentle hand tapping him on the shoulder. He rolled over and the hallway light silhouetted the man standing over him. He knew who the man was by the sound of his voice.

"Come on, Son. Time to get up else we'll be late."

"What time is it, Gramps?"

"Four fifteen and we want to be on the boat by five o'clock, so we gotta hurry. Splash some water on your face and get dressed. We'll eat breakfast at Miss Lottie's."

When he went to bed the night before, he had dressed in the clothes he'd wear to go fishing. He sat up in bed, placed his legs on the floor and bent over to retrieve his shoes and socks. He tiptoed to the bathroom and splashed water on his face.

Travis waited as his grandson crept down the stairs. He was a burly man going on sixty-five and enjoyed the summers he spent with his grandson.

"You ready? Everything's in the truck. All we need is ourselves."

"Ready, Gramps. Let's go."

Travis messed the boy's hair and they quietly left the house. "You're gonna do good this morning, Brad." He liked when his grandfather called him Brad, his favorite nickname.

They drove to the Blocker's Bluff dock and unloaded the truck. Bradley untied the boat and they cast off to sea. They fished until sunrise then returned to the marina, secured the boat, and placed their catch in the cooler.

"We had a good morning, didn't we, Gramps?"

"We sure did." He put his hand on the boy's shoulder. "You ready for breakfast now?"

"Yep, and I hope Miss Lottie has a big one ready 'cause I sure am hungry." He looked up at his grandfather. "The summer is almost over, and I'll soon be going home. I'm gonna miss you, Gramps."

He pushed the boy's hat over his eyes. "I'm gonna miss you too, Brad."

Neither of them knew that it would be their last summer together and before long he wouldn't see his mother anymore.

CHAPTER 31

Present Day

"Yes, I remember." The twin sized bed that he slept in and the small dresser with a picture of him and his grandfather the time they went fishing together were still there. "You haven't changed it much. Why?"

"Because I hoped one day you would visit me. That's why."

He felt guilty for not having tried to visit her sooner. He was away fighting a war so he had an excuse—but he could have taken a leave and visited her during all those years.

"I'm sorry I didn't, Mother."

"Bradley, would you please stop referring me as Mother. I know you were brought up that way, but it would be nice if you would call me Mom."

"I'll call you Mom if you'll stop calling me Bradley."

"What should I call you?"

"Call me Brad. Like Grandpa did."

"Okay, Brad, as long as you call me Mom. I'll also call you son if you don't mind."

"I'd like that too, Mom."

"Good, and I really do love you."

"I love you too, Mom." He took her in his arms and held her tight. "Can we talk about what happened between you and father?" He wasn't about to refer to him as dad, not after the way he was treated as a boy, and when he joined the marines.

Judy knew her marriage was one of convenience to enhance his image as well as his political and financial aspirations—and his parents' image as well. Maybe in the beginning there were feelings—which was why they had two children together. But it soon became apparent that they too were part of his sham—and to mask her son's trips to visit her father—he said the boy was away at camp learning valuable people skills. He had a story made up for everything.

She endured the cold and cruel relationship for as long as she could—but eventually couldn't bear it anymore—and ended up in someone else's bed. He couldn't have that, have her tarnish his image, destroy his ambitions and his family's reputation—and so he exacted his revenge.

"I had an affair and your father threatened to expose us if I didn't agree to his terms. I did what was best for everyone, especially you and your sister. He would have made it very ugly, and I didn't want you two to have deal with that." She took Miss Lottie's advice and left certain particulars out. "I'm sorry, Brad, I did what I felt was right. It wasn't easy knowing I might never see you again. Even your grandfather was unhappy."

He mentioned the letter Miss Lottie said she wrote him and that he never received it. Then he told her how he accidently found out about his grandfather's death.

"I stopped by the cemetery and saw the graves of Grandma and Grandpa. I'm sorry I wasn't there for you." He reached out and touched her hand.

"You didn't know so don't apologize. I'm glad you saw their gravesites." *That son of a bitch!* "Let's get beyond the past and enjoy what we have now. How long will you be here?"

"Two more weeks, but I'm getting out this October."

"What will you do after that?"

"I'll come back here and live with you if you'll have me. Unless I get a better offer." He thought about the lieutenant and what might be.

"Of course I'll have you. You're my son and don't you ever forget it. Would you hug me, please?"

He stood up and wrapped her in his arms. "I've never forgotten it, Mom."

Two decades of heartache was finally coming to an end, but Judy still had another secret.

"Mom, do you drive Grandpa's truck?"

"Sometimes, and I work on it too. If there's something I can't fix, I take it to the garage in town, and Ollie works on it. He was a good friend of your grandfather."

"I know. He told me the other day when I was there to buy a new battery for Miss Lottie's car."

"She'll never get rid of that old clinker. Your grandfather bought it for her."

"I was with him when he delivered it to her. She gave him a big hug and a kiss in appreciation."

They had another cup of coffee and then it was time for her to leave for work.

"Will I see you again?"

"Yes, you will. Would you like to go with Miss Lottie and me to Thomas' next ball game in Crofton?"

"I'd love to, when is it?"

"The last one was Friday so I suspect the next one is this Friday. I'll let you know."

She offered to give him her phone number.

"I already have your number, Mom. I looked you up on the Internet when I first got here. I planned on contacting you, but I needed for it to be the perfect time."

She kissed him. "Well, I beat you to it. There's never a perfect time for anything. Let me give you my email address too, unless you have that also?" He gave her a sly grin. "Oh. You have that too?" She watched him leave and hoped she had done the right thing by not being completely honest with him.

Lottie's car was in the driveway when he walked up onto the porch and into the house.

"You folks are back from church early."

"It was a short service, Brad. Where did you go?"

"I went to see my mom."

"How did it go?" asked Miss Lottie.

"It went well. Did you know she still has my grandfather's ride-on, truck, and trailer? She even mows her yard and works on the ride-on and the truck."

Miss Lottie grinned. "Yes, I did. Your granddaddy taught her. She mows my yard once a month too. Your mother's a hard worker."

He looked down feeling guilty. "I guess she had to be." He sat down. "Lottie, I asked my mom to come with us to Thomas' next ball game. I said it might be this Friday. Is it okay with you if she comes with your grandmother and me?"

"Absolutely, Brad." She glanced at Miss Lottie. "It'll be like a family night out with all of us together."

"Great, I'll text her later and let her know."

After lunch, Lottie and Thomas went home. Miss Lottie and Bradley sat on the porch and watched them leave.

"You satisfied now that you talked to your mother?"

"I think so." But not really, he wanted to know who it was that caused her to give up her children.

Sunday after breakfast, Molly and Porter decided to go back to the mainland so she could do some housework and he could shop for groceries in Crofton. Two nights of romance and a day of fishing Saturday were enough to relax them and recharge their batteries. They planned on relaxing at home Sunday afternoon or maybe walk into town.

They saw Harding when he came out of Judy's driveway. Porter waved to him and they caught a glimpse of her going into her house.

"That was Miss Baxter's guest, John."

"I guess mother and son had a reunion of sorts. I hope it went well for both of them."

She put a hand on his thigh. "I do too, and I regret upsetting Miss Baxter."

"You meant well, and I'm sure she'll forgive you."

"You think so? She was pretty angry with me."

He patted her hand. "Yes, Molly, she knows you meant well."

Molly drove home and they unpacked the truck. Porter took Miss Mollie for a short walk.

"Okay, John, here's the list. Get everything and if you have an accident, I swear I'll kill you myself."

CHAPTER 32

Wednesday morning, Bradley was looking forward to seeing Laurie, Jessica, and Sarge again. Miss Lottie had scrambled eggs, bacon, grits, and biscuits made for his breakfast. He poured a cup of coffee and sat down at the table.

"Morning, Grandma."

She turned from the stove with sparkling eyes. "Good morning to you. Are you looking forward to going to Beaufort and seeing those two young ladies again?"

"Yes, I am. I just hope that they're looking forward to seeing me again."

She set his plate in front of him and patted his hand. "I'm sure they will be. Just don't be too anxious, sometimes you have to let things take their course, especially in matters of the heart."

"You're probably right and maybe I'm making something out of nothing. I'll just wait and see." He took a sip of coffee.

She fixed her plate and joined him. "That's good advice. Are you happy with how things are with your mother?"

"Yes and no." Happy they finally met and talked, but he had more questions. "I'd like her to tell me what really caused the divorce and why she agreed to my father's terms."

Miss Lottie set her fork down. "It's not my place to talk about it, but if it's bothering you, we can talk about it in the morning. Mr. Johnson will be here tonight so we'll wait until he's gone."

"I love my mom and if you know something I would appreciate you telling me. It can wait until tomorrow because I have to see what happens in Beaufort today."

"I'll tell you what I know, but you'll have to talk with your mother about it." At least it would give her more time to decide just how much she wanted to tell him. "After I tell you, I hope you'll understand how difficult it was for her."

"I promise I'll try."

After breakfast, Miss Lottie cleaned the kitchen, and he went upstairs to prepare for leaving. She waited on the porch to say goodbye.

"You'll call me when you leave Beaufort, won't you?"

"I will." He gave her a hug and a kiss.

She rubbed her hands down his arms. "Drive safely."

Since the directions to Laurie's house were still fresh in his memory, he skipped the GPS. Her car was parked in the driveway so he parked on the street, walked up to the front door and rang the bell. When she opened the door, she was wearing sweat pants and a t-shirt, but she looked just as beautiful as the last time he saw her. His heart skipped a beat.

"Good morning, Sergeant. How are you?"

"I'm fine. I hope you are too. Have you been exercising?"

She looked down at her outfit. "I just came from running. Please excuse my outfit. Jessica isn't here. She and Sarge are at their therapy session. Come in and I'll bring you up to date." He followed her to the kitchen. "Would you like a glass of iced tea? I made it fresh this morning."

"I would, but I really need to use the bathroom if you don't mind."

"Use mine. Jessica isn't the neatest person, and I haven't had time to clean up after her."

"Which way?"

"It's down the hall and on your left."

He walked down the hall and entered her bedroom. It was neat and orderly—in fact it was immaculate. He walked into the bathroom and is was just as neat and tidy. Not a single female article was present but there was a faint odor of her perfume. On her dresser were three pictures. He picked up the one of a teenage girl wearing shorts and holding a basketball. It was from her high school days.

The next picture was of her in a nursing uniform flanked by her parents. He picked up the third one and looked close. She was wearing the same uniform with a cap on her head.

She stood in the doorway watching as he picked up each picture.

CHAPTER 33

When Laurie sent him to her bathroom, she'd forgotten about the pictures on her dresser.

He turned and faced her. "Oh, hell, you're an officer." She turned her head so as to avoid his eyes. "Why didn't you tell me?" He set the picture on the dresser.

She hesitated and could feel the beating of her heart. "I wanted to and didn't mean to deceive you." She looked down, started to continue, but her words were unintelligible because she was sobbing. "It's been a long frustrating year. You showed up and then Sarge and everything got confused." She leaned against the door jam and wiped her eyes.

"Oh, the hell with decorum." He walked over, took her in his arms and held her tightly. She laid her head on his shoulder.

"I'm so sorry."

"Don't apologize, you did nothing wrong."

"I violated my officer's conduct."

He realized that what happened at the hotel and being in her bedroom had violated both their codes of conduct. "It was just a one-time indiscretion, that's all." It wasn't an indiscretion for him, and it wasn't about the sex. "I didn't mean it that way."

Her face went rigid. "Is that what it was to you?" The words were out of her mouth before she realized what she said.

"No, absolutely not, but it's what you called it." He took a deep breath. "Listen to me. Dammit, I love you and I don't want you to compromise your commission."

"It's too late, I already have and we both are in violation."

"Dammit, Lieutenant!" He was furious. "No one knows what happened between us, and Jessica doesn't have to know. I'll be a civilian soon, but you have a career ahead of you. Please, don't do anything foolish."

"That's easy for you to say."

He grabbed her shoulders and shouted, "No, it's not! Listen to me. We can continue being just friends, and I'll visit Jessica and Sarge periodically. When I'm a civilian, I'll come back and you can decide if you want me. If not, I'll go to Blocker's Bluff and get on with my life."

She wiped more tears. "That doesn't solve my problem."

"It will have to. Just take some time and think about it, Lieutenant." He hoped she would, but whatever happened in the future would be up to fate. "Oh hell, it must be five o'clock somewhere, and I could use a drink."

"There's beer in the refrigerator."

He went to the kitchen, opened a bottle of beer and took a long gulp. For want of something to punch, he slapped his forehead and yelled, "Son of a bitch!" He finished his beer and got another one.

She closed the bedroom door, stepped into the shower and let the water wash away the tears. Then she dressed and joined him.

"I see you got your beer."

He looked at the empty bottle. "Yes, and I needed it. Tell me about this therapy. When did it start?"

She held her hand up when her cell phone rang. "Hey, Jess, how did your session go? I'm glad. Sergeant Harding is here. Yes, Jess he knows. We'll talk later, should I leave now? You are? That's great. Okay, forty-five minutes. Is it just coffee or are you having lunch too? We'll pick up lunch on the way home. Enjoy your date. Yes, it is a date, Jess. Bye now."

She closed her phone and smiled. "She says hello and we don't have to rush. Take your time and finish your beer. She has a coffee date with one of the members of her group."

Jessica's call was a distraction from what had occurred in her bedroom.

"That's awesome. Now tell me about her therapy, when did it start?"

"The Friday after you left. Sarge goes with her. She goes for physical therapy and counseling. Sarge has been really good for her. You did a good thing, Sergeant."

"We both did a good thing, Lieutenant."

"Yes, we did." She looked at her watch. "Finish your beer, we should leave. It's not far, but traffic can be awful during lunchtime."

He polished off his beer, put the bottles in the sink, and they drove in silence until he turned and asked her, "How did the trip to Jessica's mother's house go?"

"It went well. Sarge stayed home because her counselor suggested it might be too much for her mother, considering her situation. They had a good talk and they Skype now. We're going back in a couple of weeks. We may bring Sarge." She slowed, allowing a bicycle group to pass on her right. "How did it go with your mother? Remember I gave you an order, Sergeant." He watched as the bicycle group turned right.

"We talked, but there's still an unresolved issue. She hasn't told me the specifics of what caused the divorce. I'm going to ask her when I get back."

"Want my advice?"

"It can't hurt, especially since you're a woman, and I could use a woman's unbiased perspective."

She laughed. "I'm glad you noticed I'm a woman."

"Oh, I noticed, and a damn good looking one."

Her heartbeat quickened. "Don't rush her. Women don't like to be rushed, especially when it's something real important. It may be something difficult for her to tell her son. Trust me, Sergeant, take your time and be especially patient."

He scratched his chin. "Patient is something I'm trying hard to be. I'll take your advice. Thanks."

Jessica and Sarge were waiting when they arrived at the hospital. Laurie waved to them. Jessica waved back and said goodbye to her date. He waited to greet them.

"Hey, Brad, how are you?"

She was much different from when he first visited her. She had a huge smile, was dressed nicely, and walked like a woman in love. When they were close, Sarge bolted away from her and ran to him. He kneeled down, rubbed Sarge's head and massaged her ears.

"It's good to see you, Sarge. I see you've been taking care of my corporal." He gave Sarge a kiss on her nose and let her lick his face.

"Would you like me to do that too, Brad?" Jessica said.

He stood and gave her Sarge's leash. "No, but you can give me a big hug. Aw shit, you can kiss me too, but no licking."

Unlike when he first arrived at Laurie's house, she wrapped her arm around him, kissed him on the lips, and couldn't resist licking his cheek.

"Damn, Jess, I said no licking."

"Oh bullshit, you know you liked it, Gunny."

Lieutenant Robinson watched and was pleased to see their antics. "Okay you two lovers, let's get some lunch. Fast food okay with you, Sergeant?"

"Yes, as long as I can get a greasy bacon cheeseburger."

"Don't worry, Brad, because I'm having one too and so will Laurie."

The lieutenant drove to a fast food restaurant, ordered three bacon cheeseburgers, fries, and a plain burger for Sarge, paid, and then drove home.

Jessica told him all about her physical therapy and counseling sessions. Then she rambled on about the guy she had coffee with.

"Jessica has a boyfriend, Jessica has a boyfriend," he sang.

She punched him on the arm. "Stop it, you're embarrassing me."

They all laughed. Lieutenant Robinson was happy, yet sad that she couldn't enjoy the camaraderie with him the way Jessica could.

"You guys have fun. I have to start getting ready for my four o'clock shift." She cleared the table, put the trash in the garbage can, and went to her bedroom.

"You guys okay, Brad?"

"Sure, I'm glad you're happy, Jess."

The lieutenant came from her bedroom dressed in uniform. He smiled when he saw her.

"Sergeant, it was good to see you again. I have to leave now. I'm on day shift for the next two weeks, so I guess this is goodbye." She reached out to shake his hand. "Remember be patient with your mother."

"Yes, ma'am, I will." He shook her hand and gave her a salute. She shook her head and walked away.

"What are you waiting for, stupid? Don't let her just leave."

"What can I do, Jess? You know the rules."

"The hell with the rules. At least say a proper goodbye, you fool."

He chased after the lieutenant and caught up to her before she got in her car. "Lieutenant, wait!"

She turned. "What is it? Did you forget something?"

"I'll be back for you!"

She turned and left.

He watched her drive away and said, "I love you, Laurie," but she couldn't hear him.

Thirty minutes later, he told Jessica he had to leave.

"Will you be back next week, even though Laurie won't be here?"

"Yes, but I'll come on Thursday. It will be my last until after I'm settled at Parris Island. How about I come early and we go out to lunch"

"Why, Gunny, are you asking me to go on a date with you?" She lifted the corners of her mouth. "You hear that, Sarge? This handsome marine wants to date me." Sarge barked.

"Jess, it's just lunch."

She knew she was making him nervous and put her hand on his cheek. "I'll go on a date with you but with one condition."

He brushed her hand away. "What the hell, Jess, it's just lunch. Okay, what's your condition?"

She laughed. "You have to take me to a restaurant not a fast food joint."

"Okay, but you have to pick the restaurant, and you have to wear a dress. If I'm going on a date with you, you have to look nice and it has to be somewhere special."

Now it was her turn to be nervous. "Um, okay, I can handle that. I think. What time Thursday?"

"Say around eleven thirty to avoid the lunch crowd. What about Sarge?"

"Sarge, are you okay with me going on a date with him by myself?" Sarge sat on her hind legs, barked, and raised her paw. Jessica bent down, held it and let Sarge kiss her. "She says it's okay to date you, Gunny."

"You're something else, Corporal."

"I am, and you can hug me if you want to." Before he could respond, she wrapped her arm around him and kissed him hard on the mouth. "See you next week, handsome."

CHAPTER 34

Blocker's Bluff

Mr. Johnson arrived Wednesday afternoon and parked behind Harding's car. He stowed his bags in his room and joined Miss Lottie and Harding in the kitchen for supper. Later, the two men sat on the porch relaxing with sweet tea and pecan pie enjoying the last remnants of a sunset. He knew that Mr. Johnson was a retired army officer and wondered if he could offer any advice regarding his situation with Lieutenant Robinson.

"Mr. Johnson, you were an officer in the army, do you mind if I ask you a technical question?"

"I was, and my last assignment was with the Judge Advocate General's Corps, so I guess I'm qualified to answer most technical questions. What would you like to know?"

"It's rather delicate so I'll be direct. Can an officer and an enlisted man have a relationship if they're in different branches and the enlisted man is getting out in six months?"

Mr. Johnson rubbed his jaw. "The army and the air force have relaxed things a little. It might be permissible if they're not in the same branch or unit, and as long as it wouldn't compromise the mission or the chain of command. It's a fine line. However, the navy and marines strictly forbid it, regardless if they're in different branches. My guess is that's not what you wanted to hear."

"No sir, it's not.

"I'm sorry it's not the answer you hoped for. The enlisted man could reenlist and then they would be back in the same situation. Even if he enlisted in a different branch, it would be contrary to regulations for the navy officer. There's no way to get around the regulations. My suggestion would be for both to wait until the enlisted man is out of the service and positive that he doesn't plan on reenlisting, but, like I said, he could change his mind at a later date. Believe me, I speak from experience."

"How so, sir?"

"My wife and I had a similar situation. I was an officer and she was an enlisted woman."

"What did you do?"

"She took a discharge from the army and we married. A year later she gave me a beautiful baby girl. It wasn't long before she gave me two more. You wouldn't believe what it was like being outnumbered by three women and their commanding officer was their mother." He laughed. "My rank meant absolutely nothing to them, but I wouldn't trade those memories for anything, and their mother never regretted giving up a potential career for me."

"That's amazing, Mr. Johnson."

"It certainly is. If you want my advice, I suggest the enlisted man wait until he's completely out of the service. If what he feels for this officer is real, he should do the right thing and wait. Although he should be sure the officer feels the same way too."

"Thanks, I'm going to follow your advice." He knew that he was in love with her, but didn't really know how she felt. If it was real, in six months they'd both know for certain.

"I believe you've made the right decision."

"Thanks, Mr. Johnson." It wasn't the decision his heart wanted, but he had no other choice. He sat back in the rocker, sipped his sweet tea, and ate his pie.

Mr. Johnson stood up. "I'm turning in. I have an early drive in the morning to Charlotte. I can't wait to see my darling bride." He put a hand on Bradley's shoulder. "I hope things work out for you. Goodnight."

"Thank you, sir, I hope they do too. Goodnight. In case I don't see you in the morning, have a safe trip."

"Thank you." He went into the house to say goodnight to Miss Lottie.

"What time would you like breakfast, Mr. Johnson?"

"Could you just leave me a snack on the table? I don't want you to fuss because I'm leaving around seven."

"It's no bother. I'm up at six anyway. I'll fix you something so you can eat it at the table or take it with you."

"You're too kind to me, Miss Lottie. Any chance I could package you up and take you home with me?"

"And what would Mrs. Johnson say?

"Oh, she'd love your company." He stepped forward and kissed her on the cheek.

"Mr. Johnson, what's got into you?"

The corners of his mouth lifted. "You know Miss Lottie, all the years I've been coming here you've been so kind to me, and I just felt like giving you something special in return. Forgive me if I was inappropriate."

She smiled and took his hand. "Your apology's not necessary. You've been a wonderful guest, and I enjoy having you. Tell your wife I said you're a sweet gentleman."

"Goodnight, Miss Lottie."

"Goodnight, Mr. Johnson."

Harding got up and went into the house. "Goodnight, Miss Lottie, I'm going to turn in. I'll see you in the morning."

"Goodnight, Bradley, sleep well."

He went to his room, got into bed, grabbed his camera and thumbed through the pictures of him and Laurie until he fell asleep.

Miss Lottie finished in the kitchen and retired to her bedroom. She took the pictures from her dresser drawer and looked at them. Then she picked up the envelope that Travis Waverly had given to her.

"What do I do now, Travis?"

CHAPTER 35

During the night, he had difficulty sleeping. Mr. Johnson's advice—although accurate—left him uncomfortable. And questions still remained about the divorce. He needed to know who the other person was and why she chose him over her children. Yes, there would have been fallout but eventually he would have forgiven her—at least he felt he would have.

Mr. Johnson was up early and walked quietly down the hall so as not to wake Bradley. He set his things by the front door and went into the kitchen. Miss Lottie was fixing his breakfast.

"Good morning, Miss Lottie. I hope you didn't get up this early just for me."

She closed the refrigerator door and turned toward him. "Good morning to you. I'm always up this early when I have guests. I like to catch the sunrise. You can still see it from the backdoor."

"I'll take a look if you don't mind."

"Go right ahead. I've got everything ready for you. You can sit and eat or grab a cup of coffee and take it with you."

He walked into the pantry, opened the back door, and gazed up at the sky. A bright golden sun and a yellow sky greeted him. It brightened his spirits since it meant good weather for his long drive.

"You're right, Miss Lottie. It's absolutely beautiful and the color of that sky means I'll have nice weather for my trip." He checked his watch. "It seems I'm a little ahead of schedule so if you don't mind, I'll sit and have a cup of coffee with you. I'll eat too since you've gone to all the trouble. No sense trying to drive and eat too."

She poured them both a cup of coffee, set them on the table, and handed him a plate of eggs over easy, bacon and grits.

"It wasn't no trouble at all. There's biscuits in that basket. You relax and enjoy, I'll keep you company."

He finished his coffee, put his dishes in the sink and checked his watch again. "It's time I got on my way. You sure I can't wrap you up and take you with me?" Then he winked at her.

"If I said yes, what would I do about the young man?"

"Oh well, can I at least give you a hug?"

She scowled at him. "I'll let you if you promise not to kiss me like last night."

His eyebrows went up as he grinned. "I promise not to." He put his arms around her. Then she surprised him by kissing him on the cheek.

"Now we're even, Mr. Johnson." She winked at him.

"You're a devil, Miss Lottie. I'll see you next time."

"Drive carefully."

When he heard Mr. Johnson's car, he checked the time, saw it was still early, so he tried to get more sleep. He tossed and turned yet sleep wouldn't come so he reached for his camera and thumbed through the pictures of him and the lieutenant. He thought about Jessica and how she had made a lot of progress in such a short time. Like him she was adjusting to a new relationship with her mother. Hers had to do with her handicap, his with the truth about the divorce. His mood lightened when he came to the picture of him strumming an air guitar, and decided today he would ask Miss Lottie what she knew about the divorce. Hopefully she could shed some light on what really happened. He got out of bed, showered, dressed, and went down for breakfast. The aroma of fresh brewed coffee and bacon frying lightened his spirits. He poured himself a cup of coffee.

"Good morning. I guess Mr. Johnson left early."

She removed several strips of bacon from the frying pan and set them on a paper towel. "Good morning to you. Yes, he did. Sit down, and I'll fix your plate."

He sat and sipped his coffee. She fixed a big plate of eggs sunny side up, bacon, and hash browns, set the plate in front of him and removed the towel covering the basket of biscuits.

"Eat up. I'll make more if you want."

His eyes sparkled. "This is a lot to eat. It'll probably be enough. Would you sit with me?"

Her mouth widened. "Yes, let me get a cup of coffee. I already had my breakfast." She poured a cup of coffee and sat down across from him. "Did you sleep well last night?"

"Yes, thank you." Not really, but he didn't want to concern her.

"I wondered if maybe Mr. Johnson's comments may have bothered you." He looked down to avoid her eyes. "I overheard some of the conversation."

He reached for a biscuit. "A little, but he gave me good advice. Thanks for asking."

She reached across the table and put her hand over his. "Bradley, women are a complicated bunch and it takes a lot of patience with them. We're not all perfect and we make mistakes." He gazed into her eyes for her meaning. "Lord knows I've made my share of them." She rubbed the back of his hand. "You just returned from the war and you have a lot to understand, especially with your mother." She squeezed his hand. "Be patient. Everything will turn out okay. Trust this old woman."

He knew she was right and it had only been a few weeks since he left Afghanistan and a lot had happened since. "You're not an old woman, Miss Lottie. You're still as young looking to me as when my grandfather brought me to visit." Her eyes twinkled and she gently slapped his hand. "But you're right. I do need to put things in perspective." He thought of his mother—mothers always know best and so do grandmothers.

"I'm glad you understand. Now, you sure you don't want more? It won't take long to make more eggs and bacon."

"No, thank you, I've had enough. Is it okay to call you Grandma now?"

She rubbed his hand. "Yes, it's okay."

He smiled. "Thanks, Grandma. I'm gonna have another cup of coffee and sit on the porch."

"I'll join you after I finish cleaning up."

He left and went out onto the porch. While he sat by himself, he thought about when he would ask Miss Lottie what she knew about the divorce—maybe after lunch might be a good time to ask.

Miss Lottie finished cleaning up in the kitchen and joined him. He looked as though he was deep in thought or feeling sad.

"You okay, Bradley? You look like you lost your best friend."

He did lose his best friend but that was over a year ago, and now this thing with his mother was bothering him.

"I'm really not comfortable with my mother's explanation about the divorce. I think there's more to it than just an affair." Miss Lottie stiffened, worried he might want to know more—if so—it wasn't her place to tell him. "I'm going to talk to her tonight after supper when I know she'll be home."

She leaned back in her rocker. "Do you think that's the right thing to do? You just got together this weekend."

"Yes, it is. My leave is up soon, and I need to know before I make a decision about my future."

She remembered the letter and stood up. "Then there's something I must give you. I'll be right back." She went into the house, retrieved the envelope Travis Waverly gave her and sat on her bed.

"Dear Lord, Travis. Am I doing the right thing? You said one day I would have to give this to him, well the time has come."

She went back out to the porch and handed him the envelope. "Your granddaddy gave this to me and said I should give it to you when the time was right. I don't know what's in it, and I hope I'm doing the right thing." She sat down and watched as he opened the envelope.

He took the letter out and read it to himself.

Dear Brad,

By the time you read this you will be a man. I hope not an old man, but I hope you have the wisdom to understand what you read in this letter. Forgive me for not being eloquent when it comes to writing, but I'll do my best to tell you the truth.

There is something you need to know about your mother. She's not like other women, and her difference is something most people don't tolerate. I knew from the time she was a teenager that she was different, and I turned the other way. She's my daughter and I love her no matter what others may think.

It was this difference that caused the divorce from your father. She had to protect her children and another's, so she gave in to your father's demands and agreed to never have contact with you. It broke both our hearts; mine especially, because it meant I would never see you again.

Whatever you were told, your mother loved you and your sister and if it were possible she would have fought for her right to see you. She may be reluctant to tell you the truth, but since you now know, please find it in your heart to forgive her and love her as she loves you. If I could do it then so can you.

If you need someone to talk to about this, so you can understand, talk to Miss Lottie. She knows the whole truth.

Love, Grandpa

He turned toward her. "I don't understand what he means by my mother was different. Can you explain it to me?"

"No, I can't. That's up to your mother. But whatever she tells you, you have to forgive her. She's not perfect, but she's still your mother. And if you really love her, you'll find it in your heart to forgive her. Just like your granddaddy did."

He put the letter back in the envelope and leaned back in the rocker. "Would you mind if I sat by myself? I need to be alone with my thoughts."

"Of course, I'll go inside, and you call me when it's okay to join you. I'll bring us sweet tea and oatmeal raisin cookies." She got up and went inside.

He rocked back and forth and wondered what it was his grandfather was telling him about his mother being different?

While he contemplated what was in the letter, Miss Lottie made a telephone call.

CHAPTER 36

John Porter was at home getting ready to go out on his boat and do a little fishing when the telephone rang. "John Porter, here, how can I help you?"

Miss Lottie hesitated—unsure if she was doing the right thing— but Porter was once Travis' best friend.

"Hello, is anyone there?"

"John Porter, it's Miss Lottie. I need your help."

"Good morning, Miss Baxter, how can I help you?"

He waited for her reply but there was just a dead silence.

"Does it have something to do with Travis' grandson?"

She was surprised. "You know who he is, John Porter? How?"

"I could tell by the way you protected him from Molly. What can I do to help?"

She recalled how Travis helped Porter. "John Porter, I need you to talk with him. It's really important."

"Sure, is it about Judy?"

"Yes."

"I was fixin to do some fishing today. Why don't I see if he'll go with me, and maybe we can talk? How does that sound?"

"Seems to me that's what Travis did with you. You're a good man, John Porter."

"Thanks, I'll be right there."

Porter and Miss Mollie drove over to Baxter House. Bradley was still alone on the porch. Porter stepped up onto the porch and extended a hand.

"Name's John Porter. What's your name?"

He stood and shook hands. "I'm Brad Harding, nice to meet you, Mr. Porter. I remember you were the chief of police when I was a kid. What's your dog's name?"

"That was a long time ago. Her name's Miss Mollie and Mr. Porter was my father. Call me John, or just Porter. Mind if I join you?"

"Sure, have a seat. Miss Baxter may join us." Since Porter called her Miss Baxter, he decided it was best that he did.

Porter sat down and leaned back in the rocker. Miss Mollie sauntered over to Bradley, sat down, and extended her paw. He bent down, shook her hand, leaned down and let her lick his face.

"Looks like she's taken a liking to you, Brad." Miss Mollie barked once. "Yep, she's taken a liking to you all right." Miss Mollie lay down by Bradley and rolled over on her back. He rubbed her belly. "I'm a pretty good judge of character and I'm bettin somethings' bothering you. Care to talk about it?"

"Not really."

"You know your grandfather was a good friend of mine."

"Really? You knew my grandfather?"

"Yes, sir, we used to fish together. Say, I'm goin fishing maybe you'd like to join me and Miss Mollie?"

"If it wouldn't be too much trouble, I'd like to." Fishing may just be what he needed right now." It's been a long time."

"I imagine so. Were you deployed, Brad?" Porter also knew that's the name Travis said the kid liked to be called.

"Yes, sir, both Iraq and Afghanistan. I just finished a tour in Afghanistan."

"How long you been in?"

"Since 2003."

"Wow, guess you're going to retire one day."

"No, sir, my enlistment's up in six months, and I'm getting out."

"Had enough, I guess. Don't blame you. You ready to do some fishing?"

"Yes, sir, should I change into something different?"

"You're fine, but you may want to bring a hat. If you don't have one, I've got extras on the boat."

"I'll have to borrow one of yours. Let me tell Miss Baxter I'm going fishing."

She stood in the doorway listening to their conversation and stepped out onto the porch. "Morning, John Porter. Bradley, I overheard you say you were going fishing with him. You go and enjoy yourself. John Porter, you want me to fix something for lunch for you two?"

"A couple of sandwiches would be nice, Miss Baxter."

"Be right back with them." She went into the kitchen, fixed two sandwiches, some homemade pickles, some oatmeal cookies, wrapped them in a brown paper bag, and brought them out to the porch. "Here you are. Have a good time and catch a plenty."

"Thanks, Miss Baxter," said Porter.

At the dock they climbed on board his boat. Miss Mollie leaped aboard also. Porter put the sandwiches in the cooler with the six pack of beer and headed out to sea. A mile from shore, he dropped anchor and handed Bradley a fishing rod.

"Bait's in the bucket. I'm sure you know how to bait a hook."

"I sure do. My grandfather taught me." He reached into the bucket grabbed a mud minnow and put it on the hook. Then he cast the line over the port side and set the rod in a rod holder. Porter baited his line and cast it on the starboard side.

"Caught me a big 'un here last week." Porter reached into the cooler for two Buds. "It's five o'clock somewhere, so you might as well relax and enjoy yourself." He handed him a Bud.

"Thanks, Porter, don't mind if I do."

"Hold on, let me get that hat for you." He reached under the seat, pulled out a weathered baseball cap and gave it to him. "Pay no mind to the look of that old hat it was once lucky for me." Brad laughed and put the hat on. They sat back, relaxed, and enjoyed their Buds.

"So, Brad, how did it go with your mother? I saw you coming from her house Sunday."

"You know my mother too, Porter?"

"I sure do. I've known Miss Judy since before she got married and after she came back home because of her divorce. She's been through a lot."

He wondered if Porter knew more about the divorce than he did.

"It broke your grandfather's heart. You used to visit him in the summers, didn't you?"

Bradley took a swig of his beer. "Yes, I did, but not after the divorce."

Porter tipped his beer to his mouth. "Yeah, that's what broke his heart."

"You know anything about the divorce, Porter?"

"I know some, but you should ask your mother about it."

"I already have, but I think she didn't tell me everything. I'm going talk to her tonight and get all the facts from her."

Porter knew the real reason for the divorce because Travis confided in him about what really caused it.

"You know what, Brad? I'm not the best person to offer advice." Miss Mollie barked. "But there's one thing I know about women." Miss Mollie barked twice. "Okay, maybe I think I know." Miss Mollie barked once. "Women are a complicated species and they're not perfect, although we think they are." Again, Miss Mollie barked.

"Look, your grandfather once gave me some advice. He knew my father well, and when I came home from Nam, I had anger issues. My best friend and I served together." Porter looked out to sea and raised his pole. "He was killed during the last stages of the war and it made me madder than hell."

He took a swig of beer. "I named my first dog, Old George, in honor of him. And back then, my wife Molly, who at the time I thought would marry me but turned me down, only made me angrier."

"What did you do?"

"Your grandfather took me fishing, and we had a long talk. He made me understand that life wasn't meant to be easy and nobody was perfect. He said give it time and things would get better."

"Did they get better?"

"It took some time, actually quite some time, but now Molly's my wife, and I'm a lucky man." Miss Mollie barked. "Oh, and I also have Miss Mollie. She reminds me every day of how long I had to be patient until Molly finally agreed to marry me. When you talk to your mother, be patient and whatever you do, be supportive. You may not like what you hear, but she's your mother, and she deserves your understanding."

"Thanks, but what if it was something awful and she doesn't want to tell me?"

Porter took a swig of beer. "Whatever it is be calm about it. Tell her you can handle anything. You've been through the hell of war, so it can't be anything worse." He gave it further consideration. "Unless she committed murder."

Miss Mollie barked twice. "Better yet, say, unless she had an affair with a Martian and you have a brother or sister somewhere in outer space." Bradley laughed. "Hopefully your mother will laugh too."

"You really think that would work?"

"Hey, you're talking to someone who's married to a complicated woman. Maybe it will or maybe it won't. I'm no expert." Miss Mollie barked. "You got a better plan?"

Bradley took a swig of his beer. "No, I don't, so I guess I'll go with yours." Miss Mollie barked again. "Why does she keep barking?"

Porter laughed. "That's her way of expressing approval or disapproval. One bark means approval and you can guess what two means." Bradley's line went taut. "You got a fish on your line, Brad." He got up and grabbed his pole. "Easy now, don't get anxious and let it get away. Work with it and reel it in easy like."

It was the same advice his grandfather gave him the first time they went fishing. He gradually reeled the line in making sure the hook was set. The fish came up out of the water and he let it take some line and then reeled it in farther. It took him fifteen minutes to wear the fish down and bring it alongside the boat. Porter held the net, captured the fish and brought it on board. It was a nine pound sea trout.

He rubbed his shoulder. "Whew, damn that was some fun. Ain't enjoyed myself like that in a long time."

"Nice catch, Brad. You want to keep it or toss it back?"

He decided just like that first fish he caught, he would let the fish live to fight another day. "Toss it back. After that fight it deserves another chance."

"You caught it, so you have to unhook it." Porter handed him a pair of pliers.

He took the pliers, unhooked the fish, removed it from the net, and lowered it over the side. "I gotta say that was a hell of a lot of fun. Thanks, Porter, for everything. Is this why you brought me fishing? The same reason my grandfather did for you?"

Porter put an arm around him. "You're learning, Brad. Yes, it is."

"Well it worked." Porter's line went taut. "Hey, you got one too."

Porter grabbed his rod and carefully played with the fish until it tired and then brought it alongside. Bradley caught it in the net and brought it on board.

"You keeping it, Porter?"

"Not today. It deserves a second chance just like your mother does." Miss Mollie barked.

"Okay, I get it, Porter. Miss Mollie sure has a way of speaking her mind."

"One thing else, be sure you say you love her over and over. Women need reassurance and saying you love her is your way of reassuring her." Miss Mollie barked. "See even Miss Mollie agrees. It's time for another beer." He handed one to Bradley and opened one for himself. "We'll eat the oatmeal cookies after our beers so Miss Baxter won't know we was drinking." Brad laughed and Miss Mollie barked once.

After they finished their sandwiches and another Bud, Porter brought the anchor up and they headed back to the mainland. He moored the boat and then drove Bradley back to Baxter House.

"Remember, Brad, patience and understanding. And it's all about forgiveness."

"Thanks, Porter, I understand. Take care, Miss Mollie." She barked. He walked up onto the porch.

Porter waved to Miss Baxter, turned around, and drove home. He called Molly to let her know he was back from fishing and on his way home.

"How did it go? Did you enjoy yourself?"

"Yes, I did. I had Judy's son with me. We had a long talk and I think it helped him. I'll tell you when you get home."

"Was it like when Travis Waverly took you fishing?"

"Yes, it was. Damn woman, you got some memory."

"That's why they call me Chief and not you."

"That wasn't fair, Molly."

"I'll make it up to you when I get home." They both laughed.

Miss Lottie waited until he sat down before asking him about his fishing experience. "Would you like a glass of lemonade?"

He wanted everyone to address him as Brad, except for Miss Lottie. Somehow it felt right.

"Do you mind?"

"Absolutely not. Relax, I'll be right back." She went into the house and came back with two glasses of lemonade. "How was your fishin experience?" She took a sip of her drink.

He took a big gulp of his. "It was great, Grandma. We both caught a fish and those sandwiches were great." *Careful Brad, don't mention the beers.* "Was it your idea for Porter to take me fishing?"

She had a sly expression on her face. "It was John Porter's idea. I just asked him for help. You seemed upset about your mother and needed a distraction. I hope it worked."

He reached over and put his hand on her arm. "It did. Porter said Grandpa did the same with him. Did you know about that?"

"Yes, I did. What are you going to do about tonight?"

"I'm still going to talk with my mom, but whatever she tells me, I won't judge her. I love her, and I'm not about to lose her again."

Miss Lottie placed her hand on his. "Your granddaddy would be proud of you, Bradley. And I'm proud of you too."

But she worried if he could handle the truth about his mother.

CHAPTER 37

After supper, he helped Miss Lottie clean the table and put the dishes in the sink. He had a call to make, and his nerves were uneasy—like just before a mission. He excused himself, left the kitchen, and dialed her number.

She didn't recognize his number on her caller ID but answered anyway. "Hello, this is Judy Waverly. Can I help you?"

He hesitated and considered hanging up, but he wanted answers—more than what she had given him. "Mom, it's Brad. Can I come over? I'd like to talk with you."

Her legs weakened and she had to sit down to compose herself. "You can come on over now if you want." She became concerned that he probably wanted the complete truth about the divorce.

"I'll be right there." He hung up and his heart started pounding and so was hers. "I'm going to visit my mother now."

She stopped putting pots away. "Remember, Bradley, patience and understanding. Don't forget that she's your mother and she isn't perfect like your granddaddy said."

"I understand, and I'll be patient." He hoped he would. "I'll see you later."

Because he didn't want to walk back in the dark, he drove to her house and rang the bell.

"Evening, Brad, I made a fresh pot of coffee." She stepped aside and let him enter. "We can sit in the living room and talk." She led him to the sofa and then went into the kitchen and returned with two cups of coffee and some cinnamon buns.

"Thanks, Mom, I guess you know I like these too."

"Your grandfather also liked them." She had prepared herself—expecting he would unload on her like his father did.

A long silence followed as he measured his words and thoughts. He felt that he could do this—it wasn't like going into battle—and besides she was his mother.

"Mom, who was the man that you gave up your family for?"

Judy's complexion whitened. She knew this day would come—but had hoped it would be much later. She wasn't sure if he would understand if she told him the real truth—and worried he might be like his father.

"Mom, did you hear me? Who was the man?"

He wondered if the man was a neighbor, a parent at his school, one of his teachers, someone she worked with or maybe a client. He had all these questions, but did he really want to know? After all these years, would it make a difference or make matters worse?

Judy had her own concerns. She didn't know if she could do this, and worried that he might reject her and lose him forever. If only her father was there, he'd know what she should do.

He didn't understand why she wouldn't answer—and didn't really believe that she had an affair with their gardener—certainly not his mother—but was she really taking tennis lessons twice a week at the country club?

The silence between them was grueling. Like when a hunter awaits the doe to come within range of his arrow.

She bit her lip. "It—"

Please don't say it was my youth league lacrosse coach.

CHAPTER 38

Judy felt like her world was about to collapse, and she'd be left stranded with nowhere to go—but she had to get it out of her system.

"It wasn't—"She took a deep breath.

He waited wondering what she did those summers he was visiting his grandfather—and hoped it wasn't the tennis pro at the country club

She struggled to get the words but knew she had to.

"It wasn't a man, Brad, it was a woman," finally she got it out of her system. His head snapped back. At last the truth was out—now she waited to see if he was like his father.

More silence and what seemed like an eternity, was really only seconds.

His eyebrows hiked. "Oh, I wasn't expecting that." There went Porter's Martian plan.

She rubbed her legs. "She was married and had a family, too. Your father would have made our affair public and two families would have been destroyed. I couldn't let him do that so I did what I had to, to protect both our families."

She stared off into space and rubbed the back of her hand across her eye. He kept his silence letting her continue. "You may not think I made the right choice, but it was mine to make, and I believe I made the right one." Of that she was certain.

"Your father left me no alternative. Either way, I was losing you and EmilyKate. He had the money and the lawyers to prove I was an unfit mother. If I went quietly, at least there wouldn't be a scandal to follow you around." Had her ex given her a choice, she would have named him Travis and her daughter, Juliette, after her mother—instead of EmilyKate, after his grandmother.

He shook his head, looked down at first and then looked her in the eyes. His father also left him no choice when he chose to enlist in the marines. Growing up in his household was like having no family at all. Birthdays and holidays were celebrated with house staff, and cards were selected by his father's secretary. He rubbed his neck. He had his mother back and Miss Lottie—and didn't want to throw it all away because of her indiscretion decades ago.

His silence was tearing at her insides. "Are you angry with me?" She expected him to get up and walk out on her.

He thought about fishing with Porter, and his words that it was all about second chances and forgiveness. "No, Mom, I'm not. I love you. You made a conscious decision and you were loyal to your friend. Like I said, I love you and it's not my place to judge you. I've made mistakes of my own, and neither of us is perfect." He leaned over and wiped her tears.

"Thank you, Brad. I truly love you too. I was so afraid you would be disgusted with me and never want to see me again."

"I would never do that. I just got you back in my life, why would I want to lose you again? Besides, Grandpa would be disappointed in me."

"Right now, I'm sure he's very proud of you."

He reached into his pocket and pulled out the letter. "He wrote me a letter. Miss Lottie gave it to me. Did you know about the letter?"

"No, I didn't. But I'm not surprised. Dad told her almost everything."

"Would you like to read it?"

"Since your grandfather wrote it to you, I believe it was meant for your eyes only."

He handed her the letter. "I'd like you to read it."

As she read the letter, she sobbed uncontrollably. He got up and wrapped his arms around her. For both, decades of heartache from being apart boiled over in tears.

"I love you, Mom."

"I love you too."

She told him about her life with his grandfather after the divorce. He told her about playing lacrosse in high school and in college. He also told her about the argument with his father and his grandfather about enlisting in the marines.

"Your father and grandfather are stuck in their ways."

Both said to themselves, *son of bitches is what they are.*

"Have you talked to him since?"

"No, he made it clear I wasn't welcome in his house anymore and that was fine with me."

"You should at least write him. He is still your father."

"Legally and biologically but absolutely not in my heart. I'd rather not talk about him. You're all that matters to me."

"What about your sister?"

"I have no idea where she lives. She agreed with them and like you, I lost her."

She decided it was best to let the past stay in the past for now and let the matter rest. She had her son, and her ex could go to hell for all she cared.

"Mom, I best get back now. Miss Lottie will be worried."

"Do me a favor and tell Miss Lottie thank you so very much. She'll understand why."

He hugged her again and kissed her. She stood in the doorway and watched as he drove off and then went back in the house with a smile and a tear.

When he returned to Baxter House, he ran up onto the porch, into the house, and to the kitchen. Miss Lottie was enjoying a glass of tea and cookies.

"So, how was your visit with your mother?"

He poured some tea and sat down with her. "It went great. I followed your advice and Porter's, too. She said to tell you thank you so very much, and you would understand."

"Your mother is a sweet lady and a wonderful person."

"I know that now. Did you know about the real reason for the divorce?"

She put her hand over his. "Yes, your granddaddy told me. You're not angry with her are you? Or disappointed?"

"No, absolutely not, she's my mother and like you said, mothers aren't perfect. Neither am I. I have two wonderful women in my life now, and I love them both." He thought about Lieutenant Robinson and hoped one day he would have three.

"Good, your granddaddy would be proud of you."

They talked for a while and then retired for the night.

Friday evening he and Miss Lottie picked up Judy and drove to Thomas' ball game and joined Lottie in the bleachers. He sat next to Lottie and Judy sat with Miss Lottie. Just like last week, Miss Lottie harassed the umpire. Thomas hit a home run and they stood up, clapped, and yelled,

"Way to go, Thomas!"

After the game, they all went out for pizza. Lottie took Thomas home and Bradley drove his ladies home. He walked his mother to the door.

"Goodnight, Brad, I had a really good time. Thanks for inviting me."

"You're welcome. Would you like to do it again next Friday? It's my last time before I leave for Parris Island."

"Yes, I'd love to. I hope you'll come and visit me before you leave."

"I will and when I'm settled, I'll visit you on weekends. I have to rent a car, though."

"You can take your grandfather's truck. I'm sure he would want you to. I have my own car so it'll just sit in the garage otherwise."

"I may take you up on your offer. Goodnight, Mom. I love you."

"Goodnight, Brad. I love you too." He hugged and kissed her and got back in the car.

"You satisfied, Bradley?"

"Yes, and I owe it all to you."

She patted his leg and then he drove them home and sat in the kitchen, had a glass of sweet tea, and then later both went to their bedrooms.

Miss Lottie sat on her bed and glanced up at the ceiling. "You were right, Travis, and you would be proud of them both."

CHAPTER 39

Thursday morning, he left for Beaufort and his lunch date with Jessica. Laurie was at work, so he pulled all the way into the driveway, walked up to the front door and rang the bell. Jessica opened the door and was dressed in a bright yellow and white knee length skirt with an elastic waistband. She wore a white pull over blouse with elbow length sleeves. Her hair was cut short and she also had a warm grin on her face.

"Hi, Brad, how have you been?"

"Damn, Corporal, you look great!"

Her eyes opened wide. "Do you like the way I look? Laurie took me shopping and helped me select my outfit."

"Like it? Hell you're smoking hot and you have great legs too."

She turned five shades of pink. "Really, I am?"

"Yes, Corporal, you are."

"Stop calling me corporal. You know my name." They both laughed. "I dressed myself this morning, except for my bra. Still haven't figured that out yet." She chuckled. "I considered about going without one. You think I should have?"

"That would be a little too much, Jess. Where did you get this sense of humor all of a sudden?"

"Counseling is working. I thought losing my arm was the end of the world, but I could have lost more—like some of the other platoon members did. I'm lucky in a lot of ways. I got a second chance so why not try and be happy and laugh some?"

"Wow, what a big difference from the first time I saw you three weeks ago."

"I told my counselor about our date and he said not to be concerned about gawkers because there'll be some. Some people will look at my arm, but I should remember that I'm a combat veteran, a beautiful woman, and to ignore them. Some will be curious, some will be concerned, and, yes, some will be inconsiderate, but I should ignore them all."

"He sounds like he knows what he's talking about. You'll have to put me in the gawker category because I can't take my eyes off you." She smiled. "Come on let's go to lunch. Where am I taking you?"

"The Beaufort Classic Dining Room. It's not too fancy, and it's sort of casual. I figured if you're taking me to lunch, Gunny, I might as well make it a little fancy. I hope you have plenty of money."

He grinned. "If I don't, I can always wash dishes. What about Sarge?"

"Pets aren't allowed so she's staying home. She doesn't mind, but I have to bring her a doggy bag."

"We'll both bring her one. Let's go, so we can beat the lunch hour crowd."

"Don't worry, we have reservations. And you have to take my right arm as we enter the restaurant because you're my date. You're getting away easy, Gunny."

"It's Brad, and you really are funny."

He took her by the arm, escorted her to his car and drove to the restaurant. It was in a trendy part of the city and expensive looking cars were parked in front—it was definitely an upscale establishment.

"This looks awfully fancy, Jess. Are you sure it's casual?"

"Trust me, I asked when I made the reservation. Don't be a wuss."

He laughed, grabbed her by the arm and escorted her into the restaurant. She gave her name to the hostess, they were seated, and the hostess gave them menus. As expected several patrons gawked at her missing arm, but she ignored them.

"What should we order, Jess? Anything in particular interest you?"

She glanced over the menu. "I'm getting filet mignon but no appetizer. Then I'm ordering the most expensive dessert that they have."

He checked the price and covered his heart with his hand. "I may have to wash dishes, Jess." Then he laughed. "What the heck, I'll have the same thing."

"Told you I was going big time."

Their waitress came over and they ordered their steaks—both medium rare. For dessert she ordered a double hot fudge brownie with two scoops of vanilla ice cream. He ordered the same.

When the waitress set their plates in front of them, she looked skeptically at Jessica's.

Jessica looked down at hers and frowned. "I think I made a mistake. I should have ordered the meatloaf."

It didn't occur to either of them that she couldn't cut her steak. He reached across the table, almost knocked over their drinks and grabbed her plate. "Nonsense, I'll cut it for you."

The waitress waited as he cut her steak into bite sized pieces and handed her plate back to her. She then turned and walked away.

"Thanks, I guess I need to learn how to do it myself if I'm going to eat steak or settle for burgers." She used her fork and took a bite. "This is really good. I haven't had steak since before I was deployed, how about you?"

He cut into his steak. "Me either and you're right it's nice and juicy." Several diners nodded approval.

"Don't forget to save some for Sarge's doggy bag."

The waitress brought their desert and set them on the table.

Jessica stuck her spoon in and put some ice cream and brownie in her mouth. "Maybe I should have ordered just this." The waitress smiled and left.

After dessert, he held her arm as they left the restaurant and drove her home. He took her arm again and escorted her to the front door.

"You coming in, Brad?"

"I can stay a while."

Sarge sauntered up to greet him. "Hey, Sarge, it's good to see you." He kneeled down and let Sarge lick his face. "I see you've been taking good care of my corporal." Sarge barked several times.

Jessica gave Sarge the contents of their doggy bag.

They sat in the living room and talked about their time in Afghanistan—but not about the ill-fated mission. The topic of their conversation was on the times when the guys in her platoon played tricks on each other, especially on him.

"Jess, mind if I use the bathroom? I've got a long ride ahead of me."

"Use Laurie's; mines not fit for a man to use. There's lots of female clutter. I'm kind of sloppy."

He laughed. "Thanks, I know where it is."

When he entered the bedroom, he glanced at the pictures on her dresser. He pulled the envelope from his pocket, put it under the picture of her in uniform and then went back to the living room.

"Jess, I think I should head out now. I had a good time. You're a great date."

"I'm not spoken for so if you ever need another date, feel free to call me."

"You're something, you really are."

She walked him to the door and grabbed him by the hand. "You're not getting away without giving me a hug, Gunny." He turned and embraced her. She surprised him by kissing him full on the mouth and winked. "Something to remember me by."

"I'll never forget you, Jess." He rubbed her cheek.

She closed the door, did a little two step, and said, "What do you say, Sarge, is he a keeper?" Sarge barked two times. "Okay, I know. His heart belongs to Laurie."

Lieutenant Robinson finished her shift at the hospital and drove home. Jessica waited to tell her about her date with Harding. She told her everything including the kiss. The lieutenant laughed.

"Sounds like you had a wonderful time, Jess. I'm happy for you. I'll go change and then I'll make supper unless you're not hungry."

"I could eat something. You go change."

She went into her bedroom, closed the door, and started to undress. When she saw the envelope, she picked it up, opened it, and read the letter.

> Dear Laurie
>
> I'm taking a chance writing this letter, and I understand that you would be taking an even greater one by reading it. I hope you'll choose to take that chance.
>
> The day you came into my life was the most wonderful thing that ever happened to me. Spending time with you I learned to smile, play, laugh—and yes to love. You chased away the horrors of war and helped me see the beauty of life. To me you are that beauty. You were the catalyst to me making contact with the mother I hadn't seen in decades.
>
> Because of you I found joy, happiness, and love with family, loved ones, and dear friends. I may have eventually taken the step on my own, but you inspired me to man-up and do the right thing.

I understand fully that it's not possible for us to be together right now, and I accept my fate. But the day will come when it will be possible, and I will come back into your life. You can choose to accept me for who I am or send me on my way to my new life. I hope you'll choose acceptance, but I'll understand if you don't.

Until then, I wish you happiness.

Love Brad

She sat on the bed and wiped her tears. "Damn him!" She finished undressing, changed into something comfortable, and joined Jessica. After dinner, they took Sarge for a short walk.

Laurie didn't mention the letter.

CHAPTER 40

Friday evening, Bradley, Miss Lottie, and Judy sat with Lottie at Thomas' ballgame. Miss Lottie wasn't as nice as she was last Friday. She harassed the umpire every chance she could. Judy laughed, but Lottie and Bradley moved several seats away.

"Lottie, you feel like a candy bar? I do."

"Sure, if it will get us away from Grandma."

"Miss Lottie, Mom, we're going to get a candy bar at the refreshment stand. Can we get you ladies anything?"

"I'm fine," they both replied.

Bradley and Lottie walked to the refreshment stand. "Lottie, can I ask you something?"

She worried it might be about her grandmother and his grandfather. "Sure, what do want to know?"

"This is my last weekend here. Would you go to the movies with me tomorrow night? We can go for ice cream after."

She hadn't been to the movies since her husband passed away. "I'll have to get a sitter for Thomas, but I would love to, Brad."

"Give me your phone, and I'll put my number in it. You call me if you get a sitter."

"Should we tell Grandma and your mom?"

He scratched his head. "No, let's keep it a secret. They might object."

"Okay, but I'm uncomfortable keeping a secret from her."

"Me too, but it's best we did." He put his number in her phone. "Okay, now we best get back." They walked back to the bleachers.

"Lottie, you missed Thomas' home run. It's the last inning, and his team's winning!" Judy exclaimed.

"Oh shoot, well he'll tell me all about it later."

After the game, Thomas told her about his home run and then they went for pizza.

Saturday afternoon, Lottie called Bradley and said she had a sitter for 7:00 but she could only sit until eleven and no later.

"That's okay, there's a seven-thirty show, so I'll come by at seven."

"Okay, I'll see you then. Wait, you need my address."

She gave him her address and he put it in his phone. Now he had to make up something to tell Miss Lottie.

"Grandma, do you mind if I go into Crofton for a movie tonight? It's my last Saturday before I go back and I would like to walk around after the movie and maybe get some ice cream."

Although she was a little suspicious, especially with the phone call he'd received, she felt it would be good for him. "You go right ahead and enjoy yourself. Tomorrow I'll invite your mother, Lottie, and Thomas for Sunday dinner. That okay with you?"

"That would be great."

He drove to Lottie's house and rang her doorbell.

Thomas answered. "Hey, Marine, you're taking my mom to the movies? Cool man."

"You don't mind?"

"Nah, she needs to get out without me and enjoy herself."

"That's real nice of you, Thomas."

"I know."

He rubbed Thomas' head. Then Lottie came and they said goodnight.

"You look pretty, Brat."

"Thanks, Bratly."

They drove into town and were just in time to get popcorn and drinks before the movie started. After the movie they walked to the ice cream parlor and shared a banana split.

A sheriff's deputy entered the shop and walked over to where they were sitting. "Hey, Lottie, it's good to see you. Who's your friend?"

Harding thought he might be implying that he didn't care for her being with a white man.

"Hey, Bobby, this is my—" She almost said cousin. "This is my friend, Bradley Harding. He's Judy Waverly's son."

The deputy's eyes lit up. "No shit, excuse me Lottie. You're Travis' grandson?"

Harding relaxed. "Yes, did you know my grandfather?"

"Did I? Man he gave me part-time work during high school. I would have gotten into trouble if it weren't for him. Damn, man, your grandfather was a hell of nice guy. What brings you here?"

"I'm staying with Miss Lottie and visiting my mother while I'm on leave from the marines."

"Marines, huh, I was army. You see any action?"

"Yeah, you?"

"Two tours in Iraq, how about you?"

"Four in Iraq and five in Afghanistan."

"Damn, man, you got some sort of death wish?"

Maybe that was why he signed for so many tours. "I never thought about it that way."

"So I guess you're going all the way?"

"No, I'm taking a discharge in six months. I'm moving to Blocker's Bluff with my mom. I've had enough."

"Don't blame you. If you need a job when you get out, I'd be happy to recommend you to the sheriff. He's always looking for good men."

"Thanks, but I've had enough with wearing a uniform. Appreciate the offer, though."

"Anything for Travis Waverly's grandson, and a friend of Lottie's." He winked at her. "See ya, Lottie."

"See ya, Bobby."

The deputy started to leave but turned and said, "Hey, marine." Harding looked up. "Hooah!"

"Oorah, army." The chime on the door tinkled as the deputy exited.

"He's a nice guy that Bobbie. He was in the same unit as my husband and was one of the lucky ones."

He covered her hand with his. "I'm sorry, Lottie."

"Don't be, I'm past that. Besides he gave me Thomas."

He noticed the damp spot beneath her eye, picked up his napkin, and wiped her cheek.

"Want to take a walk?"

She checked her watch. "Sure, we still have some time."

They strolled through town and then headed back to the car holding hands. He drove back to her house, parked, and turned the engine off. She turned in her seat and he did too. Without asking, he put his arm around her, pulled her close and kissed her.

She pushed him away. "Brad, wait, there's something you should know. We can't do this." She wanted to but knew it wasn't possible.

"Why not?"

CHAPTER 41

Lottie opened the door and started to get out. "Because we're cousins, that's why." She covered her mouth with her hand when she realized she just revealed her grandmother's secret.

"What are you talking about?"

"Ask my grandmother." She was out the door and ran to her house.

He was about to go after her but she was already inside. "What the hell was that all about?" He started the engine and hurried to Baxter House.

What does she mean we're cousins and to ask her grandmother? He got out of the car, walked up onto the porch, reached for the doorknob and hesitated. *What am I supposed to say—that Lottie implied I'm your grandson? It's not possible.*

He opened the door and ran into the kitchen. "Miss Lottie!" he shouted.

She had just hung up the phone. "Stop shouting and sit down. That was Lottie and let me explain."

"I'd rather stand."

She draped her towel over her shoulder. "I'll be right back." She went to her bedroom, retrieved the pictures and returned. "I have something to show you." She handed him the pictures. "This one is of your granddaddy and me with our daughter, Lottie's mother."

He looked at the pictures "No, I don't believe you. Grandpa would never do that."

"Well he did and we both did. I'm sorry no one ever told you. But it's in the past."

"First my mother lied and now you. Does my mother know?"

"Yes, your granddaddy told her."

He set the pictures on the table. "I'm going to my room and sleep on it and decide what I should do. Goodnight." He left the kitchen and went up to his room.

She watched him sulk off to his room like a hurt child. She sat down, held the pictures in her hand and clutched them to her heart. "We lost him again, Travis." She needed to talk to someone because she couldn't bear losing him over what happened in the past. She got up, paced the kitchen nervously, picked up the telephone and made a call.

He had a restless night trying to absorb what he just learned. At 5:00 he got up, dressed, left the house, and went for a run to clear his head. He ran into town, saw the lights on in the diner, a provisions truck just pulling away, and decided to go inside for coffee.

"Morning, you're up early. What brings you here?"

"I was out for a run, Chef, saw the lights on and thought I'd stop for coffee."

"I'll get you a cup and join you." Chef Willie poured two cups and handed him his. "Hold on, I'll get you a fresh baked muffin to go with that." He went into the kitchen and called Miss Mavis over. "Something's bothering that young man. You don't think it has to do with Miss Lottie and his granddaddy do you?"

"Could be because she called me last night and said she told him. Lottie also knows. Let him be, maybe he'll get over it."

"You're right as always." He left the kitchen with a muffin and joined Harding.

"Chef Willie, did you know my grandfather?"

"Sure did. Miss Mavis and I both did. Why, is there something you want to know?"

"No, just asking."

Miss Mavis overheard his question and came out from the kitchen."Young man, is this about Miss Lottie and your granddaddy?"

He rubbed his forehead. "You know about them too?"

"Yes, we do. Miss Lottie tried to tell you, but you wouldn't listen, so I'll tell you." She told him everything she knew.

"No, Miss Mavis, I don't believe you," he yelled. "My grandfather wouldn't do something like that."

"He did, and Miss Lottie practically raised your mother after her mother died. Don't you judge Miss Lottie for something she and your granddaddy did in the past that was of the heart."

"I'm not judging, I was just asking."

She crossed her arms and narrowed her eyes. "You got no right, what with you not visiting your mother all these years and you never even came for your granddaddy's funeral."

"But, I didn't know—"

She thrust her palm at him and turned. "That's all I got to say. I got work in the kitchen. Chef, we ain't open for breakfast yet." She turned and went back into the kitchen.

"I don't understand. Is she right, Chef?"

Chef Willie was just as surprised by Miss Mavis' reaction. "Yes, she is but don't let her upset you. She means well. But the past is in the past, and you have to accept it."

"I didn't say I don't accept it, it's just—"

"Listen, your granddaddy and Miss Lottie loved each other, and folks around here loved them both. And they don't take kindly to anyone speaking ill of them."

"I'm not—"

"Like I said, it's all in the past."

They were both right even though he didn't know the date his grandfather died, he could have visited his mother, and he had no right to judge anyone.

"I have to go, Chef Willie, thanks for the coffee."

CHAPTER 42

The sun was just above the tree line when he left the diner. He ran back toward Baxter House, angry and alone with his thoughts.

He was confused and at a crossroads. He could let his anger get the best of him, go straight ahead and put the past in the rearview mirror or make a turn one way or the other and lose everything he had now.

He stumbled on the road and regained his footing.

"Son of a bitch!" He paused to take a breath and exhaled fire and smoke.

He wasn't sure who he was angrier with—his grandfather, his mother, Miss Lottie or himself. He paused, put his hands on his knees and took a deep breath.

He could pack his bags and leave Blocker's Bluff forever, or accept the fact that he had his mother again—even with her faults which she paid dearly for.

He took off again at a faster pace still angry and frustrated.

When he reached the porch, he stopped, took another deep breath and hesitated before going up the steps. Finally, he walked up the steps, reached for the doorknob and paused.

What could she say to me that would change what happened in the past?

He opened the door and walked into the kitchen. Miss Lottie was just hanging up the phone.

"Good morning, Miss Mavis just called. She didn't mean to upset you. Sit and I'll try to explain again."

He just stood there looking at her. "I'd rather not, ma'am."

She picked up a wooden spoon and pointed it at him. "Go on now, do as I say and sit!" He took a deep breath, exhaled, and sat like an obedient child.

She set the spoon down and took his hand in hers. He tried to pull it away, but she held fast. "You're gonna listen to what I have to say. You hear me?" He nodded. "Your granddaddy and me we fell in love while I was taking care of your mother and keeping his house. It was after your grandma died. We raised both our daughters and loved them both. I'm sorry if your momma and I deceived you, but we kept it a secret to protect you. And that's the truth"

"It seems everyone knows your secret, including Chef Willie."

Her hand flew to her chest. "He told you too?"

"No, he confirmed it. I'm more confused than ever now."

She grabbed his hand again. "Please don't hate your granddaddy. I can accept how you feel about me, but don't judge him. He would have eventually told you if he had the chance."

He looked at her, how he had wanted to call her Grandma, how it felt right, and now he knew why. She meant well by trying to protect him like his mother did. It was time for him to grow up and be a man.

"I'm not judging anyone, certainly not my grandfather and not you." He swiped a tear. "I just wanted a home and a place to come to after the marines and maybe a family too."

She brushed her hand over his cheek. "You have two homes here if you want. You have your momma and an extended family too. Thomas and Lottie adore you as do I." *Lord Travis, I hope he understands.*

She was right again; he did have a home and family here—unlike what he had back in Virginia. For the past decade The Marine Corps had been his family but now he had a real one and a home—but he had a decision to make. If he threw it all away, he may never get another chance.

He took her hand and gently squeezed it. "You're my family now, and I'm not going to lose any of you, especially now that I have two homes to come to after I'm discharged." He pulled her up and hugged her. "I love you, and now you really are like my grandmother." He squeezed her to him.

"I love you too."

Sunday afternoon Judy, Lottie, and Thomas came for dinner. Miss Lottie told Judy when she invited her that Bradley knew about her relationship with his grandfather.

When Judy arrived, Bradley greeted her with a warm hug and a kiss. "Mom, Miss Lottie told me about grandpa and her. I'm okay with everything, especially now that I have a family here."

She rubbed his cheek. "I'm glad. Your grandfather would be too. Now we both have a second chance to be a family here." She went into the kitchen to help Miss Lottie with supper. They greeted each other with a warm hug and kisses.

When Lottie and Thomas arrived, he greeted Lottie with a hug and rubbed Thomas' head.

"You okay, Brad? I'm sorry about the other night."

He leaned close to her ear and whispered, "Yes, cousin." Then he kissed her on her cheek.

"We have to tell Thomas."

"Tell me what, Mom?"

"Let's go outside. Brad and I have something to tell you."

They went outside and sat on the rockers. "Okay, Mom, what do you guys want to tell me? Is it about Grandpa?"

Lottie and Bradley's eyes opened wide.

"Which grandpa are you taking about, Thomas?"

"Grandpa Travis. I overheard Miss Judy and Granma talking about him. That's how I learned he was my granpa." His face lit up. "Is that what you wanted to tell me?"

"Yes, Thomas," answered Bradley. "Your mom and you are my cousins. You okay with that?"

"What are cousins, Marine?"

"Thomas, it means we're related and are family," answered Lottie.

"You mean the marine is like my brother?"

"Not quite like that, Thomas, but close enough," said Bradley.

"Cool. I like that, Marine, but I'm not calling you cousin. I like calling you Marine."

Lottie and Bradley laughed. "You can keep calling me marine if you want to, and I'll call you Thomas, Cousin."

"Bump fists, Cousin Marine." They bumped fists and turned to Lottie. "Come on, Mom, bump fists."

The three bumped fists, exploded them, and then went back into the house.

"Gramma, guess what?"

"What, Thomas?"

"This here's my cousin the marine." Everyone laughed.

"And I'm your Aunt Judy, Thomas."

"Cool, Aunt Judy. Bump fists with me." She did and even exploded his fist.

Miss Lottie put dinner on the table and they all sat down.

"Mind if I say a grace, Grandma?" asked Bradley.

Everyone gave him a strange look. It would be a first for all of them since it was something they rarely did, except on special holidays.

"Go ahead."

Make it short, Cousin Marine, 'cause I'm hungry."

CHAPTER 43

Monday after supper, Bradley called his mother to visit and say a final goodbye before leaving in the morning. Even though it was goodbye, Judy knew he would be coming back after he's discharged. She had just finished supper and told him she would make some lemonade.

"Grandma, I'll be back soon. I'm going to visit my mom." She waved to him as he left.

When he pulled up to her house, she was waiting at the door for him.

"Hey, Mom."

She reached out and wrapped her arms around him. "Hi." She kissed him on the cheek. "Come on in, I've got lemonade and cookies."

"Sounds good to me."

They walked into the house; he sat in the living room, she went into the kitchen and returned holding a tray with two glasses of lemonade and some cookies.

"When will I see you again?"

He grabbed a cookie, took a sip of lemonade and puckered his lips. "Whoo, that's tart."

She took a sip of hers and puckered her lips. "Too much lemon, you think? It's how your grandpa liked his."

"I like it this way too." He took a bite of the cookie and another sip of lemonade. "After I'm settled in my new assignment, I'll take a weekend and visit. It may be a few weeks or even a month. I'll definitely be back for Mother's Day."

She clasped her heart and put a hand on his cheek. He covered it with his hand. Both their cheeks became damp.

"I'll even get you a heart shaped box of chocolates, like I did when I was a kid."

Her heart fluttered. It had been a long time since they were together on Mother's Day and he gave her a box of chocolates.

"I'll have to rent a car first."

"You could take your grandfather's truck. It's not like I'll be driving it. I can have Ollie work on it while you're away."

"Thanks, Mom." They chatted a while before he had to leave. "I better get back. I've got wash to do."

"You're all grown up now and doing your own laundry. You've become a fine young man." She put a hand on his cheek again.

He gazed into her eyes, saw that same look she gave him when he was a young boy and knew how proud she was of him. "Thanks, Mom."

She was happy that at least now she wouldn't experience a mother's worst nightmare of two marines ringing the doorbell and standing there with bad news.

"You be safe, Son."

"Don't worry my combat days are over. I'll be safe and I'll be back. I love you, Mom." He took her in his arms and held her tight.

"I love you too." She walked him to the door, said a final good-bye, and waved to him as he drove off.

Before leaving to visit his mother he had left his laundry by the washing machine. While he visited his mother, Miss Lottie washed his clothes and ironed them.

"Grandma, you didn't have to do my laundry. I could have done it myself."

"I know, but I wanted to. How was your visit with your mother?"

"It was a good one. I told her as soon as I'm settled I'll come back for a weekend and stay with her. You don't mind do you?"

"No, you should stay with her but be sure to come by and say hello."

"I will. I'm going to turn in early. See you in the morning."

"Goodnight."

In the morning he was up early, showered, dressed, and brought his bags downstairs. He waved goodbye to Miss Lottie and backed down the driveway. When he reached the end, he looked at the sign that read *Baxter House*—the place where his life had changed and the dawn of a new life to come.

CHAPTER 44

Parris Island—May

After Harding turned in his rental, a car and driver were waiting for him—one of the privileges of his rank. He was taken to his temporary quarters at the Osprey Inn. They weren't fancy, but they weren't a tent. Before the driver left, he told the sergeant that his presence was requested at his CO's office at 0900 Thursday morning. He stowed his gear and spent the rest of the day relaxing.

He had several choices for transportation Thursday. He could use the car and driver, take the base shuttle or start walking and any number of marines would offer a ride. Since it was already there, he chose the car and reported to the CO's office as requested.

After greetings from his CO, he was informed that he could take the remaining sixty days leave before his discharge or his last day of service could be the end of his leave. He elected to have his discharge date be the last day of his leave. His CO said he would process the paperwork. Harding's leave would begin 02 August and his discharge date would be 01 October. Thus he wouldn't have to report back. He was assigned to tactical classroom training.

"You'll have a lot of free time on your hands, Gunny. If you get bored, we sponsor a youth lacrosse program and could use some help. If you're interested, maybe you could coach a team. Call this number if you're interested." He wrote a name and number on a piece of paper and handed it to him.

The CO glanced over Harding's service record. "I see by your record why you chose to get out, Gunny. That rescue mission, even though you received a field combat promotion, was a lot for anyone to handle."

Initially Harding was offered the rank of lieutenant but declined and compromised for a significant leap in rank as a non-commissioned officer.

Instead of saluting, his CO stood and extended his hand. "I'm honored to have you in my command, Master Gunny."

Harding grasped his hand. "Thank you, sir."

Three weeks later he rented a car and made a trip to Beaufort to visit Jessica. He had hoped to see Laurie, but she was on duty, so he took Jessica to lunch. He told her about his new assignment and that he agreed to coach a youth lacrosse program.

"Bet it takes your mind off some things." She was thinking of Laurie.

He half-heartedly smiled. "It helps. I'm going to visit my mom next weekend and she's giving me my grandfather's truck. I won't have to rent a car anymore."

"That's great. Guess you can come see me more often."

"Maybe, we'll see. Anything new with you?"

Her eyes sparkled. "I've had a few dates with this one guy from counseling. Nothing serious, we're just friends." Then matter-of-factly she said, "My mom wants me to come live with her in Charleston."

"Really? That's great."

"She thinks she can help me get a job, and I can go back to school and get my accounting degree. There's a VA hospital there, and I can continue my counseling. I haven't told Laurie yet."

"I'm sure she'll be happy. What about Sarge?"

Jessica frowned. "I'm not sure. Mom doesn't think we can keep her."

"I can take her but not until August. I have sixty days leave coming, and I'm taking it as of 01 August. She can come live with me in Blocker's Bluff. There's someone there who would love to play with her. Let me know what you decide."

"Thanks, but it may not be for a couple of months."

"That's perfect, Jess."

After lunch, he drove Jessica home and spent some time playing with Sarge before returning to base.

In the evening, Jessica told Laurie about her lunch with him. She didn't seem much interested in what Jessica had said.

Then, again off-handedly, she said, "I told him about my mom."

"What about your mom? Is she ill?"

"No, she wants me to come live with her."

"That's wonderful, will you take Sarge?"

"Maybe not, but Brad said he could take her in August when he has leave. If I go, will you keep Sarge until Brad comes for her?"

Sarge looked at Laurie with pleading eyes. "She really is his dog, so I'll have to if necessary."

But that means he might want to visit more, and I can't be here when he does.

CHAPTER 45

The following week, he drove to his mother's house. She had left a key in a flowerpot for him. He put his overnight bag in his room, changed into shorts, sneakers, and a comfortable shirt. On the kitchen counter were the keys to the truck, the title and registration, and a garage door opener. While he was away, she took care of transferring ownership to him.

He left the title but picked up the registration, keys, and opener. "Thanks, Mom." He went into the garage and got in the truck, backed it out of the garage, lowered the door, and drove into town to Ollie's Garage.

When Ollie saw him pull up, he recognized the old green two-door Ford pickup truck and walked over thinking Judy was driving. He was surprised to see Harding get out of the truck.

"Hey, fella, how come you're driving Miss Judy's truck?"

Harding grinned. "Actually it used to be my grandfather's truck, but my mom said I could take it when I go back to Parris Island. Can you work on it and make sure there are no problems." It felt good to let Ollie know who he was. "Can you do that for me, Mr. Jackson?"

Ollie crossed his arms and laughed. "First off, call me Ollie." He uncrossed his arms and extended a hand. "So, you're Miss Judy's son and Travis' grandson. Thought you looked a little like him last time you were here." They shook hands. "I'd be happy to look at your truck, but your mother had it in just last week. Everything checked out okay, and I put a new battery in it and changed the oil. Your mother takes real good care of it. Looks almost new."

"Sure does. Thanks Ollie, now I have to arrange a trip to get rid of my rental car."

Ollie removed his hat and scratched his head. "There's a rental agency in Crofton, maybe you can take it there. If not, I'll go with you to return it and we can come back in the truck. How's that sound?"

"I can't ask you to do that, Ollie. That's way too much to ask."

Ollie waved a hand at him. "Ain't no trouble at all. Anything for Miss Judy's son and Travis' grandson. They would do the same for me. You check with the rental agency in Crofton and let me know. What will you do about parking on Parris Island? You gotta get a decal?"

Harding grinned. "Heck no, my ID has a chip that allows me access to any military base and parking."

"Ain't that something now? Say, I'm fixin to go to lunch. You eaten yet?"

"No, sir, I just got here."

"I ain't either. I was going to the diner. Care to join me?"

"Sure, want me to drive?"

"Drive? Hell no, we'll walk. And stop calling me sir. I ain't your daddy."

"Okay, Ollie." They walked over to Willie's Diner.

"Looks like you got a friend there, Ollie," said Chef Willie when they entered. "You guys having lunch?"

"We sure are. This here's Travis Waverly's grandson."

"Hell, I know that. Sit down, and I'll bring you both the special."

He felt like family and was glad he chose to come back to Blocker's Bluff. He googled the rental agency and located one in Crofton.

"Ollie, the rental agency I got my car from has an office in Crofton. I'm going to call them and ask if I can turn my car in there." He called the agency. "They said I can bring it there, but they close at five."

"No problem we can go there after lunch."

After lunch they drove to Judy's house, retrieved his rental, went to Crofton and turned it in. Then he drove Ollie back to the garage.

"Thanks, Ollie, I appreciate this."

"Anytime, hell if it weren't for your grandfather, I'd a lost this place. The oil company wanted me to replace the underground storage tanks. I didn't have the money and was going to close, but Travis said no. He lent me the money months before he died, and I had the work done. Paid your mother back every cent too." He looked around the garage. "And Miss Judy, she being on the town counsel and with the help of the mayor, got that resort company to give me the money to fix this place up. 'Cause it helped that the mayor's daughter was married to the resort manager." He grinned.

"But I had to make it look like it did seventy years ago. Somethin bout preservin' the town's history and charm." Ollie laughed. "The whole town looks like it did in the '40s. And those petrol pumps are actually real gas pumps and they take credit cards too. In the afternoon when I take a break, I lean back on a chair under that canopy." He smiled. "Folks like to take my picture too." Then he beamed with pride and added, "My station's cleaner than the ones in Crofton."

"They did all that for you?"

"Yep, they sure did. Guess you can say I'm beholden to your family. Say, I hear tell you're getting out soon. You got a job lined up?"

"Haven't given it any thought. Why?"

"I know you can change a battery and spark plugs. Did they teach you anything in the marines?"

"I picked up a few things. I'm a quick learner."

"If you don't mind getting your hands dirty, I could use a part-time helper. I can teach you all you need to know. Doesn't pay much, but when the snowbirds come, I'll be real busy. You interested?"

"I hadn't considered working in a garage, and I don't mind getting my hands dirty. I could use the work until I decide what I'm going to do."

"We got us deal then?"

"We got us a deal." They shook hands. "Thanks, Ollie. I get out 01 October, but I have sixty days leave that I'm taking the first week of August."

"Good 'cause that's about the time the snowbirds start arriving, so you'll be busy. You come by when you're ready."

Ollie said goodbye and Harding drove to his mother's house. When he came to Miss Lottie's, he turned into the driveway, parked, and rang the bell.

"Lord Almighty, would you look at you. Welcome." Miss Lottie's eyes glowed. "Give me a hug."

He hugged her tight. "It's good to see you, Grandma. I was on my way to Mom's and decided to stop and see you."

"I'm glad you did. How long are you home for?"

"Just the weekend, but I'll be back in August. And Ollie said I could work part-time at the service station."

"Why that's wonderful. You have any plans for the weekend?" She looked at the truck. "Is that your granddaddy's truck?"

"Yes, it is. Mom said I could take it with me." He scratched his head. "It's Friday; does Thomas have any more games?"

"Tonight's his last one. Can you go?"

"Yes, I'll call Mom and see if she wants to go too. We can go together, but it will have to be in her car since the truck can only take two. Is that okay with you?"

"Lottie's coming to get me. She and Thomas are spending the night, so I'll go with her. If your mother doesn't want to go, you can go with us. I'm sure Lottie will be happy to see you. So will Thomas."

"I'll call her at work and ask her." He dialed her number on his cell phone. "Mom, it's me, Brad. I'm at Miss Lottie's. Yes, I've been home, and I have the truck. Ollie went with me to Crofton and I turned in my rental." He smiled. "Yes, Mom, I'm fine. Thomas' last game is tonight. Would you like to go with me? We can take the truck."

"I'd love to. What about Miss Lottie?"

"She's going with Lottie, so we'll meet them there. Hold on Miss Lottie wants to ask me something."

"Ask her if she would like to come for supper tomorrow. I'll invite Lottie and Thomas.

"Mom, she wants to know if we can come for supper tomorrow night. Lottie and Thomas will be here."

"Tell her yes. I have to go so I'll see you at home. I'm leaving early. Love you."

"Love you too, Mom. Mom says 'yes.'"

"Good, you have time for some tea or are you in a hurry?"

"I've got time."

They went inside, sat in the kitchen, drank sweet tea, and chatted. He told her about what his duties were at Parris Island and of coaching lacrosse.

"That's wonderful. Maybe you can coach at the high school when you're here."

"We'll see. I best get home. Mom said she was leaving early."

She walked him to the porch. He hugged and kissed her and then she waved goodbye.

Later that afternoon, he and his mother drove to Crofton and met up with Miss Lottie and Lottie at Thomas's baseball game.

"It's good to see you again, Brad," said Lottie excitedly. "How are the marines treating you?"

He hugged her and she felt good in his arms. He would have kissed her, but Miss Lottie and his mother were there. "I've got it easy," he replied. "I do some classroom instruction and have a lot of spare time so I'm coaching a kid's lacrosse team. It's a lot of fun. What's new with you?"

She stroked his arm. "That's great. Maybe you could help the high school coach next spring. The school year is winding down, and I have to find something for Thomas to occupy his summer because I'll be working. He usually spends the summers at Grandma's."

He thought about Jessica and Sarge. "I may have something for him to do. A former platoon member of mine has a dog and she can't take it with her when she moves to Charleston. I said I would take her. Maybe Thomas could look after her for me until I get out."

"Oh, Brad, he'd loved to."

"Don't say anything yet until I'm sure it will happen because it isn't positive that she'll be moving. Will Grandma mind?"

"Are you kidding? She'll love to."

"Are you two gonna just talk or you joining us for Thomas' game?" said Miss Lottie.

"We're coming, Grandma," replied Lottie. "We better go join them." They walked over and sat down between Miss Lottie and Judy. Judy patted his thigh and smiled at him.

It was the bottom of the last inning, and Thomas' team was down by one run with two outs. Thomas came to bat and hit a single. Then the shortstop, the littlest player on the team, came up to bat. The first two pitches were called balls and then he swung at the next two and missed. The next pitch was called a ball and now the count was three and two.

The coach called time out, walked onto the field and said something to him. He looked beyond third base, smiled, and then stepped into the batter's box. He adjusted his helmet, positioned his feet, banged the bat on home plate and took his batter's stance.

"Eye on the ball, now." Yelled the coach.

The batter scrunched his eyes and gave the pitcher a menacing look. This was his mission and he was determined to complete it no matter what the cost. He could become a hero or a loser and fade into oblivion. But the batter had no intention of suffering the slings and arrows of those who had never been in his situation. He took a deep breath and waited with anticipation.

The pitcher went through his wind up and threw a slider. Thomas took off running for second base. The batter swung and hit the ball. Everyone watched as it sailed over the left field fence. Thomas and the shortstop scored and the team won the game. The whole team rushed the shortstop and piled onto him like an avalanche burying a skier's cabin.

Thomas crawled out from under the pile, raced to the stands and almost tripped on his shoelace. "Mom, did you see Marcus' home run? Wasn't it awesome?"

"Yes, it was, Thomas."

"Did you see it, Marine?"

"I sure did."

Thomas lowered his head. "Too bad his mom wasn't here to see it. It's the first time all year he got a hit."

"Thomas," Brad said. "I think she did see it." He pointed to the field.

Thomas turned and saw a female dressed in an olive green jumpsuit holding Marcus in her arms and kissing him. "Wow, that's something, Marine."

"It sure is."

"I'm gonna go join the team to celebrate. If they're going for pizza after the game, can we go with them? Please, Mom."

"Thomas, we have to take Grandma home."

"Please, Mom."

"Lottie, we can squeeze Miss Lottie in the truck with us," said Judy. "It's not like we haven't done it before with your grandpa."

Lottie looked to Miss Lottie. "Do you mind, Grandma?"

"No, child, you go with Thomas. Like Miss Judy said, it's not the first time we squeezed into that truck."

"Gramma, you're the greatest, and so are you, Aunt Judy," said Thomas. "Marine, you drive safely with my gramma and my aunt, you hear?"

"Yes, Thomas, I hear you. Now go celebrate." He winked at Lottie. "See you tomorrow, Lottie."

"You too, Brad. Come on, Thomas, let's go celebrate Marcus' home run."

"Thomas."

He stopped and turned around. "Yes Aunt Judy."

"Tie your shoelace."

They left and then Bradley, Miss Lottie and Judy left also. Miss Lottie squeezed between Bradley and Judy and he drove to Baxter House.

"Thank you two for the ride. It was like old times." She patted Judy on the knee. Judy got out of the truck and helped Miss Lottie get out.

Judy walked her to the porch. "Want us to stay until Lottie gets here?"

She patted Judy's arm. "No, you go on home and be with your son. Thank you, though, but I'll be okay."

Judy kissed her on the cheek and whispered, "Good night, Momma, I'll see you tomorrow."

"What did you say to her?"

"I just said goodnight, that's all."

Saturday afternoon Bradley and Judy drove to Miss Lottie's for supper. Thomas sat on the porch steps eagerly awaiting their arrival. As soon as he saw the truck come to a halt he was up and running to greet them.

"Where you two been? I've been waiting for you."

"Well, we're here now, Thomas. Good afternoon."

"Good afternoon, Aunt Judy." She rubbed the top of his head. "Marine, you want to play catch?"

"Sure. How was the celebration last night?"

"You boys chat, I'm going inside," said Judy. Then she walked up onto the porch and into the house.

"It was awesome, Marine. We ate lots of pizza, and Marcus' mom was there. She's a captain in the air force and a pilot too." He looked down. "Marcus is a lucky kid."

He put his hand on Thomas' shoulder. "You're a lucky kid too, Thomas. You have your mom."

He smiled. "Yeah, I do, and I have you, Marine."

"That's right, Thomas."

"Let's play catch, Marine."

Thomas tossed the ball to him and he tossed it back. They played catch for a while and then sat on the porch.

"Where'd you get the truck, Marine?"

"It was my grandfather's, now it's mine."

"Cool."

Lottie stuck her head out the door. "Okay you boys, supper's ready."

"Let's go, Thomas." Then he smiled and said, "We're coming, Mom."

Lottie shook her head and they followed her into the kitchen.

Later, Bradley and Judy went home. Lottie and Thomas spent the night. Sunday afternoon Bradley said goodbye to his mother.

"Will you be home again?"

"I'll be back in two weeks."

CHAPTER 46

The next time he was home, Judy asked him if he had written his father yet. He ignored her question so she repeated it.

"Brad, he's still your father and you should at least let him know what's happening in your life since you'll soon be a civilian."

He picked up the picture of his grandfather and him taken when he was thirteen. It was the last summer he spent with his grandfather. "I know, Mom, but I just can't bring myself to forgive him."

She put her arm around him and touched the picture. "It's in the past, and you need to move on. Your grandfather would want you to." Although she said it, she wasn't sure he would want him to.

"I'll think about it" He checked his watch. "It's time I left for Parris Island."

"Okay, but promise you'll think about it."

"I will." He hugged her, left the house, got in the truck and drove off. Judy waved to him.

The next week, he decided to write his father—just a brief note. He addressed it to father—not dear father or dad. He said he was doing well and getting out in a few months and would be living in

Blocker's Bluff with his mother. She told him all about the divorce, why it happened, that he forgave her and had put it in the past. Then he mentioned coaching lacrosse and the part-time job at the service station. The last thing he wrote was to ask for his sister's address so he could write to her. He signed the letter "Thanks, Brad."

Two weekends later, during his visit with his mother, he told her that he had written his father. But he didn't tell her what was in the letter, especially about forgiving her.

"That's good, Brad, let's hope he writes back."

He turned his palms up, smirked, and tilted his head. "We'll see. Are we having supper here tomorrow or at Baxter House?"

"Baxter House, Lottie and Thomas will be there."

He thought about Sarge. "Mom, a former platoon member of mine who lives in Beaufort has a dog that has helped her deal with PTSD. She's moving to Charleston to be with her mother and can't take the dog. Would it be alright if I brought the dog here to live with us?"

She touched his arm and smiled. "Absolutely, you always wanted a dog when you were a boy. When will you bring him?"

"It's a she, Mom, and she's special. She only has three legs."

"Oh my, that's sad. Will she be okay during the day when no one is home?"

"I've already mentioned it to Lottie, and she said Thomas could watch him. Miss Lottie said he could bring the dog to Baxter House."

"That's wonderful. I can't wait to meet Sarge. When will you bring her?"

"As soon as I know if she's moving. I'll let you know."

Saturday evening Bradley and Judy had supper at Baxter House. He told Lottie that it was okay with his mother for Sarge to live with them.

"But don't say anything to Thomas yet until it's certain."

CHAPTER 47

Jessica called Harding the second week in July and said she was moving to Charleston on the thirty-first and asked if he could he take Sarge.

"I can come get her this weekend and take her to my mother's house. There's a ten-year-old boy who will take care of her during the day while my mom's at work. It will only be temporary until I'm discharged."

"Okay then, I'll let Laurie know."

He contacted Doctor Jennings, the veterinarian at CARV, and asked her if it would be okay for him to take Sarge to live with him in Blocker's Bluff. He told her about Jessica's situation.

"She's your dog, Sergeant, and partly Laurie's. Is she okay with the arrangement?"

"Yes, she's already agreed."

"Who will look after Sarge during the day?"

"My mom and a ten-year-old boy will watch her at my grandmother's house."

"You still have symptoms of PTSD?"

"A little, but I have family in Blocker's Bluff. Sarge will be for me like she was for Jessica."

"Okay. I guess Sarge has a permanent home now."

"Yes, she does. Thanks, Doc."

Saturday morning, Bradley arrived at Laurie's house. He was hoping she would be home, but her car wasn't in the driveway.

Jessica opened the door. "Morning, Brad, Laurie had to work today. I'll tell her you were here and said hello." His expression registered disappointment. "I'm sorry, Brad, I know you would have liked to see her."

He tilted his head. "It's okay, Jess, I'm here for Sarge and to say goodbye to you."

"Come on in, Sarge is waiting."

As soon as he entered the house, Sarge walked over to greet him. He bent down and let her lick his face. "You ready to come home with me, girl?" Sarge barked once. "I guess that means yes."

"Do you have to leave right away, or do you have time to chat?"

"I can stay awhile. Hey, does your mother have Skype?"

Her eyes brightened. "Yes, Laurie installed it so I could talk to my mom. Why?"

"Let me give you my email address and Skype name. We can Skype each other and stay in contact."

"I'd like that." She got a pad and pen and he wrote down the information.

She poured them each a cup of coffee and they sat and talked. She let Sarge out to do her business and then Bradley and Sarge prepared to leave.

"Time for us to go, Jess."

"Yeah, I'm going to really miss Sarge and you. Oh, I forgot, Sarge doesn't have a particular spot of her own. She sleeps wherever she wants and at night in bed with me."

He laughed. "She'll probably sleep with me too."

She looked at him sheepishly. "Um, can I give you a hug?"

"Sure, come here."

She wrapped her arm around him, looked into his eyes, and then kissed him passionately. They both took a deep breath and stepped back.

"I've wanted to do that for a long time. I owe you a lot, and I love you."

He took another deep breath. "You don't owe me anything." Then he surprised her and wrapped his arms around her and kissed her even more passionately. "Now we're even."

She breathed deeply and fanned her face. "Whew!"

"We better go now. Come on Sarge." He rubbed his fingers gently down her cheek. "Call me when you're settled, Jess."

When he arrived in Blocker's Bluff, Judy was still at work, so he went to Baxter House hoping Lottie and Thomas would be there. Fortunately, they were since Lottie was there to help her grandmother with laundry and cleaning the upstairs rooms. Thomas sat on the porch and he looked bored.

When he saw Bradley's truck, he leaped up and shouted, "Mom, Gramma, the marine's here. Come see."

He parked and stepped out of the truck. "Hey, Thomas, I have a surprise for you and a favor to ask."

Thomas ran up to the truck. "What's the surprise and the favor you want, Marine?"

He opened the door and Sarge leaped out. "Thomas, this is Sarge. She's special."

Thomas looked at Sarge's legs. "She only has three legs. Is that what makes her special?"

Bradley grinned. "Yes, and I need a special favor from you."

"Okay, what is it?"

"Will you watch Sarge for me while I'm away? I already asked your mom, and your grandma said it was okay too. What do you say?"

The boy's eyes lit up and his smile stretched from ear to ear. "Really? You bet I will. Is Sarge okay with it too?"

"I don't know, let's ask her." He looked down at Sarge. "Sarge you okay with Thomas watching you while I'm away?" Sarge barked once. "She said yes, Thomas. Say hello to her."

Thomas bent down and extended his hand. Sarge sat on her hind legs, gave him her paw and licked his face. He rubbed the back of her head and said, "Nice to meet you, Sarge. We're gonna have fun. You'll like my mom and gramma too."

Miss Lottie and Lottie stepped onto the porch. "Thomas, what's all the yelling about?" said Lottie. When she saw Bradley she smiled. "Grandma it's Brad."

He waived and walked to the porch. "Hi, Lottie, hello, Grandma."

"You come give me a hug," said Miss Lottie. He gave her a hug. "Is that the dog you told us about?"

"Yes, and Thomas and her are already friends." He turned and hugged Lottie. "He seems really happy and excited about taking care of her." Their eyes locked and they smiled.

"He does, thanks, Brad. Grandma, we should introduce ourselves to her." She called out to Thomas. "Thomas, bring Sarge here so we can introduce ourselves."

"Okay, Mom. Come on, Sarge, you have to meet my mom and gramma." Sarge followed him up onto the porch.

Lottie bent down and rubbed the dog's head. "It's nice to meet you, Sarge, I'm Lottie." Sarge licked her face and then walked over to Miss Lottie.

Miss Lottie sat in the rocker, leaned forward and let Sarge lick her face. "Oh, you are a sweetheart. I'm gonna enjoy having you visit with me." Then she rubbed Sarge's head. "You wait here, and I'll get you a treat because you're special." She got up and started to enter the house. Sarge followed her. "Well now, you want to see my home do you? Come on in. Thomas, you come to." She looked at

Lottie and Bradley. "Let your momma and Brad talk." She winked at them and then she, Thomas, and Sarge went inside.

"Can you come for supper tonight, Brad?"

"Yes, but I want to call Mom and let her know I'm here. I'll ask her if she wants to come." He called his mother. When she answered, she was still at her office.

"Brad, where are you?"

"I'm at Baxter House. I wanted Thomas to meet Sarge. She's taken to him, and apparently Miss Lottie has taken to Sarge too. Lottie wants me to come for supper this evening. Can you come too?"

"Yes, I'd love to. Should I meet you there or are you going home first?"

"I'll go home and later we can come back in the truck."

"Okay, I'll see you at home. I can't wait to meet Sarge."

"Mom says yes, so we'll be here later. I'll leave Sarge with Thomas and bring her home tonight."

"Good, let's go inside and I'll make you a sandwich."

After he ate his sandwich, everyone went out onto the porch, sat, and watched Thomas play with Sarge. Bradley checked his watch, saw it was four-thirty so he left and went home. Judy arrived a half hour later. She walked into the house and found him sitting in the kitchen with a beer.

"Don't drink too many of those or you'll spoil your appetite, and Miss Lottie won't be happy."

"Mom, it's good to see you. This is the only one I've had. I just felt like a beer." He set the bottle down and walked toward her. "Let me give you a hug." He held her tightly in his arms and kissed her cheek. "Whenever you're ready we can go to Miss Lottie's.

"Give me a minute to freshen up and then we can go."

After she freshened up, they climbed into his truck and he drove to Baxter House.

"Is that Sarge with Thomas?"

"Yes, and remember I said she was special, Mom."

She put a hand on his shoulder. "I can see. She only has three legs, but she gets around well enough." Then she clasped her hands together over her heart. "She's adorable. We'll give her a good home and she can sleep anywhere she wants. Most likely though, she'll sleep in your room."

He smiled and they walked over to the porch so she could meet Sarge.

"Thomas, introduce Sarge to your aunt."

"Hi, Aunt Judy, come meet Sarge."

She bent down and let Sarge lick her face. "Hello, Sarge, you're going to like your new home with Brad and me." Sarge barked once. "Does that mean yes?" Sarge barked once again.

"That means yes, Aunt Judy."

"Okay then, I'm going inside to say hello to your grandma and mother. Bye, Sarge, I'll see you later." Sarge sat down on his hind legs and extended her paw to Judy.

After supper, Miss Lottie suggested that the adults play cribbage while Thomas and Sarge watch television. Bradley and Lottie glanced at each other.

Lottie started to speak. "Um, Grandma..."

Judy interrupted her. "I don't think they want to play cribbage, Miss Lottie. Why don't we let them go to the movies? We can watch Thomas. I'm sure he won't mind, not with Sarge to occupy his time. We can play cribbage ourselves."

Miss Lottie looked at the two skeptically. "I'm not sure that's a good idea."

Bradley and Lottie looked to Judy for help.

"Miss Lottie, it's just the movies. Besides they don't want to spend the evening with a couple of old ladies. Let them go."

Miss Lottie knew Judy wasn't going to stop asking so she relented. "Okay, but you two make sure you come right home after the movies."

"Yes, Grandma," they both said and smiled.

Bradley and Lottie climbed into his truck and he drove to Crofton.

"Mom sure has a way with Miss Lottie, doesn't she?"

"She wasn't going to give in."

He reached over and grabbed her hand. "No, she wasn't. Lottie, it don't—"

"Don't say it, Brad."

"Aw come on, Lottie."

"No, Brad, don't." She shook her head. "Oh, hell, go ahead, you big baby."

He smiled and shouted, "Man, it don't get any better than this!"

"You're such a kid, you know that?"

"Am not."

"Are too."

"Well you're a brat."

She hit him on the arm. "So are you, now pay attention to your driving." They both laughed.

After the movies they went for ice cream and then walked back to his truck and he drove to Baxter House.

He walked around to her side and opened the door for her. She stepped down and said, "Thanks, Brad."

He had been disappointed that Laurie wasn't at home when he picked up Sarge but was happy to be with Lottie. Without asking, he grabbed her in his arms and kissed her.

"Brad, stop, you know we can't. Besides, what if Grandma and your mom were on the porch. Then what would we do?"

He looked toward the porch and saw no one there. He breathed deep. "Yeah, I guess we better." He took her hand and they walked up onto the porch. He released her hand and they went inside and to the kitchen.

"Where is Thomas, Grandma?"

She looked up, lowered her eye brows and replied, "He's in the living room watching television."

"We didn't see him when we came in. We'll go check."

Lottie and Bradley walked back to the living room and saw Thomas laid out on the sofa sound asleep. Sarge was cuddled up with him.

"Gee, Lottie, I hate to have to wake him to take Sarge home. Maybe she should stay here tonight, but Sarge will have difficulty climbing all those stairs."

"He can sleep down here. I hate to wake them both too. Let's go tell Grandma."

Miss Lottie said it was okay for Thomas to sleep on the sofa. Judy checked the clock and said it was time to go home.

"Lottie, you walk Brad out while I say goodnight to your grandmother." Miss Lottie started to protest, but Judy stopped her. "Let them say goodnight." She waved her hand at Judy and relented once again.

Miss Lottie stood up so Judy could hug her. "It's good for them to have a moment, Miss Lottie."

"I'm not so sure it is." She suddenly felt a weakness in her knees and sat back down.

"Are you all right?"

"Yes, I guess I'm tired. You go on home. Can you come for lunch tomorrow afternoon?"

"I wish I could, but I have a meeting that I can't miss."

"You work too hard."

"I have to pay the bills and when Brad comes home, I'll have two, correction three mouths to feed."

They laughed then Judy left. She walked past Lottie as she was leaving and winked at her. "Lottie, I'm worried about your grandmother. It may be nothing but keep an eye on her."

Lottie's face registered concern. "I will, Aunt Judy, goodnight."

Bradley and Judy left and Lottie went into the house and to the kitchen.

"Grandma, would you like to sit for a while?"

She got up slowly. "No, child, I'm tired and I'm going to lie down. I'll see you in the morning. You lock up."

"Okay, goodnight, Grandma."

Miss Lottie went to her room and got into bed. Lottie locked up the house, went upstairs, got a quilt and a blanket and came down into the living room. She spread the quilt on the floor and cuddled up with a pillow.

In the morning, he decided to make the trip to Parris Island shortly after breakfast. He kissed his mother goodbye and drove to Miss Lottie's to say goodbye to Sarge.

Lottie was awakened by wetness on her face. She opened her eyes and saw Sarge staring down at her.

"Oh, good morning, Sarge, where's Thomas?" She glanced at the sofa and it was empty. Then she realized that she didn't smell the usual aroma of fresh brewed coffee and bacon frying. Alarmed, she got up and went to the kitchen. Thomas sat at the table eating a bowl of cereal. "Thomas, where's Grandma?"

"She's still in bed so I poured me some Cheerios and gave some to Sarge. You want some?"

Lottie turned and hurried to Miss Lottie's bedroom. Sarge sat at the foot of the bed. Her grandmother was lying on her back with her hands crossed over her heart.

"Oh God, no, Grandma!"

CHAPTER 48

Lottie hurried to her grandmother's bedside. She felt her neck for a pulse and put her cheek next Miss Lottie's mouth to see if she was breathing.

Miss Lottie opened her eyes. "Lottie, what are you doing?"

Relieved, Lottie replied, "Grandma, I was worried you were dead."

"I ain't dead. I just didn't feel well and couldn't get up."

"Grandma, you lie there, I'm going to call the doctor."

"No don't, I said I'm okay." She started to get up but fell back on the bed.

"I'm calling the doctor, Grandma, and don't you give me any grief." Lottie grabbed her phone and called Dr. Myers. Fortunately, she had just returned home from early morning rounds at the hospital. "Dr. Myers, it's me Lottie. My grandmother is ill and she needs you. Can you come?"

"How bad is it, Lottie?"

"She can't get out of bed. I found her lying with her hands over her heart. I thought she was gone."

"Okay, Lottie, I'm on my way, and I'll call for an ambulance just in case."

When Doctor Myers arrived at Baxter House, Thomas and Sarge were on the porch.

"Is my gramma gonna die?"

"No, Thomas, she's not. Don't you worry." She hurried into the house and to Miss Lottie's bedroom.

"Edna, you didn't have to come, I'm fine."

Doctor Myers shook her head. "Well, I'm here, Miss Lottie, and I'm going to check your vitals. You lay there while I do it." She checked her pulse, heartbeat, and blood pressure. "Your heartbeat is rapid and your blood pressure is way too high. I'm going to give you some medication to help you relax." She reached into her bag and took out some pills. "Lottie, get me a glass of water. Now, Miss Lottie, after you take these pills, you're going to want to rest. You have to take it easy for a few days or otherwise I'm putting you in the hospital."

Miss Lottie raised her hand. "I ain't goin to no hospital."

"Fine, but you stay in bed and rest." Lottie handed the glass of water to the doctor. She had Miss Lottie take the pills and drink the water. "Lottie, your grandmother needs bedrest for a few days."

"I can take a few days off and stay with her."

"No, Lottie, you need to go to work. I'll be alright by myself."

"No you won't, Miss Lottie," said the doctor. "If you don't take my advice, you're going into the hospital." Miss Lottie relented.

"I'll call Aunt Judy and see if she can help too." Judy answered her phone and thought maybe Lottie called to tell her Bradley had already been there.

"What is Lottie?"

"Aunt Judy, Grandma is ill and has to stay in bed. I'm taking tomorrow off to be with her. Can you help me?"

Judy's hand went to her heart. "Oh God, Lottie is she okay? I'll cancel my appointment for today and be right over. Bradley is on his way there."

"Dr. Myers says she'll be alright after a few days bedrest. Thank you, Aunt Judy."

Bradley turned into the driveway and saw the flashing lights of the ambulance. He parked and ran to the house.

"Thomas, what happened?"

"It's Gramma, Marine. Mom's inside."

He rushed into the house. "Lottie, what happened?"

"She had a spell. The doctor gave her some medication and prescribed bedrest. I'm going to stay with her, and your mom is on her way."

"Can I see her?"

"The medicine put her to sleep. She'll be okay, Brad"

Judy rushed into the house. "Lottie, is she okay?"

Dr. Myers came out of the bedroom. "Morning, Judy, morning Brad. Miss Lottie will be fine as long as she rests. I'll send the EMTs away. You all watch her and call me if anything changes. She's a stubborn old lady."

"Damn, I wish I didn't have to go back to base."

"There's nothing you can do here, Brad. You might as well be on your way."

"Aunt Judy is right, Brad. You go. We'll text you and keep you apprised of her condition."

"Okay." He hugged his mother and Lottie and then said goodbye to Thomas and Sarge. The drive to Parris Island was a somber one as he thought about Miss Lottie. He considered making a stop in Beaufort but decided not to.

Judy and Lottie worked on plans to care for Miss Lottie.

"Lottie, you go to work tomorrow. I'll take a few days off and watch your grandmother. Thomas can stay here with Sarge and me."

"Are you sure, Aunt Judy?"

"Yes."

"Okay, but I'll come right here after work, and Thomas and I will stay here so you can go home."

"I'm not going home, I'm staying here too. You go home and get what things you need and come back. Then I'll go home and do the same."

Monday Bradley called Lottie and asked how Miss Lottie was doing. She updated him on her status and told him that his mother was staying at Baxter House to take care of her.

When word got out about Miss Lottie being taken ill, the women's guild, led by Miss Mavis, showed up at her doorstep and offered their services. Every morning a lady arrived at eight-thirty to relieve Judy and stayed until after lunch. She fixed lunch for Thomas and Miss Lottie. After lunch, another lady came and stayed until Lottie or Judy arrived.

Eventually Miss Lottie was allowed to sit on the porch, but couldn't take guests and she wasn't allowed in the kitchen except to eat. She resisted vehemently, but the ladies had known her a long time and could be just as stubborn as she was. Eventually her condition improved, but she needed a cane to get around.

CHAPTER 49

Several days before the start of his leave in August, Harding received an envelope postmarked from Virginia with his father's law firm as the return address. He opened the envelope and pulled out the single sheet of paper. His sister's name and address were the only words typed on it.

"Guess somethings never change."

He threw the envelope in the trash but kept the sheet of paper. The next day he wrote his sister and told her everything including his new home address and telephone number.

The day finally came for him to start his leave. He loaded his truck and made the drive to Blocker's Bluff. The first thing he did when he arrived was pay a visit to Miss Lottie. She and Thomas were sitting on the porch with Sarge lying between them.

"Thomas, that looks like Brad's truck. You and Sarge go say hello."

He jumped off the porch and Sarge followed him.

"Hey, Marine."

"Hey there, Thomas."

Thomas hugged him as he rubbed the top of Thomas' head. "Hey there, Sarge." Sarge sat and offered her paw. He bent down and let her lick his face. "I have to say hello to Grandma. Follow me, troop." He walked toward the porch with Thomas and Sarge marching behind him. "Hello, Grandma, how are you?"

"I'm just fine, you come give me a hug." He hugged her and sat with her. "Thomas, go get us some lemonade."

"Sarge you wait here with Marine and Gramma." He went into the house and returned with a tray of glasses filled with lemonade and set them down.

"Thomas, you're a regular gentleman."

"Thanks, Marine. Mom said I have to help around the house. Getting lemonade is one of my chores."

"Well I'm here now, so I can help too."

"Aren't you going to work for Ollie?"

"Yes, Grandma, but I can still help out, especially with any heavy chores. I'll take care of the yard. Grandpa's tractor still works, so I'll use it here and at Mom's." They sat for a while and then he stood.

"I'm going home now, but I'll be back to visit."

"You come for supper tonight; Miss Judy and Lottie are cooking."

"Sounds good, I'll see you later. Bye Thomas, bye Sarge."

"Bye, Marine."

Later he and his mother arrived at Baxter House. He played catch with Thomas and Sarge while Lottie and Judy made supper.

After the meal, Thomas and Sarge watched television while the adults sat in the kitchen.

"Brad, why don't you and Lottie take Thomas and go to the movies. We'll watch Sarge. Besides, she likes being with us old ladies."

"Who you calling an old lady? If you were younger, I'd take my hand to your behind."

"Miss Lottie, we are old ladies."

Miss Lottie waved her hand. "Shush, speak for yourself." Bradley and Lottie found the conversation amusing.

"Grandma, we really would like to see a movie with Thomas. Say it's okay, please."

She shook her head. "Okay, but you come right home after the movie."

Bradley, Lottie, and Thomas quickly left for Crofton.

"Stop worrying about those two. I'm sure Dad would approve of them going to a movie. Besides, Thomas will be with them."

Miss Lottie relented. "If you say so. Get that cribbage game so I can beat you again."

Later, Bradley, Lottie, and Thomas returned from the movie. Thomas leaped out of the truck and ran to the house. He grabbed Lottie's hand and, spun her around.

"Stop it, Brad. We have to go inside."

He lowered his head and followed after her.

Thomas told his grandmother and aunt about the movie, leaving nothing for them to tell. After ice cream, Bradley and his mother went home.

CHAPTER 50

Waking up in the same room in the house that he spent summers with his grandfather and now lived with his mother, he hadn't had a nightmare in several days. Hopefully, that would continue. Monday morning he was up early, ate breakfast and then left at 7:00 for Ollie's Service Station. The door was up and Ollie was in the bay. Ollie had already turned the gas pumps on and two cars were gassing up. He got out of his truck and walked into the bay.

"You're late. But since it's your first day we'll let it slide," Ollie said and grinned.

"What time do you open?"

"Six-thirty, the first customer has already been here. His car's over there." He pointed to the car. "Wants the oil changed and the tires rotated. Can you handle that?"

He scratched his head. "Sure, don't you have a lift?"

Ollie laughed. "Of course I do, but I hardly ever use it. If you need it, the controls are over there. I made sure he pulled in right."

Harding raised the lift and went to work. Ollie watched and then went into the office to answer the phone. Several more customers came and wanted their cars worked on. Ollie taught him what to do and by the end of the day he had the hang of it.

The next morning, he arrived at six-fifteen and waited for Ollie. Every morning he arrived at the same time and worked as long as Ollie needed him. Since Ollie lived behind the service station, he always closed up, turned the gas pumps off, and went to the diner for supper.

Before going home, Harding always stopped at Baxter House to get Sarge.

After school started and Thomas couldn't watch Sarge while he was at work, he left her with Miss Lottie. But occasionally he would bring Sarge to the station with him.

On a Saturday evening, he took Lottie and Thomas to Crofton for an early movie and ice cream. The following Saturday, just he and Lottie went into Crofton for a late movie. Judy, Thomas and Sarge watched television at her house.

Two weeks before his discharge, he and Ollie were taking an afternoon break under the canopy at Ollie's garage. Ollie rested the back of his chair against the wall while Harding sat on an old crate next to him. Each had a soda pop. Sarge was between them.

Ollie took a sip of pop. "Life sure is good, Brad."

Harding leaned back against the wall and raised his bottle of pop. "Amen, I'll drink to that." Then he took a long drink. Sarge barked once.

Ollie took another drink. "You're leave's almost up. You got any plans yet for after your discharge?"

He took another sip. "Haven't given it any thought."

"You turned out to be a damn good mechanic and I could use you full time. I'm getting too old for the heavy work, and I'm thinking of getting a tow truck. Another service I can offer, maybe even get some work from Triple A. What do you say?"

He tilted the bottle to his mouth, sipped, and then reached down and patted Sarge on her back. "What do you think, Sarge? Should I work full time for this old man?"

Ollie sat up straight. "Who you calling an old man? Bet I could whip you at arm wrestling." Ollie rubbed his hands over his arms. "Tell you what, let's arm wrestle and if I win, you come work for me fulltime. If I lose, you do what you want." He set his soda pop on the ground. "Get off that damn crate, and I'll show you who's an old man."

Sarge got up and got out of their way. Harding moved the crate between them.

"You are an old man, Ollie."

They both got down on one knee and locked hands. Ollie started to count but suddenly a car pulled up and Harding turned to see who it was.

"Three," said Ollie and shoved Harding's hand down. Then he laughed. "I win; you work for me fulltime starting tomorrow or whenever you finish mustering out."

"What the hell, that's not fair, Ollie."

"Hell, it ain't. Now who's the old man?"

Molly, Porter and Miss Mollie walked over to them.

"Hey, Chief, what's up?" asked Ollie.

Miss Molly sauntered away and joined Sarge under the shade of the canopy.

"I think I need a new battery because it was difficult starting this morning. I know I should have come earlier, but I figured you'd be busy."

"No, problem, my new full time mechanic will check it." He looked at Harding. "Get to it, full time mechanic."

He shook his head, walked over to the chief's car and lifted the hood. Porter went with him.

"Damn cheater that Ollie."

"What did he do? Pull that old one, two, shove your hand down and say three?"

"Yeah, you know about it?"

Porter laughed. "He does it all the time. What's he mean by new fulltime mechanic?"

Harding walked toward the garage. "I have to work for him fulltime when I get discharged. That was the bet."

Porter put a hand on his shoulder. "Can't be any worse. Did you have any plans?"

He grinned. "No, and I was gonna ask anyway if I could work fulltime. Damn fool beat me to it." They both laughed. Harding wheeled the rusty old cart out with the battery load tester on it and hooked it up to Molly's battery. He turned the tester on, checked the reading and then did it again. "Chief, you need a new battery."

"Check it again, that thing's so old it sometimes take two tries to be sure," yelled Ollie.

"I already did," he yelled back. "You old fool this thing is a relic." Porter laughed.

"I may be an old fool, but I would have used the newer one hanging on the wall."

"Okay, put a new one in and charge it to the town," yelled Molly.

Harding took the old battery out, put it on the cart, and wheeled it into the bay. Porter pointed to the BLT sign. Harding shook his head, exchanged the battery for a new one, and put it in Molly's car while Porter watched..

"Don't let him get under your skin, Brad, he has a good heart."

"I know and in some ways he reminds me of my grandfather. So do you, Porter."

"I'll take that as a compliment. What say next Sunday we take the dogs and go fishin?"

"I'd like that."

"Four-thirty okay with you?"

"Sounds like a plan."

Molly signed the charge for the battery. Miss Lottie leaped into the back seat and then they left. Harding and Ollie went back to reclining under the canopy with Sarge. Both were smiling.

CHAPTER 51

Mid-October

Harding waited until he received his DD214, officially discharging him from the marines, before making one last trip to Beaufort. Whatever the outcome, he knew he had a home, family, loved ones and friends waiting for him—unlike six months ago.

When he turned into Lieutenant Robinson's driveway; her car wasn't there. He parked anyway and walked up to the front door. He hoped he was doing the right thing, and she'd be happy to see him. He felt as nervous as when he was a teenager asking his first girl for a date.

"Oh hell, I might as well get it over with." He rang the bell and waited. Then he rang the bell again and again and again and waited some more. He hunched his shoulders, turned and walked back to his car.

"Guess she's not home, just my luck." He stopped, turned and took one last glance at her door. "Or maybe it wasn't meant to be."

Laurie peeked out from behind the curtain and watched as he left, wiped a tear, and went back to her laptop.

He called Lottie. "Hi, I'm on my way home. Would you and Thomas like to go a movie tonight?

"We'd love to. Thomas will be real excited."

After a light supper with his mother, he drove to Crofton, picked up Lottie and Thomas and they went to the movies. Every so often, he, Lottie, and Thomas went to see a movie. Judy played cribbage with Miss Lottie. Occasionally just he and Lottie went to a movie and for ice cream afterward. Judy stayed with Thomas at Lottie's house along with Sarge.

Things were back to normal at Baxter House. Miss Lottie was receiving guests and cooking meals for them as well as Sunday dinner for all her kinfolk and Sarge. She enjoyed spending days sitting on the porch with Sarge at her feet when Harding went to work.

He called Laurie several times but always got her voice mail and left messages. He kept trying but was disappointed she never returned his calls. The last message he left was an invitation to Baxter House for Thanksgiving and his saying that Jessica and her mother would be there.

CHAPTER 52

Thanksgiving Day

The holiday dinner was to be a special occasion at Baxter House. Aside from Miss Lottie, Lottie, Thomas, Bradley and his mother—John Porter and Molly were invited as were Chef Willie, Miss Mavis and Ollie Jackson. Jessica and her mother received a special invite and drove down from Charleston. When Harding gave them directions, he told them that they would know they were at the right house when they saw the sign that said Baxter House at the end of a long driveway. Miss Lottie gave them each a room at no cost for the holiday.

Bradley, Judy, and Sarge left for Baxter House with two pies for desert. Judy reached over and touched his leg. "How's that counselor that Doctor Myers referred you to?"

When he confided in his mother that he was having some nightmares, she spoke to Doctor Myers and asked her in confidence if she could refer him to a counselor.

He looked over and smiled. "She's great. It helps that she was a nurse in Nam and knows what it's like to see the horrors of war."

'I'm glad she's helping you."

"Me too."

He pulled up behind four cars and parked behind the last one.

"Guess we're not the first ones here."

"Doesn't look like it and that looks like Thomas waiting on the porch. Hold these pies while I get out." She handed him the pies, got out of the car, and took them from him. He let Sarge out of the car and they walked to the porch.

Thomas ran over to greet them. "Where you been, Marine, I've been waiting for you? Everybody's here. Hey, Sarge." He bent down and let Sarge lick his face. "Come on, Sarge, Miss Mollie's waiting for you."

"Morning to you, Thomas."

Thomas stopped and turned around. "Morning to you, Marine. You too, Aunt Judy."

"Morning, Thomas. Brad, let's get these pies in the house."

As soon as they entered, Porter shouted, "Where the hell you been, Harding? You're gonna miss kickoff. Morning, Judy."

Sitting with Porter were Chef Willie, Ollie, and Jessica.

"Morning, John Porter. How many beers have you had?"

"It's my first. Miss Lottie said no drinking until thirty minutes before kickoff."

She shook her head. "I'm surprised Miss Lottie even let you have beer in the house."

Porter grinned. "It's Thanksgiving, Judy." He raised his beer. "Turkey, football, the guys and a Bud. That's the American way and it don't get any better than this."

"You're an old fool, John Porter."

Then she looked around the room and saw Jessica sitting between Chef Willie and Ollie.

"Brad, put these pies on the buffet with the rest of the deserts."

"Yes, Mom." He did as she asked.

"And don't any of you boys touch those deserts, you hear me?" scolded Judy as she lowered the corners of her mouth.

"Yes, Mom," the men said.

"Young lady, you must be Jessica. Come here and let me say a proper hello." Jessica got up and walked around the men. Without warning, Judy wrapped her arms around her. "It's nice to finally meet you. Brad has told me all about you."

Jessica let out a deep breath. "It's nice to meet you, Mrs. Waverly."

"Call me Miss Judy. When you're here, you're like family."

"Okay, Miss Judy. Miss Lottie said the same thing last night."

Judy smiled and put her hand on Jessica's cheek. "And you best listen to her. You staying here with these boys or are you coming into the kitchen?"

"Miss Lottie appointed me the beer lady so I'm staying here to keep tabs on them."

Judy addressed the men with another scowl. "Don't you boys take advantage of this young lady, you hear me?"

"Yes, Mom," they said and raised their bottles to her.

"You guys will never grow up. Brad, you watch these guys and don't forget to come in and say hello to the ladies." He nodded and she went into the kitchen. "Morning, ladies, happy Thanksgiving."

"Morning, Miss Judy," they all responded.

Miss Lottie closed the oven door after checking the turkey, turned, and said, "Happy Thanksgiving to you, child. Come here and give me a hug." Judy walked over and hugged her. "This is Jessica's mother. Introduce yourself. I got things to do, and you can help her peel potatoes."

"Mrs. Towning, I'm Judy Waverly. It's nice to meet you. You have a lovely daughter."

"Thank you, but you have to call me Paula because Miss Lottie said if I'm going to spend Thanksgiving at her house with her family, I have to drop my surname like everyone else."

They both smiled. "Very well, and you may call me Judy. We don't want Miss Lottie to scold us." Then she surprised Mrs. Towning and wrapped her arms around her in a bear hug. "We're all family here, and in this family we hug a lot."

"So I'm learning." Mrs. Towning was still getting used to the way everyone treated her and Jessica. The two ladies then began their chore of peeling potatoes.

In the living room, Bradley hugged Jessica. "Good to see you, Jess. How have you been?"

"I'm good. Miss Lottie has made us feel at home. She said we're like family. You're one lucky guy."

"I said you would like her. How's your mother?"

"She's fine. Initially she was shocked with everyone, but they made her feel welcome and now she's comfortable. Miss Lottie has her helping in the kitchen."

"What's new with you, Jess? I should have Skyped you sooner."

"It's okay, I could have Skyped you, but I promise I will. I have a job in accounting where my mom works. The company works with a group called 'Jobs for Vets.' It's only three days a week, but it works for me. I'm going to school the other two days to complete my accounting degree. And I run on weekends with a group of veterans. We call ourselves—The Undefeated Runners."

"Damn, Jess, I'm proud of you."

She beamed with pride. "I still go to counseling once a week. And I take the bus to school and counseling." She grinned. "I'm self-supporting. I owe it all to you for not giving up on me that day in Beaufort."

"Jess, it's really because you didn't give up on yourself."

"Maybe, but..." Then she surprised him and put her arm around him and hugged him. "I love you, Brad."

"Oh! Well, I love you too."

"We love you too, Brad," the men shouted.

Jessica turned and put her hands on her hips. "Knock it off, you guys or you won't get any more beer."

"Aw, come on, Jess, we're just kidding," replied Ollie.

"Ignore them, Jess, they're harmless, but they're good guys and are like uncles to me."

"I know, and I like them. They're cute and treat me like a sister. It's like being with the guys in our platoon." She whispered, "How are you and Laurie doing?"

His expression changed to one of somberness. "I've called her numerous times, but I always get her voice mail. I left messages and even invited her here for today, but she never replied."

"I'm sorry, Brad, I hoped you two would."

"I guess it wasn't meant to be. We'll see though, I'm not giving up just yet." He smiled and followed with, "I have a life here and a family, and I like being a father figure for Thomas."

"His mother likes it too." She winked. "I think she's sweet on you."

"We're good friends, Jess. I used to spend my summers here when I was a kid, and we became friends."

"If you say so."

"Uh-huh," said the men.

He shook his head and hadn't realized that they were listening.

She punched his arm and smiled. "See, I'm not the only one. Anyway, I like your mom, she's really nice."

"Yes, she is. I have to go say hello to the ladies."

"Okay, I'm staying here. It's like being back with the platoon." She looked around the room. "You guys ready for another?"

"You bet," answered Porter.

"When you come back, you come sit by me again, young lady," said Ollie.

"Watch out for that old coot, Jess, he ain't trust worthy," said Chef Willie.

Everyone laughed.

"I'll get the beers, Jess. Sarge is out front with Thomas and Miss Mollie. Go say hello."

"Thanks. Don't you guys go away, I'll be right back."

Porter raised his bottle. "We'll be here."

She went outside and he walked toward the kitchen.

Porter grabbed his arm. "It's a good thing you did inviting that young lady. Your grandfather would be proud."

"He sure would be," said Chef Willie.

"I am too," added Ollie.

He lowered his head and grinned. "Thanks guys, I appreciate it." They raised their bottles. Then he went into the kitchen. "Happy Thanksgiving, ladies."

"Happy Thanksgiving, Brad," the women replied.

"Young man you come here and give me a hug," said Miss Lottie.

He gave her a big hug and then hugged Lottie.

"Happy Thanksgiving, Brad."

He held the hug longer than expected. Miss Lottie and Judy looked at each other.

"Happy Thanksgiving, Lottie." He looked at the other ladies. "Happy Thanksgiving, Miss Mavis. Same to you, Chief."

"Only one more month to go and I will be a civilian just like you. Since it's a holiday, call me Molly."

"Okay, Molly." He addressed Mrs. Towning. "You must be Jessica's mom. It's nice to finally meet you Mrs.—"

"Call me Paula, and it's nice to finally meet you. May I hug you?"

He looked at his mother, and then Lottie and Miss Lottie. They nodded.

"Sure, why not."

She hugged him and whispered, "Thank you for getting Jessica back to me."

"I wish it were under better circumstances."

"Just having her home is enough. I'm sorry about your friend."

Jessica must have told her about Pritchet. "Thanks, I appreciate that." She wiped his eyes.

"If you ladies don't mind, the guys are ready for another beer." He grabbed a six pack from the fridge. "I'm going to join them."

"Uh-huh," the ladies said.

He quickly left the kitchen.

Thomas was sitting on the porch with Sarge and Miss Mollie beside him.

"Mind if I join you, Thomas?" asked Jessica.

"No, sit next to me. Move over, Sarge. This is Sarge, she's special."

She sat down, let Sarge lick her face and rubbed her neck. "I know, Thomas, she was special for me."

"Were you really a marine too?"

"Yes, I was, and I served under Brad. He was my platoon leader and he saved my life." She had forgotten what else happened that day in Afghanistan.

"Really?"

"Yes, I'm lucky to be here."

Thomas lowered his head, "My dad was in the army, but he wasn't as lucky as you."

"I'm sorry to hear that."

"It's okay, he gave me my mom and now I have the marine and Sarge."

"You're a lucky guy, Thomas."

"Does it hurt?"

"You mean my arm? No it doesn't." He was the first person to ask her that question and surprisingly she was glad he had.

"Can I touch it?"

"Sure if you want to."

He touched her arm. "Cool. You gonna get a fake one?"

She had been thinking about it but hadn't decided if she wanted one. "Maybe, what do you think I should do?"

"My friend's dad has one, and he let me touch it. It was neat. He said it didn't change who he was. You should wait, that's what I think. But I'm just a kid, what do I know?"

"You know more than a lot of people, Thomas. I think I'll take your advice and wait."

Sarge and Miss Lottie rose up on their hind legs, placed their front paws on Jessica and Thomas' knees and licked their faces.

"You're pretty, too, just like my mom."

She kissed the top of his head. "Thank you, Thomas. That was sweet." For the first time, Jessica realized that her identity wasn't measured by the length of her arm but by the person within her. A three-legged dog and a ten-year-old boy had given her the courage to proudly face the world without ever again being self-conscious of her disability.

Miss Lottie announced that dinner was almost ready and it was time to set the table which meant the football game had to wait until later. The men brought the old dining room table in from the garage and set it up in the living room. The ladies scrambled to set the table and bring the vegetables from the kitchen. There were mashed potatoes, squash, turnip greens, and green beans. The stuffing and gravy were also placed on the table and everyone sat down except for Miss Lottie.

Bradley sat between his mother and Lottie. Miss Mavis, Chef Willie, Molly, and Paula sat next to Ollie.

"You sit next to me, Jess," said Thomas. He pointed to his right. "That way Sarge can sit on the floor between us. Miss Mollie will sit next to Porter."

"Thank you, Thomas." Lottie smiled at her; Jessica smiled back and sat down.

"John Porter, you sit at the head of the table across from me," announced Miss Lottie. Then she carried the turkey to the table and set it in front of him. "You carve the turkey now, John Porter."

He rubbed his hands together, picked up the carving knife and fork and started to carve the turkey. Miss Lottie took her seat at the other end of the table.

Everyone was about to pass their dishes around, when Thomas asked, "Gramma, can I say grace?" Everything came to a halt and a silence enveloped the room. All eyes turned toward Thomas. He reached into his pocket and took out a piece of paper.

"If you want to, Thomas," answered Miss Lottie.

"I wrote it down. My teacher said it was very good. Everyone hold hands except me since I have to read."

Everyone held hands. Lottie put her hand on Thomas's shoulder and Jessica held Porter's hand. Ollie squeezed Mrs. Towning's hand and winked at her. She turned a shade of pink.

Thomas lowered his head and started reading. "God, bless this meal and bless this family of loved ones and friends. And thank those who sacrificed to make this day possible. We are united in that we sacrificed for this exceptional country in one way or another. Watch over the men and women in uniform wherever they may be and keep them safe from harm. Amen." He folded the paper and put it back in his pocket.

"Amen," everyone echoed.

"Thomas, that was beautiful."

"Thanks, Mom."

Jessica leaned against him and whispered, "See, Thomas, you do know more than a lot of people."

Suddenly chaos erupted as dishes were passed around so Porter could put turkey on them. Some asked for dark meat and some asked for white. Ollie asked for a leg as did Bradley. Porter kept the wings for himself. Vegetables, stuffing, and gravy were also passed around.

Again all eyes turned toward Thomas as he cut Jessica's slice of turkey for her. Lottie and Bradley nodded at each other, like proud parents do.

Miss Lottie sat back and enjoyed the scene. She held the locket in her hand that Travis gave her. She opened it and glanced at the pictures of him and her daughter. Then she looked up.

Told you, Travis, everything would be okay. It just takes patience.

After dinner, coffee, and desert, the ladies cleared the table. The men dismantled the table and put it back in the garage so they could watch football. Thomas and Jessica went outside with the dogs.

They sat on the porch steps. Thomas held a ball in his hand. Sarge and Miss Mollie sat in front of him. "Okay now, I'm going to toss the ball. You two chase it. First one gets it, brings it back to me. You got it?"

The two dogs cocked their heads and stared at him as if saying, of course we got it, we're dogs not humans. Throw the damn thing.

He leaned forward and let the dogs see the ball. They both licked his face and barked. "Good dogs." He tossed the ball in the air and it landed twenty yards from the steps. The dogs ran after the ball. Miss Mollie picked up the ball in her mouth and gave it to Sarge. She took the ball and they both walked back to Thomas.

She dropped the ball at his feet.

Jessica and Thomas laughed. "Good dogs." He rubbed the top of their heads and let them lick his face. "You throw it this time, Jess."

She threw the ball, but it only went ten yards. Sarge and Miss Mollie ran after the ball. Sarge held the ball in her mouth, gave it to Miss Mollie and the two walked back to Jessica.

Miss Mollie dropped the ball at her feet.

"Good dogs." Then she wrapped her arm around Thomas and started tickling him while the dogs licked his face causing him to laugh real hard.

Bradley and Lottie watched from the doorway with their fingers laced and laughed.

"Stop, you're gonna give me a belly ache," he giggled.

After the festivities died down, Bradley and Judy said goodnight and went home. He left Sarge at Baxter House so Thomas and Jessica could enjoy more time with her.

"Your friend's a charming young lady, Brad, and very brave."

"Yes, Mom, she is, and has come a long way."

"Lottie likes her, and she really appreciates the attention you pay to Thomas. She said you're like a father figure to him." She smiled. "And she adores you, too."

He turned and smiled. "I like Thomas, and I like being a father figure to him."

She smiled back at him. "And, Lottie?"

"Mom, we're good friends." But he still had conflicted feelings toward her.

"Uh-huh." She winked at him. "You know what would have made this a great day?" His first thought was of Laurie. Judy placed her hand on his thigh. "If only your sister could have been here."

Later that night, he was awakened by his cell phone ringing. "Hey." He listened to the voice on the other end and smiled. "I'm glad you called."

ACKNOWLEDGEMENTS

This book is dedicated to the men and women who serve this great and exceptional country and to all the first responders as well. I owe my freedom and liberty to them.

As previously stated, this book is a work of fiction. Although some locations actually exist, names, characters, places and incidents are the product of the author's imagination or are used fictitiously. Any resemblance to actual events, locales, or persons, living or dead is entirely coincidental.

A number of places mentioned are actual locations but Blocker's Bluff and Crofton exist in my imagination only and on paper.

I'm grateful for the numerous websites that gave me an enormous wealth of information making it easier to do research. I took the liberty and embellished and distorted some of the information to advance the fictional characteristics of the story.

My thanks to those who anonymously provided information relevant to the sequence of events portrayed in this novel. And thanks to the inspiration from Lucy, who, like Sarge, has only three legs.

I intended to write a murder mystery, but Miss Lottie's character became the driving force behind the story. She took control of my keyboard and added that feel good home town flavor. Porter and Molly added the humor like they did in the original Blocker's

Bluff. I fell in love with Miss Lottie, and I hope you did too as she was a wonderful character to write about.

Post-traumatic stress disorder is a disease that has been around for a long time. It has become more apparent since 9/11 and the wars in the Middle East. PTSD has had a dramatic effect on the military and first responders. When I started writing this book, it wasn't meant to be about PTSD. The characters took on different personas and dictated the direction of the subject matter so I went with their direction. Events moved rapidly and that wasn't meant to diminish the severity of the disease. I recognize that treatment takes much longer, but this was a work of fiction, so I moved things along rapidly.

A special thanks to the organizations that provide service to our wounded heroes.

And to those who provided editing services, I thank you all.

32644340R00211

Made in the USA
Middletown, DE
12 June 2016